# Zayden's eyes bulged with fear

"Wait!" The desperate man leaned toward Mack Bolan as he spoke. "I'm serious. Rabin's death was a contract killing. I was the one who delivered the request. I was the courier who delivered the up-front payment, the guns, all those things."

"Nice coincidence for Kassem," Bolan said, "someone else wanting the same guy dead. And willing to pay for it, too."

"Just because someone else footed the bill doesn't mean Kassem wasn't happy about it."

Bolan considered that. Once it had become clear that the Libyans had made the kill, the big American had assumed Kassem had done the deed to get even. "Fair enough. Lots of people wanted Rabin dead. So who hired him?"

Bolan unleathered the Beretta.

"And don't tell me the intel is above your pay grade."

*Other titles available
in this series:*

| | |
|---|---|
| Strike and Retrieve | Colony of Evil |
| Age of War | Hard Passage |
| Line of Control | Interception |
| Breached | Cold War Reprise |
| Retaliation | Mission: Apocalypse |
| Pressure Point | Altered State |
| Silent Running | Killing Game |
| Stolen Arrows | Diplomacy Directive |
| Zero Option | Betrayed |
| Predator Paradise | Sabotage |
| Circle of Deception | Conflict Zone |
| Devil's Bargain | Blood Play |
| False Front | Desert Fallout |
| Lethal Tribute | Extraordinary Rendition |
| Season of Slaughter | Devil's Mark |
| Point of Betrayal | Savage Rule |
| Ballistic Force | Infiltration |
| Renegade | Resurgence |
| Survival Reflex | Kill Shot |
| Path to War | Stealth Sweep |
| Blood Dynasty | Grave Mercy |
| Ultimate Stakes | Treason Play |
| State of Evil | Assassin's Code |
| Force Lines | Shadow Strike |
| Contagion Option | Decision Point |
| Hellfire Code | Road of Bones |
| War Drums | Radical Edge |
| Ripple Effect | Fireburst |
| Devil's Playground | Oblivion Pact |
| The Killing Rule | Enemy Arsenal |
| Patriot Play | State of War |
| Appointment in Baghdad | Ballistic |
| Havana Five | Escalation Tactic |
| The Judas Project | Crisis Diplomacy |
| Plains of Fire | Apocalypse Ark |

# Don Pendleton's Mack Bolan®

## LETHAL STAKES

A GOLD EAGLE BOOK FROM

# W❂RLDWIDE®

TORONTO • NEW YORK • LONDON
AMSTERDAM • PARIS • SYDNEY • HAMBURG
STOCKHOLM • ATHENS • TOKYO • MILAN
MADRID • WARSAW • BUDAPEST • AUCKLAND

First edition July 2013

ISBN-13: 978-0-373-61562-9

Special thanks and acknowledgment to
Tim Tresslar for his contribution to this work.

LETHAL STAKES

Justice belongs to those who claim it, but let the claimant beware lest he creates new injustice...and this set the bloody pendulum of revenge into its inexorable motion.

—Frank Herbert,
1920–1986

Everyone is entitled to justice, not just the rich and the privileged. When the authorities aren't up to the task, someone has to step forward. I do not seek revenge. I avenge. There is a difference.

—Mack Bolan

# PROLOGUE

What the hell did he do now?

The question raced around Ben Rabin's mind as he sat in what should have been paradise—at an umbrella table next to the swimming pool of a four-star hotel in Athens. Instead, he chewed over the question for what seemed like a thousandth time in an hour while he puffed worriedly on his cigarette, his fourth since he sat down. He fixed his stare on the surface of the swimming pool; the water glittered under the onslaught of the midafternoon sun. His second glass of Scotch on the rocks sat, sweating, on the table. Pulling his stare from the pool, he swiveled in his chair, ground out the cigarette in an ashtray and chided himself, not for his nervousness, but for his reaction to it.

The Israeli had spent his life as a soldier. He'd entered the Israeli Defense Forces as a young man, fully intending to fulfill his minimum hitch before moving on to school so he could study international relations and eventually become a professor. His interest in foreign affairs and his keen mind had led his superiors to move him into intelligence work, where he continued to climb the ranks while attending night school. Along the way, he'd realized the spy's life suited him, and he'd ditched the idea of academia. After years of actively tracking foreign affairs and occasionally playing some small part in their direction through various espionage operations, the idea of teaching, even at a military academy, held no charm for him. A truth he understood as a middle-aged man, that had eluded him when he was younger, was that he hungered for action, to be in the thick of things.

His success in the military had led him to Mossad, the Israeli intelligence organization, where he ran operations against his homeland's Arab neighbors and especially its enemies. Under Rabin's direction, Mossad teams had assassinated more than one Hamas or Hezbollah leader, and occasionally scored a few al Qaeda scalps along the way. In the early years, it had been up close and personal: knives, snipers, poisons or bombs.

In his last years with Mossad, though, unmanned aerial vehicles had become the norm, vanquishing enemies with a trigger pulled from deep inside Israel's borders. Then there'd also been Icarus. Rabin personally had decided to name the operation for the young man who, using wings made by his father, had perished because he'd flown too close to the sun. The Icarus program had targeted scientists who'd been involved in nuclear programs in Iran, Iraq, Libya, Syria and Saudi Arabia.

Mossad agents first would "urge" the scientists to defect, or at least move on, using money, blackmail or other levers. When that didn't work, they usually found their careers cut short by other, more lethal, means. He'd orchestrated each of these operations, making all the major calls and producing results most of the time.

That made this day's indecision all the more surprising and, yeah, humiliating. Bringing the Scotch to his lips, he knocked back the entire contents of the glass and set it down on the table. The alcohol ignited a slight burning sensation before it reached his belly. Normally he enjoyed the feeling, but it barely registered with him, certainly did nothing to calm his nerves.

What should he do?

He'd been enjoying his vacation in Greece. Since he'd left government service, he'd joined the boards of a handful of Israeli defense contractors, been retained as a consultant for a couple more. For the most part, the work was easy, requiring him to share his opinions, of which he had many, in exchange for yearly compensation and tons of perks. With his background, his involvement gave these various ventures credibility, with both investors and government officials, and the products they made kept his country safe. In his mind, it was a fair trade, a way to earn real money after decades of living off comfortable, but not stellar, government pay.

When the server walked by, he gestured at his empty glass.

The trip had been an under-the-table gift from the executives at QF-17, recognition for his work as a board member of the Tel Aviv, Israel-based defense contractor. Rabin recalled how Dan Kantor, one of the vice presidents, had shown up at his home, dressed to the nines, and handed Rabin a large, brown envelope.

"It's two airline tickets," Kantor had said, flashing his 1,000-megawatt smile. "Athens, Greece. I have a suite there, in a hotel. Take some time for yourself. Take a friend." He nodded at the envelope. "There's a list of restaurants in there. You eat at any of them, put it on my tab."

"I can't—"

"You can," Kantor had replied. "You're not in government service anymore. I'm not selling you anything. Take the tickets. Take Patricia with you. Have some fun. We've had a great year. We couldn't have done it without you."

"Damn it, Dan—"

"Go."

So he'd traveled to Athens. It had been great—until a young woman had called his hotel room and everything changed.

She had said things, crazy things, and asked to meet with him and Briggs. He had almost dismissed her as a lunatic, a pitiful, paranoid person. His appointment to QF-17's board had received wide coverage in the Israeli media. That notoriety had benefited the company, allowing it to dominate the business news cycle for at least twenty-four hours. But his links to the shadowy Mossad also had sparked plenty of conspiracy theories, most of them spewed by bloggers who wrote under aliases. If she was a spy, however, she was a clumsy one, sharing conspiracy theories no rational person would believe.

Still, she'd known enough of the right things to say, information that never should have been available to her. Without consulting his companion, Patricia Briggs, and against his better judgment, he'd agreed to hear her out. If she was a kook, he figured he'd brush her off and go about his vacation without involving Briggs. If he sensed something more sinister from the young woman—a honey trap where someone tried to embroil him in a sex scandal for blackmail, or tried to hurt or kill him—he'd deal with that. Experience told him he could take out another spy with deadly efficiency.

He'd given her one option—meet here next to the hotel's pool. At first she'd balked, asking for someplace less conspicuous. Without hesitation, he'd told her no. He was already ignoring his better judgment. The last thing he needed was to encounter her somewhere off the beaten path, a place of her choosing where he'd find himself vulnerable.

He was curious, sure. Not suicidal.

So she'd relented and saw him at the hotel. When he met her, he thought it confirmed his fears that someone was trying to set him up for a honey trap. Angel Tzon was beautiful, with glossy black hair, wide, chocolate-brown eyes and a light olive complexion. Her smile dazzled even an old cynic such as himself. But he also sensed a toughness to the woman. A toughness and, unfortunately, an earnestness.

What the woman told him had blown his mind, had opened a hollow pit of fear in his stomach and left him questioning his reality.

Then she'd stood abruptly. "Think about it," she said. "I'll call later."

Donning her sunglasses, she'd turned and walked away.

The presence of the server at his side brought him back to the present. The woman set another drink in front of him and smiled. Rabin acknowledged her with a nod. The Israeli picked up the Scotch, gulped down half of it and returned the glass to the table.

Suddenly, another thought occurred to him. Where the hell was Briggs?

A glance at his wristwatch told him it had been 45 minutes since they had spoken by telephone. A chill raced down his spine. She'd promised to join him in a matter of minutes, 20 minutes at the longest. A former army colonel, Briggs was nothing if not efficient and punctual. When she said no more than 20 minutes, she damn well meant it. He called once and got her voice mail.

Go! Check on her! his mind screamed.

He gathered up his cigarettes, put them in the breast pocket of his shirt, grabbed his keys and headed into the hotel.

AHMAD AL-JUBARI OVERTURNED the suitcase and emptied its contents onto the floor of the hotel room. He knelt next to the jumble of clothing and picked through it, his hands encased in surgical gloves. Finding nothing of use, he pulled a Ka-Bar folding knife from his pocket, opened it.

A small, almost undetectable whimper registered with him, causing him to turn and look at the woman seated on the bed. She was clothed, with her hands and feet bound with duct tape. Another strip of duct tape was pressed over her mouth. Tears rolled down her face, leaving black smears on her cheeks. al-Jubari again noted she was attractive. Her blond hair fell well past her shoulders and framed her oval face. She looked younger than his dossier indicated she was, the small crow's-feet at the corners of her eyes the most revealing sign of her age. She obviously had kept herself in good shape. She had fought like hell and it had taken two of them to subdue her after they had surprised her. But they had brought her down, and now she was neutralized as a threat.

He wagged the knife's blade in her direction.

"You like it? Perhaps I will give you a closer look before we leave."

She blinked hard and looked away. He smirked and returned his attention to the suitcase's interior. The frame of the bag was insulated with a quilted lining. He stabbed the point of the blade into the fabric and jerked the blade down, slicing through the fabric and peeling it away with his free hand. He found two thin packets of U.S. dollars, sealed in plastic shrink-wrap.

He slipped the money into a pants pocket. When he finished searching the bag, he tossed it aside. They were going to destroy the place, make it look like a robbery. It was anything but that, though. They had come for a specific purpose.

He rose and moved to a nightstand. Grabbing the handle, he pulled out the drawer and found it empty. He reached for a second drawer as his cell phone began to vibrate. Scowling, he pulled it free from the belt case and looked at it, noting the number flashing on the screen.

He looked at the other man, Tariq Mustapha, who was cutting a huge gash in the mattress.

"Hey," he said.

Mustapha was barrel-chested with stick-thin legs that made him look like a bulldog from a cartoon. Adding to his bulldog appearance were the thick jowls and tiny eyes that peered out from beneath thick eyebrows. A fellow Libyan, Mustapha had served in Khadaffi's army as a commando before the regime had fallen. In recent years, though, he had become soft by drinking and eating too much, thanks to the generosity of their boss, Massoud Kassem, and his mysterious benefactor who had seemingly endless piles of money to spend.

Jubari felt disgust well up inside him whenever he looked at Mustapha. Softness and comfort made a man vulnerable, Jubari believed. For his part, Jubari had done all he could to avoid such a fate. Kassem, he knew, could be mercurial and demanding, cunning and vicious. And for that reason, he knew better than to become complacent. At the end of the day, Kassem paid for results. While he often lavished others with praise, money and women, his mood inevitably swung the other way, and he launched into relentless, often violent tirades against his people. That had led Jubari to keep the indulging to a minimum, socking away his money and always maneuvering to remain Kassem's trusted assistant.

"What?" Mustapha asked.

"He's coming."

The other man nodded and a smile pulled at the corners of his mouth. They both were going to enjoy what was about to happen next.

RABIN MADE HIS way down the corridor. He held the phone to his ear and heard it ring a fifth time before a voice—Patricia's voice—broke in.

"Hello, you've reached Patricia Briggs."

Rabin squeezed his eyes shut and ended the call. It was the third time he had gotten her voice mail and he saw no need to leave yet another urgent message for her to call.

His heart hammered in his chest as he rushed along the corridor. When he last saw her, she had already showered and dressed. Perhaps she was in the bathroom, the phone out of reach. It was possible she had turned off her cell phone, though he doubted it. He had spent decades being on call around the clock. Now, whenever he had the opportunity to be unreachable by phone, he took it.

She, on the other hand, would not do that. She was too responsible for that, always worried someone who needed her might not be able to find her. He noticed a film of sweat had formed between his palm and the cell phone's smooth back. He slipped the phone into his pocket and drew out the card that opened the electronic lock on his hotel room.

He took another look around, trying to determine if someone had fallen in behind him. He noticed nothing amiss other than the anxiety roiling around inside him. There were several people, families mostly, pushing their way through the hallways, mothers, fathers and children in bathing suits and carrying beach towels or dressed in shorts and T-shirts, setting off to visit the pool or the sights of Athens.

He reached the hotel room door and tucked the cane between his left arm and his chest. He set his right hand on the door's release handle, but applied no pressure. The curved metal felt cool against his palm. He strained his ears for a couple of heartbeats but heard nothing. Maybe she had gone out shopping and forgotten her cell phone. Two days ago, she had seen a handmade silver bracelet that she had liked in a nearby jewelry store. He had encouraged her to buy it then. She had held off, always the more frugal of the two. She had mentioned it a couple of times since then. Maybe she had finally decided to go buy it. Maybe she had left her phone in the hotel room.

Maybe he was just a silly old warhorse, jumping at shadows cast by a silly, delusional girl. Maybe.

He slipped the card into the slot and pushed down on the handle. He came through the door and found a nightmare. Strong hands grabbed him from behind and shoved him into the room. He stumbled, lost his cane. He landed on all fours, saw Briggs's and his clothing strewed about the room, saw a pair of khaki-clad legs rushing toward him.

Someone drove a kick into his chest and Rabin felt a searing pain bolt through him, heard a rib crack. The force of the blow drove him onto his back and left him gasping for air. Three men came into view, towering over him. One displayed a knife blade while a second aimed a sound-suppressed pistol at something to Rabin's left. He knew what it was before he looked, but turned his head, anyway. He saw Briggs, her mouth gagged, her cheeks shiny with tears of rage and fear. Then another kick cracked against his temple and everything blacked out.

# CHAPTER ONE

*Stony Man Farm, Virginia*

The first thing that struck Mack Bolan, aka the Executioner, as he entered the War Room was the worry etched on his old friend's face. Hal Brognola, a man who had run covert operations for the country for years, wasn't easygoing on his best days. This day, Bolan noticed dark crescents under the other man's eyes, and his shoulders were slumped. As always, his tie was pulled askew and the cuffs of his shirtsleeves were rolled up to the middle of his forearms.

The big Fed looked up when Bolan entered, greeted him with a tight smile and a nod.

Bolan strode to the nearest armchair and lowered his big frame into it.

"Where's the rest of the crew?"

Brognola, who'd been swigging coffee from a foam cup, wiped his mouth with his bare wrist.

"Bear gave a seminar at Ft. Meade last night." "Bear" was the nickname of Aaron Kurtzman, head of the Farm's cyberteam. "He'll be arriving from Maryland later today. As for Barb, she should be along soon. I called her. Judging by the sound of her voice I woke her from a deep sleep. I'm guessing she'll be along as soon as she can get herself together."

Bolan knew that Barbara Price had been fast asleep when summoned to the meeting. The honey-blonde mission controller of Stony Man Farm had been asleep in Bolan's bed, both of them resting after making love, as they often did during

Bolan's brief stays at the Farm. The soldier guessed his old friend had known—or at least guessed—he was making two phone calls to the same room when he'd begun mustering the troops. But the big Fed was too classy say anything about it.

While Bolan waited for his old friend to speak his mind, he poured himself a cup of coffee from a carafe on the table.

After a few more seconds, Brognola glanced at his watch and shrugged slightly, apparently to himself.

"Let's go ahead and call this meeting to order, shall we?" he said.

"It's your party," Bolan said.

A stack of folders stood at Brognola's right elbow while another was already fanned open on the table in front of him. He grabbed a folder and slid it across the tabletop to Bolan. The soldier took the folder, opened it and began to rifle through its contents. It contained papers and photos.

He set aside the papers, glanced quickly through the photos and was struck immediately by their grisly contents. They appeared to depict a crime scene. A wide angle shot showed a man and a woman, hands and feet bound with duct tape. Or, at least, the woman's ankles were bound. Bolan looked more closely at the man, saw he had only one leg. The left leg of his tan slacks was empty, the fabric trailing away from the body until it disappeared under the bed.

The man lay on the floor, on beige carpeting turned dark by what Bolan could only assume was blood. The woman was curled on the edge of the bed, clad only in a T-shirt. The contents of her purse had been dumped on the bed behind her. While Brognola waited, the soldier leafed through the other photos, saw close-ups of each victim's face. Even in death, the man's white hair gleamed against his tanned face, etched with deep lines; his thin lips were parted slightly.

Next, Bolan studied a picture of the woman's face, a profile. Predictably, she was pale, save for an ugly, blue-black bruise on her left cheek. Blond hair that fell well below her shoulders was spread out over the surface of the mattress. Crow's-feet at the corner of her eye led Bolan to put her age in her late 40s or just over 50. In life, he guessed she'd been an attractive woman.

"Athens police found them twenty-four hours ago," Brognola said.

"Looks like a robbery. At least, judging by all the drawers and clothes on the floor."

"*Looks* being the operative word there," Brognola replied.

"Explain."

"I'll get to that," the big Fed said. "Let me identify them first. The man's name is Ben Rabin, an Israeli. Former Mossad, former Israeli Defense Forces. We made some inquiries. Mossad's being fairly tight-lipped, but they acknowledge that he coordinated some black operations in his day. Of course, we already knew that because he'd coordinated a few of them with our intelligence services."

"Otherwise, they told us nothing."

"Right. And, really, there's no reason they should. My guess is, if they get wind of something, they'll want to deal with it on their own. Can't say I blame them for that, either. As for the lady, she's the reason you're here. Her name's Patricia Briggs. She is—or was—a retired U.S. Army colonel, but more recently had been working as a private contractor. Her specialty was weapons systems design. According to her Pentagon file, she was a genius at that sort of thing before she retired and kept working on it after she left the military. She was a huge asset for our country."

Bolan nodded.

"Apparently, the two were in Greece for a vacation," Brognola said.

"Together, I assume?"

"Right. Rabin, like Briggs, did a lot of work in the private sector, though mostly for Israeli companies and security agencies, as you can imagine. Their one link professionally was they sat on the board of QF-17. Heard of them?"

Bolan shook his head. "Never."

"Not surprising," Brognola replied. "They fly pretty low under the radar. In the U.S., at least, though they did get some funding from our government. That was Briggs's role on the board, in fact. When the U.S. agreed to sink money into it, we also encouraged the company to put an American on the board. The White House and the DOD wanted to know how our dollars were being spent."

"And also dig up useful information."

Brognola grinned. "Consider it giving your friend a hug and picking her pocket."

"I'm hiding my shock."

"Way of the world," Brognola said, shrugging.

"Did she find anything useful?"

"Just her relationship with Rabin. They met a year ago, started dating and eventually became inseparable. Kind of a nice turn of events for her. Her late husband was an Army colonel, too. He was killed by a roadside bomb in Baghdad. Two years later, her son, who was in the Army infantry, was shot and killed by the Taliban. She had no other kids, no other family. By all accounts, she went through hell."

Bolan studied the crime-scene photo, his mind momentarily imagining the terror that must have consumed both Briggs and Rabin in their final moments.

"Looks like she went through hell again," Bolan said.

"Agreed," Brognola said with a nod.

Bolan pushed the photos away and leveled his gaze at his old friend.

"This is awful, Hal," he said. "Don't get me wrong. But if there's more to it, lay it on me. If it's a murder and a robbery, even a horrible one, it's probably a police matter. I'm not a detective. If you want me to mobilize…"

"I need to give you more, right?" Brognola asked. "Trust

me, there's more to it, or at least someone thinks there is. Hell, I think there is. Otherwise, we wouldn't be having this conversation."

Brognola drank some coffee and set it back down.

"What I've given you is the public, albeit a less sanitized, version. But there's more to know."

"Okay."

"Forty-eight hours ago, meaning a day before the murder, a CIA asset contacted her handler," Brognola said. "This particular asset happens to be a high-priced call girl. She draws a wealthy clientele, some of whom are foreign visitors. That puts her in touch, if you'll pardon the expression, with some of the more interesting men traveling through Athens.

The big Fed paused for a moment, then took a roll of antacid tablets from a pocket, removed two and popped them into his mouth. Then he stuck the end of the unlit cigar into a corner of his mouth.

"The local CIA station chief recruited her. Because of her job, she has a lot of up-close-and-personal contact with some unsavory people. And, for that matter, some high-profile politicians, executives and dignitaries, folks we like to keep an eye on."

"And she's willing to name names."

Brognola nodded affirmatively.

"Very altruistic," Bolan said.

"Very profitable. We pony up serious money for that information. It's always reliable. She likes the cash and doesn't want anyone to issue a burn notice on her."

"Okay, so she's legit. So what?"

"So she called up the Athens station chief. Said one Massoud Kassem stopped by for some slap-and-tickle action about forty-eight hours ago."

"A day before the murders."

Brognola nodded again.

Bolan said, "This is the Libyan? The intelligence chief?"

"The same. Part of Khadaffi's inner circle. One or two slots down from the main spy chief. Handled most of their domestic intelligence. We both know what that means in a dictatorship."

"Hooking car batteries to a guy's balls."

"Exactly. And kidnappings. And murder, of course. Guy was—is—an animal. When Khadaffi got a bullet to the brain, this guy found himself out of work and definitely unwelcome in his home country."

"And you think the two are linked, his arrival and their murders?"

"We suspect it. Kassem fell off the grid for a while. But, from what Langley has pieced together, he surfaced six months or so ago in Algeria. Apparently, he reinvented himself as a gun for hire, gathered some of his old colleagues and a few new recruits and started his own Murder, Inc."

Brognola paused, took a sip of coffee and made a sour face.

"God, that's so awful, I'd swear Aaron made it. Anyway, at first no one sweated it. He mostly was taking jobs from his former colleagues, high-level Libyan bureaucrats, pissed they no longer were in charge and looking to settle a score or two. It wasn't pretty or nice on our part. But other than sharing information with Interpol, we weren't about to send in the Marines to wax this jerk. Frankly, we weren't actively gunning for him. And a few of his kills helped us more than they hurt. One or two of the jerks he killed were up to their neck with al Qaeda long before the revolution."

"Then things went wrong."

"Don't they always? Yeah, our friend wasn't just another pretty face. He was a damn good assassin. And good at building a strong organization on top of that. Next thing we know, he's out freelancing for the Iranians, the Syrians, the North Koreans, anyone who can meet his price, which is considerable."

"And you think he killed Briggs and Rabin?"

Brognola shrugged. "Not sure. It's possible he traveled to Athens for the scenery and a little nookie. I wouldn't bet rent money on it, though. He's got at least a dozen international police or intelligence agencies hunting him. Makes travel a little riskier."

"And there were no other deaths in Athens that could be attributed to him?"

"Not that we know of. It's possible he knifed someone, dumped them in the river and the police just don't know about it. Anything's possible, right? But there's some history here that makes him the likely hitter."

"That being?"

Brognola slid another photo across the table. Without picking it up, Bolan studied it. In it he saw an up-close photo of Kassem dressed in a tuxedo. Bolan surmised the picture was old. Kassem's hair looked darker and was cut short, with military precision. The skin of his face was smoother. He had his arm looped over the shoulder of a younger man, also clad in a black tuxedo. Unlike Kassem, the younger man wore wireless glasses with small, rectangular lenses, and the angle of his head showed his hair nearly reached his collar. But the resemblance between the two was unmistakable.

"That's Kassem's son. The picture was taken at a party Khadaffi threw years ago."

"Is he on the run, too?"

The big Fed shook his head.

"No, he isn't running or walking. Not on this earth, anyway. He died a couple of years ago. He liked the good life, just like his old man did. They found him in a hotel room in France, dead. According to what the cyberteam pulled together, he was doing some blow with a hooker and overdosed. That was the official report, anyway."

"And the unofficial report?"

"Well, the kid was smart. He had a PhD in physics and

worked in Libya's nuclear program when it had one. Israel at the time was trying to, um, slow down Libya's progress."

"So Mossad waxed baby Einstein? Is that theory, or—"

"It's fact. Sure, Israel denies the hell out of it. But we have it on good authority that Mossad did the deed."

"Meaning?"

"I got confirmation from the upper reaches of government."

"I thought you were the upper reaches of government."

"Higher."

"Wow."

"Impressive, right? Here's the kicker, though. Rabin supposedly was the guy running control on the mission. Mossad ran a program called Icarus for years. The aim was to keep the Israelis the only nuclear power in the Middle East. It was a collaboration, actually. Mossad, CIA and MI-6. They'd target nuclear scientists in these countries, especially Iran and Iraq, but other places, too. It was a blunt instrument. They'd get leverage over someone—money, women, men—and give them the option of defecting. For a lot of them, they could live with betraying their country—"

"But they couldn't do it for Israel."

"That's where the U.S. and Britain came into the picture. A lot of these guys hated us, but they hated Israel more. We'd work a deal with them, so long as we got all the information."

"And the ones who didn't take a deal?"

Brognola shrugged. "Most ended up dead. The Israelis' bargaining strategy was to give them a bad option and an even worse option."

"Is that what happened to Kassem's boy?"

The big Fed set his unlit cigar in a glass ashtray and shook his head.

"No, they just waxed him. The thinking was they'd never get the son of a high-ranking Khadaffi official to turn. Not only was that a death sentence for the son, but probably for Daddy and the rest of the clan."

"So it's a revenge killing."

"That's the theory. If so, that makes Briggs's death even more tragic. She had nothing to do with junior's death. She was just in the wrong place at the wrong time."

Bolan stared into his coffee cup. The coffee was nearly gone. But through the dark liquid he could see a few grounds resting on the bottom of the cup. He pushed it away. His stomach burned, not from the coffee, but with anger. Mental movies, brief flashes of the horror the lovers had suffered before Death finally wrapped them in its cold embrace continued to roll through his mind as he and Brognola had talked.

"The Man wants you to shut Kassem down. If you can find out who ordered the hit, so much the better. But he wants it known that our country won't stand for this sort of thing. That, if you hurt one of ours, we'll come at you and destroy not only you, but your organization."

Bolan nodded his understanding. He was only too happy to serve up payback.

"I'll leave as soon as I can," the Executioner said.

# CHAPTER TWO

*Athens, Greece*

The elevator doors parted and Bolan stepped onto the thirtieth floor of the luxury apartment building.

A large oval-shaped mirror framed with dark wood was fixed to the wall opposite the elevator. Bolan caught his reflection in it. He wore a black Armani suit, a powder-blue shirt, a black tie and black wingtips. His Beretta 93-R was stowed in a shoulder rig underneath the suit jacket. Black shades covered his icy blue eyes. In his left hand, he gripped a leather briefcase that contained his .44 Magnum Desert Eagle, along with extra magazines for both weapons.

Though Brognola had provided the soldier with a decent dossier, he wanted more information about Kassem. Since Kassem had made a point of visiting a call girl while he was in town, Bolan figured she might be a good place to start. Figuring she might not take a reservation from the U.S. Justice Department, Brognola had enlisted help from Leo Turrin. Another of Bolan's old friends, Turrin had run prostitutes for the Mafia even as he'd been working undercover for the U.S. government.

The way Bolan understood it, the woman, Kristina Mentis, only took referral business. Keeping her customer list short shielded her from the cops, the creeps and the pimps, Turrin had explained. She was a master of her craft and had enough repeat business to keep two of her busy, according to the semi-retired wiseguy. Turrin, through mutual contacts, had reserved some quality time with Mentis. It had required Bolan using role camouflage, adopting his persona as a Black Ace enforcer for the Mafia. Hence the high-dollar suit and master of the universe attitude he sported.

He reached the door and raised his hand to knock when he noticed it was open slightly.

Scowling, Bolan reached under his jacket, drew the Beretta and pushed lightly against the door with his fingertips. The heavy wooden door swung inward and the soldier brought up the Beretta, gripped with both hands, to chest level and slipped inside the penthouse.

His eyes traveled first to the man who lay crumpled on the floor. What had been a white T-shirt now was stained red, part of the fabric torn open from a bullet's exit wound. A pistol lay on the ground, inches from curled fingers. The pool of blood forming underneath the man gleamed under the fluorescent lights. The soldier heard anguished cries from a woman, accompanied by a man's raised voice. Bolan headed in the direction of the sound.

As he moved, he swept his gaze over the apartment, noting that long curtains had been pulled closed over its tall windows, allowing only small cracks of light to enter. Unless Mentis doubled as a vampire, Bolan guessed she kept the curtains drawn to guarantee her guests some measure of privacy. Or at least an illusion of such, since she shared her client list with the CIA and probably several other intelligence agencies.

He moved over the highly polished floors, wove his way between the luxurious pieces of furniture toward dual stair-cases that curled up from the first floor to the second.

As he neared the staircases, he caught a whiff of cigarette smoke, noticed the whitish haze that hung above him. Another cry pierced the air, and Bolan's first instinct was to rush up the stairs. He checked himself, though, knowing he didn't want to announce his arrival with heavy footfalls. When he reached the midway point on the stairs, he heard someone clear his throat, cough. The floor creaked slightly under the weight of footsteps. Bolan froze, his body coiled to respond, the Beretta's muzzle seeking a target.

A heartbeat later, a man built like a professional wrestler came into view. An unlit cigarette stuck out from his thick black beard, and he was raising his lighter to it. He stood at the railing and swept his eyes over the floor below. Deep creases formed in his forehead as he apparently sensed something amiss. He caught sight of Bolan in his peripheral vision, and his head whipped in the big American's direction. His fingers opened, and a blue disposable lighter fell to the floor. The now-empty hand stabbed underneath his jacket, clawing for hardware.

The Beretta chugged. A single 9 mm round drilled into the guy's forehead. Even as the gunner collapsed to the floor, Bolan continued moving up the stairs, his eyes and ears alert for more danger.

When he reached the landing, he saw the gunner lying in a heap on the floor, his foot still twitching.

Only two doors were visible. Bolan glanced in the first. He saw that the room contained a wooden desk topped with a blotter, a laptopwith an attached monitor, and a desk lamp with a green shade. A couple of filing cabinets stood against a wall. The soldier saw no threats and moved to the next door.

A man's voice exploded from the other room.

"What did you tell them, woman? Answer me, damn it!"

Bolan slipped through the doorway and into the room. He quickly noted the dark wood paneling, the massive bed, the chandeliers and the large-screen television running a porno.

The sound of someone gagging and the splashing of water drew Bolan's attention to an open door on his left. He moved up to the door, which stood partially open, and stole a glance around the doorjamb. A man stood with his back turned toward the door, bent over.

"You like this, bitch?" the man said, his voice loud and taunting.

Bolan came around the jamb and through the door, the new vantage point affording him a better view. The man stood in front of a bathtub, his legs spread apart. In the space between his legs, Bolan could see the hunched-up form of a woman. The man was pushing her head into the water. Her hands were pressed flat on the edge of the bathtub, the muscles of her back visible, as she pushed back against her attacker's superior leverage. Water sloshed over the side of the bathtub and spread over the tiled floor.

The man was still shouting. "You talk too much! You know that? Too damn much."

Mentis was fighting for her life and losing.

The soldier crossed the room. With the attacker's hands locked on the back of Mentis's neck and head, Bolan didn't worry about whether the guy was armed. His left hand snaked out and grabbed a shirt collar. The big American yanked hard, drawing the guy backward. Before the thug could wrap his mind around what was happening, the soldier spun him a quarter turn and hit him hard in the right temple with the bottom edge of the Beretta's grip. The guy's eyes lost focus, his legs went rubbery and Bolan shoved him back against the nearest wall.

From the corner of his eye, Bolan noticed the woman, gagging and coughing, had pulled herself from the tub. She was crawling on her hands and knees toward the door.

In the meantime, Bolan knelt next to the unconscious thug, stretched him out flat on the floor and bound his hands behind his back with plastic restraints. The soldier got to his feet and exited the bathroom.

SHE REACHED OUT with a shaking hand for a bottle of vodka. Bolan put his hand on hers to stop her.

"No," he said. "Not right now. I need to ask you some questions."

She turned and looked at the door. "Basil!" she yelled. "Basil!" She turned her eyes on Bolan. "Where the hell is Basil?"

"Skinny guy in the white T-shirt?"

"Yes."

"Dead. They shot him."

Her lips tightened into a hard line and tears glistened in her eyes. Burying her face in her hands, she sobbed. Bolan stood by, but said nothing. After a minute or so, she peeled her hands away and looked up at him.

"You starting to get it now?"

She squeezed her eyes shut and nodded.

"Good."

He jerked his head toward bathroom.

"The guy in there. You know him?"

She nodded. "His name's Harambi. Abed Harambi. He works for one of my clients."

"Kassem?"

She licked her lips and hesitated.

"I know about Kassem."

"Know what?"

"The people who set up this meeting, they didn't tell you why I'm here?"

"They said you were looking for someone. They didn't tell me anything else."

"Your friend Kassem—"

"He's not my friend, you bastard."

Bolan made a dismissive gesture. "Whatever. You know what he does for a living right?"

She shook her head. Bolan guessed she was lying, but he decided to let it slide.

"He kills people," Bolan said. He saw something flicker in the woman's eyes and guessed he'd struck a chord. But he didn't press the issue; he was trying to misdirect her. "Kassem's been trafficking in weapons. He's been sitting on a pile of stuff he stole from Libya before they tossed his ass out of the country for good.

"At first he sells a few things in Syria, Pakistan and northern Africa, and my bosses, they don't give a shit. We'll take money from people in those countries, sure. But it's not our core business. Shit, they have enough weapons in Africa, we might never sell anything there."

The woman remained silent.

"Unfortunately for Kassem, he stepped out of line. Way the fuck out of line."

"What did he do?"

"Started selling stuff to the cartels. Shoulder-fired missiles, assault rifles. Hell, these assholes all but have a key to the government armories in that country. But what they need, we sell them."

"Who's we?"

"I think you know. At least you know enough or we wouldn't be talking. Anyway, that Libyan prick has stepped over the line, way over it."

"You're here to warn him? To stay off your turf?"

A grim smile ghosted Bolan's lips. "Warn him? Put him in the ground is more like it."

She shuddered.

"You want me to help you kill him?"

"Help me?" Bolan laughed. "Hell, help yourself." He jerked a thumb toward the bathroom. "That little prick in there? The one I hogtied? There's a million of him. For whatever reason, Kassem is pissed at you. I walk away from you now, and you'll have some other asshole shoving your head in a tub tomorrow."

"I'll hire another bodyguard."

"Make sure you give him life insurance."

"You're a bastard."

Bolan shrugged. "Wrap your head around this. I don't want you to kill anyone. Just do what you do best."

"You mean?"

"Not that. Just sit here and wait on someone else to kill you."

MENTIS WANTED TO take a shower, put on some fresh clothes and a little makeup. Bolan had agreed to it. Without her asking, he grabbed the unconscious thug by the collar and dragged him from the bathroom into the office next to her bedroom. He sat the guy up in a rolling armchair, the back of which leaned against a wall. The gunner still hadn't stirred. Bolan used the secure satellite phone he carried to call Brognola and request a cleanup team for the apartment.

The soldier sat on the edge of the desk and thought about Kristina Mentis. He knew she was shaken and rightfully so. The callousness he was showing her fit with his cover, but didn't sit well with him. He knew the lady was in hell. Maybe some of it was self-inflicted. Whatever. Bolan wasn't a puritan and he wasn't about to judge Mentis for her occupation or her life choices.

No, he wouldn't judge her, but he was going to use her as bait. She was his only lead at the moment.

Bolan walked over to the thug trussed up in the chair. The guy's lips were parted and drool trailed from the corner of his mouth.

With an open palm, the soldier slapped the guy once across the face, hard enough that it sounded like a branch breaking. The thug's head whipped to one side and his eyes snapped open. He turned and glared at Bolan, the drool replaced with a line of blood, arms straining at the plastic restraints.

"Hey, slick," Bolan said. "Rise and shine."

"Who—"

"Am I? I'm the best friend you just met."

The thug continued to glare at Bolan, but remained silent.

"See, you just woke up in hell. One where studs like you—you know, the ones who drown ladies in bathtubs?—they die a very slow death." Bolan reached into his pocket and withdrew the pearl-handled switchblade he'd taken from the man. He opened it and studied the edge of the blade. "Here's the deal. I've killed a lot of people. Far away. Up close. Doesn't matter. But they had it coming. You? You and your little buddy out there. The dead one? You come in here, the two of you, to kill a working girl."

Bolan's arm shot forward and the blade sliced through the air an inch or so from the guy's left ear. The blade bit deeply into the wall. The man's eyes bulged and he inhaled sharply, jerked his body away. A smile ghosted Bolan's lips and he pulled the knife from the wall.

"I know, right? You almost die, it scares you. Even a tough guy like you. If you hadn't already pissed yourself when I kicked your ass in the bathroom, you'd sure be pissing your pants now, right? That's what fear does to people, makes them lose control. Makes them do dumb things."

"You speak bullshit," the man said. "You don't scare me."

Bolan shrugged and yanked the knife free from the wallboard. He slit the restraints, then folded the weapon and stuffed it into his hip pocket.

"Not sure I buy that. But, okay, maybe pissing your pants gets you off. Whatever. To each his own. The point is, I have a decision I need to make. And you're going to help me. I killed your buddy out there." The guy in the chair swallowed hard and Bolan smiled at him. "I'd just as soon put you in the ground, too. But I came a long way to find your boss, have a little talk with him. Here's my dilemma. Do I kill you right here or let you deliver a message to your boss?"

The guy licked his lips. "I can deliver a message for you."

"Figured you might say that." He walked to the door and stopped just short of it. "Okay, here's the message. Tell Kassem I know what he did and I'm looking for him. Tell him Matt Cooper is hunting for him. Go."

The man went.

Bolan heard fabric rustling, smelled cigarette smoke and turned. Mentis stood at the top of the stairs. By now she had dried her hair and applied a bit of eye makeup and lipstick. She had wrapped herself in a satiny red bathrobe that reached just to the top of her thighs. She stood on the top step, arms hugging her midsection, a cigarette poking from between the first two knuckles of her right hand. A thin line of white smoke rose from the tip of the cigarette and curled toward the ceiling.

"Is he gone?"

Bolan nodded.

"What now?"

"We move."

"To where?"

Bolan shook his head.

"You'll know soon enough. Just trust me on this."

"You're a criminal."

"I'm also the only thing you've got right now."

He expected more pushback from her. Instead, she turned and started toward her room.

"Let me pack."

Is THIS MY FAULT?

The thought careened through Angel Tzon's head as she read the headline for what seemed like the thousandth time. "No New Leads in Double Homicide," the headline said. In the forty-eight hours since Rabin and Briggs had been murdered, she had read every story she could get her hands on about the investigation. While she cared if the killers were caught, she was also looking for any references to Rabin's meeting with an unidentified young woman. She was that woman, and if the police were looking for her she wanted to know as soon as possible.

So far, she had seen nothing in media reports. She took little comfort from it, though, since police often held back information from the press during investigations. They could be looking for her right now. If they were, if they questioned her, arrested her, it would ruin everything. As badly as she felt about the murders, this all was so much bigger than that.

She read the first couple of paragraphs again. The police were still referring to the case as a robbery/homicide, at least publicly. She considered that a good thing, an indicator they had no idea what they truly were dealing with.

She brought her tea to her lips and stared over the rim of her cup at her surroundings. The hole-in-the-wall café was crowded, dark and noisy. A bar ran the length of one wall. A half-dozen round tables stood in the center of the dining area, accompanied by a handful of booths tucked along one wall. She was seated in the last booth, a location that afforded her a view of the front door and a large window that faced the street.

The patrons were all adults, all dressed in casual business attire, and she guessed they were the workday lunch crowd. They chatted among themselves animatedly and seemed to ignore her, which is exactly what she wanted. She wanted to blend in and have time to think. There was so much happening so quickly, she needed to figure out her next move.

Her cell phone vibrated against the surface of the wooden table. She recognized the number flashing on the screen immediately, picked it up and brought it to her ear.

"Hello?" she said.

"It's Sandra," a voice said.

"About time," Tzon said. "I called three hours ago. Under the circumstances, you'd think I might get priority status."

She heard Pearson exhale on the other end of the phone.

"Sorry, Angel," Sandra Pearson replied. "I'm trying to

make sense of all this myself. I haven't been avoiding you. This all has moved in a direction we never anticipated."

"Tell me about it," Tzon replied.

"Look, I know you're pissed, but keep your head on straight. We can work this out."

Tzon bit down on a profane reply. "Okay," she said. "Bring me up to speed."

"Like I said, I am still trying to make sense of it, too. Dale has been hacking the local police department and I've been working my Interpol sources."

"And?"

"The police don't know about you."

Tzon exhaled and felt the tension in her shoulders loosen a bit.

"That's good, at least," she said.

"But it doesn't solve our larger problem."

"QF-17."

"Right. As best we can tell, the players are still moving in the same direction they were before Rabin and Briggs were killed. Whether they killed those two is open to debate. But whether they benefit from the deaths is not," Pearson said.

"So we're back at square one."

"Not necessarily. We do have a lead that has popped up."

Tzon raised an eyebrow. "Well, tell me, damn it."

"Dale got a call an hour or so ago from one of his sources. Apparently, a man named Massoud Kassem was in town at the time of the murders. Does that name mean anything to you?"

A cold sensation raced down Tzon's spine.

"He worked for Libyan intelligence. Pretty high up the chain."

"That's him. Any idea why he might have been there?"

Tzon shook her head even though Pearson couldn't see her. "I have no idea why. I assume he got purged with the rest of the Khadaffi regime."

"He did. I found a classified Interpol bulletin calling for his arrest."

"Why?"

"Doesn't say. I don't get the impression it has to do with his former job in Libya. I think it would be clearer if that were the case."

"True. Is he still in the country?"

"Can't tell for sure. He was traveling under an alias. But here is something even more interesting."

Pearson always liked to build the suspense, and it drove Tzon crazy. She wanted to snap at her boss, but forced herself to drink tea instead.

"If this really is Kassem's alias, then it looks like he also made a trip to Brazil in the past month. And guess who he met with while he was there."

"Jiang Fang."

"Right."

"Wow."

"Could be a coincidence."

"You know I don't believe in coincidences."

"I know."

"This could be the link."

"*Could be* being the key words there. We need more information."

"Fair enough. Any thoughts on where to look next?"

"Here's what I'm thinking you should do."

AFTER SHE ATE, Tzon returned to the hotel where Briggs and Rabin had been murdered. As she passed through the revolving doors and into the lobby, a shiver passed through her. For a moment, she could smell Rabin's cologne, tainted by the smell of stale cigarettes. She could hear his derisive laughter as she'd tried to explain the dangers he and his partner faced. His reaction had surprised her; she'd thought—or at least hoped—their shared nationality would have bought her some credibility with the former Mossad man. Obviously it hadn't or he might still be alive.

She crossed the lobby and moved to the front desk.

A young woman with short, spiky blond hair, stood behind the desk staring down at something. Tzon cleared her throat and the woman looked up, smiling. The smile morphed into a scowl as she identified her visitor.

"Angel," the woman said.

"Isadora," Tzon said.

"I suppose you want to see him."

Tzon nodded. The clerk picked up the phone, punched in a couple of numbers and fidgeted while she waited through a couple of rings. Tzon heard someone on the other end answer the call.

"She's here," Isadora said. "Yes, her. No, Christos, I didn't say anything to her. Of course I'll send her back. I'm not a damn child!"

She slammed down the phone and gestured at the door behind her with a jerk of her head.

"He's in his office."

"I can find it."

Tzon walked around the desk and through a swing door. She always found the corridor on the other side of the door jarring. The lobby and the rooms were luxurious, almost breathtakingly so. The administrative offices were clean, but barren: white walls and neutral brown carpet, outfitted with steel desks and filing cabinets, all painted black, cardboard file boxes stacked against the walls.

She found the door to Christos Kellis's office, knocked once and went inside. Kellis, a small man with an immaculately trimmed goatee, stood behind his desk, shrugging on his suit jacket. The framed picture of his wife and three children that stood on a table behind his desk had been turned around. Classy.

He flashed Tzon a smile and came around the desk, arms open.

"Angel, welcome," he said.

Tzon let him hug her and kiss her on the cheek. He planted a second on her neck, and she felt her skin crawl. But she forced a small moan and pushed herself against him. He let his open palm slide from the middle of her back down to her waist. She pushed him away gently, turned her head to avoid another kiss.

"Not today," she said. Or any other day.

"You said last time…"

"I know," Tzon said. "I'm just so upset."

"Come here, then," he said. He tried to wrap his arms around her. She deftly stepped out of his arms, and when he moved for her again, she pushed an open palm into his chest to stop him. She'd spent countless hours studying Krav Maga and could send him crashing to the floor with strikes to the groin or throat. As much as she'd have loved to see the philandering jerk writhe in pain, she needed his help.

"I can't." She forced a tear, let him see it roll down her cheek then turned her head and cast her eyes down.

"Did Isadora say something? She means nothing to me."

Isadora, the desk clerk, was not his wife. She was just one of several hotel employees the little sleazeball boned during work hours, she knew.

Tzon shook her head.

"Nothing like that," she replied. "It's this murder."

"Murder?"

"The one here. The two people."

"Oh, that. Yes, it's terrible. I've caught hell from corporate over the whole thing. The press keeps coming by and asking questions, harassing the patrons. It's hell. But how does that affect you?"

"Well, there's a newsmagazine, one in America, that wants a story on the murders."

"That's good, isn't it?"

"Of course it is. I mean, well, it would be. But the editor there is screaming for more details. You know how they are."

Tzon guessed he had no idea what editors were like. But he nodded his head agreeably.

"You want some quotes from me? They'd have to be off the record," he said. "I'm not allowed to speak to the media. Corporate strictly forbids it."

"Yet here I am in your office."

He gave her a lewd smile. "Our relationship is so much more than professional."

Tzon felt a laugh brewing. She hid it by covering her mouth with an open hand and coughing.

"So," he said, "you want some quotes?"

She nodded. From what she understood, he was off work the day of the murders and had been kept away from any details by a team of corporate security specialists who'd flown in from the States to assist the local authorities. Everything he spouted had already been reported in various newspapers. He was just regurgitating what he'd read elsewhere while staring at her chest. Tzon forced herself to smile and nod and jot notes in a notepad while he talked, occasionally fantasizing about jamming a pen into his eye.

"Was that helpful?" he asked.

"Very much," she lied.

"So you feel better now? A little more at ease?"

She knew where this was going. Pushing up her left sleeve with her right hand, she gasped. "I have a deadline to make," she said.

"A deadline? Now?"

"I'm afraid so. By the way, the lobby has security cameras, right?"

"Of course."

"So there's footage," she said. "From the morning of the murders."

"Of course."

"I'd like to get it."

"What? I can't give you that."

"Why not? No one needs to know where I got it."

"Everyone will know where you got it. Who else here would give it to you? Certainly not Isadora."

"Fair enough. But I won't spread it around. I just want to look at it. Maybe there are some clues."

"Clues? I gave it to the police. Let them solve the murders."

"I'm not going to solve the murders. I just want to look at footage. There have to be details on there that would help my story."

"But my quotes…"

"Are great. But you can never have too much information. Do you have the footage?"

He nodded. "I have a copy. But I don't know whether I should give it to you. What good would come of it?"

"You'd have my gratitude," she said, "and all that comes with it."

Ten minutes later, she left his office with a thumb drive in her purse that included the security footage. She'd send it to Washington and then move to her next stop.

CHRISTOS KELLIS STARED at the door after Tzon had left his office. His neck and cheeks burned with anger and humiliation. He knew the woman was playing with him, using him for information. She knew what he wanted. She'd gladly dangle it in his face but always told him no. It pissed him off, but he'd tried to look past it, figuring she'd relent sooner or later.

Apparently not. She just wanted to make a fool of him. She was probably laughing at him even now.

Fine. Two could play at that game.

Walking back around his desk, he pulled open the lap drawer. He rooted around in it for a few seconds before he found what he was looking for—a business card. He turned it over and read the name: Detective George Pappas.

Before the murders, he'd never heard of Pappas. But the man had been assigned to investigate the murders and had asked for Kellis and his people to call him with any new information, including press inquiries.

*What the hell?* Kellis thought. Pappas would harass Tzon a little. More than likely, he'd harass her a little and tell her to stay away from his witnesses. He might push her to share whatever information she had dug up on the murders, but he'd push it no further. The guy was a cop and he had rules to follow.

As for Tzon? If she wasn't going to give in, Kellis had no use for her.

He made the call.

THE PHONE'S RECEIVER sandwiched between his left ear and his shoulder, Pappas listened to the hotel manager as he recounted the woman's visit. Kellis was speaking rapidly, the speed and pitch of his voice rising the longer he spoke. The woman obviously had gotten under the man's skin. Knowing what he did of the hotel manager's reputation as a lothario, Pappas guessed it involved sex or the refusal of sex. Little else sustained the man.

Pappas was seated in a rolling chair behind his desk, his feet propped up on the desktop. The agitated man on the other end of the line was speaking quickly, and Pappas found it difficult to keep up. He closed his eyes, hoping in vain that by shutting off one sense he might enhance another.

When Kellis took a breath, the detective piped up. "This woman claims to be a journalist."

"She's a journalist."

"You've seen her work."

"No, but she told me she is a journalist. She had business

cards. Her business cards say she's a journalist. She must be a journalist."

"I can buy business cards that say I'm the pope. It doesn't make it so, my friend. You get my meaning?"

The other man said nothing.

"This journalist? She works in television? Newspapers? Internet?" Pappas pressed.

"Television. Well, she's pretty enough to be on television. Beautiful, actually. But she writes for magazines."

"Such as?"

"I don't know. One in America."

Pappas rolled his eyes.

"But you don't know the name?"

"No. I can scan in a copy of her business card and email it to you."

"I'd like that. Did she ask you any questions? Ask about the progress of the investigation, any of that sort of thing?"

"No."

"Did she ask to speak with other employees? Patrons?"

"No. None of that. She just asked a few questions and left."

"So she just came in, fluttered her eyelashes and left?"

"Well," the other man began before he fell silent for several seconds.

"Well, what?"

"She asked for some footage from our cameras."

"And of course you complied."

"I could lose my job for this," Kellis said. The detective got the impression it was the first time this had dawned on the hotel manager.

"It's the same footage you gave us, correct?"

"It is."

"I told you to destroy extra copies, didn't I? You realize this is a police investigation and that you're interfering with it? You gave us the original file. Why didn't you destroy the extra copies?"

"I don't know."

"Perhaps because you could trade them for sex or money. You've done that before, haven't you? At least the money part. It takes a lot of cash to maintain so many girlfriends."

"That's a damned lie!"

"Of course it is," Pappas said. "How many other copies have you handed out?"

"None." Something in the man's voice told Pappas he was telling the truth.

"I'm going to send someone over," Pappas said. "I'll send you his name. You will let him into your office. He will comb through your IT system and make sure there are no other copies of the surveillance tape. You understand?"

"This man, he will be a police officer?" Kellis asked.

"Of course," Pappas lied. "Give me two hours and we will clean up this mess."

He slammed down the receiver, looked at the ceiling and shook his head in disgust. Another damn mess to clean up, always another mess. From the moment he'd heard Kassem was coming to town, he'd known disaster would follow. The minute he'd heard about the hotel murders, he'd stepped up and volunteered to investigate them.

A sane man would have run the other way, but he couldn't do it. Without being told, he knew what he needed to do— run interference on the investigation, make it so the damn thing ended up unsolved. At the same time, he was to keep his ear to the ground and make sure he could report back to Kassem's handlers on the progress of the investigation. In espionage, they'd call him a double agent. In police work, he got no such glamorous title. He simply was a crooked cop, a man guilty of betraying not only his comrades, but also his oath of office. Or a crook.

At some point that had bothered him, but that was a long time ago. Now he just did as he was told and money arrived in one of the accounts he maintained at different banks. Sometimes, getting the money was easy; he simply looked the other way. Other times, when a fire broke out, he had to take a more active role.

This was one of those times. His gut told him someone would die. Not by his hand. But with his knowledge, with his help. Bringing his feet to the floor, he leaned forward, opened the bottom right desk drawer and drew a silver flask from it. Unscrewing the cap, he raised the flask to his lips, tipped it and took an extra-long swallow of the whiskey. It tasted good, so he took another swallow before he replaced the cap. He stood the flask on his desk and stared at it for several seconds without really seeing it.

Now would be a hell of a time to grow a conscience, wouldn't it? Make a stab at redemption. Stop Kassem and the other killers slithering through Athens, his city, the one he'd sworn to protect. Hunt the bastards down before they could draw more blood. Shove them in jail or maybe just gun them down, dispense justice himself.

Sure, it'd be a hell of a time to do all that.

He belched and the taste of whiskey filled his mouth again. He scratched absently at his scalp and smiled. Who the fuck was he kidding? He was a kept man, one with several owners. Like Christos, he had a propensity for sticking his dick in places it didn't belong. Unlike Christos, his extracurricular activities had been filmed by spies and crooks alike, leaving him vulnerable to blackmail. So, yeah, he could make a stand. But over the years it had gotten so much easier to crawl, and the view from the bottom wasn't so bad.

Screw it.

He reached for the phone and dialed a number.

# CHAPTER THREE

Scowling, Sandra Pearson chewed her lower lip and stared at the phone.

Tzon had sounded afraid. That worried Pearson, of course. Caution while in the field was one thing, fear another, as far as Pearson was concerned. But even worse, the Israeli woman had sounded wary and distrustful of Pearson, an old friend and ally. The distrust hurt, of course. Pearson's concerns went well beyond her feelings, though. When an operative stopped trusting, it became too easy to isolate and withhold information.

It got people killed.

Pearson already had gone through that hell once on this mission. It was the first time since the end of the cold war that the Pearson Center had lost someone in the field. The first time she'd sent someone to die. She'd always known it was a risk, which didn't lessen the pain and guilt one iota.

She'd been sitting in the operations room for hours, drinking coffee and foregoing meals. Her eyes felt grainy from lack of sleep and her thoughts drifted back to her empty stomach with increased regularity. Still she turned to her PC and began scouring the internet for more information about the murders. Food and sleep sounded wonderful, but she couldn't bring herself to take a break. Not with everything going on.

Strong hands came to rest on her shoulders, startled her.

"A little tense, are we?" Dale Roberts asked, the Briton's voice subdued.

Her shoulder muscles loosened and she exhaled deeply.

Reaching her right hand across her chest, she patted the top of his left hand.

"Just worried," she said.

"About?"

"Angel. She's out there alone. She's scared."

"Comes with the territory, love. The girl—sorry, the woman—knew the stakes when she put up her hand and volunteered. She's not exactly a novice at this sort of thing, you know. She was a war correspondent. Daddy was an Israeli commando. She knows how to get herself out of trouble."

Pearson nodded slowly, reluctantly.

Roberts continued. "She did what she needed to do. She made contact with Ben Rabin. She told him everything he needed to know…"

"And now he's dead."

"What's the saying? You can lead a horse to water, but you can't make him drink? You passed along the information. The stubborn old fool didn't listen. Had he listened the minute she'd told him, called his superiors at the company, he and his American girlfriend still would be alive, sipping ouzo and fucking like wild beasts at the hotel."

"Dale!"

"Sorry, love, spent too many years in too many shitholes, up to my waist in blood and mud to be delicate. If he'd listened to Angel, he'd be alive. One way or the other, he'd be alive."

"What do you mean, 'One way or the other'?"

He pulled his hands away, spun her in her chair so she faced him. He crossed his arms over his chest and stared down at her with his pale green eyes. From what he'd told her before, he was at least part Irish with a ruddy complexion and reddish-blond hair and matching beard. His thin lips turned up at one corner in a cocky half grin.

That same cockiness had almost led Pearson to turn him away when he first approached her about a job with the Pearson Center as a controller. Pearson liked confidence, but had always met arrogance with caution, if not outright contempt. Arrogance and overconfidence bred mistakes. That was bad enough with an operative, but was intolerable from a controller.

Still, he'd come highly recommended. John Thomas, one of her late father's contacts in MI-6 and a fellow cold warrior, had hooked them up. He said Roberts had experienced "a setback" while operating in Afghanistan that had led to him bailing from the SAS. When she'd pressed for specifics, Thomas had demurred because the specifics were secret. "He's a good bloke and just needs another chance," the man had said. "Trust me. I've known you since you were a girl. If I thought even for a minute he was unreliable, you and I wouldn't be having this conversation."

Though she'd hated not knowing the full story, she'd honored Thomas's request and had brought Roberts on board. It had worked out, perhaps better than expected.

"What?" Roberts said.

"Sorry?"

"You're smiling. Just a bit, but you're smiling."

"So?"

"So, what are you thinking?"

She rose from the chair and moved in close, looping her arms around his neck. The top of her head reached just to the tip of his jaw. She laid the side of her head against his chest and closed her eyes.

"I'm thinking I'm tired and hungry," she said.

"Sliced turkey in the refrigerator. Just brewed a pot of coffee. There's a six-pack of dark beer if you want something a little stiffer."

She tilted her head up at him and smiled. "Definitely something stiffer," she said.

He nodded once. "Definitely."

She squeezed him one last time, then pulled away.

"First food," she said. "And maybe coffee. So I can stay awake."

"Staying awake won't be a problem. You definitely should eat, though. Keep up your strength."

"You hungry?"

He nodded at the computer. "Let me take care of a few things here," he said. "I already ate. Give me an hour or so to wind those things up. I'll meet you upstairs after that."

"Hopefully, I'll still be awake," she said.

"Your loss if you're not," he said.

She rolled her eyes. "I'll manage somehow."

He jerked his head toward the door. "Go eat."

She patted him on the stomach, exited the operations room and made her way to the elevator that would carry her to the first floor.

A FEW MINUTES later, Pearson sat at a table in the kitchen. She chewed a small mouthful of a turkey wrap. She'd selected bottled water because the thought of downing another cup of coffee made her stomach churn. She knew even a single beer would put her to sleep. A few bites of food had helped calm her nagging hunger. It had done nothing to dispel the sense of dread gnawing at her gut, however.

As she thought about it, she couldn't blame Tzon for her suspicions. Just a couple of weeks ago, another of their operatives had been killed in Hong Kong. He'd been the first to catch the chatter about the trouble being raised by a small ring of Chinese spies. He'd passed along what he knew to Pearson, which had set everything else in motion.

Resting her elbows on the table, she laced the fingers of both hands together and rested her forehead against her knuckles. Tears stung her eyes. She closed them, only to have an image of his dead body, bruised, streaked with dark, dried blood, flash in her mind's eye.

Her eyes snapped back open. She picked up a paper napkin and dabbed at the corners of her eyes.

The police in Hong Kong said he'd run afoul of Chinese organized crime. Pearson had no doubt about that. He was a high-level fence who spent most of his time associating with mobsters, terrorists and crooked bureaucrats. Though it often left him in a precarious position legally, it also gave him access to the kind of information the Pearson Center wanted.

So maybe he hadn't died specifically because of his links to Pearson's operation. Maybe. But, without his involvement with Pearson, he would have been somewhere else, somewhere much safer. He'd be alive.

Tzon wasn't an idiot. Only a small handful of people knew about the Pearson Center's activities. If someone had betrayed him, it was possible the leak had come from inside her organization. She'd considered the possibility of betrayal, had even asked Roberts to investigate. He'd done just that, and by his own admission, had found no signs of a mole in the organization.

So here she was—one dead operative and no idea how it had happened. She had other people working in other parts of the world. But this situation with QF-17 was the only one that'd turned deadly for her.

She thought of her father and her grandfather before him, wondered how they might've handled the situation. Her family had amassed much of its fortune by operating a shipping company and by making automotive parts. Robert Pearson, Sr., a man known to unwind with a few drinks, had expanded the family's holdings during Prohibition by shipping bootlegged alcohol into Maryland and Virginia. As World War II threatened to draw the United States into the conflict, Pearson had retooled the family factories so they churned out parts for rifles and tanks, rather than roadsters. By 1942, her grandfather's old friend Colonel William Donavan, father of the Office of Strategic Services, had conscripted Pearson's boats and cargo planes to smuggle people and weapons behind enemy lines.

In addition to his being an unrepentant drunk, Pearson later came to realize her grandfather was an adrenaline junkie who'd taken easily to espionage. When World War II ended, he'd found he couldn't stay away from it, but he also didn't have the ability to work for someone else. That was when he'd established the Pearson Center. On the surface, it was a think tank and a foundation that studied international issues and gave generous research grants to some of the world's best foreign policy experts. That was the cover, anyway. While most of the scholars on the center's payroll had no idea of the organization's dual role, a few were keenly aware of its purpose. The center's inner circle included several journalists, former intelligence and military officers, and law enforcement officials willing to travel the world, gathering information vital to U.S. security. The center then forwarded the information to the CIA, FBI and NSA to follow up on.

Since they'd never find themselves hauled before a congressional committee to testify as to their methods, they bent a lot of rules in search of the truth. Pearson's father, Robert Jr., had stepped into the organization during the Vietnam War. Like his father before him, Robert Jr. had spent as much time as possible traveling the world, locking horns with the Soviet Union and its proxy states, rather than manning a desk in the Beltway. They'd turned up stunning information on occasion, which they passed along to the U.S. government, asking for neither money nor recognition in return.

After the cold war, Sandra had continued to run the organization, keeping the focus almost entirely on gathering intelligence. Like the others before her, she spent much of her time rubbing elbows with the denizens of Washington, D.C.'s upper reaches while also carrying out intelligence-gathering operations. The center employed a handful of analysts, all of them experts in their fields, and a few researchers. Otherwise,

Pearson spent much of her time running operatives, such as Angel Tzon, in foreign countries.

Even after 9/11, the center had left the bloody work to legitimate intelligence agencies.

Then she'd received the tip about QF-17 and that all changed.

A part of her wanted to order Tzon to come back immediately. Pearson's intuition told her the situation was going to get worse. And with Tzon now casting a wary eye at Pearson, Roberts and the others, she was in more danger than ever. Still, the woman was good at digging up information and Tzon wanted to know more about the murders, more about the other things unfolding behind the scenes. If anyone could secure such information, it was Tzon.

Pearson just hoped her old friend was okay.

THREE HOURS LATER, Dale Roberts stood, fully dressed, at the foot of Pearson's bed and stared down at her.

The woman lay on her bed, a sheet draped over her curves, and snored softly. Normally, she was a light sleeper and given to occasional nightmares. Roberts had helped her into a deep slumber by adding bits of a sleeping tablet to her wine. He'd used it sparingly, just enough to deepen her sleep without making her groggy in the morning and arousing her suspicions.

The thought caused a smile to ghost his lips. He doubted she'd ever suspect him of anything bad. Despite her education and her intellect, she trusted easily. He guessed it was the optimism that came from growing up a millionaire. In a profile of her authored by his handlers, some psychologist had blathered on about a "father wound" or some such bullshit, as well as the loneliness inherent in leading a double life as socialite and spy. She presented a hard exterior to protect herself, the assessment had stated. But once she'd opened herself up she was likely to ignore signs of betrayal, making her a perfect target.

The Briton didn't know about all that crap. He just knew the woman was smitten with him and he was going to ride it for all it was worth. He'd been sent in to infiltrate her operation. The Chinese were paying him handsomely to do so, too, shifting the money to a bank account in the Cayman Islands. He'd already made his way into her bed and if he could also tap into her trust fund, so much the better.

And he'd leave no one behind to complain, either. He planned to put her in the ground, if at all possible, but hadn't figured out how to make it happen yet. He'd considered hiring a hit man, but professional pride had blocked him from doing so. After all, he had been one of MI-6's best wet work specialists back in the day. Knives, guns, drugs. He'd used them all while hunting Iraqi insurgents in Basara after the U.S., Britain and other coalition forces invaded the country.

After he left MI-6, he'd moved to Africa and sold his services as a mercenary and assassin to the highest bidders. Roberts had worked with John Thomas, a friend of the Pearson family, for years. Thomas had retired from active service before Roberts had moved to Africa to pursue what he jokingly referred to as "private practice." The older man would've been aghast had he known the details of Roberts's activities there.

Jiang Fang's first stab at recruiting Roberts had failed. The Chinese spy had secured proof of Roberts's involvement in bombing a school in Sudan that had killed a dozen children. Jiang had presented him with the evidence and demanded his cooperation. Otherwise, Jiang had said, he'd expose Roberts, leave him ruined.

Roberts had laughed at that. "I was ruined a long time ago," he'd told Jiang. "You want my services? You bloody well can pay for them like everyone else does, you cheap prick."

Jiang had paid and was getting his money's worth.

Roberts had already sold out one of Pearson's operatives. And, before the night was through, he'd sell out a second.

Pearson rolled onto her side, her back facing him, and moaned softly. She really was too trusting, he thought. She was in way over her head, playing with the big boys. By the time she realized it, it'd be too late.

TZON STEPPED INTO her small apartment and bolted the door behind her.

Setting her keys and purse on a table next to the door, she kicked off her shoes and enjoyed the feel of the cool, flat floor against her aching soles. After her meeting with the hotel manager, she'd spent the rest of the day tracking down several other leads, none of which panned out.

A long, hot bath, capped by a gin and tonic, sounded ideal. She rolled her eyes. Wishful thinking. A hot shower, a pot of coffee and several more hours surfing the internet sounded more likely. Maybe she'd fall into bed by 3:00 a.m. Maybe.

Before she could take another step, her cell phone rang. She made an exasperated sound and retrieved it from her purse. Her brow knitted in confusion when she saw the number. The Pearson Center was calling again. What the hell? She'd emailed Sandra an hour ago and told her the day had been a bust.

"Sandra?"

"Better," the male voice replied.

"Dale?"

"Smart lady. How'd you know?"

"There's exactly one person at this number with a British accent."

"Like I said, smart lady."

Patronizing piece of crap. How Sandra could stand him mystified Tzon.

"Speaking of accents," she said. "Did you just call to hear mine or do you have actual business to deal with?"

"Well, aren't we frosty."

"It's been a long day and I'm nowhere near done with it."

"You're right," Roberts replied. "You're not."

"Save the man of mystery routine for some other woman. Get to the point or call me in the morning."

If Tzon's sharp words bothered the Briton, he gave no indication.

"I've got a source for you. Actually, Sandra dug him up. I'm just passing along the name."

An edge of suspicion crept into Tzon's voice. "Why didn't she call me herself?"

"How the hell should I know? You want the tip or not? Maybe earn out that overly generous salary of yours?"

"Son of a…"

"Bitch? Was thinking the same of you. I'll text you with the information." Roberts hung up.

Tzon gritted her teeth and stared at the phone for a couple of seconds. A beep announced the text from Roberts. She opened the message and read it. The hairs on the back of her neck prickled and her scowl deepened. Was he kidding?

Apparently, she had a late night ahead of her, but it wasn't going to be spent in the apartment. Slipping her shoes back on, she grabbed her purse and keys and exited the apartment.

FORTY-FIVE MINUTES LATER, Tzon guided her car down a darkened street. Peering through the windshield, she sized up her surroundings. Old factory buildings, most of which had closed during the recession and never reopened, lined the street. Chain-link fences surrounded most of the properties. In some places, vandals had cut through the fences and sprayed graffiti on the shuttered factories. Second- and third-floor windows had been shattered by rock-throwing vandals. Tzon parked her car under one of the only streetlights still working on the avenue.

Letting the car idle, she sifted through her purse until she found what she was looking for—a small-frame Glock pistol. She took the pistol out of her purse and set the bag on the passenger seat.

Roberts's message had been cryptic, giving the source's name and the address of the rendezvous point. She'd recognized the address immediately. The dilapidated area had become a magnet for smugglers and drug dealers because it was close to the docks, but not heavily traveled or populated.

A sense of dread gnawed at Tzon.

She had already sent Roberts a text message asking him to verify the address after she'd left her apartment. He'd sent a terse confirmation. She could understand a source wanting to meet in an inconspicuous place, away from prying eyes. But this made no sense.

She got out of her car just as another vehicle, a black SUV, turned onto the street. The engine growled halfway through the turn and tires squealed against the pavement. Tzon quickly found herself pinned in the glare of the headlights. The righteous anger she'd felt dissipated, replaced by a thudding heart and blood pounding in her ears.

Before she could react, similar vehicle sounds arose behind her. She wheeled around and saw a low-slung black sports car, headlights lancing through the darkness, bearing down on her from the opposite direction.

For a couple of heartbeats, she froze and weighed her options. She'd walked into a trap—or been led into one if her suspicions about Roberts turned out to be true. Regardless, here she was, up to her chin in trouble and no idea what she was up against. Should she run? Where the hell would she run to? She didn't know the neighborhood, other than a few of the streets themselves. If she tried to melt into the maze of alleyways and side streets that wound their way among the rotting structures, she would likely end up lost. If she looked for shelter in one of the failing structures, she almost certainly would injure herself.

If she held her ground? Maybe they'd just talk to her, pass along information about the murders. If they legitimately had information to share, anyway.

Or, finding a woman alone, they might peg her as helpless, try to rob her—or worse. She wasn't helpless. One, maybe two attackers, she could handle. After that, all bets were off.

The black SUV rolled toward her. The driver stopped the big vehicle next to her car, parking the right fender next to her passenger-side door, blocking it.

The rear door on the driver's side of the SUV opened. A pair of men crawled from the back, one after the other. Tzon felt her body tense, her fingers tightening on the pistol's grip. She wanted to run, but remained still. Her arms hung at her sides. She pressed the Glock against her right thigh and watched as the men walked around the SUV. The combination of the streetlight and the headlights created enough light that Tzon could see the faces of the men approaching her.

The driver was a small, slightly built man who hung back, crossed his arms over his chest and watched. The two who had crawled from the back of the SUV were a mismatched pair. One of them, deep wrinkles set at the corners of his eyes and lips, moved toward Tzon and smiled coldly at her. If she had to guess, the man with him stood several inches over six feet tall. The handle of a pistol jutted up above his belt. He halted a couple of feet from Tzon and regarded her with a cold-eyed stare.

Dragging his gaze over her from head to toe, he said, "Roberts said you wouldn't come," the man said. "I knew you would."

The man's words hit her in the gut like a sucker punch and her mind reeled. The whole thing had been a setup from the word go. Like a fool, she'd hurled herself headlong into it.

The smaller man stepped toward Tzon. Her body immediately tensed.

She raised the Glock and leveled it at the point of his nose.

"Stop," she said through clenched teeth.

He smiled.

"You don't want to do that," he said.

"Like hell," she stated. "Say what you have to say, get your ass back in your car and let's all go home. And stay out of my space or I'll blow your head off."

Traces of a smile played on his lips.

"Really?" he said. "You think you could kill me?"

"Yes."

She heard her own voice and, to her surprise, it sounded calm, as level as the gun barrel aimed at the man's face. Her breath was coming in smooth pulls. Any tremors or weakness she'd felt in her knees had disappeared.

She guessed her body would shake and her chest would tighten again later, once the threat had passed. That was one thing she knew of herself: she did well under pressure. It was only after the crisis had passed that she fell apart.

Footsteps sounded behind her. She guessed it was one of the occupants from the second vehicle, making a play to help his friend.

She jerked her head over her shoulder.

"If he takes another step," she said. "You lose your head. Think about it."

Her target looked over her shoulder and nodded once. The footsteps stopped.

"There," the man said. "We can all be agreeable here, can't we?"

"I was told you have information for me."

"Is that what he told you? Roberts?" The man clapped his hands four times in fake applause. "He does know how to spin a tale, doesn't he?" He shook his head gently. "I am too harsh. Actually, we do have information for you, though probably not what you wanted to hear."

Tzon felt sweat slicking the palm of her gun hand. The man looked past her to the man standing behind her again.

That man took another step in her direction. Tzon squeezed the Glock's trigger. The weapon barked once and sent a bullet crashing into the face of the man who stood in front of her.

She swung the Glock toward the stocky man, fully prepared to take him down, too. She saw that he'd already lined up a shot on her. I'm going to die, she realized. A scream of terror formed in her throat, never to escape. The bullet punched through her sternum, her heart, killing her instantly.

KASSEM PRODDED THE woman's limp form with the toe of his boot. As best he could tell, the shot had been a good one, straight through her heart. Blood already was draining onto the asphalt, pooling around her body, gleaming under the streetlight's glow.

He'd hoped to handle things differently. Not that she'd ever been going to live through the night, of course. But he'd wanted to take her into one of the buildings and kill her there. Doing so would have delayed the discovery of the body and exposed the physical evidence to the ruinous effects of time. Unfortunately, the option had been taken away from him. Plus he had one of his own people dead, giving him a second corpse to deal with.

From the corner of his eye, he saw Mustapha approaching him. The guy had already stowed his weapon and zipped up his jacket.

Kassem turned and scowled at his lieutenant.

"I didn't want her killed here," Kassem snapped. "Not in the open."

"She was going to shoot me," Mustapha protested. "I had no other choice." He jerked his head at the dead man sprawled a few feet away. "Ali never should have engaged her. He should have kept his mouth shut and let you handle it."

"Ali was a fool," Kassem replied. "He thought he still was in Libya, where he could do whatever he wanted. Now he has left us a mess to deal with. Damn him!"

"What should I do with his body?"

Kassem ground his teeth. He knew the dead man was a devout Sunni Muslim and his body needed to be dealt with quickly and appropriately. Kassem was a Muslim in name only, just one of the many ways he'd disappointed his pious mother and father. He'd just as soon throw the idiot into a garbage bin. Such behavior would not sit well with the more devout men in his group. A couple of them, he knew, would consider any affront to Islam ample justification to betray Kassem in one of a thousand ways.

"Get his body out of here," Kassem said, his voice hushed. "But deal with it appropriately."

"Understood."

He pivoted on his heel and returned to his car, a black BMW roadster. Gunning the 255-horsepower engine, he left the carnage behind him and headed for the apartment he maintained in Athens.

Athens was one of the few places where he traveled without a security detail. Several years ago, Kassem had set up a false identity here as a mining executive. The cover allowed him to travel to Africa and South America without drawing much interest from local authorities. It also explained his lengthy absences between trips to Greece. Kassem had learned how to build a successful cover while working for Libyan intelligence. That skill had kept him alive. He'd kept the identity even after the Libyan government had been overthrown, though he used it much more sparingly.

The Athens job, at first, had seemed perfect. It was easy money and it gave Kassem the chance to exact revenge on the man who'd killed his son. But it was quickly turning into something complicated, with too many moving pieces to manage.

Once he'd left Libya, Kassem had turned to assassinations and smuggling because he understood those things well and they were, from his point of view, simple. Not always easy, but simple. If you killed someone, make it look like an accident or misdirect the investigators to another suspect. That'd been his plan with the killing of Rabin and Briggs. The Israelis had plenty of people wanting to settle a blood debt with him. It was just a matter of picking the right one. However, Jiang had insisted they make it look like a robbery. Kassem had followed orders and collected his pay. But the job had kept growing, forcing him to remain in Athens too long so he could cover his tracks and those of his employer.

With three murders linked to him, every fiber of his being screamed for him to leave the country, to return to Brazil and wait for things to cool down. Unfortunately, he couldn't do it—yet. His employer had told him in no uncertain terms that he'd left behind another loose end that required his attention.

Kassem had agreed to handle the problem. Having served as part of Khadaffi's regime, he'd learned the value of keeping his mouth shut and taking orders. While he did it less and less these days, Kassem's latest employer shared several qualities with Khadaffi, not the least of which was his demand for blind obedience. Kassem guessed that not giving the man what he wanted could have fatal consequences. Kassem was neither a coward nor a fool. He knew the man who'd hired him had ties to the Chinese government and organized crime. And the Libyan had little appetite for acquiring either of those groups as enemies.

So he'd do as he was told. He'd spill more blood in Athens. Then he'd get the hell out of here. There was something bad happening and he wanted to get as far from it as he could.

# CHAPTER FOUR

*Brazil*

Why hadn't he heard from Kassem?

Jiang ground his teeth together as he considered the question during the elevator ride from his penthouse to the ground floor. The doors slid apart and a couple of the men from Jiang's security detail marched into the lobby and scanned it for threats. After a couple of seconds, they gestured for Jiang to follow. He exited the elevator and began his morning march across the marble floors. His entourage included six guards, all of them former special forces soldiers from China and North Korea. Underneath the specially tailored jacket of his $3,000 suit, Jiang also carried a Beretta PX4 Type 4 Compact pistol on his right hip.

His eyes hidden behind sunglasses, Jiang swept a trained eye over the lobby, looking for threats. His people were some of the best soldiers the two countries had to offer. But he also knew he had to be vigilant. He could trust his own people only so far. Guards got lazy, apathetic. Or they could turn on you. Only a fool truly turned his security over to another man. If he ever truly found himself under threat, Jiang considered those around him bullet stoppers and little else.

The air outside felt hot and moist even at this early hour. The air was tinged with exhaust fumes and traffic already was beginning to slow to a crawl in front of his building.

He saw his Rolls-Royce Silver Wraith idling in front of

the building. The driver jumped from behind the wheel of the black limo and held the door open for Jiang.

Jiang sauntered up to the vehicle, scowled at the man, and began to climb inside. Even as he settled into his seat, he saw the familiar smile of Wong Mei-Xing and smelled her familiar perfume.

One of the guards climbed into the front passenger seat. The other gunners split into two groups and stuffed themselves into a pair of silver sedans that would ride in front of and behind the Rolls.

The custom-made Rolls had a pair of bench seats, situated across from each other, in the passenger compartment of the vehicle. Dressed in a red business suit, Wong was seated across from Jiang. Her legs were crossed and the hem of her skirt had hiked up just enough to reveal a few inches of thigh. Her glossy black hair was pulled back into a ponytail. She wore little makeup other than the bright-red lipstick that matched her suit.

"Hello, love," she said.

He acknowledged her with a nod and she didn't bother waiting for more. The two had been lovers for several years, though Jiang tried to keep it a secret publicly. He'd told her it was for safety reasons. That was true. His wealth and his ties to the Chinese government made him a target for criminals and spies. And, while he guessed some knew of their relationship, he saw no need to draw attention to it.

Besides, downplaying their connection also helped him avoid any uncomfortable questions from his other sexual conquests, of which there were many. With her knees pressed together, she balanced a short stack of folders on her thighs.

"I haven't heard from Kassem," he said. "What's the situation?"

"Trouble," she said.

"Go on."

Sighing, she flipped open the top folder. "Apparently, he's drawn some attention to himself."

"Meaning what, exactly?"

"The job he did for us in Athens? Someone is onto him and is trying to take apart his organization."

Jiang scowled. "American or Israeli?"

"We don't know for sure," she said, shaking her head. "But we're guessing it's the Americans."

"Because?"

"He was with an American informant the night before the murder."

"Who?"

"A woman. A call girl. Her name is Kristina Mentis. Apparently, he made a stop there the night before. He does that when he is in Athens."

Jiang crumpled the briefing paper in his hand. When he spoke, his words came through clenched teeth. "The same prostitute every time he goes to Athens? And an American informant on top of that? The damned fool knows better."

"He *should* know better," she said. "But men are blinded by a beautiful woman. She can cloud their judgment and make them do stupid things."

"Some men are blinded."

She nodded. "Not you, of course."

Jiang listened for irony in her voice, but heard none. That pleased him. Unlike Kassem, he was focused and driven, a man who enjoyed the company of a beautiful woman, but knew better than to lose his good sense around one.

"We could eliminate him," Wong said.

"You're right. We should eliminate him. Absolutely. But we will not."

She gave him a surprised look. "Because?"

"He's too useful to us."

"Really? In what way? From where I sit, he seems like a liability."

Jiang sighed and shook his head in a pitying way.

"It's obvious, really, isn't it? I have leverage over him. That makes him an asset, not a liability. Otherwise, I'd have him killed. As it stands, we can get him to do what we want."

"Except when he's having paid sex with informants and drawing the Americans' attention.

"That only makes him more valuable."

"I don't follow—"

"The more they focus on him, the less they look for me."

"Misdirection."

"Yes."

Wong nodded approvingly.

"So we do nothing?" she asked.

"Ridiculous," he said. "We're still engaged in this. There's no reason to sit back and hope it works. But if someone's coming for him, I want to be there. I want to see them in action."

"You want to use Kassem as bait."

"Yes."

"And what of our enemy? Once you've seen him in action, what then?"

"We kill him."

She crossed her legs and studied him for several seconds.

"What if it's the Americans? What if you draw their wrath by killing one of their own?"

"Apparently, I already have done that. Indirectly, anyway. Or more to the point Kassem has drawn their wrath. I just plan to do something about it."

"Taking action," she said, "could expose your larger plans."

"Hoping the storm just passes could do the same thing. Kassem already has put us on the radar. But, if I do this right, the Americans will chalk it up to Kassem and his people."

"You hope."

He shrugged.

"Hope is not something I partake in. I plan. And, if this plan doesn't work, I have other ways of dealing with this."

Wong nodded, but said nothing. She knew he had blood on his hands, gallons of it. He'd spill more if required. He didn't consider himself bloodthirsty. But he also wasn't squeamish or sentimental when it came to others, including the woman sitting in front of him. He simply didn't care one way or the other. Ordering someone killed or pressing his thumbs against their windpipe as their face turned purple, it all was the same to him. He had no nightmares. He wasn't troubled by the faces of those he'd killed. It was as though they'd simply dissolved into the ether, as though they'd never existed.

When it came to the American woman and the former Mossad chief, he felt the same. Or, more to the point, felt nothing. He hadn't bound them, tormented them, slashed their throats. He had ordered the hit, had studied the pictures of their corpses, had paid the bill. But their deaths didn't haunt him.

Jiang always had been ambitious. The son of farmers, he had always wanted more and had been willing to do whatever it took to get it. When his parents were killed in a flood, he'd been sent to an orphanage in Beijing and later joined the People's Liberation Army before he'd become a spy.

His superiors had lauded him more than once for his cool detachment and his patriotism. He liked his money and the lifestyle it afforded him, one that exceeded his parents' wildest ambitions and modest achievements. But he also wanted his country to succeed. Not so much because of some simple love for his homeland, but because he couldn't stand the notion that another country would achieve more. He didn't want to be second in anything, and he didn't want to come from a country that lagged in second place. China had made strides in recent years. He wanted it to go even further.

That was why that couple had needed to die in Athens. He'd kill a thousand more just like them, if necessary.

"You have that look," Wong said.

He blinked, and her face, which he'd already been looking at, came back into focus.

"What look is that?"

"You're planning something."

"I plan to make a couple of calls. I want people—our people—in Athens tonight."

# CHAPTER FIVE

The apartment was small and nondescript, located on the building's third floor. Bolan walked up to the apartment's door, the wood marred with deep gouges and scratches, and halted. The soldier reached under his jacket, drew the Beretta and motioned for Mentis to wait.

Already stressed, the woman's eyes widened, but she nodded her understanding. He gently twisted the knob, found it unlocked and pushed the scarred wooden door open. He passed through it, and nodded for Mentis to follow.

The door led into a smaller room, the size of a modest walk-in closet. A second door stood on the other side of the room, a numeric pad fixed to the wall next to it. He punched in a code and when the bolt released, he pushed the door open.

As he walked through the door, a shape registered in the corner of his eye. He turned around and found Grimaldi standing in the doorway. The lanky pilot leaned against the doorjamb, arms crossed over his chest. He had ditched his pilot's jumpsuit and dressed in faded jeans and a polo-style shirt and tennis shoes. A Browning Hi-Power pistol rode in a shoulder rig. His mouth was turned up in a wide grin.

"Bang," Grimaldi said.

"You were supposed to stay at the plane."

"Fly all the way to Greece and cool my heels in the pilot's lounge? What's the percentage in that? Not when I can take in the sights." His eyes drifted past Bolan and settled on Mentis. He unleashed his most disarming smile in her direction. "And speaking of sights, I see you found our friend."

"I did."

"She come willingly?"

"Considering her other options," Bolan said, "she decided she couldn't live without me."

She smacked him on the arm. "I'm right here, you jackass."

Bolan shrugged. "Make the lady a cup of coffee," he said to Grimaldi.

"Don't you have anything stronger?"

"Sit," Bolan said.

She hesitated, chewing on her lower lip for a couple of seconds, before she walked to a nearby armchair and sat. Grimaldi suppressed a grin and headed to the coffeemaker. Bolan waited while the pilot poured two cups and handed them over.

The soldier strode over to Mentis. She didn't look at him, but instead was hugging herself again, her gaze fixed on a spot on the floor. He cleared his throat and she looked up at him, blinked a couple of times and took the coffee.

"You okay?"

"Like you care."

"I care enough," the soldier said. "You saw nasty stuff, got slapped around today. That's not something you just bounce back from. I get that."

"You're all heart."

"Just trying to help," Bolan said.

"A mobster with a heart. You seemed perfectly happy to kill."

"Happy, no. But was it necessary? Yes."

"What do you want from me? How long are you going to keep me here?"

"Not long," Bolan said. "I'm guessing our friends will make their play quickly. We'll neutralize them and go on our merry way."

"Neutralize them? As in kill them?"

"Yeah."

"Good. I don't want them coming back for me."

"That won't be a problem," the soldier said. "If all goes as planned, you won't see them again. Same goes for us. Once we disappear, you never saw us. You never met us. Got it?"

"I should be so lucky."

"Trust me," Bolan said.

She laughed bitterly. "Sorry, all out of that," she said.

Bolan nodded. "Fair enough."

He moved to a nearby couch, sat on the middle cushion at the front edge.

"What do you know about Kassem?" he asked.

"Nothing," she said. "He became a client while he still lived in Libya. That was before they threw him out, along with his crazy boss."

"You know what he does now?"

She gave an irritated shrug. "Lives off the money he stole, I guess. Isn't that what people do when they go into exile?"

"I think you know more than you're telling me."

Her cheeks flushed red.

"He has other interests," she said.

"Like killing people."

She chewed on her lip.

"Look, why involve me in this? I'm nobody. He has sex with me once in a while, gives me money for it. It's not like he tells me why he is here or what he is doing."

"Fair enough," Bolan said. "That doesn't mean you don't know anything. You catch any snatches of phone calls, see any receipts, anything?"

"You sound more like the police."

"Not even close. I just want to find the guy and take him out."

"Why?"

"Consider it a business decision," Bolan lied.

"It's very nasty business."

"Said the working girl to the hit man. Bottom line is, he

has it in for you. I'm guessing it wasn't because you don't do good work. You want to tell me about that?"

"Not really."

"I think you should."

"Why? So you can help me? For some reason, I'm not expecting that to happen."

"Help me and help yourself. I told you I'd protect you, but I want something in return."

She scowled. "Nothing comes for free, does it?"

"I just want information. That's all. Tell me what you need to know and we're good."

She sighed. "What's the question?"

"When Kassem comes to town, who else does he see?" Bolan asked. "Has he mentioned any names to you before?"

Mentis's forehead wrinkled slightly and she seemed to consider the question. She started to shake her head, but checked herself.

"Wait," she said. "There's one guy he keeps in contact with. His name's Zayden. Jamal Zayden."

"And they talk why?"

"Zayden is an electronics expert. He has a crappy little cell phone shop, but he supposedly is a genius when it comes to electronics. One time, when my cell phone died, I mentioned it in passing to Kassem. Two days later, a package arrives from Zayden's shop and it's a new cell phone."

"When was that?" Bolan asked.

"Two weeks ago," she replied.

"You talk about him on that phone? Maybe call someone he'd rather you not talk to?"

"I'd never do that on a cell phone. How could you even accuse me of such a thing? Do you think I am an idiot?"

Bolan figured she was lying, but he let it pass. "I'm just wondering if that's why he came after you," Bolan said. "That's all. Do you have an address for Zayden?"

# CHAPTER SIX

Something felt wrong. Xu Chin slid back the cuff of his sport coat, checked his watch and scowled. Kassem's kill team had entered the building thirty-three minutes earlier, parking in the underground garage, and had yet to leave the building. Considering their mission—killing a prostitute and a security guard who was strictly amateur hour—that was a long time.

Seated on a bench across from the hotel, the garage's exit in his line of sight, Xu had waited for them to leave so he could tell his handler they had completed their mission. As best he knew, Kassem's people had no idea he was there, making sure they accomplished their mission. And, if all went well, they never would know. He would just disappear, file a report, ship it to Beijing and go about his day.

If all went well.

A couple more minutes and several unread pages flipped by and a scowl tugged at the corners of Xu's mouth. His mind began churning through the possibilities. Had the guard turned out to be more formidable than originally thought? Word was he was just a young man with a gun, one paid with alcohol, sex and a place to stay, a guy to scare the johns, should one get a little overzealous and push for more than his money's worth. The woman spent most of her time either in bed or drunk, mixing the two as often as possible. Neither should have put up a fight.

Motion from across the street caught his attention and prompted him to look up. Instead of the green van he'd hoped to see, a red compact car caught his eye as it braked for a couple of seconds before rolling into traffic.

He closed the magazine, rolled it up and tucked it under his arm before he rose from the bench. Slipping a hand into the pocket of his khaki pants, his fingers wrapped around his cell phone. He walked a few paces down the street, turned and stared into the wide display window of a men's clothing store, pretending to survey the gray suit displayed there when actually he was staring at the garage entrance's reflection.

A second vehicle, this one silver, rolled into view. Sunlight hit the chrome of the car's grille and the reflected gleam winked at Xu. What the hell? He recognized the vehicle as a silver Mercedes, the same kind of car Mentis drove. Had they taken her car? It took everything he had not to whip around and look at the vehicle. Instead, he forced himself to remain still and allowed the seconds to pass as the car rolled up the street behind him. As it neared him, he let the magazine fall from beneath his arm to the ground, pages fanned open, fluttering in the light breeze. When he bent to pick it up, he stole a three-second glance at the car. His vantage point, combined with the sedan's tinted windows, prevented him from seeing anything other than the silhouettes of two people, one seated at the wheel, the other in the front passenger seat. However, he stole a glance at the license plate and confirmed it was indeed Mentis's car.

He walked up the street, keeping his gait casual, lingering a couple of seconds at another store window before moving on. When he reached a four-way intersection, he turned left and started down another street while also entering a speed-dial code with his thumb.

Pressing the phone to his ear, he heard three clicks as it passed through as many cut-out numbers before it began ringing.

A man's voice, raspy and flat, answered on the fourth ring. "Hello?"

"Something's changed," Xu said, his voice even.

"Tell me."

"A car just passed."

"And?"

"It belonged to your aunt."

"My aunt shouldn't be driving."

"Yes."

The man on the other end of the line remained silent for several seconds. Xu felt a knot of fear form in his stomach. He swallowed hard, but said nothing.

Finally the other man spoke.

"We can't let this continue."

"Of course."

"Deal with it."

"As you wish."

"You took the measures I suggested. With her car, I mean?"

"Of course."

"Good. Then you can find her?"

"I believe so."

"Believe so?" The menace was evident in the other man's voice.

"I will find her," Xu promised.

"Was she alone?"

"No, someone else was in the car. I didn't get a good look. The windows are tinted."

"Get help, just in case."

"Consider it done."

"I'll consider it done when you deliver," the other man said. "Not a minute sooner."

The line went dead.

Xu punched in another phone number and waited for several rings before a male voice sounded on the other end of the line.

"What?" the man asked.

"Shut up and listen," Xu said. "We have an issue that needs

to be dealt with. Gather the others. I'll give you the details later."

The other man knew better than to ask questions. When Xu called, it was because he needed someone to spill blood.

"Where and when should we meet?"

Xu thought about it for a couple of seconds before suggesting a time and place. He terminated the call, pocketed the phone and continued heading for his car, which was parked a couple of blocks away.

Even before Kassem's people had slipped into the building, Xu had found the woman's car and placed a tracer in it. At the time, it had almost seemed a waste of time and equipment. Kassem was an assassin, one who'd surrounded himself with other professional killers. Murdering a prostitute, particularly one who could place him in the country at the time of a double homicide, should have been easy enough. Putting a tracer in the car was really a way to follow the woman if she left the apartment before her deadly visitors arrived, a way to cover his ass if they screwed up the job.

Well, they had screwed up the job, unless the woman had just risen from the dead. So Xu's move to cover his ass was about to pay dividends. In his business, that meant he would get to live another day. The woman, on the other hand, wouldn't be so lucky.

# CHAPTER SEVEN

Bolan sized up the cell-phone shop from across the street. The store was located on the ground floor of a four-story brick building. The building next door, a movie theater, stood dark, the windows boarded up on the first two floors. The exterior was covered in graffiti that had been worn dull by time and weather. Bolan guessed it was a remnant from the riots that had shaken Athens earlier in the decade, when the country was plunged into recession.

The soldier walked another two blocks past the store. Once he'd put some distance between it and himself, he crossed the street and began to backtrack to the cell-phone store, his eyes constantly sizing up his surroundings. An alley opened to his right, two buildings shy of the phone shop. He turned down the alley and followed it until it opened into a service road that ran behind the stores.

A man leaned against the back door of the phone store. He smoked a cigarette and stared at a spot on the pavement. Bolan wasn't sure if the guy was a store employee, hired muscle or just someone who'd stopped for a smoke break.

The soldier reached the theater and glided along the rear wall. He was almost on the loiterer before the guy sensed his approach and whipped his gaze in Bolan's direction. Straightening, he plucked the cigarette from his mouth and threw it into a puddle where it died with a hiss. The guy turned toward Bolan, and his hand moved to the edge of his jacket. He swept the tail of his jacket back and glared at Bolan.

Before the guy could say anything, Bolan flashed his Justice Department ID at the man. It was fast enough that the guy couldn't actually read it, but Bolan guessed he could tell it was an official ID.

"You speak English?"

"Show me the badge again," the man demanded.

"So you do speak English."

"You must be a detective," the man replied.

Bolan showed the guy the badge again.

"Why is the U.S. Justice Department here, Mr. Cooper?"

"I'm on loan to Interpol."

"And Interpol wants what with us?"

"There's no us," Bolan said. "I'm here for Zayden."

The man held up a hand to stop Bolan

"You should have used the front door," the man said. He nodded at the building. "I'll go through here and tell him he has a visitor. You go through the front door like everyone else does."

Bolan nodded his understanding and threw a roundhouse punch that caught the guy in the jaw. The man's knees buckled and he sank to the ground. A search of the man turned up a .40 Glock pistol and a couple of spare magazines. He pocketed those items and bound the man's hands with plastic restraints.

As he rose to his feet, Bolan grabbed the guy by his jacket collar and dragged him toward the door. With his free hand, Bolan fisted his Beretta.

The soldier entered the rear door and found himself in a storage room. He laid the unconscious man down and headed into the main shop. A man was seated at a worktable, various cell phone components spread over it.

The top of his head was bald, the dark exposed skin of his scalp contrasting with the white hair that ringed his head. Bolan swept his gaze over the store. A long glass counter filled with cell phones, tablet computers and MP3 players bisected the room.

Bolan crossed the room. The sound of footsteps prompted the other man to spin on his chair and see who was coming. The soldier grabbed Zayden and shoved him hard, toppling the stool. The guy struck the ground with his rear end. He gritted his teeth and swore.

The soldier reached down, grabbed a fistful of the man's shirt and yanked him upright. He drove a fist into Zayden's gut and the guy belched out air.

Releasing the guy's shirt, Bolan stepped back and let him fall to the ground. The soldier moved around the counter, turned the dead bolt on the front door, pulled the shades. When he returned, Zayden was sitting up, his arms wrapped around his stomach.

The soldier stopped a couple of paces away from Zayden and pointed the Beretta at the guy's head.

"I'm looking for Kassem," the soldier said.

The guy replied by blurting out something in Arabic.

"Cut the bullshit," Bolan said. "I know you speak English. You studied at MIT."

Zayden's eyes narrowed and he scrutinized Bolan as though the guy had just materialized there.

"Who are you?" Zayden asked.

"We'll get to that. Where's Kassem?"

"I don't know."

"Bull. You deliver messages for him. You provide satellites and other gear for him."

"Really, I don't know," the Libyan said, licking his lips.

"Pretty crappy gig," Bolan said. "For a man of your credentials. Pay must be good or every now and then Kassem throws you a hooker. Is that it?" He paused for a few seconds. "I mean, he must be doing something for you, if you're willing to die for him like this."

"Die for him? What are you talking about?"

Bolan shrugged. "I want to find Kassem. You know where

he is. You're not telling me. I think you can figure out the rest."

"I don't know where he is. And if I did know I wouldn't tell you."

"Why?"

"Because he'd kill me."

"You're not paying attention. I've scored lots of kills already. I'm just getting warmed up." The sweat that had beaded on Zayden's scalp trickled down his forehead and into his right eye. The salty liquid caused him to squeeze the eye shut for a couple of seconds before he reopened it. When he spoke again, an urgent tone had crept into his voice.

"I don't know where he is."

"What do you know? What other operations does he have here in Athens?"

The guy scowled. "He runs weapons."

"Okay. Does he do it out of the back of his van? Give me some specifics."

"He has a warehouse near the docks. He supposedly has a big deal coming in. I didn't hear it directly from him. But one of his men came by to pick up a phone and said they had some people coming into town to make a buy."

"What kind of people?"

"Chechens."

"Names."

The man shook his head. "I don't have any names. This guy wasn't high up. He knew general information. But Kassem doesn't share many details with his people until the last minute."

"You have relatives back in Libya? Anyone you would go see?"

The creases in Zaydan's forehead deepened. "A few. None in Tripoli. My brothers and a sister in Misrata. I have to sneak in to see them. I'm not welcome there under the new regime.

But I have gone back a couple of times. One of my brothers has lung cancer."

"Lucky you. You're going back again."

"What?"

"Sure," Bolan said. "At least, that's what you're going to tell Kassem. Your brother's condition has gotten worse and you're going home to see him. You'll be out of pocket for a few days. Does he have a backup courier?"

"Not in this region. If he has one somewhere else, I don't know about it."

Bolan gave the Arab a hard stare, but got the impression the man was telling the truth.

"When do I leave?"

Bolan shook his head. "You don't. You're staying right here."

"But you said—"

"You're not leaving the country. Unless I decide it's going to help me. You think I am going to let you run loose in Libya. Maybe get caught there. Or duck away and warn Kassem that I'm coming. Forget it. But you will tell Kassem that you're sneaking back into Libya. That way, if he can't reach you, it won't make him suspicious."

Zayden's eyes widened. "Then what are you going to do with me?"

"Don't worry," the American said. "I won't kill you. Unless you do something stupid. I'm giving you over to the CIA for safe keeping. They're going to ask you more questions. But at least you'll still be alive."

"Bullshit. I'm going to fall into a black hole. I'll never be seen again."

"You'll be breathing. That's more than can be said for Ben Rabin and Patricia Briggs."

"That's what this is about?" Zayden snapped. "Those two? You did all of this over an Israeli—a Jew—and some American bitch?" Bolan felt a knot of anger form in his stomach and a desire to close the distance between himself and Zayden, to break his jaw.

"Yeah," he said, "I did all this for those two. And before this is over, I'm going to do much, much worse to Kassem. You want to live to see how this plays out? Shut your damn mouth and I'll deliver you into the CIA's loving arms. I told you you'd live. I never promised it would nice. It's the best offer you're going to get from me."

"I didn't kill those two," Zaydan protested.

"Which is why you'll end today vertical," the soldier replied.

Zaydan, his shirt now dark with sweat, eyed Bolan uneasily.

"What now?" he asked.

"I hand you over to the CIA."

"Where will they take me? You said I wouldn't be killed."

"Wrong. I said I wouldn't kill you. Precision in language, Jamal. It's important."

"Bastard."

"Nothing personal," Bolan said, shrugging. "I'm going to see your boss and I like to travel light. You'd get in the way. Besides, I am guessing the CIA will be happy to discuss some of your past activities."

"I'm not afraid of the CIA."

"Then you're an idiot. Me? I'd call our friends in Israel. I'm guessing they would love to have a crack at you."

Zayden swallowed hard.

"Mossad?" he asked.

"Sure," Bolan said. "You're not afraid of them, are you? You said it yourself, they're just a bunch of Jews."

"You're bluffing."

"Keep telling yourself that if it makes you feel better. I don't care what you believe."

Zaydan studied Bolan's face for a few beats. Bolan guessed he wanted some sign as to the soldier's intentions, though the soldier did his best to keep his expression stony. Finally, he looked away from the big American's face and fixed his gaze on some spot on the floor, occasionally shifting in his chair. Bolan leaned against the service counter. He guessed that whatever visions of Mossad captivity Zayden had conjured up were way worse than any story Bolan could spin to scare the guy.

"They'll kill me," Zayden said, his voice soft.

"Not immediately," Bolan said.

The other man jerked his head up and gave Bolan an imploring look.

"You can stop this," he said. "If you said something to the CIA, they would keep me, wouldn't they?"

"Maybe."

"You and your CIA contacts could keep me from going to Israel, if you wanted."

"I could make a few phone calls, I suppose, and put in a good word for you."

Zayden exhaled loudly, and his shoulders sagged with relief.

"Thank you."

"Whoa, I said I could. It doesn't mean I will. I only promised not to kill you. I didn't promise to be your travel agent. Once I hand you off, they can bury you in a landfill for all I care."

"I have information," Zayden said.

"You gave me your information. Don't jerk my chain."

"I didn't tell you everything."

Bolan scowled. "So you held out before, but now you're ready to open up. How convenient."

"I told you what you asked. That doesn't mean I told you everything you'd want to know. Precision in language, isn't that what you said?"

"Okay, tell me what you know."

"You'll make sure I don't go to Israel?"

"Depends on what you tell me. If the Israelis find out we have you, they may decide they just can't live without you," Bolan said, shrugging. "And they can be pretty damn persuasive."

"Not good enough."

Bolan crossed his arms over his chest and scowled.

"Fine," he said. "Tell me what you know. I'll make sure we don't hand you over to Mossad."

"Or the Israeli government."

"Or the Israeli government. Just spit out what you know before I change my mind."

"You think Kassem did this murder for himself, don't you?"

"Sure. Rabin killed his son."

"You're wrong. Kassem was working for someone else."

"Nice try," Bolan said. He reached into his pocket for his cell phone. "Enjoy Tel Aviv."

Zayden's eyes bulged with fear. He leaned forward when he spoke. "Wait!" he said. "I'm serious. Rabin's death was a contract killing. I was the one who delivered the request. I was the courier who delivered the up-front payment, the guns, all those things."

"Nice coincidence for Kassem, someone else wanting the same guy dead. And willing to pay for it, too."

"Just because someone else footed the bill, doesn't mean Kassem didn't enjoy it."

Bolan considered that. Once it had become clear that the Libyans had made the kill, the big American had assumed Kassem had done it to get even.

"Fair enough. Lots of people wanted Rabin dead. So who hired him?"

"I'm not sure. Don't look at me like that. I really don't know. I shuttled the messages and the supplies, but it wasn't like I was intimately involved. I was a cut-out. They brought me in after they'd struck a deal. I just handled details."

"You were talking to yourself the whole time."

"I'm not saying that. All I am saying is that I don't know who hired Kassem. That was above my pay grade."

# CHAPTER EIGHT

"How's your girlfriend?" Leo Turrin recognized Grimaldi's voice immediately.

"I'm going to kick your ass."

"Trouble?"

"Good news is she hates me. Bad news is I'm trapped in the apartment with her. Have you heard from—" He almost said Bolan's name, but caught himself. "You heard from Cooper?"

"Negative. You getting antsy? He's only been gone an hour, maybe a little more."

"Hey, if I wanted to be confined in small spaces with a woman who hates me—"

"You would have stayed home, right? Look, just hang in there for a couple of hours with little Miss Sunshine. Then I'll take over. You can spend hours staring at the exterior of a building. It hasn't moved yet, by the way."

"How long?" Turrin asked.

"Two hours. Three, tops."

Turrin sighed. "Okay."

"Who knows? Maybe all the butting heads is just a front. A little sexual tension. Play your cards right, you could get lucky."

"Luck has nothing to do with it when you're paying."

Turrin heard Grimaldi chuckle before the pilot terminated the connection.

He set his phone on a nearby table and shrugged. Grimaldi was right. What was the worst thing that could happen in two hours? Pulling a crushed pack of smokes from his pocket, he shook the last one into his palm. Scowling, he crumpled the pack into a ball and tossed it into a white plastic trash can in the corner.

Lighting his last cigarette with a disposable lighter, he peeked into the living room and saw that Kristina Mentis was sitting in an armchair. A cup of coffee sat on a small circular table next to an ashtray. She hadn't moved from where she sat since he'd arrived.

THE VAN ONLY vaguely registered with Grimaldi the first time it circled the block. The Stony Man pilot was seated at a small table outside a coffee shop located across from the safehouse. A cup of heavy black coffee sat nearly untouched on the table's circular top, next to his cell phone. Against his better judgment he had struck up a conversation with a pretty brunette at the table next to him, forcing him to split his attention between the safehouse and the thirty-something British woman who was emitting positive vibes, the full force of her dark eyes focused on him.

"Your work sounds fascinating," she said.

"It's the best," he said. What had he told her again?

"How many funds do you manage?" she asked.

Oh, that's right. "Several," he said. "Only high-net-worth people. The dollar amounts are insane. Their bank accounts equal the GDPs of small countries."

The white van circled by again, this time more slowly. Alarms began to blare in the pilot's head. Could be they were just looking for an address so they could deliver a package or clean the carpets or something. Could be, but maybe not.

"Do you practice socially conscious investing?"

"More like semi-conscious," Grimaldi replied, his attention now entirely on the van.

"Excuse me?"

He glanced at the woman. "What?"

"You said you make semi-conscious investments. What does that mean?"

Grimaldi drew himself up from his chair. "Sorry," he said. "I have to go."

"Why?"

"I have a phone call."

"Your phone didn't ring."

"Um, it will," he said. Reaching into his pocket, he drew out some money, tossed it onto the table and picked up his phone. With his free hand, he grabbed the handle on his duffel bag, slung it over his shoulder and, with long strides, wove his way through the tables populating the café's patio.

Grimaldi saw three men file through the door of the apartment building.

All three had raven-colored hair and dark complexions. A fourth man, who looked Asian, was holding the door for them. Once they were inside the building, he followed them.

Grimaldi felt his heart hammer in his chest. He sprinted across the street, his long legs moving him with quick strides. He was unzipping his duffel bag as he closed in on the apartment building. He dipped a hand into the bag and felt around until he found the pistol grip of an Uzi. His fingers curled around the weapon's grip. Thirty seconds later, he was through the door and crossing the lobby.

The faint sound of shoes scuffing against the linoleum floor registered with him, along with the faint odor of cologne and traces of mold. If the place had been in use, bustling with activity, he never would have heard the footsteps, so he counted himself lucky in that regard. He hoped the intruders had also triggered the silent alarm, alerting Turrin to the coming threat.

Grimaldi heard more footsteps on the stairs. He moved to the stairwell and began climbing up, taking the steps quickly and quietly. As he moved, he swept the area in front of him with the Uzi and looked for a target.

Without pausing, he cast a glance over his shoulder. As he'd moved up in the safehouse, he'd looked for spotters, but saw none. However, he also realized there could be more gunners outside. It was possible the hit team had looked for multiple ways to enter the building.

Before he could continue that train of thought, gunfire crackled upstairs. The sound spurred Grimaldi, sent him surging to the next floor.

THREE MINUTES EARLIER, the lights inside the apartment had blinked twice in quick pulses. Turrin froze and swore under his breath. The lights told him someone had breached the building without using the right access code. He set down his coffee and headed toward Mentis. When he grabbed her by the biceps, she winced. He yanked her to her feet.

"Hey, you son of a bitch," she said.

"Stow it," Turrin growled. He jerked his head toward the bedroom. "Get in there. Shut the door and lock it. Don't open it until I tell you to."

Her irritation dissolved. Her eyes widened and her lips parted to ask a question.

"Go," Turrin said sharply.

She nodded once, turned on her heel and headed toward the bedrooms.

Turrin crossed the room to where a Benelli shotgun leaned at an angle against the wall. He hefted the shotgun, clicked off the safety and headed for the front door, the gun tucked in at waist level.

There was a chance, but only a slight one that Bolan or Grimaldi had triggered the alarm without thinking. He doubted those guys would make such an amateur play, though. He wondered fleetingly why Grimaldi had missed the intruders. Why hadn't the pilot called to warn him? The hell with it, Turrin decided. A million things could have gone wrong.

He'd figure out the communication problems after he'd dealt with the situation at hand.

He had more critical worries.

Like staying alive.

Just as he rounded the corner and the front door came into view, something struck it hard. The blow jarred the door, but didn't knock it inward. But another hit or two like that would probably send the door crashing in. Turrin positioned himself at a 45-degree angle, raised the shotgun to his shoulder, leveled it at the door and waited for the inevitable blow.

The next strike broke the lock and sent the door swinging inward. The knob and dead bolt flew in separate directions. A hulking man, a black ski mask pulled over his head, bulled his way through the door. A submachine gun was tucked in next to the man-mountain's ribs.

The Benelli cut loose with a peal of thunder. The blast tore into the man's chest and stopped him cold before it tunneled through his torso and exploded out his back. The big man collapsed to the ground, his foot twitching as he experienced the last throes of death. A second shooter followed the hulk through the door. The guy triggered his Uzi and sent a spray of bullets zinging just past Turrin. The stray rounds lanced into walls and flattened when they struck a window made of bullet-proof glass.

Turrin thrust himself sideways but swung the Benelli's barrel in the direction of the intruder. The shotgun blast struck the Uzi-wielding thug in the face, effectively decapitating him and knocking him off his feet.

An unseen force slammed into his ribs on the left side. Fire lanced through his chest and he sank to the floor, his breath stolen by the impact. He'd been shot, his mind screamed. He tried to catch his breath, to swing the Benelli around and take down another attacker. But the gun suddenly seemed too heavy and his arms too unwilling to bear the weight.

He felt more pain lance through his torso. The force

knocked him over, so he was lying on his side, struggling to catch his breath. His fingers fumbled for the pistol holstered under his jacket, but he couldn't locate it. Black spots were whirling in his vision. He tried to push himself up off the floor, but his arms wouldn't respond. Finally, he stopped trying to lift his head and let his face lie on the floor, grateful for its coolness. A heartbeat later, everything went black.

# CHAPTER NINE

Xu stared at the fallen man, who lay on his side, his blood pumping onto the floor. The guy had his arms wrapped around his midsection and had drawn his legs in close, in a fetal position. The American continued to twitch. Xu raised his pistol and prepared to fire a final round into the guy's head.

He heard something crash in the back of the apartment. His eyes whipped in the direction of the noise. It sounded like it'd come from the bedrooms. Raising the weapon in a two-handed grip, he started forward.

Before he took his third step, he heard the crack of gunfire outside the apartment and swore. He weighed whether to leave the apartment and help his comrades fight or to focus on killing the woman, which is what he'd been hired to do.

It was really no choice.

He continued rolling toward the bedrooms.

The apartment was small and he moved through it quickly. He felt his pulse quicken with each step, not from fear, but from anticipation. He'd never heard of the woman before today and had only the vaguest idea why she needed to die. And, frankly, he didn't much care why Jiang had handed down a death sentence on the bitch. He just wanted to stare into her eyes as they bulged with terror, her cheeks streaked with tears, as he shared her last seconds with her. Given enough time, he would have loved to hear her beg for her life, listen as she bargained with him, enjoy the sweet sound of her voice growing louder and more brittle as hysteria overtook her when she realized her pleas fell on deaf ears.

He'd stand there, omnipotent, and listen for a while before putting a bullet in her head.

Unfortunately, he didn't have the time for such a luxury today. Instead, he needed to make the kill and get the hell out of here.

Xu reached a pair of doors, one open, the other closed. A glance inside the door to his left revealed a sparsely furnished room—a bed covered in a simple floral print bedspread, an unfinished white pine dresser, an oval-shaped mirror fixed to a wall. The closet door was closed. Moving into the room, he crept across the wooden floor to the closet, grasped the knob and flung the door open. Other than a few plastic hangers hanging from the clothes rod, he found the small space empty.

Satisfied, he exited the room and crossed the hall to the second door, paused before it. He imagined the woman cowering inside the room, her heart hammering in her chest when she saw his shoes interrupt the line between the floor and the bottom of the door. The thought triggered a pleasant flutter in his stomach.

He rested a hand on the knob, turned it slowly. Though he still heard fighting elsewhere in the building, it sounded distant, replaced by the work at hand. He twisted the knob, freed the door and shoved it forward. It hit the wall with a heart-stopping crack.

He followed it, gun raised.

Cold eyes scanned the room. Its interior was nearly identical to the other one. After a couple of seconds, the buzz of anticipation faded. His forehead creased, puzzled.

Where the hell was she?

Instinct prodded him to turn even before his mind identified the sound of a shoe scuffing against the floor and the grunt of exertion. He spun in time to see a clear glass bottle arcing downward toward his head. The woman, her face a mask of fear and anger, gripped the bottle by its neck. It cut through the air like a hand ax.

Jerking his head and torso to one side, Xu lashed out with his hand to block the attack. His wrist collided with hers. Pain lanced down through his arm from the point where bone struck bone. And, even though he'd expected it, the pain caused him to grunt. In the meantime, the woman yelped and drew her arm back as though it'd been burned. Her fingers uncurled from the neck of the bottle. It plummeted to the floor and exploded into shards.

Xu's lips twitched in an approximation of a smile.

He stepped forward and Mentis shrank back. His left hand snaked out and he grabbed her by the arm, fingers digging into her triceps muscles.

"Bastard!" she screamed. Her free hand rocketed around in a vertical arc at his head. Grabbing her wrist, he jerked her forward and took her balance so she fell onto all fours. She started to move, to scramble to her feet. But before she could, he raised the pistol and pointed it at her head.

She opened her mouth to speak. He knew what was coming. The inevitable protests, the frantic pleas. She surprised him when a scream suddenly erupted.

He cut it off with a single shot.

# CHAPTER TEN

When he heard the first shots crack, Grimaldi bounded up the steps, driven by concern for his friend's welfare. He saw the door hanging wide-open and initially heard no other noise. He crossed the landing and passed quietly through the apartment doorway.

A hardman stood several feet from the door, his back to Grimaldi. The guy had to have sensed the Stony Man pilot's approach because he wheeled, seeking a target with his weapon. What he found was death. Grimaldi's Uzi stuttered out a fast burst, the bullets stitching a ragged line across the man's torso. He stumbled back a couple of steps before his body collapsed in on itself, folding to the floor.

Grimald stepped over the corpse. The gun smoke now hanging in the air stung his eyes. He crept past the entryway and through a short corridor that led into the kitchen. What he saw in that room brought him up short. Turrin lay on the ground, a dark red stain spreading out from a bullet wound just beneath his rib cage.

The pilot moved to his friend and knelt next to him. Turrin's breath was coming in strained pulls. His skin looked pale and Grimaldi guessed the guy was about to slip into shock. A white dish towel was looped through the handle of the refrigerator door. Grimaldi snagged it, folded it up and pressed against the wound.

A quick glance around for a blanket or some other cover for the injured man turned up nothing. He peeled off his leather jacket and placed it over his friend. He wanted to stay put and apply pressure to Turrin's wound. However, another worry nagged at him.

Where the hell was Mentis?

A scowl fixed on his face, he gathered up the Uzi, rose to his feet and took a couple of steps.

A woman's scream cut through the apartment, was almost immediately swallowed up by the thunder of a gunshot. The sound spurred Grimaldi to move toward the bedrooms. He reached one of the doors and could see from an angle that part of the frame had been splintered where it apparently had been kicked in. Holding his breath, he listened for a moment. The hum of car engines and the distant wail of a siren, louder than at any other point in the apartment, reached him.

Someone had opened one of the bulletproof windows.

The Uzi leading the way, Grimaldi swung around the door frame. In an instant, his eyes swept over the room's interior as he assessed what he faced.

A man was climbing through the window. His legs straddled the windowsill and one foot was planted on the bedroom's hardwood floor. When he saw Grimaldi, he brought up his weapon in a blur and squeezed the trigger. Bullets lanced through the door and missed the pilot by inches. His own weapon chattered, but the quickly placed line of fire missed the shooter by more than a foot. It pounded into the wall. The man disappeared through the window.

It was only then that he noticed a foot clad in a black pump jutting from behind the bed. Muttering a curse, he rushed into the room, rounded the bed and founded Mentis sprawled on the floor. A bullet had punched into her forehead and passed through her skull before exploding from the back of it.

Grimaldi's stomach lurched. He turned his gaze away and shook his head and moved toward the window. The shooter had used an emergency rope ladder to climb down two stories to a rooftop below. Grimaldi saw the man sprinting across the rooftop. Before he could react, the sound of heavy footsteps and a halting gait reached his ears. He whipped around in time to see Turrin appear in the doorway. Grimaldi saw the man sway on his feet and started to move toward him.

Turrin fell heavily against the door frame and seemed to hang there, like a puppet suspended by a single string. He started to say something, but his strength gave out and he collapsed under his own weight. Grimaldi rushed to help him.

RETURNING FROM HIS interrogation of Zayden, Bolan rolled up on the safehouse in his rental car. He saw ambulances and other emergency vehicles parked outside the building, lights flashing. Police had blocked off the street with metal barriers and several officers milled around outside the building. A small crowd of onlookers was lining up outside the barriers, talking among themselves or shooting pictures of the house with their cell phones.

The soldier swore under his breath as he pushed through the crowd. He pulled his Justice Department credentials from his pocket and was holding them as he moved past the barricades. A young police officer rushed to him, placed a hand on his chest to stop him and said something in rapid-fire Greek. The soldier felt an urge to shove the guy out of the way, but checked himself. Aside from the fact that he had no fight with the officer, one of the rules in his War Everlasting was that he would never knowingly hurt a police officer, even in self defence. Besides, the guy only was doing his job.

Before Bolan could make his next move, a man, hair gray at the temples, eyes deep brown, came up behind the officer. The older man, a plastic ID card of some kind clipped to his lapel, set a hand on the officer's shoulder and said something Bolan didn't understand. The young officer looked at the older man, then to Bolan and back to the older man. Finally, with a shrug, he turned and walked away toward a knot of other officers and paramedics gathered next to an idling ambulance.

"My name is Detective George Pappas," the older man said

in heavily accented English. He nodded toward the other officers. "I will make sure you have full access to the scene."

Bolan nodded his thanks and moved past the guy. The detective, short and plump, fell in step beside Bolan. The soldier noticed the man seemed to have trouble keeping up with him.

"One of the men," he said. "The short one, he was injured. It was a wound in the torso. He lost a lot of blood. I am not sure whether any organs were damaged. The paramedics whisked him away and I have not yet heard from the hospital."

Bolan nodded. "The others?"

"The tall skinny one? He is fine. The woman?" He shook his head sadly and his jowls quivered. "I am sorry. She is dead. There was no saving her. Whoever did this, they wanted her dead."

By now Bolan was walking up a short set of stairs leading to the apartment building's front door. "You said 'whoever did this.'"

"Yes. Your friends. They have people who want them dead? Enemies?"

Bolan knew the truth was way too complex. "Be more specific," he said.

"They have enemies in Chinese organized crime?"

"No," the soldier replied. "Why?"

"The shooters—at least the ones who were left behind— appear to be Asian, maybe Chinese. I saw a couple of tattoos. I think they're Chinese organized crime. Our forensics people will get fingerprints and pictures, try to run down identities."

He paused and scrutinized Bolan for a few seconds. The soldier kept his face impassive.

"Any of this registering with you?" Pappas asked after a couple of seconds.

"Every detail," Bolan replied.

"So why are Chinese mobsters attacking your friends? Is that why you're in the country? You're looking into organized crime?"

"No."

"Care to say more?"

"No."

The detective's eyes narrowed and his lips pressed into a thin line.

"I have dead bodies upstairs," he said, "and an injured man in the hospital, and you're not going to answer questions?"

"Pretty much," Bolan said.

He wheeled around the detective and moved up the steps, taking them two at a time. He couldn't see Pappas, but he could hear the other man behind him, shoe soles slapping against the stairs.

"You're going to have to make a statement," the man said to Bolan's back.

The soldier didn't bother to turn. He could hear the edge of irritation in Pappas's voice. Probably in the detective's world, Bolan would have to make a statement. But the soldier knew with a couple of phone calls, Brognola would have him on a flight out of Greece while high-level officials from both governments talked tough on the telephone or at a local embassy, pretending they were smoothing things over, solving things. However, Bolan knew the American president could pick up the phone and convince the Greek administration to look the other way, which would trickle down to Athens PD and Pappas. The detective never would see any of this happening, of course. He'd just get word from his boss to steer clear of the murder investigation, that it'd been kicked upstairs. Judging by what Bolan had seen of Pappas, the portly cop would probably shrug and find some other case to investigate.

Bolan reached the top floor. Moving with long, quick strides, he moved through the entry and into the kitchen. He stepped over a couple of bodies, each covered with a blanket. Both were too big to be Kristina Mentis. They only vaguely registered with him. He rolled through the kitchen and into the living room where he found Grimaldi. The pilot was perched at the edge of his seat, in the middle of the couch. His face was a stony mask as his eyes bored into a spot on the wall in front of him.

Two forensics officers were working the room.

When Bolan entered the room with Pappas behind him, Grimaldi flicked his eyes up at his old friend before dropping his gaze to the floor.

"You okay?" Bolan asked.

"Better than her," the pilot said as he jerked his head toward the back of the apartment.

"What happened?"

Grimaldi opened his mouth to reply, but before he could speak, someone called from another room.

"George!"

A short, stocky man strode through the kitchen. He wore a black suit with a light blue tie. His coppery-red hair was combed straight back off his forehead, exposing a sharp widow's peak. Freckles dotted the man's wide, pale face.

"Michael," the detective muttered.

Bolan didn't recognize the guy, but he noticed right away that Pappas's shoulders slumped and he took a step back from Bolan.

"Everything okay?" the red-haired man asked.

"Lovely," Pappas said, his voice indicating anything but.

"Anything you need from my friends?"

"I don't think so," Pappas muttered.

"Fine," the man said. "We're leaving now."

"Of course."

# CHAPTER ELEVEN

*Alexandria, Virginia*

"Hal, you don't look a day older."

Carl Chapman, an FBI agent, thrust a hand toward Brognola.

"Carl," Brognola replied, "I won't dignify that lie with a response."

Chapman grinned and so did Brognola. The men shook hands before Chapman returned to his seat and gestured for Brognola to join him.

The big Fed settled into a chair and ordered coffee from a passing waitress. As the two men made small talk, Brognola noticed a folder lying on the table next to Chapman's left elbow. If Chapman had picked this table, he'd found one in the farthest corner of the restaurant, well out of earshot of others. He immediately wanted to ask the other man about the folder's contents, but checked himself.

Chapman, a counterintelligence agent with the FBI, had called Brognola a few hours ago and asked to meet. Brognola had agreed. The two men went way back, had trained together at Quantico back when gray hair and stiff knees were some other guy's problem. Brognola had risen through the ranks of the Justice Department while Chapman had stayed an agent because he had no interest in being anything other than an investigator.

The waitress brought Brognola coffee and refilled Chapman's cup. Once she disappeared, Brognola leaned forward in his chair and rested his elbows on the table.

"So, how can I help you, Carl? I assume you didn't call 'cause you were missing me."

Chapman smiled again, but this time it seemed forced.

"Look, Hal," he said, "I've got some information for you."

"The folder?"

"We'll get to that. Obviously, I have a boss. A chain of command, and I am completely going around that. I hate to ask, but…"

"It's all off the record," Brognola said. "We're just two old buddies having coffee and shooting the breeze. Besides, if your boss wants to make an issue out of it, well, I'm his boss. I'll happily explain that to him. Who is your boss, by the way?"

Chapman grinned. "Hank Purcell."

"That horse's ass? How did he get promoted?"

"You know how it works."

"Okay, what did he do?"

The other agent shook his head. "He's not the problem. I mean, he's a problem, but he's not *the* problem. I wouldn't call you out here just to bitch about my boss. You're a busy guy. I know that much, even if I don't know what you do all the time."

Brognola let the comment pass. Instead, he drew his unlit cigar from his mouth and set it on the white tablecloth.

He drank his coffee and let the silence grow between them.

Chapman stared into his coffee as though gathering his thoughts.

"Look, I have some information, and I'm not sure what to do with it."

"Tell me," Brognola said. "We'll figure it out."

"Okay, I've got a line on a Chinese spy."

"That's good news, right? You hunt spies for a living."

"It's complicated. This is a well-connected spy. Well, actually, it's a spy who's boning a well-connected U.S. citizen, one who has buddies in the upper ends of the major political parties."

"Shit," Brognola said.

"Yeah, and apparently this douche bag has been feeding information to the Chinese for years. He's British, here on a visa. Normally, we could swoop on him in a minute."

"But?"

Chapman's face flushed. "I'll get to that."

Brognola nodded. His stomach roiled and he knew it was more than a reaction to the coffee. The tone of his old friend's voice told him he was going to hear something bad. His hand drifted underneath his jacket and into an inside pocket for a roll of antacid tablets.

"Still got a bad stomach? Of course you do. This job will give it to you, right? Anyway, this guy has been sending information to the Chinese. One of my informants flagged me on it a little more than a month ago. That's not very long for a counterintelligence case. Even the ones where the perps are strictly amateur-hour can take months to pull together. But things started hot on this one and never cooled down."

Shifting in his seat, Chapman slid the folder across the table to Brognola. The big Fed picked it up and found it was fairly thin. He fanned it open. Several pages of paper were fastened to the right flap. He recognized the top sheet as an investigator's narrative and assumed it was Chapman's work. On the left flap, a stack of photos was attached to the folder with a silver paper clip. He pulled the photos free, and pushing away the coffee cup, arranged them in a line on the table.

The first photo was of a Caucasian with thick black hair, high cheekbones and a wide forehead. His lips were twisted into a smirk.

The second photo depicted an Asian male, and the third a woman with lustrous hair that framed an oval-shaped face. Even in a photograph, her sea-green eyes radiated intensity and intelligence. An intricate diamond necklace was looped around her neck and matching earrings dangled from her ears. If the rocks were real, Brognola guessed her jewelry cost three years of his salary.

Brognola put her age somewhere in the mid-30s. He thought he recognized her, but he couldn't put a name to the face.

"Nice-looking lady, right? Her name's Sandy Pearson. Actually, she goes by Sandra. Sandra Pearson. You recognize her face or her name?"

Brognola shook his head.

"She runs in a little different circle than us humble public servants," Chapman said. "Her family has a long history in this country. They're very wealthy, very well connected." Chapman nodded at the picture. "That lady there? She could just sit back and count her money. She doesn't. She still involves herself in the family business as a board member. And she does a lot of philanthropic work."

"Philanthropic work? What kind of causes?"

"Stuff having to do with children, mostly," Chapman said. "Her pet cause is fighting human trafficking and sex slavery. She's gotten a lot of attention for it over the years. But it was mostly in the society pages of the national newspapers. She travels around the world, has a network of other people who do the same thing."

"Travels around doing what?"

Chapman shrugged. "Giving speeches to the UN, kicking world leaders in the shins over their human rights records, that kind of stuff. When she isn't doing that, she spies."

Brognola peered up from the photo.

"Say what?"

The FBI agent grinned.

"You heard me right. She spies. For us. It's sort of a tradition for the Pearson family. Her daddy did it. So did her grandpa and grandma. World War II, the cold war."

"So whose assets are they? CIA? NSA?"

"They…" Chapman looked over Brognola's shoulder and smiled broadly. A moment later, the waitress appeared at Brognola's left elbow and offered refills on their coffee, which both men accepted. When the waitress finished and walked away, Chapman stared after her for a few seconds until she had moved out of earshot before he continued speaking.

"They sort of freelance," Chapman said. "At least, that was the best information I could get. I'm sure you have a higher clearance level and could get more details. But from what I was able to dig up, they mostly gather information. Her predecessors did some operational stuff, like helping the OSS smuggle weapons into Nazi-occupied territories or helping defectors escape from behind the Iron Curtain. My understanding is that this young lady doesn't do much of that."

"But she does some?"

Chapman spread his hands. "Honestly, I don't know. What I do know is she gathers a lot of good information while she's traveling the world as a professional do-gooder. She brings that information back here and passes it along to the CIA or the State Department's intelligence shop. Some of it's probably come across your desk, and you didn't know where it came from."

"I'm a bureaucratic mushroom. They keep me in the dark and feed me shit."

"Like the shit you're feeding me, Hal? Fine, play it spooky. A lot of what she finds out is focused on organized crime groups and other scum involved in human trafficking. That means she also shares information with friendly countries like the United Kingdom, Australia, Canada and Israel. From what I understand, she and her network find some pretty good information, too. A lot of these people are former investigators—police, private detectives, reporters—that kind of thing."

"So we think she loves us, but she still likes to date around," Brognola said. "Not a good arrangement."

"I agree. But with a lot of this stuff, there's really not much the U.S. can do. She gives the U.S. right of first refusal, if you will. Her organization has a good reputation. They turn up actionable intelligence. Pearson has served as a backchannel communicator for us, carrying some high-level information to other countries. There's no evidence she has done anything against America. And have I mentioned how connected she is?"

"Not in the last five seconds." He popped two more antacids into his mouth and reached for the cigar resting on the tabletop.

Chapman started to pull a pack of cigarettes from his shirt pocket, then checked himself and pushed them back out of sight.

"God damn no-smoking restaurants. Who the hell serves coffee and doesn't expect a guy to light up? Anyway, here's the issue. Among the various and sundry scumbags this lady tracks are the triads, specifically the Chinese mobsters most tied into human trafficking. That's all well and good. She shares what she learns. Unfortunately, her buddy, Roberts, is doing the same thing. But he's reporting it back to the Chinese. Specifically, he's passing it along to Jiang Fang."

"Where's Jiang taking it?"

"Not sure yet. But here's the important thing." He reached across the table and took the folder from Brognola. He leafed through several papers, paused at one, nodded and handed the folder back to the big Fed.

It was a printed copy of a story from the *New York Times*. Brognola read the headline, "Israeli Journalist Killed in Athens." He checked the date and saw it happened the day before the strike on Bolan's safehouse.

"Tell me what I'm looking at," Brognola said.

"The victim, her name is Angel Tzon. She's Israeli."

"I see that." Brognola didn't want to look his old friend in the eye. While he hadn't heard about this murder, he knew Chapman would pick up that something about the story was striking a chord.

"You notice it says 'former' journalist? That's because in the last few years she's been working for Pearson as an investigator."

"Okay."

"She's the second person with a connection to Pearson to die in the last month."

"Okay."

"Both of those people were tracking some aspect of the same triad and its human-trafficking operations. Both ended up dead."

"And you pieced all this together. By yourself while keeping it from your superiors?"

"Hey, I'm good."

"You are good. You're also full of it."

Chapman gave his old friend a lopsided grin. "Fair enough," he said. "Look, I got a tip that Roberts was passing information to Jiang about a month ago. That information came from the Russians. A Mafia guy in New York got it from one of his relatives in Tel Aviv, passed it along to me. These guys fuck each other over all the time. You know how it works. They wanted me to send our organized crime guys after the triad."

"So you'd leave his people alone," Brognola said.

"Precisely. The guy in New York points me to this clown. Paul Woods. Paul's a fence. Not just any fence. He doesn't do the small-time stuff like a stolen laptop or a game console. He thinks a lot bigger—stolen cargo from freighters, containers swiped from warehouses, that kind of stuff."

"American?"

"He is. But his base was Hong Kong. Mommy was a diplomat who dragged him all over Asia. Longest he's been in the States was to attend Princeton for a year. He got kicked out. Smart guy, but he didn't apply himself."

"Made Mom proud."

"I know, right? I say, good on him if he didn't fit in. I never liked the Ivy League schools, either. Here's the weird thing, though. Paul's a thief and by most accounts an arrogant douche bag. But he has a soft spot for kids. Don't look at me like that. I'm not saying he's a perv. What I mean is, he's a crook and deals in hot merchandise. But he still had his mom's 'I'm gonna change the world attitude.'"

"How so?"

"He'd sell fenced goods for the triad, the Russian mafia and a bunch of other scum, okay? Put a little money in their pockets, cozy up to them. Ply their people with hookers, drugs and alcohol. Then he'd turn around and pass along any information he got to Pearson. Guy had a set of brass clangers on him, if you ask me."

"Good on him, I guess."

"Maybe. He did good things. Maybe it counteracted the bad stuff, leveled out the Karmic balance and all that crap." Chapman leaned in. "But it also got him killed. One day, he just disappears." Chapman snapped his fingers. "A few days later, some guys working at a water-treatment plant found his body when it got tangled up in some of the equipment. The general theory is he got whacked because of his organized crime ties and dumped into the sewer. Judging by the lack of an investigation, I'm guessing it was some of his triad buddies who popped him and now the government is turning a blind eye to the whole thing."

"You're guessing?"

"It's an educated guess. Hey, did I tell you the guy weighed 350 pounds? I'm guessing the rats and the fish thought they'd hit an all-you-can-eat buffet when they found this guy."

"You're all heart, Carl. So the problem, I guess, is this

guy had some good information, but now he's dead and you can't get to it."

Chapman's eyes dropped and he stared at a spot on the tablecloth.

"Not precisely."

Brognola's stomach churned harder. He popped a couple more antacids into his mouth and ground them into a mint-flavored paste with his teeth and his tongue.

"Then what is the problem?"

Chapman fidgeted for a couple of seconds, absently stirred his coffee.

"I got the call on this guy a couple of weeks ago," he said. "At that point, I'd never heard of him, Pearson or anything else related to the complaint. But once I started digging, I got worried. I mean, this lady has some high-powered friends, right up to the White House staff. If someone in her organization is leaking to the Chinese, that's a big damn deal. I figured I'd better rattle some cages, fast. I booked myself a trip to Hong Kong. I tracked the guy down at his office. He slammed the lid of his laptop closed the minute I flashed a badge. Then he says he doesn't have to tell me anything. Says if I keep harassing him, he's going to call the U.S. Consulate and complain. Blah, blah, blah. I tell him he should stick to eating truckloads of cheeseburgers and leave the law to the professionals."

Brognola covered his face with hands.

"Keep going," he muttered.

"Granted, it wasn't my best moment. Anyway, I realize this guy isn't going to tell me shit. I could push harder, but I don't want to. I'm trying to keep the whole thing as low key as possible for as long as possible."

"Because that's your trademark."

"Was that called for? Like I said before, this guy won't tell me anything. I don't have the patience to fight with him. I thank him for his time, leave his office and four hours later follow him to his apartment. When the lights finally went out," Chapman snapped his fingers, "I'm in his apartment."

"You broke in."

"I didn't say that. I said I was in his apartment. How I got in is irrelevant."

"Just finish the story."

"All right. I am in the apartment by means known only to me. The apartment has speakers wired in all the rooms. Woods is piping this crazy white noise through it. All I hear are beach sounds—crashing waves, seagulls, that kind of crap."

"Point."

"Okay, the point is I found the laptop and I took it. I scoured the freaking thing and found all sorts of good stuff in it."

"None of it admissible in a court of law."

"Wussy. It's all good stuff. Really good stuff. Some of it pertains to his fencing operation. Some of it pertains to his work with Sandra Pearson. And it turns out the guy is crazy paranoid. He's been spying on his own people, including Roberts and Pearson. He's got hours of digital recordings of Roberts talking to Jiang and a couple of other known Chinese agents. He's got pictures of the guys meeting. He even has a listing of Pearson's other operatives. If you have three of Pearson's operatives dead, I'm not sure what it means, but it's nasty."

"Where's the laptop?"

"I have it."

"I want it."

"Look, Hal. I acquired it."

"Stole it."

Chapman pressed the curled fingers of his right hand against the heel of his left palm. Brognola heard the knuckles crackle.

"What're you going to do with it?"

"Use it."

"How? It's illegally obtained evidence."

"Let me worry about that."

"This particular triad is a dangerous organization, Hal. No offense, but you don't spend a lot of time on the street these days."

Brognola had been kidnapped, injured and almost killed more than once during his years with the Farm. But all the details were classified. As far as Chapman knew, Brognola did nothing other than sit behind a desk.

"Again," Brognola said, "let me worry about that."

"I want a piece of this," Chapman said, his neck and cheeks flushing.

"Give me the laptop and your notes. Forget this ever happened. Trust me. I am doing this for your own good."

The other guy exhaled loudly. "I'm in trouble, right?"

Brognola shook his head. "As far as I'm concerned, we had coffee and talked about the Washington Nationals. After that, my memory gets fuzzy."

"You know I haven't done this before. Steal evidence, I mean. I feel crappy about it."

Brognola knew his old friend well enough to know the guy was telling the truth.

"You're a good agent, but stay away from the black-bag stuff."

"Okay, Dad."

He reached under the table and Brognola heard the crunch of paper. A moment later, Chapman's hand came back into view, holding a paper grocery sack, the top folded and rolled down several times. He set the bag on the table.

"Don't let the packaging fool you. The contents are invaluable."

The big Fed pushed his chair back from the table, stood

and picked up the bag. "Thanks for the coffee and the conversation."

"Let me know how it works out."

Not likely, Brognola thought.

# CHAPTER TWELVE

Exile had been good for Kassem, Bolan decided.

Perched on the rooftop of a dilapidated warehouse, his form partially obscured by the parapet running the perimeter of the roof, he stared down at a shorter but newer commercial building. The warehouse Bolan eyed was sprawling, its exterior freshly painted white, the grounds well manicured. There was a helipad on the building's roof.

Kassem used the warehouse as a transit point for shipping the SA-7 shoulder-fired rockets and other hardware he'd smuggled out of Libya before Khadaffi's regime had fallen, according to information unearthed by Stony Man Farm.

The soldier had spent the past few hours watching the facility. He'd counted a half-dozen guards walking the grounds, at least one sitting in a guard shack at the front gate and one on the warehouse roof at all times. None wore uniforms. Instead, all were dressed in street clothes—blue jeans, khakis, polo shirts and the like—but they all traveled armed with AK-47s, MAC-10s or Steyr submachine guns carried in plain view. After the shift change, the squad grew to eight, all males, all similarly armed.

With night approaching, Bolan had hoped for the opposite. Many times, he'd found security forces diminished overnight, in part because there were fewer duties beyond the basics. The gates were locked. Fewer people were coming and going, which meant fewer IDs to check, fewer vehicles to inspect. But Kassem's people had beefed up security. That triggered alarm bells for Bolan. Maybe they anticipated a late-night shipment and needed the extra people.

From what Bolan understood, Kassem's people were supposed to cut a deal this night with a Chechen terrorist who wanted the RPGs to use on the Russians. According to the information the soldier had dug up, the Chechen was supposed to make an appearance himself. With that kind of star power on hand, Bolan hoped Kassem would show up, too. That way Bolan could wax the guy and head back to the U.S. to handle the next looming crisis, whatever that may be.

The northern faces of the garage and the warehouse stared back at Bolan through the fence. He could hear the growl of the tractor-trailer rigs as they idled on the other side of the garage. Bolan estimated a fifty-yard stretch of pavement, faded and broken, stood between him and the fence. The area was poorly lit and offered enough shadows to cover his approach.

His surveillance told him the guards walked the perimeter fence once every hour, with each patrol taking less than fifteen minutes. They'd just finished such a check about twenty minutes ago. If they kept to their routine, he had plenty of time to penetrate the fence before a sentry passed his way.

If—

Bolan had fought too many battles in his War Everlasting to trust routines. Since they appeared to be on high alert, it was possible a guard might decide to shake things up and run a second patrol. Or Bolan could trip a sensor and suddenly find all the guards bearing down on him at once. The worst-case scenarios were endless. Whatever. Most battle plans went to hell once you hit the ground, anyway.

The soldier traversed the pavement, taking care to melt into the shadows as he moved. As he neared the fence, he pulled a small canvas duffel bag from his shoulder and, with a grunt, tossed it up and over the chain-link barrier. It hit the grass-covered ground with a thud.

Drawing a small pair of bolt cutters from inside his jacket, the soldier made a T-shaped cut in the fence. He peeled back each side and crawled through the opening. Picking up the duffel bag, he moved to the garage, edged along its exterior until he stood within a few yards of one of the idling trucks. Pulling the duffel bag from his shoulder again, he gave it a toss and it skidded across the concrete until it disappeared beneath the truck.

He kept moving, hoping to take out at least a couple of guards before anyone found the hole in the fence.

The soldier wove his way between the trucks. Though they gave him cover, the rumble of the engines would rob him of his hearing. When he reached the truck's cab, he knelt next to one of the tires and peered around the bumper.

He held the Heckler & Koch MP-5 SD-3 subgun with both hands and watched as a pair of guards approached him. Neither looked in his direction. Instead, both seemed focused on the garage. Though each carried a submachine gun, the muzzles of the weapons were angled toward the ground.

The soldier inched the H&K's barrel around until he'd lined up a shot on one of the men. The MP-5 coughed out a fast burst. A ragged line of red dots seemed to suddenly open up across the man's chest, his body jerked under the onslaught.

The second man swore, a lit cigarette falling from his lips. His SMG swung up, looking to deal death even as he scrambled to acquire a target. A second burst from the MP-5 punched into the guy, stitching him from right crotch to left clavicle. Unfortunately for Bolan, the guy's dead finger spasmed, tightening on the trigger. A burst exploded from the weapon and the slugs pounded against the exterior of the garage at Bolan's back, chipping away at the brick and peppering him with brick fragments.

Once the weapon stopped firing, Bolan got to his feet and backtracked between the rigs. He moved along the rear of the trailers until he reached the edge of the last one and paused. One of the bay doors jerked and began rolling downward.

Four guards surged through the door before it closed, their weapons searching for targets.

The soldier laid down another burst from the MP-5 and the punishing barrage mowed down two of the gunners before they'd covered much ground. The sudden demise of their comrades caused the remaining two to halt in their tracks and fire wildly at Bolan. The first volley of gunfire lashed over the soldier's head, missing him by several inches.

He dived forward to escape the inevitable second wave of rounds. When he hit the concrete, the impact pushed the air from his lungs and caused it to hiss out through his clenched teeth. More rounds lanced into the concrete around Bolan and forced him to roll to avoid the murderous rain. The soldier emptied the H&K's magazine, dragging the weapon in a tight horizontal line. Some of the slugs tore into the shoulder of one of the shooters. A crimson spray exploded from the man's wound. The impact spun him a quarter of a turn and his SMG fell from his grip.

Bolan released the MP-5, letting it hang on its strap. At the same time, he yanked the Beretta from his shoulder rig, flicking the fire selector switch to 3-round-burst mode.

Muzzle-flashes blazed from the remaining thug's weapon as he tried to burn Bolan down. Whether it was inexperience or the stress of combat Bolan would never know, but the barrage whistled past the Executioner's temple, missing him by an inch. Bolan responded to the lucky stroke by snapping off three rounds from the Beretta. The Parabellum manglers drilled into the guy's torso and caused him to stagger before he crumpled to the ground in a boneless heap.

The big American ejected the Beretta's partially spent magazine and fed another one into the weapon's grip. Holstering the pistol, he reloaded the MP-5.

As he set out for the warehouse, Bolan guessed he'd eliminated at least two-thirds of the security force and it was time to finish this strike. Behind him, the soldier heard the squeaking of metal, followed by the slamming of a truck door. He wheeled around and saw that someone had climbed into the cab of one of the Mercedes trucks.

The truck's 375-horsepower engine growled and the brakes hissed as the driver disengaged them. The vehicle lurched forward, sliding out from between the other rigs. Was the driver trying to get away? The thought caused Bolan to hesitate. He didn't want to fire on an unarmed truck driver, even if the man had been shipping weapons for Kassem.

The hesitation nearly proved fatal. The truck curved right and began to gain speed as it left the other vehicles behind. Bolan heard the driver shifting the transmission and the engine whine before the vehicle launched into a wide turn that was going to put Bolan face-to-face with the big rig's grill.

In the same instant, a hand protruded from the driver's window. The nickel-plated surface of a pistol caught the glare from a streetlight and winked at Bolan.

MOVE! BOLAN'S MIND screamed.

The soldier darted left. In the same instant, he raised the MP-5 and squeezed off two fast bursts. The slugs slammed into the truck's cab, sparking as they glanced off the steel skin and careened into the night. The big machine's engine growled and the cab's front end veered toward the soldier. He found himself bathed in the glare of the rig's headlights as it bore down on him.

The subgun coughed out another swarm of bullets. The slugs drilled through the windshield and a series of spider-web cracks spread across the glass, but the truck didn't slow.

Bolan moved again, figuring agility was his best weapon against the lumbering truck. As he sprinted, he stowed the MP-5 and fisted the Desert Eagle, cocking the hammer as he brought it around and squeezed off several shots. The .44-caliber boat tail slugs drilled through the truck's grille and into the radiator. The Executioner knew a damaged radiator would cripple the truck, but probably not in time to help him.

With his free hand, the soldier reached into his jacket and drew out a detonator.

Heart pounding in his chest from exertion and adrenaline, the soldier stood his ground for what seemed like forever as the rig continued to barrel toward him. Thunder pealed again as the Desert Eagle fired twice more.

One of the shots glanced off the vehicle's bumper while the other missed completely.

Bolan cared little about whether he struck the vehicle. He simply wanted to keep the driver engaged for a couple more heartbeats.

The man behind the wheel apparently realized the danger he faced. Tires squealed against the pavement as the driver stomped the brake. The truck slowed. Bolan sprinted out of its path, diving forward and hitting the ground in a roll. He simultaneously flicked a switch on the detonator. A small red light on the box winked.

A loud boom exploded from beneath one of the parked trucks. Bolan stayed on the ground long enough to ride out the shock waves.

Boiling columns of orange flame rose skyward, engulfing the trailer of the nearest truck. The force thrust the vehicle's trailer into the air, metal groaning before it snapped loose from the cab. It crashed back to earth, the flaming carcass shuddering as it struck the ground. Bolan kept moving. He knew the flames would ignite the fuel tanks of the other trucks as well as a nearby diesel pump.

As the driver tried to stop the vehicle, it launched into a sideways slide toward the flaming motor pool.

The big American jumped to his feet and continued toward the warehouse. A glance over his shoulder told him the cab of the truck that had tried to run him down was now fully engulfed in flames.

While he sprinted for the building, he reloaded the Desert Eagle. He rolled up on a gray exit door, tried the handle and found it locked. He aimed the Desert Eagle at the lock, squeezed the trigger. The bullet drilled through the lock. Bolan hastily holstered the gun and unslung the MP-5 before he yanked open the door and moved inside the warehouse.

One of the men spotted Bolan, raised his subgun and squeezed off a single shot. The round lanced through the air just over the warrior's head. At the same time, another of the gunners wheeled and swung a pistol in Bolan's direction.

The Executioner held his ground and squeezed off an extended burst at the gunners. The 9 mm fusillade caught both men and they withered under the swarm of bullets. Stray rounds smacked into the vehicle, piercing its hood, windshield and grille.

Chechen terrorist Anzor Sadulayev, a black briefcase in one hand, was frantically trying to open the driver's door. Bolan took him down with another burst.

The soldier checked the downed men again, making sure they were dead. Satisfied, he slung the MP-5, fisted the Beretta and walked toward the nearest forklift. His eyes continued to scan his surroundings for other threats. He could hear sirens wailing in the distance and figured the numbers were falling fast now. He needed to finish his work here and get out.

Slipping the strap of his war bag from his shoulder, he knelt next to one of the forklifts, opened the bag and drew out a thermite charge. He slipped it under the gas tank of the vehicle, set the timer, repeated the process at the other forklift, setting two thermite charges for good measure before he tossed the bag aside.

The soldier started for the door but hesitated. He pulled his sat phone from his pocket and walked to the vehicle and snapped a picture of Saulayev's face, figuring Brognola would want to pass it along to other agencies in the government. He pocketed the phone and started to turn for the exit. He paused, took a second look at the black briefcase that had fallen from the man's grasp when the Chechen terrorist had crumbled to the ground. Grabbing the handle, he picked up the briefcase and headed for the exit.

TEN MINUTES LATER, the soldier was sitting in his rental car. He pulled out his sat phone and punched in the number for Stony Man Farm, waiting while the call went through a series of cutouts. Brognola's voice, gruff and weary, answered on the first ring.

"Striker?"

"Good to hear your voice. Sounds like you're turning Athens on its head. Was our information good?"

"It was. Found weapons in the place and our Chechen friend was there to make a deal with Kassem."

"Did he get what he came for?"

"No, but he got what he deserved."

"Even better."

"I'll send you a picture."

"Good. You get free and clear from the site?"

Bolan turned the ignition key and the car growled to life.

"I did. You gave the locals a heads-up about the thermite? I would have called the police dispatch, but figured the language barrier would have put us back."

"We ran it through some channels. They were pissed about the operation, but to hell with them. I know you didn't want firefighters rushing into a building stockpiled with weapons and ammunition. I'm guessing they'll set up a perimeter around the place and let it burn."

"Be best for everyone."

"Except Kassem. I suspect you're giving him the granddaddy of all ulcers."

"Just a down payment on what he's going to get."

After a few seconds, Brognola said, "Where's your head, Striker?"

"Come again?" Bolan asked.

"You sound dark. Darker than usual."

"Forgot to take my lithium."

"Funny guy. You know what I mean, damn it. You sound pissed off. The hooker, are you stewing about her?"

Bolan didn't answer.

"That's it, isn't it? You told her you'd protect her and you didn't. She's dead and one of your friends got hurt in the process."

"How is Leo?"

"He's fine. But don't change the subject. Answer my question. Where's your head?"

"Right where it needs to be, Hal. Seriously, I'm good on this one. I haven't forgotten why I am here or what Kassem did."

"I know you haven't forgotten the mission, Striker," Brognola replied. "Truth be told, if you want to kill Kassem for killing the call girl—"

"Her name was Kristina."

"Kristina. Sorry, you know I didn't mean anything by it."

"Sure."

"But you want to kill Kassem for what he did to her. Or for Leo getting caught in the cross fire, fine. More power to you. Your motives aren't my business at the end of the day. I know you'll get the job done.

"My point is, just keep your cool. You're a good soldier. If you're pissed, fine. Just don't let it cloud your judgment."

"Understood," Bolan replied.

By now, he'd put enough distance between himself and the fire that he felt comfortable pulling over. He wheeled the car into a parking lot, guided it between a red compact car and a black van.

"This is bigger than Kassem," the Executioner said.

"Yeah, it is."

"You get any identification on the bodies?"

"We did. Chinese nationals. Again, no surprise. We could tell by the photos they were of Asian descent. We ran their names, pictures and fingerprints through every database we could find."

"Get any hits?"

"Couple of them. Apparently, they both spent time in the United States as university students a decade or so ago. One in New Mexico, the other in Hawaii."

"Hardship duty."

"Yeah, send me, send me. Anyway. The first guy, Lo Aiguo, ended up getting the boot from the U.S. The State Department yanked his student visa, the whole nine yards, and sent him home. But not for poor grades. Apparently, our young friend was studying physics, with a special focus on the nuclear side of things."

"I think I know where this is going."

"You'd be right. He started asking a lot of questions of people, especially a couple of adjunct faculty who'd worked in high-level jobs with the Department of Energy. The FBI got wind of it and started quizzing him. Before things got too hot and heavy, though, the Chinese apparently threatened and begged until some bureaucrat somewhere decided it was easier just to pack up the bastard and send him back to Beijing. Once he left the country, the CIA picked up his trail and followed him off and on for several years. They were able to piece enough evidence together to prove he worked for the Ministry of State Security."

"Chinese intelligence? Surprise."

"Baffling, right? Our other friend, Wu Han Chung, has a nearly identical story. Wu attended a university in California. He got caught nosing around the campus labs where they were conducting government-funded research into super-computers. This time, the Chinese decided to be shitty about it. They nabbed an American student, accused her of spying and we had to trade."

"Was she?"

"Was she what?"

"A spy."

"That's for me to know and you to find out." The big Fed stated.

Brognola continued. "So Wu went to Beijing, disappeared from view. A couple of years later, he reappeared in Hong Kong, which is where things get interesting. He began keeping company with Huang Dingxiang. Same went for Lo."

Brognola paused. Bolan got the feeling this was supposed to be an "aha" moment,

"I have no idea who this third guy is," Bolan said.

"Sorry," Brognola said. "I keep seeing dispatches about this guy come across my desk. I forget other people occasionally leave their offices and do actual missions. Huang is a mid-level spy handler with the MSS. One of his specialties, apparently, is rehabilitating some of the washouts."

"Like our two friends."

"Yeah. According to the files, neither of these clowns had an advanced degree in the sciences. That was part of the reason they got caught. They asked pretty ham-handed questions and drew a lot of attention to themselves. Pretty sloppy work, especially for the Chinese."

"Good for us, though."

"Sure. From there, these guys teamed up with their new handler. That was when they started getting involved with things that were a little more, um, kinetic."

"Like killing people," Bolan said.

"I believe wet work is the appropriate vernacular," Brognola said. "They mostly focused on what the Chinese government considered troublemakers—dissidents and government critics. Apparently, they excelled at this. We all have to have a trade, right? But even if they weren't rocket scientists—or nuclear physicists or whatever—they still were highly intelligent and patriotic. A bad combination if you're the opposition. But they racked up a dozen or so confirmed kills as a team."

"Before today."

Brognola paused. "Yeah, before today."

Bolan's eyes felt gritty from lack of sleep. He squeezed them shut for a couple of seconds, reopened them, and his vision seemed to sharpen.

"Odd thing is," Brognola stated, "Huang doesn't usually operate in Europe. He focuses on Latin America. China's been trying to make inroads there for a bunch of reasons. If I was a political scientist, I'd explain it all to you. Huang's been more low-key there, though. Spends more time pushing for trade deals and greasing palms with hookers and alcohol than he does waxing people. That said, the CIA still believes his team has knocked off a couple of Chinese human rights activists who bitched too loudly about its expansionist policies."

"'Expansionist policies?' Now you sound like a political scientist. Does he have a home base?"

"Rio de Janeiro, Brazil," Brognola said. "Lives pretty damn well, too."

"You have a location for him?"

"The cyberteam's running traps on him right now. It's possible he was in Athens, too. Regardless, if he lost a couple of people, he'll be communicating about it. Barb contacted her old employers at NSA and asked them to keep their eyes and ears peeled for him. No small task. But we'll turn up something."

"Let me know when you do," Bolan said. "In the meantime, I still need to deal with Kassem."

# CHAPTER THIRTEEN

*Algeria*

It hadn't taken long for the fire to rip its way through the warehouse's interior and eventually eat its way through the roof, releasing long tongues of orange flame and choking the sky with plumes of black smoke. Windowpanes bowed under the onslaught of heat and eventually burst out in a shower of glass shards. Fire hoses released long jets of water that pushed back against the flames and contained them, but didn't extinguish them.

Seated in a wingback chair, Kassem stared at his computer monitor and followed each agonizing moment as the fire destroyed the structure and its contents. The losses, he guessed, would reach into the millions of dollars. The building itself was expensive. Its contents—an arsenal of weapons smuggled out of Libya before rebels had toppled Khadaffi's regime—would make up the bulk of the money lost, though. A bottle of bourbon and a glass sat on his desk within easy reach. Kassem filled the glass halfway, but left it untouched for the moment. In the past hour, he'd already downed two glasses. The alcohol had done nothing to douse his quiet seething. Instead, it only had aggravated the acid roiling in his stomach.

A knock sounded at the door.

"Enter!" Kassem snapped.

The door opened and Mustapha entered the room. The stocky ex-soldier approached Kassem's desk, but avoided his eyes.

"I have news."

"Fuck your news," Kassem said. "Explain again how this happened."

"The American—"

The quiet rage boiling inside Kassem spilled over. He slammed an open palm on the desktop. "Idiot!" he said, "I know it was the American. I want to know how he did this. I give you people and money and guns. Yet one man sweeps in and does this to your people. I ask again. How the fuck—" he pounded the desktop again, this time with the flat edge of his fist "—does this happen?"

Kassem noticed Mustapha's fingers curl into fists, his cheek muscles bounce, as he clenched and unclenched his jaw. Kassem guessed he was humiliating the other man, but didn't care. Maybe if he enraged Mustapha, the bastard would do his job.

"He took them by surprise," Kassem said, "didn't he?"

Mustapha acknowledged the question with a faint nod. "They were more focused on keeping the Chechen hidden from public view. They weren't expecting a one-man death squad to scale the fence and burn the place down."

"You're an idiot. They were idiots. Now I've lost a warehouse and tons of weapons. Well played."

"It gets worse."

Kassem felt himself stiffen.

"How could it get worse?"

The other man raised his eyes and looked directly at his boss.

"I got a call from Sadulayev's people. He brought along a suitcase full of currency, a million dollars."

"He was supposed to transfer the money electronically!"

Shrugging, Mustapha said, "He wanted to hand over at least some of it in cash. I guess it makes— made—him feel like a big man to carry around a suitcase full of money."

Kassem jerked a head toward the image of the burning warehouse displayed on his computer monitor.

"So it's in there, reduced to ash?"

The other man shook his head. "Apparently, the American walked off with it."

Kassem felt his rage ebb slightly, edged out by confusion.

"So now he's a thief?"

"It's more complicated than that. Apparently they heard you hired the American to kill Sadulayev so you could keep the money and the weapons."

"That makes no sense. If I did that, I'd lose money on the deal."

"The Chechens were told you didn't expect Sadulayev to pay, so you set him up. You planned to kill him and take the money."

"Who told them all of this?"

Mustapha shrugged again. "I have no idea, but apparently this person also told them you are working both sides of the fence, taking their money and working for Russian intelligence."

"And they believed that?"

The other man nodded. "Their leader's dead. They want someone to blame. I tried telling them the Americans did it. Once someone mentioned the Russians, it was all over. They're too paranoid."

"Damn it," Kassem said. "Who's in charge now?"

"Magomed Umarov."

Kassem gestured at the telephone on his desk. "Call him. I'll explain things to him."

Mustapha shook his head slowly. "He wants to meet with you in person."

"Fuck him."

"He insists. He says he wants to look you in the eye when you tell him that you didn't set the whole thing up. Otherwise, he won't change his mind."

Kassem shook his head in disgust. He had too many other things to worry about without adding this to the list. And yet, Kassem didn't want to lose the other man's business. Finally, he relented.

"Set something up with him."

## CHAPTER FOURTEEN

*Baltimore, Maryland*

Rosario "Pol" Blancanales wheeled the rented Chevrolet into the parking lot outside the Restwell Motel, selected a space and backed into it. Killing the engine and the headlights, he swept his gaze over the motel—a pair of one-story, L-shaped buildings with redbrick facades. The skin of a black Mercedes parked in the far corner of the lot gleamed from the light of a street lamp. A rusted red pickup truck with wooden side rails on either side of the bed, a yellow Honda and an orange Volkswagen also stood in the lot. All the cars appeared to be empty.

Exiting the car, he felt a rush of cool air against his face. A .40-caliber Glock pistol was stowed in a shoulder holster underneath his brown leather bomber jacket. A small-frame SIG-Sauer pistol was strapped to his right ankle and a folding knife was hidden in the pocket of his jeans. Though not expecting trouble, he had decided to travel armed. He was supporting one of Striker's missions and his old friend tended to draw violence.

He scanned the motel-room doors until he found the one with a rolled-up newspaper in front of it. That was his destination. He doubted the Restwell Motel offered amenities like a newspaper, especially since most guests probably paid by the hour. But, even if it did, it was just before midnight and the next edition for local newspapers wouldn't hit the streets for hours.

Walking up to the door, he stepped to one side of it. His hand slipped underneath his jacket, not actually grabbing the Glock, but putting his fingers within grabbing distance. He rapped on the door with the knuckles of his left fist.

"Who is it?" a woman's voice called.

"Delivery," Blancanales said.

"Of what sort?"

"Overnight mail," the Able Team warrior replied.

A moment later he heard a dead bolt click open and the rattle of the door chain being pulled aside. The door parted a few inches and Blancanales saw a woman's face—or the right half of it, anyway—staring at him from behind the door.

"You're from the Justice Department?"

"Yes."

By now Blancanales had moved his hand away from his gun and instead drew out a leather bifold case from inside his jacket. He flipped it open so the woman could study his fake Justice Department credentials. After a minute or so, she nodded with satisfaction, opened the door and stepped aside to allow Blancanales to enter.

Once he was inside, he heard the door close and turned to see Sandra Pearson locking it.

In her left hand, she clasped a small black revolver, its muzzle pointed at the floor. Blancanales assumed it had been hidden behind the door. She turned and gestured toward the bed.

"Please," she said. "Sit."

"I'll stand," Blancanales stated. "I'm a little antsy in enclosed spaces. Especially when the other person is holding a gun."

"Sorry," she said.

Reaching her gun hand around, she slipped it into the waistband of her jeans.

"I'd offer you a drink—" she began.

"But the roaches already drank your stash?" Blancanales replied, flashing a smile.

She glanced around the room then gave him a faint smile.

"I know, right? I'm going to bathe myself in rubbing alcohol before I get in my truck."

Blancanales's mind flashed to the rusted truck sitting in the parking lot.

"That's your truck?" he asked.

"What, you thought I'd drive a black Mercedes here? Maybe wear an evening gown?"

"But not a diamond-studded tiara. Sorry, I made an assumption."

"Apparently, you know a little about me."

"I know enough," Blancanales said. "Heiress to an alcohol fortune. You have a doctorate in international studies from Yale. You left your brother to hawk alcohol while you pursue the family's other business. The spooky stuff."

She sighed and smiled ruefully. "Nowhere near as spooky as I'd like," she said. "Mostly jetting around the world, chatting up foreign diplomats and passing along what I hear to my friends in Washington."

"But spooky enough that you're carrying a gun."

She shrugged slightly, a forced lightness in her tone. "A woman needs her accessories."

Blancanales allowed himself a grin. Despite her wealth, intelligence and Ivy League education, he didn't sense any pretenses from the woman. He liked her instantly and knew it would only make his mission here that much harder.

"I brought you something," he said. He reached into the left hip pocket of his jeans and noticed she took a step back, widening the distance between them. He extended a hand to her, palm open, a flash drive in it. She moved forward again, took it from his hand and studied it, as though she could discern its contents by looking at it.

"It's proof," Blancanales said.

"Of?"

"Of what I am about to tell you. You're going to want that later."

"Why?" Pearson queried.

"Because you probably won't believe it the first time."

BLANCANALES RETURNED A half hour later.

He balanced a drink carrier holding two cups of coffee in one hand. In his other hand, he clutched a white paper sack filled with cheeseburgers. While away, he'd kept an eye on the parking lot and noted the same cars still stood outside the motel. He paused at the motel-room door, set the bag of burgers on the cracked pavement and dug the room key from his jacket pocket.

Opening the door, he retrieved the food and stepped into the room. He found Pearson where he'd left her, seated on the edge of the bed. She turned and looked at him. Though her cheeks were dry, her eyes looked red and she clutched a wadded tissue in her right hand.

Blancanales flashed his best disarming smile and closed the door.

"Is this true?"

"I'm afraid so," he said.

She squeezed her eyes closed and shook her head resolutely. He set the food and drinks down, crossed his arms over his chest and watched.

"I can't believe it," she said. Her eyes snapped open and she gave the Able Team warrior a challenging stare. "I don't believe it."

"It's true. You need to trust me."

"Or?" Pearson asked.

"Or not. Either way, it's the truth and it needs to be dealt with."

She balled her hands into fists. "Damn it."

"I can run you up the chain, if you'd like. You want to talk to the attorney general? The CIA director? Higher?"

"You can raise those people on the phone?"

"I can't. My boss can. I'd prefer not to have to go that route. But it can be done."

Her shoulders sagged and she shook her head.

"What now? I suppose you need to arrest him."

"Something like that."

Her stare hardened.

"Meaning?"

"Something bad's happening. He's part of it. We need to take him."

"Take him. Arrest him?"

Blancanales shrugged.

"And once you take him? What then?"

"Talk to him. He has information and we need it."

"You're going to hurt him," Pearson said accusingly.

"It depends on how he wants to play it, frankly."

She rose from the bed, slowly and deliberately. She crossed her arms over her chest and met Blancanales's stare.

"I can't let you hurt him."

"It's not up for debate," he said, his voice even. "I can promise he'll have a choice. Either he tells us what we need to know or he gets his ass kicked. But he gets a choice."

She licked her lips.

"You're serious?"

"I am."

"I can't believe this."

"At least I'm giving him a choice. Those operatives, the ones he betrayed? They had no choice. They died because of what he did. No second chances. No debate. Just torture then death."

That seemed to hit her like a slap to the face. Her eyes glistened and she turned her gaze toward the floor. "I can't believe I didn't see this."

Blancanales stayed silent. He'd just laid a lot on the woman, upended her entire world. He guessed she needed time to wrap her mind around it. Unfortunately, they didn't have that kind of time.

"You'll help us?"

"He's not going to go easily," Pearson warned.

"Meaning?"

"You saw his background?"

Blancanales nodded.

"Then you know what kind of man he is. He's killed people before. He'll do it again, if necessary. If he feels like he's cornered. Whoever you send needs to know this."

"I think we've got that one covered."

DALE ROBERTS WAS two sips into his whiskey when his phone buzzed. Reluctantly, he set aside his drink, took up the phone. A glance at the screen told him the call was coming from an unidentified caller. He scowled, turned on the phone and brought it to his ear and identified himself.

"They know," said a male voice, flat and cold.

Roberts recognized Jiang's voice immediately. His stomach clenched and he stiffened in his chair. Jiang almost never made his own calls to operatives, preferring instead to rely on a network of couriers and informants.

"I said—"

"I know what you said," Roberts replied. "Who knows?"

"In sixty seconds, you'll get a knock at the front door. Answer it."

The line went dead.

Roberts slipped the phone into his pocket. The shock of Jiang's call had worn off, replaced by the weight of his words. *They know.* Pulling open the lap drawer of the mahogany desk, he reached inside and pulled out a SIG-Sauer P-226 pistol sheathed in a leather holster. He clipped the weapon to his hip just as a knock sounded on the door. Exiting the study, he descended the stairs and headed for the front door. With his hand resting on the SIG's grip, he stopped at the front door. Standing to one side of the door, he reached over and unlocked it, turned the knob and pulled the door open.

The door swung aside to reveal an Asian man dressed in a worn black leather jacket, snakeskin cowboy boots, faded jeans and navy-blue turtleneck. The man's scalp was shaved bald; the ridge of his nose was crooked where it had been broken. Roberts noticed his visitor's eyes flick to the SIG before he looked back at Roberts.

"I was sent," he said.

"Get in here," Roberts snapped, "before someone sees you."

The man crossed the threshold and Roberts shut the door, twisting the dead bolt to lock it. The man had put several feet between himself and Roberts. His arms hung loosely at his sides, his fingers curling and uncurling into fists. Roberts couldn't tell whether the rhythmic movement signaled a nervous tic or impending violence.

"Talk," Roberts said.

"They know about you."

"So I hear. Give me specifics."

"The woman. The one you betrayed. The Americans have contacted her."

"Sandra?"

The man nodded.

"When?"

"Maybe an hour ago. Maybe a little more."

"Shit. How did this happen? I covered my tracks."

The guy shrugged. "Who cares? They know. They're on their way here and you need to deal with them."

"'They?' Who the hell is 'they?'" Roberts asked.

"She was contacted by a Justice Department agent. She met with him at a motel and now they're on their way here. You can deal with this, right?"

Roberts shot the guy an eat-shit-and-die look. "Of course I can deal with it. Hell, I took it this far, haven't I? C'mon upstairs. I have something to show you."

Roberts led the man up the stairs to the second floor. He retraced his steps from just a few minutes ago, but when he reached the study door, he walked past it and entered the next door down the hall. He flicked a wall switch and an overhead light flared to life. The room contained a single bed, a small oak dresser and a few other items of furniture. Roberts marched through the room to the walk-in closet. He moved inside and on the wall opposite him was a steel door sealed with an electronic lock.

He punched a code into an alpha-numeric keypad and the lock box emitted a small beep. The door slid aside, disappearing into a recessed area in the wall.

The door opened into a room about twice the size of the closet. A variety of shotguns, submachine guns and semi-automatic assault rifles hung from the walls. as he studied the room's contents, his eyes settled on a pair of Thompson machine guns and a Schmeiser machine gun. From what he recalled, Pearson's old man had an affinity for World War II-era weapons, and these, along with a few handguns from the era, were what remained of his collection, much of it sold after his death.

He looked past the relics and his eyes settled on a pair of Spectre M-4 submachine guns. He pulled one down, handed it to his new companion and took the second one for himself. He stuffed a magazine into the Spectre, then chambered a round. His companion grabbed a magazine and loaded his own weapon. Roberts found an olive-drab shoulder bag, slid extra magazines into it and looped the strap over his shoulder.

He was vaguely aware of the man next to him grabbing more magazines for the other Spectre.

Roberts's eyes lit on the Thompson machine guns again. Both weapons were immaculate. Pearson's father had loved them and kept them cleaned and maintained. Even after his death, she had continued the tradition, hiring a gunsmith to check the guns over and replace parts. Roberts had made fun of her for it on more than one occasion, dismissing it as useless sentimentality and a waste of money. He pulled down one of the weapons, the weight of which never ceased to surprise him. Finding one of the drum magazines, he loaded it into the weapon.

Without a word, he moved past the other man, exited the confines of the weapons room and doubled back through the hallway. There was nothing to discuss. They knew Pearson and her new friends would be coming from the ground floor, though it remained to be seen whether they would enter through the front or rear door of the house.

She would deactivate the alarms, that much he knew. But it didn't matter. He had eyes on them and they wouldn't know that. They would assume he was unaware of their approach. Unaware and alone. They wouldn't live long enough to be surprised.

CARL LYONS, BLANCANALES and Pearson reached the large white double doors of the mansion. Both men had their pistols drawn. While Pearson busied herself with the lock, Blancanales turned and checked their six. He swept his eyes over the lush lawn, along the top of the security fence, but found nothing. They'd sealed the gate behind them, and Pearson had been able to reactivate the alarms through an app on her cell phone. They should be secure.

Still a sense of uneasiness gnawed Blancanales, a sixth sense forged in the hellfire of combat.

He elbowed Lyons, who was the leader of the urban commando unit known as Able Team, based at Stony Man Farm.

"Something doesn't feel right," he said.

Lyons nodded.

"It's quiet," the big ex-detective said. "Too quiet."

"Did you really just say that?" Blancanales asked.

"Seriously," Lyons said.

He turned to Pearson. "Don't you have a security team that patrols the grounds or something? Or at least a contract service that cruises by and checks the locks on the front gate?"

She nodded. "We have two night watchmen. One's a Marine and the other a retired Washington, D.C., police captain. I don't live on the grounds anymore, and we don't want to leave all the sensitive documents and the computer systems unprotected."

"Plus, someone might steal your caviar," Lyons said.

"God you're a dick."

"Lady, you have no idea."

She turned to Blancanales.

"I don't speak caveman. Can you please translate the grunts for me?"

"Where are your guards? You give them the night off?" Blancanales asked.

She shook her head.

"Does boy wonder have the authority to give them a night off?" Lyons asked.

"Yes, damn it, he does."

"If someone called in sick, you'd know about it?"

"They'd call me directly, and I'd have to call the other one in as a replacement."

"He kept them home," Lyons said. "Maybe to keep them out of the cross fire. More likely because they'd fight for their boss."

"Yeah," Blancanales said.

He glanced at Pearson. Her eyes were fixed on a spot on the ground, her brow furrowed. She chewed gently on her lower lip. A few seconds passed before she spoke again.

"He planned to kill me," she said to no one in particular. "He was going to betray me."

"Nothing personal," Lyons said. "He screws everyone, apparently."

She glared at Lyons, but Blancanales gestured for both of them to stand down.

"Save it for Roberts," Blancanales said.

Nodding, she turned and finished unlocking the door.

THE DOOR SWUNG inward. Lyons bulled his way through it. The Able Team leader had stowed his Colt Python, instead pulling the Auto Assault 12 shotgun from its carrying case, discarding the case in some nearby shrubs. The weapon, outfitted with a 20-round magazine, was capable of firing 300 rounds per minute with a muzzle velocity of 1,000 feet per second.

When Pearson saw the shotgun, she started to protest, but Blancanales interceded. The door was open and the time for discussion had passed. He entered the house on Lyons's heels. Holding his Glock pistol at chest level with both hands, Blancanales swept the weapon over his field of fire. Pearson followed the other two inside the mansion and softly closed the door behind her. She quickly reset the alarm, probably out of habit. Blancanales shrugged it off. At least that way, if someone tried to follow them inside the house, they'd likely set off the alarm, making a sneak attack at least a little more difficult. Unless, of course, that prick Roberts turned the alarms off.

The house itself was at once opulent and predictable, exactly what Blancanales would expect from an old-money family. Marble floors, paintings by European masters, portraits of distinguished-looking men and women. A woman in one of the portraits looked similar to Pearson, albeit older and dressed with the formality of a 1960s First Lady.

"My grandmother," Pearson whispered. Blancanales nodded, but his eyes continued to rove over their surroundings.

From the corner of his eye, he saw Lyons wheel to the right, the AA-12's barrel hunting for a target. He followed the Able

Team leader's line of sight, started to bring around his own weapon, but checked himself when he saw Lyons's target. A suit of armor, a shield decorated with a family crest hooked to one arm, a broadsword protruding up from the other hand, stood alongside one of the walls.

Lyons whipped his head in Blancanales's direction. "A suit of armor?" he whispered. "Seriously?"

"You saved us, amigo," Blancanales said, grinning.

The group covered the first floor and began climbing the stairs, with Lyons in the lead.

As Lyons neared the top of the steps, a wide area he guessed was the size of his first house opened before him. Red carpeting covered the floor. An antique love seat, three chairs and a grandfather clock were clustered in one corner. Several doors lined the walls.

Before he could exit the stairs, though, a doorway to his left flew open. An Asian man, a submachine gun gripped tightly to his body, darted through it. Jagged orange-yellow flames spat from the barrel of the submachine gun. The rounds whistled just past Lyons's head and shoulders.

Throwing himself to the ground, he squeezed the AA-12's trigger. The weapon thundered out a half-dozen 12-gauge slugs. Spent casings cascaded to the ground as the volley of slugs pounded into the man's chest, vaporizing his torso in a red haze.

Even as Lyons climbed to one knee, they heard a crack from downstairs, this one sounding like a door being kicked from its hinges. No alarm wailed and Lyons had to assume that Roberts had switched the system back off.

The thudding of footsteps rose from the first floor and prompted Lyons to chance an over-the-shoulder look down the stairs.

What he saw kicked his heartbeat into overdrive and caused blood to thunder in his ears. A half-dozen or so fighters, all armed and dressed head to toe in black, were converging on their location from the first floor.

The weapons they carried were silent, though Lyons guessed that would change once they had clear shots at him and his friends.

Already he noticed that Blancanales had brought his MP-5 into view and was whirling toward the new threat. Pearson also was aiming her handgun down the stairwell, apparently trying to acquire a target.

"Freeze!" someone yelled from behind.

Given the choice between freezing and fighting, Lyons nearly always chose the latter and this time was no different. He thrust himself sideways and hit the ground in a roll. Lying on his stomach, he began to raise the AA-12.

Roberts had dropped to one knee and was swinging the barrel of his weapon in Lyons's direction. In an instant, the former cop tagged the weapon as a Thompson SMG and felt his heart skip a beat. The last thing he wanted was to tangle with a flurry of .45-caliber ACP rounds.

But here he was.

The automatic shotgun roared and released three more slugs. The hastily placed shots sailed past Roberts and punched through the wood-paneled walls. One drilled through a portrait of one of Pearson's dearly departed relatives, giving the stodgy bastard a third eye in the center of his forehead.

Though he missed his target, Lyons at least threw Roberts off his game, forcing the man to thrust his body sideways. The guy landed on his side and triggered the Thompson. Flames and steel-jacketed slugs spewed from the weapon's barrel, the wild shots drilling into the ceiling, chewing into the wooden banisters. Roberts rose up onto one knee and cut loose with another round of autofire that kept Lyons pinned down. Before the Able Team commando could respond, though, Roberts was on his feet. The traitor sprinted to one of the doors and disappeared through it before Lyons could line up a decent shot.

Hauling himself to his feet, Lyons stalked in the other man's direction.

CROUCHED ON THE stairs, Blancanales swept the MP-5 in a tight arc as the weapon punched out a volley of autofire, raining death on the hardmen who had tried to ambush them from behind. The deadly onslaught from the German-made SMG forced most of the shooters to scatter.

One stood his ground, a black grease gun fitted with a sound suppressor tucked tight against his body. The hardman squeezed off a burst from the weapon, the rounds stabbing through the air just inches over Blancanales's head before they pounded the stairwell at his back, splintering wood and ripping carpet.

Blancanales squeezed off a burst from the MP-5. The slugs lanced through the air and pounded the guy in the torso. The swarm of bullets caused him to jerk in place until Blancanales eased off the trigger.

By now, Pearson had joined the fray. She was aiming her pistol through a space on the safety rail and squeezing off shots. Blancanales climbed to his feet just as two more shooters came into view. Maneuvering the H&K in a figure-eight pattern, he stitched the two hardmen, killing both. He saw Pearson duck for cover and eject the magazine from her pistol. He turned in her direction and squeezed off a couple of quick bursts of cover fire to allow her a chance to recharge her weapon. When she finished, he reloaded the MP-5 and headed toward the first floor.

By the time he reached the bottom of the stairs, he'd spotted two more of the shooters working their way in his direction. The MP-5 flared to life again, this time stitching both intruders. In addition to his two kills, he saw two other black-clad corpses on the floor and found himself impressed with Pearson's performance under fire.

He realized someone was approaching him from the rear. He spun, saw it was Pearson and acknowledged her with a nod. He noticed she had a few scratches on her face, probably from the splinters blasted off when bullets struck wood.

He noticed a blankness in her eyes, as though she were stunned. He gave her a tight smile.

"You okay?" he asked.

She nodded.

"You ever kill anyone?"

She shook her head.

"Just on the shooting range." She glanced at the corpses sprawled on the floor, averted her gaze almost immediately, as though stung.

"I'll get over it," she said.

"Yeah, you will," Blancanales replied.

"Let's find Dale," she replied.

Blancanales watched as she turned on her heel and headed toward the stairs. He figured he should let Lyons know they were on their way. Before he could key his throat microphone, though, gunshots sounded from the second floor.

Pearson, who was closer to the stairwell, sprinted upstairs with Blancanales a couple of steps behind.

DALE ROBERTS RETURNED to the study and locked the door behind him. He scanned the room's contents until his eyes lighted on a heavy oak table covered with several short stacks of paper. Crossing the room, he grabbed an edge of the table and, with a grunt, yanked up on it, toppling it.

From outside the door, he could hear the crackle of gunfire through the floor. He had no way of knowing how the fight was going, though he imagined that in the end sheer numbers would win out, leaving the federal agents and Pearson dead.

He crouched behind the heavy table and fed a new magazine into his SMG. The shotgun-toting Fed who had followed him upstairs had taken down Jiang's agent without hesitation. No shouted warnings or flashed badges. He'd simply slain the man. Roberts had run in black ops circles long enough to know that when a guy did that, he likely had a government sanction, the kind that allowed someone to kill a man without questions being asked.

Sweat beaded on Roberts's forehead and trickled into his eyes, prompting him to blink hard. What the hell had he inserted himself into? He always had worried that his activities with Jiang could spark some questions and bring some unwanted attention. But he'd guessed it would come in the form of a couple of FBI agents knocking on his door and frogmarching him into a federal prison.

At worst, he'd assumed he'd spend the money he'd squirreled away in his Cayman Island accounts on some high-priced lawyers to bail him out. Maybe they'd revoke his citizenship and send him back to London. But he knew he could start over at the drop of a hat, move to the Middle East or some African shithole where he could spy or coordinate dirty-tricks operations for some two-bit dictator.

But in none of those scenarios had he expected to die.

Before he could ponder his situation more, something thudded hard against the door. His heart seemed to stop. He turned and looked at the door. It still stood. He aimed the Thompson at it and stroked the trigger. The antique submachine gun thundered and flames lashed out from the barrel. He stitched a figure eight on the door, the bullets tearing through the ornate wood. When the weapon finally clicked empty, he ejected the magazine and reached for another one.

Before he could finish reloading, though, something heavy struck the door again, causing it to burst inward in an explosion of wooden shards.

Just as he slammed home another magazine of ammo, the blond Fed with the shotgun bulled his way through the door, a snarl on his lips. He swung the automatic shotgun in Roberts's direction and squeezed off three rounds.

Roberts ducked behind the table for cover. The shotgun boomed again.

LYONS DREW DOWN on the oak table and triggered the AA-12 three times. The slugs struck the tabletop, simultaneously shoving it forward and disintegrating part of it.

The Able Team leader kept his weapon trained on Roberts's position, but held his fire. He wanted to see if he'd hit the guy or if the cowardly Brit would crawl out from behind the table and surrender. Either way, from his way of thinking, it was a win-win.

"Roberts!" Lyons shouted. "Climb out of there and let me see your hands! Go!"

A second ticked by, then five more. Lyons felt his anger rising and he weighed whether to unload the AA-12 on his target. He'd pulverize the guy, eliminating any possibility of an interrogation, but he'd also eliminate the treacherous bastard. In a perfect world, he would have chosen the latter course of action, turned the guy into a greasy smear on the floor and driven to the nearest club for a cold one. But he also knew Bolan was in the field. The guy needed information, any information he could get, and the best thing Lyons could do was capture this SOB for questioning.

He saw the top of Roberts's head come into view from behind the table. Lyons tensed. Roberts stood, a Spectre SMG clenched in his right hand by its pistol grip, the barrel pointed skyward. The fingers of his left hand were wrapped around something.

"Put it down, Poindexter," Lyons warned.

Roberts shooting hand was a blur as it dropped and he swung the SMG's barrel toward Lyons. Before Lyons could react a pistol cracked from behind him and two holes opened up in Roberts's torso, causing the guy to drop the Spectre and stumble backward. The guy fell to the floor and his hand opened. A small black box about the size of a cigarette lighter fell from his fingers onto the floor, a red light blinking on it.

Lyons wheeled around to face Blancanales and Pearson.

"Run!" he shouted.

The two ran from the room. Lyons bolted over to Roberts who lay on his back, writhing in pain. The former cop drove a big fist into the guy's temple and the Briton fell unconscious. Just as he threw Roberts over his shoulder, he heard peals of thunder as explosions ripped through another part of the house.

Lyons carried the guy from the room and headed for the stairs. He wanted him alive long enough to interrogate. After that, all bets were off.

# CHAPTER FIFTEEN

By the time the first fire engines rolled on the scene, Lyons, Blancanales and Pearson had exited the house. Roberts lay on the ground, moaning in pain. Pearson's shot had passed through Roberts's shoulder, apparently without striking bone, coming out clean on the other side.

Stripping off his leather jacket, Blancanales draped it over the injured man's torso. He'd already applied a field dressing to the wound. He guessed Roberts teetered on the edge of unconsciousness and he wanted to make sure the guy stayed warm. He was a treacherous bastard, but Blancanales wanted to make sure he lived so they could interrogate him later.

He glanced up and saw Pearson staring at her family's home, now engulfed in flames. Her arms were crossed over her chest and Blancanales thought he saw her shoulders shaking, though it was hard to tell for sure in the light from the flickering flames.

When Lyons had gathered up Roberts, he'd found a detonator of some kind next to the guy's fallen form. He guessed Roberts had planted thermite charges of some kind in the house and had hoped to use the explosions to cover a last-minute escape.

A half-dozen or so firefighters, each togged in full turnout gear, burst through the front gate. A couple of them carried heavy firehoses while a third pointed at a hydrant and shouted. A couple of paramedics were next through the gate. When they saw Roberts lying on the ground, they darted toward the injured man. Blancanales rose to his full height when they reached him. One of the paramedics dropped to one knee and began checking Roberts's injuries while the other turned to Blancanales.

"What happened to him?" the paramedic asked.

"Gunshot wound," Blancanales said. He flashed the guy his fake Justice Department credentials.

"Whole place is a crime scene," he said. "You can tell your people not to worry about finding other survivors in the house."

The guy scrutinized the credentials for a couple of seconds, then nodded his understanding. Blancanales saw Pearson and Lyons standing next to, he assumed, the fire captain. Pearson was gesturing toward a couple of chrome hydrants that stuck up from the ground and saying something Blancanales couldn't hear. The fire captain nodded occasionally.

Blancanales reached into his pants pocket for a cell phone and grabbed some distance from the others. He punched in a number. The call passed through several cutouts before he heard a ring.

A woman's voice answered.

"Hello," she said.

"Hey," Blancanales replied.

"You get him?"

Blancanales hesitated. "Yeah, we got him."

"That doesn't sound like a victory celebration in the background, Pol," she said. "What's going on?"

Blancanales told her about the shootout, the fire and Roberts's injuries.

"Sounds complicated," Price said.

"That a euphemism for fucked up?" Blancanales asked.

"Maybe. You need us to send a cleanup crew?"

"Lawyers, guns and money," Blancanales said. "The crap didn't hit a fan. It struck a wind turbine and covered half of Wonderland in the process. We're probably going to need a couple of lawyers and a few FBI agents to seal down the scene. The Chinese may also be asking questions before the night's over. If they're smart, they'll be quiet. But who knows?"

He could hear Price exhale on the other end of the line.

"Wow," she said. "Anything else?"

"Coffee," he said. "It's going to be a damn long night."

IT WAS NEARLY dawn before Blancanales and Pearson arrived at the hospital. Lyons had headed back to the Farm, as his skills were needed elsewhere.

Unlike most metropolitan hospitals, the halls here were only sparsely populated with a handful of doctors, nurses and other support staff. The facility catered to an elite group, members of the U.S. Congress and their families, and there were only a couple of politicians who needed an overnight stay.

Pearson had spent most of the drive over in silence with the woman staring ahead through the windshield while Blancanales drove. Roberts had been sent to a secure room on the second level of the hospital. During the elevator ride to Roberts's floor, she finally broke her silence.

"The congressional hospital? You guys must really rate."

"We figured this was the best spot for him. He had some pretty serious backup at your house. Now his cohorts are likely pissed off at him. If they decide to take him out, the last thing we want is a gunfight in some public hospital, surrounded by innocent bystanders."

She nodded. The elevator reached the level and the doors slid open. They exited the elevator car and headed for Roberts's room.

"How are you doing?" Blancanales asked.

"I found out my lover is a spy, I lost my family's estate and I killed a man tonight. Otherwise, my life's a fairy tale."

"Stupid question, I guess."

Blancanales reached over and patted her shoulder gently. She gave him a weak smile.

"It's okay," she said, shrugging. "You meant well."

"Are you sure you want to see him?" Blancanales asked. "The wound's a little fresh, and I'm not talking about his shoulder."

"I'll be all right. I want to hear from his mouth why he did this. Why he betrayed me and everyone else. I need to know that, I guess."

Blancanales nodded his understanding.

"You're a bastard," she said to Roberts. "I can't believe this is who you really are." She whipped toward Blancanales. "And you—I trusted you! You realize I've lost everything, don't you?" Blancanales ignored her. He could sympathize with her, but he also knew they had bigger things to deal with than her wounded pride.

"What does Jiang want? What was his connection with the killings?"

"Killings? You mean the couple in Athens?"

Blancanales nodded.

"You're really that dense?" Roberts shook his head. "They meant nothing. Jiang doesn't care about them. Not specifically, anyway. They were just there. If it hadn't been them, it would have been someone else."

"Explain."

"Jiang wanted their board seats. He didn't care whether they lived or died. They had a chance to sell out, but they wouldn't do it. So Jiang took them out."

"What was so important about their board seats?" Blancanales pressed.

"They both were executives with QF-17." Roberts began to speak slowly, as though addressing a child. "QF-17 makes defense equipment for the Israelis and it has an American division. They're making a high-level missile shield and China wants the technology."

"Why not just steal it?"

"Steal it? Sure, and pretty soon someone figures out you stole it. The horse is out of the barn, sure, but they lock the doors behind you and you have to start from scratch."

"He wanted someone on the inside."

"Close, but not quite. He wanted to own a piece of it. That was the most important thing. Own a piece of the company, own the technology and all the information it had accumulated over the years. And no one would realize it."

"I assume QF-17's not the only target, then?"

"Well, look at you. You're finally thinking. No, it's not the only target. Jiang has been grabbing pieces of companies all over the world, particularly the United States and Britain, but also France and Russia. He plans to be like a vacuum and sweep up all this high-level technology. In most cases, he has only accumulated small holdings in companies, but he plans to buy bigger shares. He'll do it incrementally—"

"So he doesn't make anyone suspicious."

"Right."

"That much we already knew," Pearson said.

"How?" Blancanales asked.

"I heard things along the way," she said with a slight shrug. "A couple of my people in the field heard about this Chinese national who was trying to infiltrate the defense industry. We had very little to go on, though. It mostly seemed like rumors, pretty fantastic ones at that. Angel tried to tell them about Jiang, tried to warn them. But the old man wouldn't listen. He treated Angel like she was crazy."

She stared down at the ground and shook her head. "If he only would have listened."

"You were too late," Roberts said. "Jiang wanted those seats and he wasn't going to let anyone stand in his way. By the time Angel warned them, they were already targets."

"You told him," Pearson said. "You told Jiang what we knew."

"Yes."

"And that doesn't bother you?"

"Not particularly."

She wheeled around and stormed out of the room.

"I think I upset her," Roberts said.

Blancanales ignored him. "How does Jiang do it?"

"No magic. Shell companies, reverse mergers, all the usual tools. Then he uses those to buy up shares of the businesses he wants."

"Okay, so why the change in tactics? I mean, if he usually acquires things slowly, why would he be so aggressive about QF-17?"

"The Chinese didn't want to wait for the technology, I guess. Not like he ever told me those things, but that is my guess. With the U.S. focusing harder on Asia, it stands to reason they want to get as much of our technology as possible."

"They wanted to analyze it."

"Probably. All I know was this was a high priority for them. They wanted it dealt with."

"Who's his face?" Blancanales asked. "I assume Jiang doesn't go around buying companies himself, right? At least, not ones in the defense sector. That would set off all kinds of alarm bells."

"Max Blackwell."

"Blackwell. The hedge-fund manager."

"Impressive. I didn't think you actually read anything."

"What's the connection?" Blancanales asked.

"Don't know. Maybe he has pictures of Blackwell mating with a chicken. Honestly, I don't care."

"In other words, he never told you. Probably because he knew what a conniving piece of shit you are."

"Blackwell, from what I understand, is a greedy son of a bitch. If he's involved in it, it must be lining his pockets or at least not upsetting his ability to make money. He has to have some reason for doing it. Otherwise the risk is too great."

"But you don't know what it is."

"No."

Blancanales wasn't sure he believed the guy, but he also knew it didn't matter. He had enough leads to move ahead. And he guessed he wasn't going to get much else out of Roberts at this point.

Roberts cleared his throat. "Okay," he said. "I've told you what I know. Now what kind of deal are you prepared to make?"

"Good question," Blancanales said, a cold edge in his voice. "I'm going to take care of you. Trust me."

Roberts detected the change in the other man's voice. His eyes narrowed and he scrutinized the warrior's features. "Meaning?"

"Meaning you're about to disappear from the world, never to be seen again."

"You said earlier—"

"I said you wouldn't go to federal prison. You won't. Not in this country. I made some calls earlier this morning, checked some things out." Blancanales glanced at his watch. "From what I understand, you stuck your hands in some bloody business in Africa a few years ago, sold guns and explosives to North Sudan. Those same weapons were used to slaughter a village. Guess South Sudan's still pissed. They want to speak with you about it."

Roberts's eyes widened. Though his lips parted slightly, it was several seconds before he spoke. "You can't do that."

Blancanales shot the guy a wink. "Be good."

He turned and left the room, Roberts shouting after him.

BLANCANALES SHUT THE door behind him. Pearson, prompted by the injured man's shouting, turned and gave Blancanales a questioning look. With his right hand, he cupped her elbow and guided her away from Roberts's room.

"What the hell was that about?" she asked.

"I suggested he might be going overseas."

"London?"

"Sudan."

Her face registered surprise. "Oh."

"We can't do it," Blancanales said. "The guy's head is too full of secret information to stick him in a foreign jail. But he doesn't need to know that. Let him sweat. He deserves at least that much."

She gave him a thin smile. "Thanks," she said.

"It doesn't bring back your house."

She shrugged and stared at the floor as they moved.

"I can get another house."

"Or your friends."

"Who died because of me."

"How do you figure?"

"I was the one who was too damned dense to realize he was working against us. I thought I was better at reading people. I guess I was wrong."

"It happens," Blancanales said. "You can't blame yourself."

She whipped her head in his direction. "And who should I blame?"

Blancanales jerked a thumb over his shoulder. "You could start with the creep back there. Speaking of which, what do you know about Max Blackwell?"

"Just what I've read in the financial press. Inherited a small fortune and made it into a larger one. His grandfather started a plastics company after World War II. The family sold it after he died. Blackwell's mother was the prototypical idle rich person. Never worked a day in her life. Had no idea where the money came from, only that it was always there. The guy she married, Max's father, Herbert Blackwell, wasn't much better. Supposedly, he had some kind of gambling problem and kept a stable of women throughout Manhattan."

They stopped at the elevator and Blancanales pressed the up button.

"Apparently, the parents had spent most of the money by the time Max graduated from Harvard. But he is an investing genius. He took what was left and grew it back into big money—leveraged buyouts and other deals. Pretty amazing, really, at least on the surface. But the official story neglects to mention something important."

"Which is?"

"He's got all kinds of organized crime connections. He launders their money by funneling it through his business transactions and then takes some off the top for himself. He owns a cargo-shipping business that is mostly legit, but also moves drugs, weapons, cash and people for Mexican cartels and Chinese organized crime gangs. He has a chain of auto dealerships that launder money for his buddies."

The elevator doors slid open and they stepped inside.

"You gleaned all that from the financial news?" Blancanales asked.

She shrugged. "Most of it. But we ran in the same circles. We even attended some of the same events."

"Polo matches? Fox hunts?"

She punched him in the arm, but smiled.

"Charity events and art auctions."

"You've met him personally?"

"No. That doesn't mean I couldn't go talk to him, though. I could use the mutual-friends ploy to get an audience with him."

"If he's mixed up with Jiang, he knows who you are."

She thought about it for a few seconds before nodding in agreement. "You have a better idea?"

"I do."

# CHAPTER SIXTEEN

"Michael" had turned out to be Michael Kelley, a CIA officer working out of the embassy. He had led Bolan and Grimaldi to his vehicle, a black Humvee with diplomatic plates. Unlocking it remotely, he walked around to the driver's side and climbed into his seat. Bolan sat shotgun while Grimaldi seated himself in the back.

"George," Kelley had said, "is not a bad guy. He just gets a little feisty sometimes."

"It seemed," Bolan replied, "like he was trying to do his job."

"That's what I mean by 'feisty,'" Kelley said. "George likes the ladies, the ouzo and poker. I have the goods on him. Plus, he took a couple of bribes from me, so now I own him on that. When I tell him to shut his mouth, he needs to do it."

Starting the Humvee, Kelley drove the other two Americans to the Athens Hilton, then guided the vehicle off the street and onto a wide driveway. He parked in front of a line of sliding-glass doors, reached to the floor and pulled on something. Bolan heard a muffled click from the trunk and the lid sprang up.

"You two have a nice stay," Kelley said. "See if you can keep the killing to a minimum."

"Should be easy with no guns," Grimaldi muttered.

"You'll get your guns eventually," Kelley replied.

The Stony Man warriors exited the vehicle. Bolan glanced up at the hotel. If for no other reason, the building was striking because it looked so modern in a city known for its ancient architecture. Kelley had secured their bags earlier. The soldier pulled his bag from the trunk, along with a black leather shaving kit. He handed the kit to Grimaldi who gave him a puzzled look.

"No, really, I brought my own," the pilot said.

Bolan gave him a tight smile. "There's a Colt Chief's Special, an ankle holster and a couple of speedloaders inside," the Executioner said. "Sort of a last resort gun. It'll hold you over until Kelley scores new weapons for you."

"A snubnose? What, you didn't have a derringer?"

"I was afraid it would be too heavy for you," Bolan replied. "Just take it."

Grabbing the rest of their bags, they entered the lobby and headed for the front desk. Grimaldi set his suitcase at the front desk and headed for a kiosk where a man was selling coffee and pastries. Bolan checked himself in under his Matt Cooper alias. When Grimaldi returned, he carried two paper cups filled with coffee, handed one to Bolan. Once Grimaldi had checked into his room, the two men boarded an elevator, headed to the tenth floor and split for their rooms.

According to the desk clerk, Bolan's room offered a view of the Acropolis, the distinctive citadel that looks down on Athens. The soldier had feigned interest, but left the curtains drawn closed. He'd seen the complex of ancient buildings before. And after the events of the past several hours, he had little interest in playing tourist. Instead, he seated himself on the edge of his bed and used his satellite phone to call the Farm.

A second later, Hal Brognola answered the call.

"You like the accommodations?"

"Better than what I left behind," Bolan replied.

"Tell me about it," the big Fed said. "Just got off the phone with the Man. He's not happy. Cabinet secretaries and high-level bureaucrats are whining about the situation over there. Not to mention the Greeks themselves. Apparently, they expected this to be handled with a softer touch."

"What? Like a ricin pellet fired from an umbrella? I tend to make a lot of noise, Hal."

"The Man understands that," Brognola replied. "He still wants this handled. And I've got your back on this, too. You don't have to worry about that. As for the locals, they've promised to look the other way for the moment."

"But you can't guarantee how long it will last."

"Yeah," Brognola said.

"Understood," Bolan said. "Give me twelve hours."

"I can do better than that," Brognola said. "I got a call from Langley, maybe thirty minutes ago. Apparently, your friend, the station chief there in Greece, told them we were short on information regarding our friend Kassem and his whereabouts. They're sending someone to help."

TWO HOURS LATER, a knock at the door jarred Bolan from a light sleep. The soldier was awake in an instant. The Beretta lay within easy reach. Shrugging on the holster, he drew the pistol, rose from the bed and crept across the room to the door.

He took a quick look through the peephole and saw a small man, his skin light brown, eyes and hair black, standing in the corridor outside, looking expectantly at the door. With the distorted view offered by the peephole, Bolan couldn't tell for sure whether the man was hiding a weapon underneath his suit jacket.

The soldier opened the door several inches until the chain stopped it and sized the guy up. A nauseating mixture of cologne and stale cigarette smoke reached Bolan's nose. The guy wore a well-tailored navy-blue suit, a powder-blue shirt and a necktie with diagonal stripes of blue and gold. His hair and goatee were cut with precision. He flashed Bolan a smile that did not reach his eyes.

"You are Matt Cooper?"

"Yes," Bolan said. "Omar Sabri?"

"I am."

Brognola had arranged the meeting with Sabri, a Libyan intelligence official, and even had sent a photo—albeit a dated one—of the guy. Bolan studied the man's features for a few more seconds until he was comfortable the guy was Omar Sabri. Then, unhooking the chain, he opened the door wide and gestured for the guy to come in. The guy's eyes flicked to the Beretta and he hesitated in the doorway.

The soldier slipped the Beretta back into the holster and Sabri entered the hotel room. Bolan nodded at a pair of wooden armchairs that stood alongside one wall.

"Sit," he said.

Sabri moved to the chair farthest from Bolan, backed up to it and sat down.

"I was told to meet with you," Sabri said, crossing his right ankle over his left knee.

"Told or ordered?"

"I have a full schedule," Sabri replied. "But I will make time for you, of course. You wanted information on Kassem?"

"Yeah. What do you know about him?"

"You are looking for him?" Sabri asked.

"Yeah."

"Because he killed the woman and the Jew."

"Them and many more," Bolan stated.

"Yes," Sabri said. "Kassem's list of victims includes people in my own government, including the freedom fighters who stood against the tyrant Khadaffi. He's been killing people for years. But only now, now that he killed a Jew, does the United States care about him."

"Drop it," Bolan said, "or you'll regret it."

Sabri glared at Bolan.

"You feeling me?" Bolan asked.

The Libyan stared at Bolan another second or two before his gaze dropped to the floor.

"I suppose," Sabri said, "we didn't come here to discuss geopolitics."

"I suppose not."

"And we all benefit if Kassem dies."

"That goes without saying."

From what Brognola had told him, Sabri was a former member of the Libyan Islamic Fighting Group, an organization with ties to al Qaeda. The soldier didn't know all the intricacies of the ties between the two groups. But he knew enough to realize he didn't trust the man sitting before him.

"Kassem is a monster," Sabri said. "He's killed many innocent people. Many of those he killed because Khadaffi had told him to do it. Others? He simply killed them because he could or because he wanted to. Because they'd looked at him wrong, insulted him, whatever. He's evil."

"At least we agree on that."

"My people? The new Libyan government? We want him dead. We want him to suffer for the pain he inflicted on his countrymen. That's why we are helping."

Bolan nodded his understanding.

"You'll find Kassem is cold-blooded and a murderer. But he also wants to survive. I tell you this for one reason. So you know the right buttons to push. His only loyalty is to those who can hurt him or hold sway over him."

"Like Khadaffi."

"Yes. Kassem isn't an idealist or a nationalist. All he wanted was power, or at least to live in the shadow of power. Had another dictator replaced Khadaffi, Kassem likely would have allied himself with that man. We didn't need someone like that running around the country. People with his skills and training, but with no loyalty, they can be a danger to a fledgling government. Besides, he had blood on his hands, the blood of the Libyan people. We wanted him gone, preferably dead and gone.

"He has a small army at his main compound. And he has no allegiance to any of them. If he had 100 soldiers, he'd put every one of them between you and him. You will have to slaughter every last one of these people if you want to get to him. He's like an animal—he wakes up every day with one goal. Survival."

Sabri eyed the American for a couple of seconds. "You have killed before."

"Yeah."

"But you don't like it."

"I don't enjoy it," the soldier said. "I accept it."

Bolan left it at that. He'd taken many lives in his War Everlasting and he knew he'd take more. His targets were killers, jackals who preyed on the weak, who served evil. He neither harbored regrets about the body count he'd racked up nor took pride in it. He considered himself a soldier; and some soldiers killed. He was one of them.

"You do not anticipate the hunt, the infliction of pain," Sabri said, studying the warrior's face, apparently for some signal he was right. Bolan kept his expression flat and his mouth shut.

After a couple of seconds, Sabri leaned back in his chair, smiled and clapped his hands together. "No answer? No matter. I know I am right in this."

Bolan leaned forward and pinned Sabri under his gaze.

"Here's something else you ought to know," he said. "You're not smart enough or skilled enough to try to poke around inside my head. You want to play mind games, go somewhere else. You want to share some intelligence with me so I can solve our mutual little problem? Great."

"Here is what I am driving at," the other man said. "Kassem just kills people. Men, women, children, he doesn't care. They're no more than cattle to him. It's not that he particularly enjoys it. But he also doesn't mind doing it. It's like putting on his shoes."

"Putting on his shoes?"

Sabri nodded.

"It's just something he does, day after day."

"But not for much longer."

"I hope you are correct."

The man reached inside his suit jacket. Bolan felt himself tense as the guy searched around for something. Sabri retracted his hand, which was balled up in a fist, extended it toward Bolan and uncurled his fingers. In Sabri's palm lay a black, rectangular thumb drive.

"This is for you," the Libyan said.

Bolan took it from the other guy's hand and closed his fingers around it.

"You can open it up now," Sabri said.

"Later," Bolan replied.

In his bags, the soldier carried a second laptop that had no passwords, telephone numbers or other information associated with Stony Man Farm. It was, for all intents and purposes, an off-the-shelf computer, one that he could plug in media from, say, a Libyan intelligence agent without risking a back-door entry into Stony Man's system.

"It's a dossier on Kassem," Sabri said. "We've been tracking him for some time, as you can imagine. We'd love to—what's the phrase?—frog-march him into a court in Libya and make him pay for his crimes there. I'd strangle him myself. It would give our people some peace knowing another of their tormentors had died."

"But you won't?"

The other man shook his head. He leaned forward, and when he spoke, he dropped the volume of his voice, as though there were more people in the room.

"Khadaffi still has friends in some parts of Libya," he said. "When we get a public face, a man from the old regime, for example, it's good to kill him in front of everyone. It gives the people a sense of closure and brings peace to the country. But, as I said, he has allies, too. If we kill him, it makes those allies angry. It causes unrest among a group whose time has come and gone. We have to weigh whether a public death will have the desired effect."

"Or just piss off a small group of insurgents. Got it. It sucks when putting down a mad dog causes a dip in the poll numbers."

"It's not like that."

"Just tell me where he is and we'll go our separate ways."

Sabri sighed. "He's in Algeria. He has a villa in the southern part of the country. It's about fifty acres. It used to belong to a high-ranking French official, until he decided to leave the country. What I said about killing 100 men to get to him? It wasn't an exaggeration. Not by much, anyway. He has a force of between forty and fifty people protecting the grounds. Most are former Libyan military officials while the rest are mercenaries. You're lucky. He used to have a few young soldiers who ran the grounds, but that no longer is the case."

"How young?"

Sabri shrugged. "Fifteen, maybe sixteen years old." A thin smile played on his lips. "So you are squeamish."

"I have limits."

"And they are?"

Bolan rose up from the bed and jerked his head toward the door.

"You just reached one. Get out."

## CHAPTER SEVENTEEN

Once Bolan closed and locked the door, he walked back to one of his bags, lifted it and placed it on his bed and withdrew a laptop.

Lifting the lid, he booted up the laptop, set it on a small, circular table. He dropped into a chair and waited for the machine to finish turning on. He didn't like being used as a pawn for the Libyan government, even if it was the new-and-improved version. But he also didn't want to spend forever playing whack-a-mole with Kassem. So, yeah, he'd make a deal with one devil if it meant taking out another one. He inserted the flash drive into a USB port and opened it, searching through its contents, most of which were in English. A plan began to formulate as he looked through the files.

"Ask the Russians for help?" Brognola said, his tone incredulous. "You're kidding."

"No," Bolan said, "I'm not."

He was speaking with his old friend via sat-phone. Bolan continued. "I just need some information."

"More like high-level intelligence. From the Russians."

"I killed one of their pests," Bolan replied. "That should carry some weight with them, don't you think?"

Bolan heard his old friend sigh.

"I know a couple of guys in the GRU," Brognola said, "who don't absolutely hate us."

"A ringing endorsement."

"You take what you can get in this game."

"If it helps, you can tell them to take credit for what happened in Athens."

"I'm sure they'd love nothing better than to claim credit for killing a group of Libyans and Chechens in a sovereign country. All while causing millions of dollars in property damage. The press over there is calling it an arms deal gone bad."

"That's sort of true."

"Yeah, but I still don't think the Russians want credit for it."

"Not officially," Bolan said, "but at least they could go through back channels and tell the Chechens it was a Russian operation."

"They could do that now, without helping us," Brognola replied.

"True. C'mon, Hal, work with me."

"Look," Brognola replied. "Here's how I can frame it. You—or the United States—just eliminated one headache for them. Now the Chechens have anointed a successor and we're offering to take him out, too. The Russians can take credit and it costs them nothing."

"That's pretty close to what I suggested."

"Close," Brognola replied, "but I added some panache."

"You're all about the panache."

"Bet your ass. Let me make the call."

Bolan hung up the phone and looked at Grimaldi, who stood at the window, curtains open, and stared at something.

"Looking at the Acropolis?" Bolan asked.

Grimaldi shot Bolan a sidelong glance then turned his gaze back on the window and nodded affirmatively.

"You haven't said anything," the pilot said.

"Said anything? About?"

"I was chatting up a woman when I was supposed to be doing surveillance," Grimaldi said. "Now the lady's dead and Leo's in the hospital. I'd say I pretty much screwed the pooch on this one."

"The guys who hit the safehouse, they're dead, too," Bolan said. "You did that. You and Leo."

"The killer got away."

"Because you stopped to help your friend. I would have made the same play under those circumstances."

"Fair enough," Grimaldi said, shrugging.

"As for the woman, the one you were talking to, how much of that was about getting laid and how much was aimed at blending in?"

"Seventy-five percent of my attention was on getting laid. Twenty-five percent was focused on establishing good cover."

"Bullshit," Bolan said. "I know you're kidding. But let's be realistic. If your head wasn't in the game, you would have been drinking coffee, trying to get into that woman's pants, your thumb firmly in your ass, when the first shots were fired."

Grimaldi looked at Bolan again. His scowl held for a couple of seconds before it finally faded and a grin tugged at the corners of his mouth.

"For the record," he said, "I never stick my thumb in my ass. Bad tradecraft."

While he waited in the hotel, Bolan spent time poring over the information provided by Libyan intelligence. Apparently Kassem, for all his failings, at least was a realist, one smart enough to know lots of people wanted to see him dead. That had led him to buy a sprawling 8,000-square-foot home from a French diplomat in a barren part of Algeria. The place was surrounded by a massive fence, the grounds prowled by mercenaries. The Libyans had put the number at roughly four dozen, which matched the one the intelligence agent had shared with Bolan. The tally included not only shooters, but also drivers, cooks and other support staff.

The house itself sounded like something from a paranoid man's wet dream. The property was surrounded by mounds of earth, making a direct attack by a vehicle impossible. A series of concrete barriers also was arranged around the house itself. The first floor windows were barred.

From what Bolan could gather, the place was a hard site and a well-guarded one at that. It also had a panic room of sorts set up below ground. Bolan's only chance was to infiltrate the outer perimeter and pursue an attack after that.

Using the secure sat-phone, Bolan contacted Brognola.

"Before you ask," the big Fed said, "I talked to the Russians."

"And?"

"They're sending the information you wanted. The President made the request and told them it was for the State Department's intelligence arm, part of a nonproliferation task force. Gave them some BS story about the Chechens trading weapons with the Mexican cartels. Not sure whether they bought it, but they gave us the information."

"Good," Bolan said. "Thanks for the help."

Brognola cleared his throat. "Just for the record," he said, "I still think this is a bad idea."

"Duly noted."

"Duly noted and discarded."

"Nothing personal, Hal. It's just the best option I have at this point. Just flushing him out didn't work. Apparently, I need to be more aggressive."

"Thank God," Brognola replied. "You're usually such a shrinking violet."

Bolan allowed himself a smile. "Sure, the shy, retiring type. That's me."

"That will make the Russians happy. If it gets ugly, they'll consider it a public relations coup. Good luck."

Bolan said goodbye and ended the call. Closing his eyes, he leaned his head back and massaged the bridge of his nose with his thumb and forefinger. He knew the plan was faulty, but it was the best among some bad options. The Executioner wanted to hit Kassem's place, kill him and get out. He knew the guy was running scared, whipsawed by the attack on his arms-trafficking operation and the attacks on his people.

The soldier opened his eyes and set the sat phone on the seat next to him. His mouth set in a grim line, he thought of his injured friend, Leo Turrin, and felt his blood boil. The undercover Fed would be okay. Bolan took cold comfort in that knowledge.

All the Stony Man warriors fought because they chose to. They each had different reasons, though they all considered it both a duty and an honor to wage war against the savages who wanted to drag civilization into darkness, who spilled blood for pleasure and profit. Every one of them raised a hand and volunteered on a daily basis.

They bickered, complained and joked. But at the end of the day not one of them would do anything else or walk away from a battle. They were pros, damn straight. They were also heroes. So, yeah, Turrin had known the score when he'd answered the call. The guy had been with Bolan long enough to know the risks, the class of killer the Man from Blood hunted. He knew he could get dragged into the maelstrom at any second.

That didn't make Bolan feel even a little better about his friend's injuries.

So, yeah, he'd answered the call. He'd gotten hurt. Kristina Mentis had answered the call, not because she wanted to, but because she had no other options, at least no good ones. Bolan had promised to protect her and he failed. Where the Turrin shooting filled Bolan with righteous rage, Mentis's death left him with another friendly ghost that he had to live with.

He needed to focus on the mission. He needed to learn who had hired Kassem and why the entourage hitting the safehouse had included killers with ties to Chinese organized crime.

But first, he needed to find Kassem and settle a blood debt.

# CHAPTER EIGHTEEN

*Algeria*

"I'm not sure whether to drive it or flush it," Grimaldi said.

Bolan eyed the white Toyota SUV, its side panels dented and rusted, and nodded. "Yeah," he said.

"Did the CIA guy in Athens do this?"

"Probably," Bolan said. "Maybe it was the ambassador. She wanted to burn it in effigy by the time we left."

"Not very diplomatic."

Bolan started for the vehicle. "C'mon," he said over his shoulder. "You've driven worse."

He opened the front passenger door, heaved his duffel bag into the back of the vehicle and climbed into the front seat. Grimaldi walked around the front of the SUV, stared at the scarred hood, scowled and shook his head. While Bolan waited, he folded himself into the driver's seat.

The pilot pulled down the sun visor and a pair of keys fell into his lap. Slipping a key into the ignition, he fired up the engine. Bolan had expected it to run as rough as it looked. Instead, the motor gave off a confident, steady growl.

Grimaldi's scowl melted, giving way to a smile. He shot Bolan a wink.

"Well, well," he said. "The old girl has some life left in her. I take back everything I said about you, sweetie."

Slipping the car into drive, he stomped the accelerator and the SUV surged forward.

Like the engine, the air-conditioning and the GPS system worked fine. Within a half hour, Grimaldi had parked the SUV in front of a squat building with a flat roof. A sign above the door said something in French. Bolan already had seen a translation in his intelligence packet and knew it said Apex Traders and Exporters.

The soldier swung open the door and stepped out of the SUV's cool interior. The heat crashed against him like a wave. Perspiration immediately beaded along his hairline, on the back of his neck and between his shoulder blades.

Bolan entered the building, followed by Grimaldi. The building's interior was only slightly cooler than outside. Ceiling fans whirled lazily overhead. A pair of gray-and-white box fans that stood on the floor seemed to do little more than stir up the hot air.

Bolan wore blue jeans, a black T-shirt and sneakers. Over the T-shirt, he wore an unbuttoned short-sleeved shirt to hide the hardware he carried. The Beretta was stowed in his shoulder holster and the Desert Eagle in the small of his back.

Grimaldi was similarly attired. He carried the .38 revolver in an ankle holster.

Even before the door closed behind them, Bolan saw a woman uncoiling from behind a desk. She flashed them a wide, disarming smile. At the same time, a pair of German shepherd dogs lumbered out from behind the desk. They were panting from the heat, but their eyes were alert and locked on the two men.

"We're looking for Maggie," Bolan said.

"You found her," the woman said. "Lucky you."

Still smiling, she came out from behind the desk and approached the two men. The shepherds at her sides moved in tandem with her. As she approached, Bolan studied her. Her hair was bleached almost white, at least it seemed white against her golden-brown skin. Bolan found himself momentarily distracted by the confident swing of her hips and the swell of her breasts against the fabric of a sleeveless white T-shirt.

"You must be Matt and Jack," she said.

"I'm Matt," Bolan said. He jerked his head at Grimaldi. "That's Jack."

"What brings you here?"

"Peace," Bolan said, "and tranquility."

She nodded. It was the coded exchange that confirmed they were her contacts.

"Michael Kelley called me a little while ago," she said. She glanced at a thin gold watch looped around her wrist. "Guess you guys were already wheels up by then. He gave me a shopping list. I found as much as I could, considering the short amount of time he gave me."

She said something in German to the dogs. In unison, they sat and continued to stare at Bolan and Grimaldi. She brushed past Bolan and walked to the door.

"I'm sure you two are legit," she said. "But just in case, let me assure you I can tell you're both packing. Matt you have a gun under your shirt, Jack on your right ankle. If you try anything, those dogs will rip your throats out before you clear leather. Or maybe they'll just chew your balls off. I let them handle the details."

She bolted the front door and turned, her smile wide.

"We're clear on that, right?"

"Crystal clear," Bolan replied.

She retraced her steps, walking back past the Stony Man warriors. She moved around a counter and walked up to a steel door that stood behind it. She gave another command to the dogs, who hesitated for a moment and then ran to her.

"Matt, you and Jack can come, too," Maggie said. "Just don't soil the rugs."

A device that Bolan recognized as a thumbprint reader was moored to the wall next to the steel door. Maggie pressed her right thumb to the sensor plate. The device chirped and Bolan heard a bolt click. The woman pulled the door open, stepped aside and gestured for the two men to enter.

Even before he reached the door, he could feel cold air escaping the room, cooling the perspiration on his face and arms. He passed through the door and found himself inside another room, cramped, clean and outfitted with another steel door. Maggie shut the first security door behind her, opened the second and passed through it. Bolan, Grimaldi and the dogs all followed her. She uttered another command and the shepherds moved to opposite corners of the room and lay down.

Bolan's ice-blue eyes took in the room. A large circular table stood in the center, surrounded by leather wingback chairs. An assortment of assault rifles, shotguns and submachine guns were lined up in rectangular spaces, secured behind locked glass doors. Several drawers were built into the walls. A pair of blue duffel bags stood on the table.

Maggie gestured at the bags.

"The one on the right is yours," she said to Bolan. "The Steyr submachine gun was easy to come by. The M-4 with the grenade launcher is my last one. I also have a Barrett sniper rifle I can cut loose if you want it. Some grenades. Fortunately, your shopping list was pretty easy. I didn't have time for anything too exotic."

She moved to the second bag, separated the straps and unzipped it. She yanked it open and pushed it in Grimaldi's direction.

"It's all yours, Jack. You have a Spectre, an M-4 and a 12-gauge shotgun, double barrel, sawed down. A couple of Browning Hi-Powers, too."

"My brand," the pilot said, grinning.

"You need us to pick up the tab?" Bolan asked.

"You don't owe me anything. Kelley's people paid the freight. He sends it to Washington, runs it through some front companies and the money comes to me. I can bypass the whole nasty oversight thing that way."

"Thanks," Bolan said.

Studying Bolan's face for a couple of seconds, she turned and made her way to one of the drawers built into the wall. She unlocked it, pulled it open and pulled a steel-gray plastic case from the drawer. She offered it to Bolan who took it.

"You're hunting Kassem, if my contacts are right. Don't bother opening the case," she said. "It's a CO2-powered dart gun and some tranquilizer darts—in case Kassem has dogs patrolling the grounds. Some people don't like to shoot dogs. I'm one of them." She shrugged. "Others don't mind. If it's not an issue…"

"It's an issue," Bolan said.

Her full lips widened into a smile.

"Kind of figured as much. Or I wouldn't have offered it."

"Meaning?"

"I have a good sense about people. When the dogs confronted you, you stood still. A lot of people when they see these two?" She gestured at the dogs. "They freeze, draw in on themselves. But they do it out of fear. That's smart. You two stayed still, but you weren't scared. You didn't want to give them a reason to attack."

"True," Bolan said.

"Because you didn't want to hurt them," she added.

Bolan nodded in agreement.

Maggie continued. "Like I said, I have a good sense about people." She nodded at Grimaldi. "Take Jack over there. He'd hump a porcupine if its ass shook when it walked."

"Hey!" Grimaldi said.

She held up her hands, palms forward, in a placating gesture. "I'm not here to judge," she said. "But tell me I'm wrong."

Grimaldi opened his mouth to speak, but checked himself. He looked at Bolan. "Damn, she read me like a book."

# CHAPTER NINETEEN

Bolan blended into the shadows of an alley that lay between a small grocery and a book store/tea room.

He was watching a small apartment building that stood across the street, waiting for his target. A glance at his watch told him it was about 1:00 a.m., probably too late for Abdelazis Farsioui to be out walking the streets. The guy was the apparent owner of the bookstore, which mostly sold jihadist books and CDs and DVDs filled with the fiery rantings of radical Imams.

In the time since he and Grimaldi had acquired their weapons, Bolan already checked the bookstore and found it locked and seemingly empty. He assumed Farsioui was either asleep in his apartment or maybe out with his cohort, though the latter scenario seemed unlikely at this hour.

Aside from his day job as a bookseller, the Algerian also served as a link for the various jihadist elements circling the globe. According to the intelligence reports Bolan had secured from Stony Man Farm, the guy often housed Islamic terrorists who were on the run. He also transferred messages between the various factions and was considered a trusted courier, a smart man and a true believer, supremely confident in the war he was fighting. While Bolan considered the Algerian a worthwhile target, he also was just a small piece of Bolan's larger mission.

According to the information Brognola had secured from the Russians, Bolan's strike on Kassem's warehouse in Athens hadn't deterred his customers, the Chechens, in their quest for weapons. Instead, the group's new leader—Magomed Umarov—wanted to meet directly with Kassem in Algeria and buy his weapons from the man himself. That made Umarov valuable to Bolan.

So the soldier was going to reach out to the Algerian this night.

Bolan keyed his throat mike.

"Give me a sitrep, Ace."

"All quiet over here," Grimaldi replied. He was scouting the rear of the apartment building. "I don't see any lights on in our guy's apartment. I also don't see any guards. A little surprising considering the circles he runs in."

"They're probably inside," Bolan replied. "Word is he travels with at least two guys at all times."

"How do you want to play this, then?"

"Direct approach," Bolan said. "I go in through the front. You keep an eye on the back in case he climbs out a window or does something else. I'll call you once I've taken him down."

Bolan glanced at his watch. "I'm going in sixty seconds."

The soldier crossed the street. Though he'd acquired the other weapons, he'd left them in his vehicle. The Beretta remained stowed beneath his shirttails and out of sight while the Desert Eagle was hidden inside a backpack strapped to his back. The pack also contained several stacks of cash that he'd taken from the briefcase he'd pirated from Sadulayev.

When the soldier reached the front door, he tried the knob. The door was locked. Reaching into the pocket of his jeans, he pulled out a rectangular leather case about the size of a case for business cards. From it he took a slim, flat length of steel and went to work on the lock. The lock was cheap and gave in quickly, allowing Bolan easy access to the building.

Entering, he appraised his surroundings and found them unremarkable. The lobby was sparsely furnished, but clean. The air was tinged with the smell of some kind of floor cleaner and the swirl marks from a mop were evident on the tile. A dozen or so mailboxes were built into the wall to Bolan's left. He saw no elevator in evidence, only a wide stairwell to his right. No cameras or other security gear, such as motion detectors, were visible.

Keeping the Beretta pressed against his leg, he crossed the lobby and headed for the stairs. Along the way he keyed the throat mike again.

"I'm in. I'm going upstairs."

"Need me to follow?" Grimaldi asked.

"Negative. Keep watching for sudden exits," Bolan replied.

The soldier climbed three flights of stairs before reaching his destination. Farsioui's apartment was at the end of the hallway. A man with jet-black hair and an olive complexion leaned his back against the wall next to the door and smoked a cigarette. The file on Farsioui had included photos of his security entourage, and the profile of the guy at the door matched one of the guys in the file. Bolan glided along the wall for a few steps and the guy seemed oblivious to his approach, directing most of his attention to blowing smoke rings at the ceiling.

The soldier cleared his throat. The guy whipped his head in Bolan's direction, giving him a hard look that probably sent small children scattering for cover, but left Bolan unmoved.

The big American raised the Beretta. The steel immediately evaporated from the guy's expression. His mouth gaped open and the cigarette fell to the floor. In the same moment, his hand stabbed down at his waistband.

The Beretta coughed once and a small red hole opened on the man's forehead, the force knocking him off his feet.

Bolan knelt next to the corpse and patted him down. In the waistband of his jeans, the guy had been carrying a .357 Desert Eagle. Bolan thought fleetingly of the irony of a jihadist arming himself with an Israeli-made weapon, decided it would be lost on the stiff sprawled on the floor and continued his search. He found a cell phone, a wallet, loose change and a half-empty pack of cigarettes in the guy's pants pockets. A small silver key was stashed in the breast pocket of the guy's shirt. Bolan hoped it opened the apartment door.

Uncoiling from the floor, he tested the door, and after confirming that it was locked, used the key to open it.

He pushed the door in gently and found it opened into a large room that appeared to be a combination dining area and living room. An oval-shaped table, covered with papers, scattered magazines and short stacks of books, stood along one wall, ringed with three chairs. On the other side of the room, a man reading a newspaper was seated on the couch, his feet propped up on a coffee table. Moving the paper over a few inches, he peered around it, apparently expecting the other guard. When he saw Bolan, he dropped the newspaper, yelled something in Arabic and began clawing at a pistol stored in a shoulder holster.

The Beretta released another Parabellum slug that drilled into the bridge of the man's nose. The bullet pounded through the back of the man's skull in a spray of crimson flecked with brain matter.

The hurried thud of footsteps told Bolan another man was coming. An arched door led from the living room into the rest of the apartment. Bolan glided across the room, pressed himself against the wall next to the door and waited.

An instant later, Farsioui barreled through the door.

"What is going on?" he asked.

Almost as soon as he'd uttered the last word, he saw the dead man and halted in his tracks. Bolan's quarry was dressed in shorts and a T-shirt. The warrior guessed the man had been roused from sleep by his guard's cry.

Bolan aimed the Beretta at Farsioui's back, just between his shoulder blades. The soldier saw his own partial reflection in a mirror fixed to the wall across the room, part of his body obscured by the Arab. In almost the same instant, Farsioui spotted Bolan in the mirror and, startled, spun to face him.

He raised his hands. Bolan saw Farsioui's eyes drift toward the front door.

"Forget it," Bolan said. "Your guard's on a one-way trip to hell. You're about to join him."

Farsioui's eyes narrowed and he seemed to regain his composure quickly.

"What do you want?" he asked in English.

"Help," Bolan said.

"You kill my friends, my brothers, and you want help? You're insane."

"Brothers? More like guard dogs," Bolan said. "Please spare me the indignant routine. I have no patience for it. And, in case you haven't noticed, I want your help, but I'm not asking for it. I'm not much in the asking mood at this point."

The other man studied Bolan for a few seconds, possibly searching for weakness or mercy. When he found neither, he gave the warrior a curt nod.

"Okay," he said.

"Smart man." Bolan gestured at an armchair. "Sit."

The guy seated himself in the chair. Bolan put himself between his prisoner and the dead guard, the latter of whom still had a holstered pistol. The Executioner didn't want Farsioui to make a play for the unattended gun. With the Beretta still trained on his prisoner, Bolan reached into his pocket, withdrew a handkerchief and, wrapping the cloth around the fallen guard's pistol, pulled it from the holster.

Farsioui eyed the pistol like a dog eying a cheeseburger. Bolan slid it into his waistband and pocketed the handkerchief.

"Well," Farsioui said, "you have my attention. What kind of help do you hope to get from me?"

"Sadulayev. The Chechen. You heard of his death."

A slight shrug. "Perhaps."

"And you know his replacement, Magomed Uramov, is coming here," Bolan said, glancing at his watch, "to Algeria, in a matter of hours."

The other man said nothing, just shrugged again.

Bolan considered shooting the SOB in the foot, but decided against it. When the situation called for it, the soldier killed with cold precision. Intimidating a prisoner also didn't bother him. But he didn't inflict misery just for the sake of doing it. Soldiers killed; savages tortured.

Keeping the Beretta trained on the other man, Bolan slid the backpack from his shoulders. He set it on the arm of the couch and unzipped it with one hand. Farsioui watched in silence as Bolan pulled a bundle of cash from the bag and tossed it into the jihadist's lap.

The man stared at the money for a couple of seconds, threw a questioning glance at Bolan then returned his attention to the cash. He turned it over in his hands, scrutinizing it.

"What is this for?" he said finally.

"A down payment," the warrior said.

"For?"

"Your help. There's more, too."

"You cannot buy a man of God!" Farsioui snapped. He kept his eyes and fingers locked on the cash, however, letting the soldier know he'd already made a sale.

"What are you?" Farsioui asked. "Are you CIA? I won't inform."

The soldier shook his head. "I'm not CIA," he said. "I'm a businessman."

Farsioui jerked a thumb at the dead guard. "Interesting form of business."

A cold smile ghosted the soldier's lips.

"It got your attention, didn't it?"

"Yes, I suppose it did."

"But not your silence."

The other man pressed his lips into a thin line and glared at Bolan, but stayed silent for several seconds.

"No reply?" Bolan said. "About damn time."

"You're a bastard," the other man said.

"So I've been told. Here's the pitch. The Chechen was buying his weapons from Kassem. You admitted that you knew he died."

The other man nodded.

"How many men died in that little fiasco?"

"I'm not sure."

"The newspapers said it was at least a dozen."

"What's your point? We know who pulled the trigger."

Bolan was genuinely curious. "Really?"

The man straightened a little in his chair and gave Bolan a disgusted look.

"Of course. You want to come in here and talk about this and you have no idea who did it?"

"I assumed it was a rival gang," Bolan lied.

The man leaned forward slightly in his chair and his voice dropped a bit in volume.

"It was the Jews," he said.

"Bullshit."

"Of course it was. It was Mossad. It had to be. Anyone with a pulse could figure that out. It was one of their special hit squads. They wanted to take out Kassem." His expression hardened. "That would have been fine with me. Kassem served an apostate regime. God already has judged him, and he'll die for what he's done."

"But the Chechens were innocent," Bolan said, derision evident in his voice.

"They were soldiers. Freedom fighters, actually."

Bolan smirked. Farsioui glared at him, his forehead creasing.

"What are you smiling about?"

"They were killers," Bolan said. "I know their names. They

shot up a school bus in Moscow three years ago with AK-47s. Five people were killed, including the driver and four children. Twelve more injured."

Setting his jaw, Farsioui pressed his palms into the seat cushion and started to push himself up. Bolan wagged the Beretta's muzzle and the man froze for a second before sinking back into the chair.

"Here's the point," Bolan said, his voice flat. "Kassem screwed up. Now your buddies have lost one of their big shots and a couple of foot soldiers. Plus, they have no way to buy weapons."

"Again, your point?"

"Like I said, I'm a businessman. I can help them."

Realization dawned in the other man's eyes.

"You want to sell them weapons."

Bolan nodded.

"And you're willing to sell them weapons?"

"Yes."

"Even though you don't agree with their cause."

"Yes."

Scowling, the other man studied Bolan. "You would do this because?"

"Because I want the business. I have a couple of warehouses full of weapons in Qatar. I could have shipments in the air in a matter of hours." He snapped his fingers. "Just like that."

"And you need me because?"

"Because you're someone they trust. If I knock on their door, they're going to be suspicious. Hell, they may just kill me. I want to talk to Magomed Umarov. You give me an intro and I'll be golden."

"Golden?"

"Good. I'll be good. They'll listen to me because I am with you."

"If that's all you wanted from me," Farsioui said, "why didn't you just ask?"

Bolan gave the other guy an incredulous look. "What? Just knock on the door, hand you a business card and tell you I was selling arms? Don't be a damn fool. You never would have given me the time of day if I'd done that."

"So you came here and killed these men. You threatened to kill me."

Bolan nodded. "I did. I wanted you to know something. I wanted you to know what I am capable of. I'm happy to sell you and your buddies all the weapons they can handle. I can get my hands on some amazing shit. And I am happy to slide you some cash as a finder's fee. But if you turn on me—" the warrior nodded at the corpse on the couch "—you're next."

The other man's face stayed stony, but he swallowed hard before nodding in agreement.

"I understand," he said.

"Good," Bolan replied. "Keep it that way."

# CHAPTER TWENTY

Minutes later, Bolan summoned Grimaldi up to the apartment. The pilot dragged the dead guards into one of the bedrooms, along with the blood-soaked couch cushions and a soiled rug. Farsioui sat on the couch, fingering the stack of cash, and staring at the floor, apparently lost in thought. Bolan figured the worst thing he could do was to give the guy time to think. Better to keep him on his toes.

"What's eating you?" Bolan asked.

"I still don't know that you're legitimate," Farsioui said.

Bolan pulled a cell phone from his pocket, flipped it open and navigated to the picture file. He found several pictures of a warehouse interior filled with crates. A couple of the crates sat open with AK-47 rifles arranged inside. In another picture, a couple of shoulder-fired missiles were arranged on a blanket, on the floor of the same warehouse. Stony Man's cyber team had pulled the photos from somewhere and forwarded them to Bolan.

He tossed the phone in the guy's lap. Laying an open hand on the stack of cash, the guy picked up the phone and studied the pictures.

"That's my warehouse in Qatar," Bolan said. "Flip through the pictures if it makes you feel better. I'd let you speak with my customers, but most of them really don't like to get calls from strangers, if you know what I mean."

Farsioui handed the phone back to Bolan. He still didn't look convinced, but Bolan decided to let it ride. He only needed the guy to provide an introduction. After that, the guy was useless to him. Before Farsioui could continue to question the soldier, Grimaldi walked into the room. He looked at his watch, then at Bolan.

"We need to go," he said. "Did our new buddy make the arrangements?"

Bolan shook his head.

"He's suddenly decided he wants references," Bolan replied.

"Due diligence," Grimaldi said. "I like that. And you told him?"

"Our customers don't want to talk to him."

Grimaldi shot the Algerian a glance. "That a good enough answer? If you want to push the subject, we can just pop you in the head and dump you with your buddies."

"You need me too much to do that."

"Everyone's expendable," Bolan said. "If you cause too many problems, we can just wax you and find someone else who is just as connected."

"What do you want me to do?" Farsioui asked.

"That's the spirit," Bolan replied. "Make the call and tell your buddies you want to meet them. In two hours."

"Two hours? They're meeting with Kassem in four hours. They don't have time to deal with you."

"Tell them to make time," Bolan said.

FARSIOUI FELT HIS stomach plummet when the icy-eyed man ordered him to stand after the call was completed. He hesitated, but only for a moment before hauling himself to his feet. The guy wagged the barrel of his Beretta at the door.

"C'mon," the man said.

"We're going to the bookstore now, right?" Farsioui asked.

The big man nodded.

The other intruder, the lanky one, stood next to the door, his palm resting on the knob. When Farsioui neared him, he held up a hand for the Algerian to stop. He did. The man opened the door, poked his head through it and looked side to side before he exited the apartment, gesturing for Farsioui to follow him.

The Algerian moved into the corridor. His gaze fell on the wall, the white paint splattered crimson with his guard's blood and other life fluids. His stomach lurched and his chest grew tight, as though someone had wrapped it in steel bands and drawn them tight.

He could feel the other American coming up from behind. Farsioui forced himself to draw a shallow breath and continued to move.

Think, he told himself. Don't panic. It's just a few hours before dawn.

Once people began to stir and leave their apartments, they'd see the blood and call the police. Whether that was a good thing remained to be seen. Many of the officers who were aware of his involvement in Islamist causes turned a blind eye to his activities because they agreed with him. Others, the apostates, also were happy to ignore his activities— so long as he paid them hush money. So chances were they'd look the other way when it came to his connections. They'd ask as few questions as possible and take it at face value that the Americans had come to rob him. If the questions got too embarrassing, he would have to fork over some money, including the cash from the Americans, to make the problems go away. He could afford it; he had cash of his own. He had the stack from the American. He had sources in Saudi Arabia, the United Arab Emirates and elsewhere willing to pony up money, too. They'd either do it because they shared his beliefs or because he'd threaten to turn them over to their own governments. Either way, he'd have their help.

But first, he needed to deal with the Americans.

He had a plan for that, too.

Inside the bookstore, beneath the counter on which the cash register stood, was a pair of loaded 9 mm Ruger handguns. He'd never been robbed. In fact, his reputation as a friend of al Qaeda and other Jihadists seemingly isolated him from criminals. However, he knew he was on the radar of several foreign intelligence services, especially those of the United States, the United Kingdom and Israel. Therefore, he also assumed it was only a matter of time before they sent a team either to kill him or kidnap him and take him somewhere for interrogation.

Regardless, he hadn't planned to go willingly.

If someone came for him, he'd go out with guns blazing.

By the time they'd crossed the street, perspiration was beading along his hairline, dotting his upper lip. He started for the front door, but the American with the icy eyes grabbed him by the shoulder, shook his head and gestured with a nod toward the alley. Farsioui shrugged off the other man's hand, but moved into the alley.

"Side door," the man directed.

The Algerian walked to the door, fished his keys from his pocket and sorted through them until he found the right one.

The slender man stood at his right shoulder and watched his every move. The big bastard was positioned at his other shoulder, watching their rear flank.

Once inside, Farsioui flicked on a wall switch and an overhead light clicked on, bathing the place in white glow. A desk stood in one corner. Boxes, open and half-filled with CDs, DVDs and books, lined a couple of the walls. Farsioui pocketed his keys and started for the door that led into the main part of the store.

"Where are you going?" the big man asked, his voice a growl.

"The front room," Farsioui replied. Worried his eyes might signal his intent, Farsioui didn't bother to look at the other two men.

"I need to turn on the lights. You must have heard me tell the Chechens I would have the lights on."

"Go ahead," the guy called after him.

By the time he'd taken a couple more steps, he realized the slender man had fallen in behind him. Farsioui clenched his teeth. He knew he was going to have to kill both men. Having someone shadow him, though not unexpected, might make it more difficult to get the guns.

"I can turn on the lights by myself," Farsioui muttered. "I don't need help."

"You're amazing," the other guy said. "This I have to see."

Slowing only slightly, Farsioui pressed his fingertips against the swing door that led into the selling area of the store. It fanned open at his touch and he moved through it, heading for the checkout counter and the weapons.

GRIMALDI KNEW THE guy was just being too damn helpful.

Sure, they'd killed two of his guards with cold efficiency. That would intimidate anyone, even a man who ran with terrorists and other cold-blooded killers. Maybe the guy just was being agreeable to save his own skin.

Maybe the guy bought their story about being arms merchants looking for an easy score. Maybe the stack of cash had clouded his thinking.

Maybe.

More likely, though, he was smart enough to realize he was screwed.

He had to suspect they'd kill him if things didn't go their way. Or if something happened to the Chechens and word circulated about that, Farsioui just as likely would end up dead.

So, no, Grimaldi wasn't buying the whole Mr. Helpful routine. He guessed Bolan wasn't, either.

Grimaldi poured on the speed, his long legs covering the floor quickly, as he tried to catch up to the other man.

"Hold it, Chuckles," Grimaldi said.

When he came within a few feet of the other guy, Grimaldi's hand snaked out and he tried to grab at the other man's shoulder. Farsioui ducked his shoulder and the pilot's fingers ended up grabbing empty air. In the next instant, the Algerian was darting across the floor.

Grimaldi muttered a curse. His hand disappeared under his shirttails and drew the Browning Hi-Power pistol from its holster.

Farsioui vaulted over the counter and disappeared for an instant. When he came back into view, he was brandishing a pair of black pistols, swinging both in Grimaldi's direction.

The Browning barked once. The slug caught the other man in the forehead, just above his left eye. The force whipped his head to the side, even as the round burst through the back of his head. He collapsed behind the counter.

Grimaldi, his gun still held in front of him, closed in on the counter. Reflected in one of the windows, Grimaldi saw the storage room door swing open and Bolan come into view, the Beretta in his grip.

The pilot went around the counter and found Farsioui sprawled on his back, his head turned to the left, hiding the bullet's entry point. Blood pooled on the floor around the fallen man's head.

"Damn," Bolan said.

"Sorry, Sarge."

"You had to do it," the soldier replied. "He was about to kill you."

"This won't sit well with the Chechens," Grimaldi said.

"We'll think of something."

Just then, a pair of black SUVs rolled to a stop outside the bookstore.

## CHAPTER TWENTY-ONE

"We need Umarov alive," Bolan said.

Grimaldi nodded his understanding. Bolan slid the backpack from his shoulders and began moving for the storeroom. He gestured for the pilot to follow him. Unzipping the bag, he drew out the Desert Eagle, still sheathed in a holster, and clipped it to his belt. He pocketed some extra magazines for the pistol. The bag also contained a few more packets of cash and a flash-bang grenade.

He heard a fist beating against the front door and someone shouting Farsioui's name. A second later, the dead man's phone began to ring. Bolan knew they needed to move quickly. The longer they waited, the more likely Umarov and his people would get nervous. If they left, it'd rob Bolan of his chance to enter Kassem's compound unnoticed. Also, he'd likely have to wait another twelve or more hours until dusk so he could have the necessary cover to breach the facility.

Bolan guessed at least a couple of Umarov's people would circle the building, looking for a second entrance. He pressed a hip against the door's release bar, pushed it open, slipped through it and glided along the side of the building. He was headed for a large steel trash receptacle that stood next to the building. Grimaldi split off and headed in the other direction.

Bolan heard voices and crouched behind the trash bin. A second later, a pair of men rounded the corner. They walked several yards apart from one another and each carried a pistol. That they were brandishing their weapons told Bolan they were starting to get nervous.

The numbers were falling faster. He had to end this quickly. He emerged from behind the trash bin. As soon as he was visible, the other men stopped in their tracks and began raising their weapons.

The Beretta coughed out a pair of 3-round bursts. The Parabellum rounds drilled into the nearer man and caused the guy to jerk in place for an instant, as though suddenly beset by a swarm of bees. The man collapsed to the ground.

Umarov's second thug was already on the move. He darted left and raised his pistol. Before he could snap off a shot, though, the Beretta chugged out six more rounds that chewed a ragged line from right hip to left shoulder. The guy's knees went rubbery and his run turned into a stumble before he fell face-first onto the ground.

Bolan marched to the edge of the building and peered around its edge. He studied the two SUVs. The farthest from him idled at the curb; its lights extinguished, a street lamp reflecting off its sleek black skin.

Condensation from the air-conditioner had begun to pool on the ground, creating a dark spot on the concrete. The closer SUV was silent. A man stood outside the latter vehicle, smoking a cigarette. Bolan had a clear shot at the guy, but held off.

If the guy went down and those inside the second SUV, namely Umarov, saw it, they'd react and possibly cost Bolan the entire operation.The soldier needed at least one of the vehicles intact.

He activated his throat mike.

"Ace, what's your location?"

"Other side of the building. Staring at the SUV, the one pumping out exhaust."

"Got a count?"

"Negative. The windows are tinted so dark, Dracula could drive the thing at high noon. Can't see a damn thing."

"Must be someone important inside," Bolan said.

"Right. Should we just keep watching them?"

"Let's engage them. Try a frontal approach. I've got your back."

"Will do."

Bolan peered back around the corner. An instant later, Grimaldi stepped from the alley and moved toward the SUV with the engine running. The front passenger-side door swung open and a hardman in a pair of jeans and a black T-shirt stepped from the vehicle. The guy strode toward Grimaldi.

From Bolan's vantage point, he could see the man had his hand resting on the grip of a pistol that was tucked into the waistband of his pants. Grimaldi held up both hands, palms facing forward, and flashed the guy a smile.

Bolan emerged from the alley and quickly moved around behind the SUV. The Beretta chugged out a trio of 9 mm shredders that tore into the torso of the man in front of Grimaldi.

Even as the guy crumpled to the ground, Bolan was moving along the side of the SUV toward the driver's door, which hung open. He pushed his way into the door in time to find one of the hardmen climbing over the console so he could fold himself into the driver's seat. The thug spotted Bolan and started to bring around his hand, which clutched a pistol.

Bolan was close enough to bring the Beretta down in a chopping motion and strike the guy in the temple with the pistol's grip. The thug's body went slack. Bolan grabbed a handful of his jacket and yanked him from the vehicle. The guy's body struck the pavement with a thud. Bolan pushed himself through the door and shoved the Beretta over the driver's seat headrest toward Umarov.

The Chechen was clawing underneath his jacket for a pistol. At the same time, Grimaldi yanked open the back door and pressed the barrel of his weapon against Umarov's sweating temple.

Umarov slowly drew his hand from inside his jacket and raised both hands.

"What do you want from me?" he asked calmly.

"Road trip," Grimaldi said.

# CHAPTER TWENTY-TWO

"You're late," the guard said. "Everything's okay, yes?"

"We got lost," Umarov said. "Fucking GPS. Doesn't help at all when one of the roads is blocked by a tree. We had to go out of our way. We ended up lost."

The man nodded but seemed to stare at Umarov as though memorizing his features. Bolan wondered whether the guy had realized something was amiss.

"I thought you were bringing a second vehicle, too." He cast a glance behind the SUV. "Where is it?"

Umarov licked his lips and paused. Bolan's right hand began to inch toward the butt of the Desert Eagle. The weapon was tucked between the seat and the console

Grimaldi piped up before Bolan could act.

"Where's the other SUV? We'd like to know the same damn thing. We flew into this hellhole, flew in because we had to clean up your mess from Athens. We arrive and you have reserved us one car. One fucking car! Had to leave half our crew at the airport. They took a taxi to our hotel. We shouldn't have to be here, arguing with a low-level guard, but here we are. Now you want to grill us about it? Fuck you!"

The guard stared at Grimaldi for a couple of seconds. Finally, he nodded once.

"That is unfortunate," he said. "I will pass along word of your troubles to the ones who made the travel arrangements."

"Do that!" Grimaldi said. "Later. First, tell us where to meet Kassem. Then get the fuck out of our way!"

The guy looked angry, but he said nothing. He took a couple of steps back from the vehicle and gestured at the guard shack for them to open the gate. A couple of seconds later, it slid back jerkily. Bolan rolled up his window and drove the vehicle inside.

"I can't believe they let us in," Umarov said.

"You sound disappointed," Bolan replied. "Hey, there's no reason for them not to. The guard probably had seen your picture. He knew you were coming. Why wouldn't they allow you into the compound?"

"I did okay?"

"Brilliant," Grimaldi replied. "Especially the part where the guard said something and you froze up like a deer in the headlights."

"A what?"

"Never mind," Bolan said.

"I did as you asked," Umarov said.

"Yeah," Bolan replied.

"Then you will let me go. When this is all over, I mean." Bolan said nothing.

"I asked—"

"I heard you," Bolan said. "Shut up."

"You can't kill me!"

"I've seen your file," Bolan said. "You've had your hands in at least a half-dozen bombings. The combined death toll on them was around eighty men, women and children. Kids, Umarov. Little children."

"I'm fighting a war," the Chechen protested.

"That makes two of us," Bolan said in a graveyard voice.

Ahead, another man, this one armed with an assault rifle, gestured for Bolan's attention.

The soldier tapped the brake and the vehicle slowed. The guard poked a finger in the air, indicating that Bolan should turn the vehicle to the right. Bolan turned the wheel to the right and found they were on a driveway that wound its way toward Kassem's house. He guessed that the structure was at least three stories tall, white-painted brick. Black shingles covered the structure's roof, and the grit on them caught the morning sunlight and glinted.

Concrete slabs covered much of the ground sloping up toward the house. Closer to the building, flagstone covered the ground, interrupted occasionally by small shrubs. Black spotlights jutted from the ground. As best as Bolan could tell, there was no easy way to sneak up on the house since there was no cover.

To one side of the house, a helicopter stood on a landing pad.

Another sentry guided Bolan to a big, rectangular pad of asphalt where several other cars already were parked.

The soldier counted seven vehicles. They included a red BMW convertible, a blue Mercedes sport coupe, two Hummers parked about ten feet apart and three dual-cab pickup trucks, all black.

The soldier thumbed open his seatbelt and climbed from the SUV. He walked around behind it and thumbed a button on the key fob. The rear hatch sprang open. A pair of large briefcases lay in the rear compartment. Bolan popped the latches on the bags. In the meantime, he heard two of the car's doors slam shut. Two seconds later Umarov stepped into view with Grimaldi just behind him, a hand on the guy's shoulder.

Bolan reached into the case closer to him and withdrew the Steyr submachine gun. Next, he grabbed the canvas shoulder bag that contained extra magazines for the Steyr as well as flash-bang and fragmentation grenades and slipped it over a shoulder. In the meantime, Grimaldi hefted the Spectre, slammed home a magazine and charged the weapon. They'd left the M-4 and the shotgun secured in their vehicle.

Umarov stared at the weapons like a dog eyeing a steak.

Grimaldi smacked him in the back of the head.

"Don't even think about it," Grimaldi warned.

Since Bolan and Grimaldi were ostensibly part of Umarov's security detachment, Bolan wasn't worried about carrying a weapon in Kassem's compound. The Libyan assassin's people may balk, but Bolan guessed they'd tolerate it since Kassem was one of their paying customers.

Bolan quickly would find out if he'd miscalculated.

An engine's growl reached Bolan's ears and prompted him to turn his head toward the noise.

He saw a brown Jeep rolling out of Kassem's personal compound bearing three men. The driver guided the vehicle across the asphalt and braked a dozen or so yards from Bolan and his two companions.

A man with bushy black eyebrows and a thick mustache of the same color glared through the windshield at the soldier. The gawker climbed from the Jeep first and strode across the pavement toward Bolan and the others. A pair of young men, both armed with AK-47s, stepped from the vehicle next.

The soldier recognized Mustapha, one of Kassem's closest lieutenants, from the file the Libyan government had provided. Mustapha shot quick glances at Bolan and Grimaldi before he turned his attention to Umarov.

Bolan sensed someone staring at him.

He shifted his gaze to the guards and saw they were regarding him with a cold stare.

One was tall and gangly, his thin arms tipped with too-large hands. The other man was thick in the arms and shoulders with a crooked nose and thick jowls. Bolan noted their foreheads were thatched with scars. If they were child soldiers from Africa, as he suspected, he guessed that the scars marked where the kidnappers had sliced them open and slipped drugs into their systems. It was a common trick among the human vermin who forced kids to become soldiers and commit atrocities against their own people.

Bolan's felt his stomach clench with anger. He'd spent his entire adult life as a soldier, a warrior. But he'd walked that path after he'd had a childhood, and after he'd had a life with his parents, brother and sister. He'd lost his parents and his sister when he was young, too damn young. He'd been robbed of his family, no doubt. But he hadn't been robbed of his childhood. He guessed the two young men were damaged goods, but he'd do his best to take them down without killing them.

He glanced at Grimaldi, who also was studying the young men. Bolan guessed his old friend was thinking along the same lines.

When Mustapha reached them, he dropped a big hand on the Chechen's shoulder.

"The guns were unnecessary," Mustapha said, his tone stern.

Umarov shrugged, but said nothing.

"Kassem wants to speak to you," Mustapha said. "He wants to open his home to you, show you his hospitality. But he will not like me bringing armed strangers into his house."

Umarov looked over his shoulder at Bolan, then looked back at Mustapha.

"You are right, of course," the Chechen said.

Umarov took a couple of steps forward. Bolan tensed and cleared his throat.

The Chechen ignored him.

Then things went to hell.

# CHAPTER TWENTY-THREE

Umarov's hand snaked out and he grabbed Mustapha's pistol, yanked it free from the holster.

The Chechen wheeled around, bringing up the gun as he moved. Bolan cleared leather before his opponent could finish the turn. The Beretta sighed and a single round punched into Umarov's forehead.

Before the body struck the pavement, Bolan was moving. He saw the pair of young gunners unsling their assault rifles and run toward the strike zone. Bolan fisted the Desert Eagle and squeezed off several shots at the young men. Even though the bullets flew high over the young guards' heads, the sound and fury from the Desert Eagle caught their attention and brought them up short in their advance. Grimaldi joined the play, firing the Spectre at the young men and forcing them to ground.

Bolan by now had stowed the Beretta and had fisted a flash-bang grenade. Pulling the pin, he tossed the weapon at the pair. They saw the object arcing at them and froze. The bomb struck between them, unleashing a white flash and a sharp crack.

The Executioner surged toward the disoriented guards. The skinny kid was closer. He had pushed himself onto all fours. His head turned up and his eyes stared at Bolan, though the big American's approach didn't seem to register with him. Bolan hit the fallen guard behind the ear. His arms and legs went rubbery and he folded to the ground.

The heavyset guard was sitting on the ground. He held his

AK-47 by its pistol grip, the barrel aimed skyward. His head was tilted forward and he looked dazed. Bolan again used the Desert Eagle as a blackjack and knocked the guy unconscious.

Something whizzed past the soldier's ear. He threw himself sideways, struck the dirt and rolled.

Bullets sliced through the air above him. Bolan, lying on his stomach, spotted the source: Mustapha had pried his gun from Umarov's cold dead hand and was trying to line up a shot on the Executioner. Suddenly, Mustapha's body began to jerk and a ragged line of red holes appeared on his chest. Bolan saw Grimaldi dousing the guy with a sustained burst from the Spectre.

The big American hauled himself to standing in time to see a dozen or so armed men running across the compound toward them. He recalled the warnings he'd received from the Libyan intelligence agent—that Kassem would put every last one of his people through a meat grinder before he'd face Bolan.

The warrior holstered the Desert Eagle, took up the Steyr and waded into the fight.


KASSEM WALKED INTO the bedroom, paused in the door and gaped at the young woman seated on the edge of his bed. She was young, certainly younger than twenty, he guessed. Whatever, he'd stopped caring about such things a long time ago. If he'd ever cared at all.

He studied her lush, black hair, which hung in loose waves. She glanced at him with deep black eyes, then back to her folded hands, which rested in her lap, and studied her thumbnail. Her legs were crossed tightly at the knee, protectively it seemed and her raised foot levered up and down quickly. Her lips were full and painted with a deep red lipstick.

"You look nervous," he said.

She shook her head.

"I'm fine," she said without looking at him.

"Good," he replied. "I'd hate for you to be uncomfortable."

After all, I paid good money for you, he added mentally.

She flashed him a weak smile.

"I'm fine. My parents, they have the money you promised them?"

He nodded. "Of course."

He stepped up to her and saw her visibly tense. His hand reached out to stroke a shoulder and she shrank from his touch. So it was going to be that way. Apparently, he was going to have to break her in—like a spirited horse. Fine, he could live with that.

He'd even enjoy it.

He grazed his fingertips along the smooth skin of her shoulders. When he reached for the strap of her negligee, he curled the first two fingers underneath the thin fabric, ready to give it a hard pull.

The rattle of gunfire outside the house stopped him cold. Suddenly, the phone on his belt began to buzz.

"What's going on?" he muttered.

Drawing his hand from the young woman, Kassem yanked the phone from his belt. He raised it to his ear.

"I hear gunshots! What the fuck is happening out there?"

"We're under attack!"

He vaguely recognized the voice, though he couldn't put a face to it. One of Mustapha's toadies, he decided.

"Attack? Who?"

"We don't know."

"Where's Mustapha?"

"Dead, sir."

Kassem clenched his jaw, squeezed eyes shut for a full second. When he opened them again, he said, "How many people are hitting us?"

"Two, maybe three. They came in with the Chechen."

"Wait, the Chechen did this?"

"No, they killed him. He came in with them, but they shot him dead."

Kassem suddenly felt light-headed. Two people against a high-security compound filled with mercenaries? Who was that crazy? He had plenty of enemies, but it had to be that bastard from Athens. Other questions whirled around his mind. How had they found him? Could this damned guy burn through a few dozen trained killers? Should he jump on the chopper and have them airlift him from the facility?

Stop it, he told himself. You're not going to let one man, no matter how capable, drive you to ground. Not when you have this kind of security. The bastard deserved to burn for what he'd done in Athens. Kassem wanted the man's head on a pike and he wanted it while the skin was still warm.

"What should we do?" the security man asked.

"What do you think? You kill him! You hit him with everything we've got, if necessary, but you kill him. I want to feed his corpse to my dogs! Understand?"

"Yes, sir!"

Kassem slid the phone back onto his belt. He thought he felt the young woman staring at his back. He turned and found her staring with wide eyes.

"What?" he snapped.

"Are those gunshots? They sound like gunshots. What—"

"Should you do? Try not to get hit," he said, shrugging. He slammed the bedroom door behind him, forgot the woman almost immediately and headed for the elevator. The way he figured it, he could try to overwhelm his foe with sheer numbers. If that failed, he had a small arsenal in the basement, enough to pulverize an army.

Surely, it was enough for two men.

BOLAN CROUCHED BEHIND a concrete barrier and fed a fresh magazine into his submachine gun.

Bullets hammered into the barrier as Kassem's men unloaded their weapons at Grimaldi and the big American. Bolan guessed that once he wound his way through the barrier, he'd have another 100 yards or so to cover before he'd reached the Libyan's stronghold.

One hundred yards of open ground, no cover, just him and Grimaldi up against a few dozen well-armed mercenaries.

Then he'd have another fight on his hands once he blitzed his way into the house.

It was a damn suicide run.

One well-placed shot and the warrior went down, his endless war ended. Maybe today was the day. Only one way to find out.

Bolan snatched a frag grenade from inside his pouch, yanked the pin and lobbed the bomb over the barrier, folded himself up behind the barrier for cover. A couple of beats later, the orb exploded, filling the air with bits of flesh-ripping razor wire. As the roar of the explosion died down, the big warrior uncoiled from the ground and stole a look around the side of the barrier. Several of Kassem's fighters were scattered around the battlefield, balled up the ground, draped over the nearest concrete wall, clothes and flesh shredded by the grenade's blast.

A couple of the fallen still lived, and their agonized moans became more evident as the reverberations from the blast died away.

Still in a crouch, Bolan wound his way through the concrete structures. He wanted to take out the wounded with shots to the head or heart.

Before he could cover a few yards, though, more gunfire rang out to his left. He whipped around in time to see three of Kassem's killers advancing in a ragged line. The soldier had no time to do anything other than react. He squeezed the trigger on his submachine gun and swept the weapon in a waist-high arc. Hot brass rained to the ground around him as the vicious volley of bullets scythed down the approaching gunners.

The soldier reloaded his SMG on the move and sprinted for the house. He climbed the short set of stairs leading to the front door. Breaking open the M-4 grenade launcher, he thumbed an incendiary round into the breach and snapped the weapon closed. The door hung wide-open. Bolan guessed Kassem's thugs had left it open as they rushed outside to confront the intruders.

Bolan moved into the foyer. A massive chandelier hung overhead. The floors were polished hardwood, the walls painted a sterile white, the monotony only broken by an occasional painting hanging on the wall. The soldier heard hushed voices to his left, emanating from a corridor there.

Following the sound of the voices, he moved into the narrow passage and saw two doors on the left and another on the right.

The soldier glided along the wall until he reached the first door to his left. He paused at the frame and could hear the voices inside, both speaking in rapid-fire Arabic. The soldier surged through the door and found a pair of Kassem's gunners, both staring out the front windows.

Bolan raised the M-4 to his shoulder and cored a round through the head of the closer man. The second guy whipped around, fumbling with his AK-47, but Bolan already had lined up a shot on the guy. The M-4 crackled twice more. Red geysers of blood sprang up from the man's chest as the rounds drilled into his heart. His body slumped and the weapon slipped from his grip.

The soldier started for the door, when he heard footsteps in the hallway outside. Bolan moved to the nearest wall and waited. A second later, a man came through the door and stopped short when he saw the dead men lying on the ground. Bolan jabbed the M-4's warm muzzle into the man's neck.

The man dropped his weapon and his hands went up.

"Where's Kassem?" Bolan asked. The man hesitated. Bolan prodded him again with the rifle. "Do you speak English? Where's Kassem?"

"Downstairs," the man said. "We're up here fighting and he's down there."

Bolan nodded. Raising the M-4, he drove the butt into the back of the guy's head. The guy collapsed to the ground.

The soldier turned on a heel and moved through the house. He'd studied the layout of the house before making the hit. He moved through a large living room, passed through the kitchen. The sound of someone coughing caused him to hesitate at the door leading from the kitchen into a dining room.

The soldier glanced around door frame and saw three more shooters, positioned around a set of double doors.

The soldier went through the door in a crouch. The guards saw him moving through the door and scattered. The M-4 chattered and one of the guards wilted under the hail of autofire. A second guy squeezed off a couple of rounds from a pistol. The bullets whizzed past Bolan, but forced him to dart left. At the same time, he fired off another burst that ripped through the guy's chest and sent him crashing to the floor. The third guy was trying to line up a shot from Bolan. But the Executioner was faster and he put the guy down with a burst to the stomach.

Bolan walked up to the double doors and saw they were sealed closed with an electronic lock. He knelt next to one of the guards. A security card was attached to a lanyard around the man's neck. Bolan pulled it over the guy's head. Rising to his feet, he swiped the card through the reader. When the lock snapped open, he pushed the door open and moved through the opening.

The report had indicated the entrance to the panic room lay beyond the bookcase. Bolan began removing books from one of the shelves until he found what he was looking for, a small red button recessed into the wall. He pressed it and the bookcase slid aside slowly.

The soldier moved through the door and onto the steps.

KASSEM CROUCHED BEHIND a stack of crates, his pistol clutched in his fist, and waited for the American. His tongue felt thick and dry. His heartbeat thudded in his ears, the noise heightening his tension as it threatened to drown out the telltale sounds of his adversary's approach. The skin of his palms felt moist against his pistol's grip.

He wasn't scared, he told himself. Cautious, maybe, but not scared. He'd faced death a dozen times in his own life, and he'd killed many times more than that. He was cautious, he reassured himself. His body was under stress and he was just reacting.

The sound of steel wheels rolling on a track reached him. In an instant, he recognized the sound as the opening of the first-floor door. His shoulders tensed and fingers tightened around the pistol's grip. By the time it'd stop rolling on its tracks, Kassem was in motion, stepping out from behind the crate and circling the outer perimeter of the room. When he found a spot where he could watch the stairs at an angle, he stopped.

It was the perfect vantage point for a kill.

Through the spaces between the steps, he could see the American's right foot come into view, press noiselessly on the top step, followed by his left foot. Kassem was glad he'd taken up his current position where he could track the other man's descent.

He watched the intruder creep off the steps and drop into a crouch. The guy was pivoting his head and the muzzle of an assault rifle to his left.

His pistol extended in a two-handed grip, Kassem tried to line up a decent shot at the big man's back. Trying to put a shot through the stairs at his current distance was risky though. Once he fired off a round, he'd lose the element of surprise and possibly buy the other man enough time to react.

Kassem drifted to his right, his pistol held steady. As he circled behind his target, he lined up his shot. His finger tightened on the trigger.

BOLAN MOVED FROM the stairs onto the bare concrete floor. He dropped into a crouch and moved the M-4's muzzle over the room while also listening for signs of Kassem. The hair on the back of his neck prickled and an icy finger raced down the length of his spine.

Acting on instinct, the soldier threw himself into a sideways roll. As his elbows made contact with the ground, he heard the bark of a handgun. Bullets lanced through the air overhead.

By the time Bolan came to a stop on his back, he saw Kassem in motion, his hands grasping a pistol, the barrel swinging in Bolan's direction.

The M-4 cut loose with a swarm of 5.56 mm fury. The deadly barrage missed Kassem by inches, but spurred him to squeeze off another wild shot and sprint for cover behind a nearby stack of crates.

The Executioner hauled himself from the cold concrete and unleashed another hail of bullets at the fleeing figure. Bullets chewed into the concrete walls and the gunfire seemed deafening in the cramped quarters.

When Bolan saw Kassem complete his wild dash and disappear behind the crates, stacked tall enough to loom over the soldier's head, he knew he was going to have to take out the man with an up-close shot.

So be it.

The warrior paused long enough to slam a fresh magazine into the M-4 before he took his first steps toward Kassem. The Libyan tried to capitalize on the pause, popping around the side of the crates and snapping off a couple of rounds from his pistol. The rounds flew wide and buried themselves in the walls behind Bolan.

The Executioner rewarded the other guy for his efforts by squeezing off a burst from the M-4. The autofire pounded into the crates. Wood splintered under the withering hail and forced Kassem to draw back under cover. Bolan continued to squeeze off short bursts at Kassem's position, shooting one edge, then the other, keeping the Libyan pinned down.

Gray-white smoke hung in the air. It would have stung the warrior's eyes had he not been so hopped up on adrenaline.

Switching the nearly empty M-4 to his left hand, Bolan fisted the Desert Eagle. He was just a few feet from Kassem's position. The Libyan uncoiled from behind the crates and swung around them. His right arm and half his face and torso were visible as he raised his handgun.

In the same instant, the Desert Eagle let loose with a peal of thunder. The jagged yellow muzzle-flash illuminated Kassem's face, a mask of shock as the .44 round punched through his sternum and drilled into his heart. He folded to the floor in a dead heap.

Bolan gave Kassem one final look before turning away.

THE SOLDIER QUICKLY searched through the contents of some of the crates until he found one packed with thermite grenades. He scooped up four, stuffed them into a canvas pouch that lay nearby and looped the bag's strap over his shoulder.

Returning to the first floor, he headed for the front door. As he passed a stairway, the sound of muffled voices—one male, one female—emanating from the upstairs brought him to a halt. He listened for a few more beats. The female's voice sounded loud and agitated. Filling his free hand with the Beretta, he marched up the stairs and headed in the direction of the voices.

He came up on a closed door. Through it, he heard the

female speaking in rapid-fire Arabic. The man laughed and retorted in the same language, his tone harsh and dismissive.

Bolan lashed out with his foot. The sole of his shoe hammered against a spot just to the left of the doorknob. Wood splintered and the latch gave in. The door swung inward, Bolan following right behind it.

The soldier sized up the situation. One of Kassem's hardmen had backed a naked young woman into a corner. His fingers wrapped around the woman's slender wrists, he was pinning her arms against the wall. Bolan could tell at a glance she was young.

The thug and the young woman both whipped their eyes toward Bolan. The hardman's lopsided grin melted away when he saw the grim warrior and the dual pistol muzzles locked on him. The guy paused. Then he did something stupid. Releasing the young woman's wrists, he made a play for a pistol holstered on his hip.

Before the guy's fingertips reached his sidearm, Bolan's Beretta chugged. Three Parabellum slugs drilled into the man's chest, each eliciting a red geyser of blood. He faltered for a second before his knees gave out and he folded to the ground.

The young woman's lips parted and a scream erupted from her. She looked at the dead man, then Bolan. Tears had left her cheeks streaked with mascara. Bolan holstered the Beretta. The other hand, filled with the Desert Eagle, hung loosely at his side.

He moved toward her, pulling a sheet from the bed as he did. She screamed again and shrank against the wall as he drew closer.

The warrior dropped the sheet on the floor in front of her.

"It's okay," he said. "I'm here to help."

She looked at him, her eyes still wary. But her hand grabbed for the sheet and she wrapped herself in it.

He extended his hand again and she drew back from him.

Up close he got a better look at her face and put her age at less than twenty. The realization only reignited his disdain for Kassem, though he shoved it aside almost as quickly.

He backed away, giving the young woman some space, and jerked his head toward the door.

After a couple of seconds of hesitation, she stood tall, the sheet clutched tightly at her throat, and exited the room.

Bolan escorted her from the building and left her in Grimaldi's care. He returned to the front door and drew two of the thermite grenades from his pouch. Yanking the pins with his teeth, he tossed the bombs through the door and ran.

## CHAPTER TWENTY-FOUR

"Another beer?" Grimaldi asked. Bolan nodded. The two men were seated in the cabin of the jet Hal Brognola had arranged for their mission. It had been two hours since the raid on Kassem's stronghold. Grimaldi stood, moved to the refrigerator and retrieved two bottles of beer. Lowering himself back into his seat, he unscrewed the cap from one of the beers and handed it to Bolan, and kept the other for himself.

Bolan pressed the cold glass bottle against his forehead and shut his eyes.

"We did okay back there," Grimaldi said.

"We did okay."

"But there's more to do."

Bolan opened one eye and looked at the pilot. "Yeah, more to do."

"So where to next?"

"Rio de Janeiro," Bolan said. "Allegedly our friends have operations there. Bear and the cyber team are doing some digging on that. We should hear something from them soon."

He glanced at his watch. "In a few minutes, in fact."

A few minutes later, Bolan finished his second beer and refused a third from Grimaldi, who was digging in the refrigerator for his fourth.

"Aren't you flying?" Bolan asked.

"Not yet. Takes at least two more beers before that happens," Grimaldi replied, grinning. "I'm going outside for a smoke."

"Fine, I have a call to make," Bolan said.

Pinching the neck of the beer bottle between his index and middle finger, Grimaldi uncoiled his lanky frame from the seat and headed for the cabin door. Bolan activated his sat phone and tapped in the number for Stony Man Farm.

Barbara Price eventually answered. "Striker?"

"Hey," he replied.

"It's good to hear your voice."

"Likewise. I figured Hal would be briefing me."

"Hal is on a plane to Ohio," Price said. "Leo was transferred by the U.S. Air Force to Germany. Now he's on a plane to Wright-Patterson Air Force Base in Ohio."

"Ohio? As if he hasn't suffered enough."

Bolan heard a smile creep into Price's voice. "Nice," she said. "Leo's doing okay. The doctors have removed the bullets. There shouldn't be any permanent damage, as best anyone can tell. No damage to his internal organs, thank God. He was lucky Jack showed up when he did. Otherwise, he'd probably be dead."

"Agreed," Bolan replied, his voice flat.

"You don't sound relieved," Price replied.

"Glad as hell about Leo. But I'm not relieved. The man who did this is still out there. And he's obviously not working alone. This was a major security breach. We need to figure out how they located the safehouse. Waxing Kassem accomplished part of my mission, but now we have the others to worry about. I need to find them before they go to ground."

"And you may get the chance."

"Explain."

"Huang? The handler for the shooters? Apparently, someone using one of his aliases popped up in Athens. The name was on a credit card that was used to rent the van driven to the safehouse. They also bought a couple of hotel rooms and a few other odds and ends. U.S. intelligence has Huang on a watch list. That's how we know this. Anyway, someone operating under the same name chartered a jet out of Athens a few hours before the hit on the safehouse. The flight didn't leave until an hour after the hit, though."

"Enough time to get from the safehouse and to the airport. Where was the plane headed?"

"According to the flight, they were headed for Brazil, to the Rio de Janeiro-Galeo International Airport, to be more specific. It's at least a thirteen-hour flight so they most likely touched down hours ago, left the plane and melted into the woodwork."

"Do we have more on Huang?"

"Precious little," Price replied. "A lot of it is almost boilerplate for a Chinese spy. He attended a military academy. Spent maybe ten years in the People's Liberation Army, in its intelligence division. He analyzed flight computers and guidance systems for foreign missiles and aircraft."

"Smart guy?"

"Reasonably so, if his dossier is to be believed. Not a genius, not a moron. But the Chinese thought he was better suited to fieldwork. Apparently, he was volatile and didn't like being locked in a lab somewhere. They made him into a recruiter."

"Which is how he met our shooters."

"Right. We've got surveillance film from the safehouse. We sent it to NSA and they've been processing it down to the last detail. It allowed us to get a good look at the guy who shot Leo and Kristina Mentis. My former colleagues at NSA had been trailing him for a few years, building a dossier on him."

"Our friend have a name?"

"He does. Xu Chin. Former special forces for the PLA. He loved to fight, but he was a crappy soldier."

"Meaning?"

"Like the guy who recruited him, Xu's pretty volatile. Volatile enough that he slapped a colonel."

Bolan let out a low whistle.

"Sounds like a good way to get executed."

"I know. Right? But I guess this particular colonel's star was falling at the time. He was considered lazy, not terribly dedicated to the powers that be. The best information we have says Xu was reprimanded and reassigned. He was never thrown out of the army, though."

"Weird."

"And the colonel he hit ended up dying six months later."

"Surprise," Bolan said, his voice sounding anything but. "Was he shot in the head?"

"Hard to tell for sure. According to the official report, a gas leak in the building caused an explosion. The authorities wrote it off as a fluke."

"You said the 'official report.'"

"Who says men don't listen? Unofficially, and this is all anecdotal, there were rumors it wasn't an accident. Not in the press accounts, of course. Chinese media's too controlled for that.

"Right."

"But the colonel's death definitely left some tongues wagging."

"We know that how?"

"Getting there. Be patient."

"Sorry."

"The murder was awful. It was quick but deadly, destructive. That colonel lived in an apartment building with his family. The explosion gutted most of the building's interior. What was left was destroyed by fire. The official toll was ninety dead and thirty missing."

"Jesus," Bolan said. "Just to get one guy?"

"Yes."

"If he did it," Bolan said, "he's crazy."

"Crazy but committed. He took out an entire building to get one man, one who, in the grand scheme of things, wasn't very important."

"But Xu wanted him dead. So he did all that just to get even?"

"That's the most logical guess. If you believe it's murder, the most logical motive would be revenge. But I made some calls and that's not the case. I talked with people I know at NSA, a couple of China experts. They said the colonel was a marked man. He'd fallen out of favor with the party and actually was spying for us. Things are too murky to know for sure. But the belief is Xu was recruited to kill the colonel. Three other officers who'd been spying for us all went down within a month or two after that. Two were quote-unquote accidents. The other died slowly from radiation poisoning."

"They think Xu waxed all these guys?

"At least two of the three. Radiation poisoning wasn't exactly his style."

Bolan leaned back against the headrest and exhaled deeply. "So where does Xu fit on the pyramid?"

"He's mostly muscle," Price said. "In the last few years, his links to Chinese intelligence have frayed somewhat and he's been getting his hands dirty in organized crime. But he's the one who does all the dirty work for Jiang."

"I want to find him," Bolan said.

"We have a couple of leads. I'll send them your way."

# CHAPTER TWENTY-FIVE

The opening riff of a three-chord rock song ground out from the telephone and prodded Max Blackwell awake. His hand lashed out from beneath the covers and slapped at the night-stand, trying to grab the phone.

On the third try, his palm smacked down on the phone. Fingers encircled it and, rolling onto his back, raised it to his ear and forced his eyes open. The room was dark and his brain still fuzzy from the seemingly endless servings of bourbon and water he'd downed the evening before. His tongue felt thick, dry, and his throat was raw from cigarettes.

"Who the fuck is this?" he said. He tried to make his voice sound like an angry growl, but it came out as a brittle croak.

"Phase two," Jiang said.

Blackwell's eyes snapped open. His heart pounded in his chest and the sudden rush of adrenaline cleared his mind instantly.

"Is this—?"

"Shh! Phase two."

"It's early."

"Yes."

"Care to explain?"

"No."

By now, Blackwell was sitting up in bed and he flicked on a light. He was only vaguely aware of the slender form next to him stirring beneath the sheets.

"Tell me what has changed!" Blackwell snapped.

"Everything," Jiang said. "But especially the timetable."

"Fuck, I need more time!"

The phone went dead.

Blackwell threw off the covers, swung his legs over the side of the bed and sat on the edge of the mattress. The woman who'd been sleeping next to him before the phone call had rolled onto her side. Her hand reached out and her fingertips grazed against the small of his back, her eyes squinted to keep out the light.

He turned his gaze on her and vaguely remembered, through the fog of booze, hooking up with her last night. Her skin was tanned a pleasant gold color. Her ash-blond hair was thick, but cut short.

"Baby, what's wrong?" she asked, her voice thick with sleep.

"You still here?" he asked. He grabbed a handful of the sheet and ripped it away, exposing her. She immediately brought her hands up to cover herself. Anger flashed in her eyes and she shot out of the bed.

"You're an asshole!" she shouted.

Her turquoise cocktail dress was pooled on the floor where she'd shed it a few hours before. He grabbed the silky fabric and threw it at her. He stalked across the floor, stopping only long enough to scoop up her shoes, open the door and heave them into the hallway. She crossed the room with an unsteady gait and he guessed the apple martinis she'd guzzled the previous night still coursed through her body. She was obviously in no shape to drive, and he was in no mood to care. It wasn't unusual for him to throw out his conquests at some point in the night; it was as routine as brushing his teeth.

He guessed one of his night maids would likely intercept the woman before she left, fill her full of coffee and call her a taxi. He cared little as to what happened to the women he tossed from bed. But he also didn't need a lawsuit. The woman hesitated at the door, wheeled around and began to unload with an obscenity-laced tirade. Blackwell gave her a hard shove that sent her sprawling into the hallway. He slammed the door and locked it. Predictably, she started beating her fists against the wood panels, but he quickly tuned her out. Eventually, she'd give up or the maids would whisk her away.

Whatever, he thought. So long as I don't have to see her again.

After his shower, Blackwell climbed into his private elevator, which carried him to his basement office. He'd remotely started the coffeemaker and the room smelled of Kenyan coffee. He poured a mug, then walked to his desk and sat in the wingback chair, the black leather creaking softly under his weight.

Three LED-screen televisions were fixed to the wall. All were tuned to financial channels, and like all the televisions in the mansion, ran continuously, the sound muted.

His eyes focused on the middle television, which was tuned to CNBC, primarily because of the pretty redheaded female anchor. It was only after a second his eyes roamed to the graphic in the corner that read "Plane Crash!" Leaning forward, he picked up a remote and used it to raise the volume.

"Authorities say the pilot, Nuri Frankel, an Israeli businessman, died in the crash. His wife of twenty-three years also perished in the crash, which remains under investigation."

A picture of Frankel shaking hands with a former U.S. Secretary of Defense flashed on the screen. Judging by the picture, the bespectacled Israeli was slim, with a pale complexion.

The news anchor continued. "Mr. Frankel was considered an expert in the commercialization of military technology. He spent twenty years in the Israeli military before he retired and joined the private sector. He sat on the boards of three defense firms. The largest of those, QF-17, you may remember, lost two other board members when they were murdered in Athens, Greece, during a robbery. Authorities there have yet to solve that crime."

Blackwell rolled his eyes at that one. They hadn't solved it because the detectives were on the take or being blackmailed by Jiang, Kassem or someone else involved in the conspiracy.

He sipped at his coffee and stared over the rim of his mug at the middle TV. The screen was split and the anchor now was talking with a reporter. The reporter stood on the deck of a boat, the wind rippling the fabric of his jacket and tousling his hair.

Behind the reporter, Blackwell noted several boats clustered in the distance. He assumed they were rescue and recovery craft.

"Sarah," the reporter was saying, "authorities here believe it could be weeks before they can piece together what happened. However, they already have dispatched dive teams to secure the in-flight recordings. Frankel was an accomplished pilot. As a younger man, he flew fighter jets. And he'd devoted much of his post-retirement time and wealth to flying. People we've spoken with say they were surprised to hear he'd crashed."

The reporter fell silent and flashed a smile. Blackwell rolled his eyes again. As if anyone expects a crash, he thought.

"But they do believe it was an accident?" the redhead asked.

"They say they have no reason to think otherwise. A mechanical failure of some kind seems the most likely cause. Back to you, Sarah."

Within seconds, Sarah had forgotten all about the plane wreck and instead was discussing stock futures and what a slight decline in the Nikkei's closing might mean for American trading.

By now, the other networks were running their own segments on the plane crash. Blackwell watched those, but none had any fresh information. That was fine with him. He already knew everything he'd needed to know about the accident before he'd seen the first story on television.

Frankel was a good pilot, one who'd done his own flying for decades. He also usually had a copilot fly with him in case a heart attack or some other unforeseen crisis put him out of action.

Frankel wasn't to blame for the crash. No, his executive jet had fallen from the sky for one simple reason: Jiang's people had sabotaged the engine because they'd wanted him dead. From what Blackwell knew the murder was nothing personal. They'd picked Frankel because his love of flying made him a likely candidate for an accidental death. Frankel simply was collateral damage, his wife and the copilot barely an afterthought. One other member of QF-17's board, an American industrialist who liked auto racing, had been selected to die until a broken ankle put his race on hold.

Now Frankel was dead, though. It meant things were moving forward.

THREE HOURS LATER, Blackwell's desk phone rang and he answered it.

"Hello?"

"Is this Mr. Blackwell?" The voice on the other end of the line spoke English with a heavy accent.

"This is he."

"This is Abrehem Havaya, chairman of QF-17."

"The defense firm?"

"Yes."

"This is a surprise," Blackwell lied. "I saw the news item. The one about Mr. Frankel. A terrible thing. You must have a million things on your mind right now."

"Yes," Havaya said. "A terrible thing. We're all in a bit of shock, as you can imagine."

"Of course," Blackwell said.

Blackwell heard a rumble on the other end of the line as the man cleared his throat.

"You must be wondering why I called, especially at a time like this," Havaya said.

"Especially."

"As you can imagine, we have several projects in the works. They're very critical to our long-term growth. Nuri was intimately involved in those. People think of him as a military man, but he was also a genius when it came to finance. My understanding was he was self-taught. An incredibly intelligent and disciplined man."

Oh, God, Blackwell thought, must I know all this about this loser? How could anyone be self-taught and be any good? He stifled a yawn.

"Really?" he asked, feigning interest.

"Yes, a remarkable man, actually. I cannot even calculate the magnitude of this loss."

I can't calculate my boredom, Blackwell thought.

"Anyway, forgive an old man for his grief," Havaya said. "The point is, we have some important things coming up in the next year. I could tell you more, if you'd sign a nondisclosure agreement. But needless to say, the plans pertain to corporate finance and mergers. You come very highly recommended."

Naturally.

"And we'd like you to join the board. Would you consider doing that?"

Blackwell paused a couple of seconds for effect before he said, "Of course I will consider it. Send me the appropriate forms and we can discuss this at greater length."

"Wonderful," Havaya replied. "My assistant will send them immediately. We'll be in touch."

Havaya may have been a bore, but he was efficient. The forms arrived in Blackwell's email inbox within thirty minutes. Blackwell printed the documents and signed them almost immediately. However, he sat on them for a couple of hours—ample time for him to read the documents—before scanning them into his computer and sending them back to the Israeli. Then he went back to his room to sleep off his bourbon hangover. Three hours later, when he returned to his office, he found he'd been booked on a flight to Tel Aviv. He ordered one of the maids to pack for him. Then he leaned back in his chair, lit up a cigarette and gazed at the ceiling.

It was all coming together.

WHEN JIANG HAD first approached him about this whole effort, Blackwell thought the guy was bat-shit crazy. Jiang had shown him the money, though. The mysterious Asian had provided more than enough for Blackwell to buy stakes in several defense-technology firms. From what he'd told Blackwell, Jiang had used a series of shell companies to make those buys. They'd created another company, one that, on paper, Blackwell controlled.

Jiang remained in the background, but made all the decisions that mattered. For the most part, it had worked well enough that Blackwell had decided to stop questioning Jiang's motives. Sure, the guy was from a country that was, to be charitable, not allied with America, and he was focused on the defense industry with a laserlike focus. But how much damage could one guy do? Was Blackwell a traitor for helping Jiang?

He stubbed out his cigarette, the move extinguishing any questions from his mind, too. The question arose occasionally, but Blackwell never entertained it for long. It had to be greed. Defense companies made money. Jiang wanted to make money. End of story, right?

What Blackwell did know was everyone had a price. Even the rich guys like him—hell, especially guys like him—had a price. Maybe it was cash, gold or real estate. He loved all those things. But Jiang had figured out Blackwell's price without ever having met him.

Fear.

Fear of losing everything.

Jiang had worked him like a pro.

Two years earlier, Blackwell had met a woman in a night-club. She'd changed his life forever and not for the better.

The music had pounded so hard it felt as though it'd shake his heart loose and the air reeked of a noxious mixture of spilled beer, perfume and sweat. It'd been a long day. He'd gotten shelled in the markets and decided to stop at a favorite watering hole for alcohol and to score a little ass. He'd slammed down two bourbons and was waiting for the waiter to bring a third when the young woman had marched up to his table and introduced herself.

She was Asian. During the conversation, she'd told him she was a first-generation American, the daughter of Chinese immigrants. He'd believed it at the time. Or, more to the point, had cared very little about her background. He just wanted to get laid. Her background, her hopes, her dreams—that crap mattered not at all to him. They were just things to feign interest in until he scored the prize.

Looking back, he guessed she'd lied about damn near everything she'd told him. They'd spent a few more hours at the club, her sipping Manhattans and him pounding bourbons, before she'd invited him back to her hotel room, where he proceeded to bang her brains out.

He'd crept out of her hotel room in the predawn hours and promptly forgotten about her.

A month later, almost to the day, Blackwell had started getting calls from Feng Dai, who said he had an incredible business opportunity for him. He'd blown the guy off until he'd started calling his cell phone. Only a small handful of people knew the number. None had a reason to give it to a salesman. That had irritated Blackwell enough to give the guy an audience, if for no other reason than to chew him out.

Feng arrived fifteen minutes late for the appointment, togged in an expensive gray suit and a blue tie, hair lacquered with copious amounts of hair gel. He'd walked past Blackwell's receptionist and into his office and began arranging a laptop on the oval-shaped coffee table.

Blackwell had shot up from his chair, cocked his fists on his hips and glared at the other man.

"What the hell? Who are you? Are you Feng Dai?" he asked.

"Yes."

"What the hell are you doing? You can't just storm into my office like this!"

"I told you, I have a proposition for you," Feng said without looking at Blackwell. He jabbed a finger at one of the chairs arranged around the coffee table. "You should come closer."

Blackwell's jaw almost struck the floor. Had this son of a bitch just told him where to sit? In his own office?

Blackwell's hand reached out for his desk phone. "I'm going to have you kicked out," he said.

The man made no move to stop him. Instead, he shrugged and stared at the laptop's screen as he waited for the machine to boot up.

"Suit yourself," he said.

"I don't have time for this bullshit!" Blackwell shouted.

"You should make time."

"Did you just tell me what to do in my own office, you bastard?"

A faint smile ghosted the other man's lips.

"I did," Feng said.

Blackwell gestured at the guy with his middle finger. He yanked the phone from its cradle and began punching in numbers. Before he could complete the sequence, he heard what sounded like the moans of a man and woman making love. The woman kept saying something in a language he guessed was Chinese. What in the hell? Had this guy just fired up a porn video on his computer?

Feng turned the laptop in Blackwell's direction so the

screen was visible to him. In a window centered in the middle he saw a naked man on top of a woman. The woman's face, her eyes, squeezed shut, and part of her right shoulder were visible. Her fingertips were digging deeply into the man's back, which was shiny from sweat. It had taken him a couple of seconds to place the woman's face. Much easier to identify had been the full-color tattoo on the man's shoulder blade. A family crest. His family crest.

He leaned back in his chair, stunned.

"You filmed me?" he said.

"Yes."

"You son of a bitch!" Blackwell said. He forced the words through clenched teeth.

"Shall I leave?"

"What do you want?"

"You know what she's saying, right?"

Blackwell shook his head. All he could remember was she'd had a damn good time, courtesy of him. Sure, it'd struck him as a little odd that she'd spoken English at the nightclub, but switched to Chinese in bed, he'd quickly forgot about it. As long as he got off, he didn't care whether she spoke English or Swahili.

"It's Mandarin Chinese," the man said. "She's saying, 'Stop, please stop' in this sequence."

Blackwell's neck flushed scarlet and it climbed up into his cheeks.

"That's bullshit," he growled. He began jabbing his finger at the other man as he spoke. "It was consensual. She didn't try to stop me. Besides, I couldn't understand her. I would have stopped otherwise."

"How does the expression go? Oh, yes. Tell it to the judge."

Blackwell started to uncoil from his chair. Feng gestured for him to remain seated. Still trying to wrap his mind around all of this, Blackwell complied, dropping back into his chair.

The Chinese man reached inside his jacket and drew out

a folded document. He set it on the table, unfolded it and smoothed out it with the heel of his right hand before sliding it across the table. Blackwell trapped it under his hand, picked it up from the table and began to scrutinize it. His jaw clenched and unclenched as he read it. An angry knot had formed in his stomach as he reached the end of the second page.

"It's an affidavit," Feng said.

"I know what it is. I can read, damn it!"

"It says you raped her."

"I said I can read, damn it!"

Blackwell crumpled the document and whipped it at Feng, who made no attempt to catch it. Instead, he let it strike his sternum before it bounced off and fell to the floor. Feng shot him a pitying smile that only heightened Blackwell's feeling of impotence.

"I know what this is!" Blackwell said. "It's a damn setup!"

"Very astute."

Blackwell had held Feng's gaze for several seconds and had found nothing there. The man obviously wasn't intimidated. In fact, he seemed more amused by Blackwell's distress than anything else. Finally, the investor let his shoulders sag and threw a glance at the ceiling. He felt something unusual—helplessness—and he didn't want Feng to see it in his eyes.

"What do you want?"

"Want? To make it go away, you mean?"

"Yes, to make it—and you—go the fuck away. How much money do you want?"

The other man shook his head. "We don't want your money," he replied.

"Bullshit, everybody wants my money."

"We want something else."

"What then?"

"We need your help."

"What kind of help?"

"You'll know when we ask."

"And if I say no?"

"That poor young woman will call the police."

"And I'll tell them I'm being blackmailed."

"By whom? By her? She never asked you for anything. Even after you raped her."

"I didn't rape her! And, yeah, maybe she's not blackmailing me. But you guys sure as hell are."

"And just what 'guys' are we?"

"I have your name."

"An alias."

"I can hire private detectives to hunt down your real identity. Your face has been recorded multiple times since you entered this building. I have your fingerprints on my office door."

"Feel free to try. It's your money and you have plenty to burn. But I am a ghost. You'll never find anything about me." The man paused for a couple of seconds, but his eyes never left Blackwell's. "Look, we can continue this discussion, which is pointless. You can offer us a thousand protests. We have thought of them all. It's really best if you submit. That way, we can focus on the future. Work with us and you might actually make some money. Work against us and it will go badly."

Blackwell bit off an angry reply and rubbed his chin with his thumb and forefinger.

"How much money are we talking about?" he asked the man also known as Jiang Fang.

That was when Blackwell had taken his first steps into Jiang's conspiracy. At the time, he hadn't realized its depth or its ultimate goal of infiltrating the U.S. and Israeli defense industries. And he hadn't really cared, either. For once in his life, he'd just followed someone else's orders, using Jiang's money to buy stock in cutting-edge tech firms, doing all his work through a multilayered veil of shell corporations.

Jiang had followed through on his promise, too. He'd put

money in Blackwell's pocket, respectable sums, all under the table. On the rare occasions when Blackwell began to ask questions, Jiang or one of his agents would remind him about the video and the affidavit or they'd list the half-dozen or so federal crimes he'd committed while working for Jiang. They'd melt away, return to China and leave him holding the bag.

His curiosity evaporated, like droplets of water on a desert highway.

After a while, he'd decided it was best to shut up and let them use him. Even now, as things had begun to turn bloody, Blackwell still felt it best to stick with the program. So long as he didn't become part of the body count, he no longer cared how much havoc Jiang unleashed. And from what he'd gleaned of Jiang's plans, the havoc would be considerable.

# CHAPTER TWENTY-SIX

Aaron Kurtzman's fingers moved over the keyboard and he kept his eyes locked on the monitor. Deep furrows lined his forehead. He scowled, but hummed a classic rock tune softly.

Barbara Price stood behind him, staring over his left shoulder at the screen. Every few minutes, she'd utter the first couple of words of a question or try to offer a suggestion. He'd gesture with his hand for her to be quiet. "Sorry," she'd mutter. They'd fall silent for several minutes while he continued pounding the keys.

After forty-five minutes, Kurtzman's hands suddenly lifted off the keyboard. He thrust his fists into the air.

"Success!" he shouted.

"You found it?" Price asked.

Kurtzman nodded. He tapped the tip of his index finger against the screen. "There it is," he said.

She followed where his finger was pointing and read the screen. Names, all of them corporations and limited liability companies, were listed on the screen. Maneuvering his mouse, Kurtzman clicked through several windows, all of which also contained lengthy lists of names.

"There must be hundreds of names," Price said.

"At least," Kurtzman said.

"This is good?"

"Sure. These are all companies that have some kind of link to Blackwell, Kassem or any of the assorted other yahoos Striker has come across. Once we dig deep enough, I'm guessing we'll find Jiang has some kind of connection with most of these companies. There also are the legitimate companies Jiang set up for all his import-export work in South America."

"You think it will help Striker find Jiang?"

Kurtzman shrugged. "Maybe. Not necessarily. Are there addresses and other information in all these documents? Sure. Plenty. That's all well and good. And we can analyze all that stuff and see what we find out."

"But you have other ideas?"

"Yeah," Kurtzman replied with a nod. "I'm thinking Jiang needs money to accomplish his mission. You can't buy stock in companies if you don't have money."

"Sure," Price said.

"So now that we have these names, I can start backtracking some more. Figure out where Jiang keeps his money and under whose name. That sort of thing. Given enough time and the right software, I probably could dissect his entire organization, chart it like I owned it."

"Do you have the right software?"

"Absolutely," Kurtzman replied. "You know we have the very best."

"Do you have enough time?"

"Hell, no. I barely have enough time to scratch the surface. There's no way I am going to piece together everything we need in a day or less."

Price scowled. "Thanks," she said, "for getting my hopes up."

"Hey, I'm good. But even I have limits. Even if the entire team worked on this full tilt, we wouldn't be able to pull it all together in less than forty-eight hours. That's working full-time with no breaks, backtracking every lead. Then we'd have to hack into some of the most secure banks in the world."

"You can't do it?"

"I can do it. Just not all in a single day."

Price signaled her understanding with a nod. He held her gaze for several seconds.

"This would help the big guy, right?" he said.

She nodded.

"All right. Give me a couple of hours. I'll turn the others loose on it, too. We'll see what we can dig up."

Price smiled and patted her old friend on the shoulder.

"Thanks," she said.

Kurtzman shrugged.

"He's going to need intel when he reaches Brazil. Let's make sure we have it for him."

KURTZMAN SLURPED COFFEE from a foam cup and drummed the thick fingers of his free hand on his desk. The computer had been running through a complex operation and had ground to a halt while it talked to a bank in the Bahamas. The longer his computer seemed stuck, the more anxious he became. That he hadn't been denied access immediately was a good thing. Still, it seemed to be taking forever.

The hum of computers, the quiet clicking of keyboards, the murmur of a half-dozen cable news networks and other sounds gelled into an undercurrent of white noise that permeated the operations center. Because of that, and his intent focus on the contents of his own computer monitor, Kurtzman didn't notice the sound of Price's footsteps until she was within a few yards of him. A moment later he caught a whiff of her subtle perfume, which she used sparingly.

She came to a halt a couple of feet behind him. He could tell by the reflection of her face, visible on his computer monitor, that she was staring intently at him.

"Tell me something good," she said.

"I don't have—"

Existing windows blinked closed while new ones flickered open on his screen. A smile pulled at the corners of his mouth.

"Scratch that," he said. "We have ignition."

"What is it?"

"I just broke into a Bahamian bank," he said. "I know what you're thinking. Someone's going to get caught."

"That wasn't what I was thinking," Price said. "But set my mind at ease, anyway."

"Encryption's strong enough that the chances of them tracing this back are nil. But let's say for the sake of argument that, they do. If they track the first IP address, it'll look like the attack came from London. If they figure out there's nothing there and they push harder, they will find another IP address for a computer in Indonesia. And each time they dig, they will get hit by all kinds of attacks from third-party computers we have networked all over the globe. They'll get hit by denial of service attacks, that sort of thing. Eventually, it would shut their whole system down. Of course, most of the scorched-earth stuff probably won't happen."

"Because?"

"Because they would never be able to track the intrusion in the first place. I worked this whole thing up with some eggheads from the NSA. Just been waiting for a chance to try it out. And here we are. My guess is, the bank managers will never realize the system has been breached."

He took another sip of coffee.

"We hope they never realize they were breached. It would make our lives easier."

"Agreed."

"I mean, strictly speaking, what we're doing isn't legal. And as best we know, this bank hasn't broken any laws, right?"

"Strictly speaking, you're right." Kurtzman craned his neck and looked past Price at the others in the room. "If a lawyer was here, I'd tell you to ask for a legal opinion. But I don't see one."

"Never one around when you need one."

"So you're comfortable with this?"

She grinned. "You know I was already comfortable. If I was worried about slavishly following the law, I'd go back to NSA. I just like hearing you explain your latest dirty tricks in detail."

"Well, now you've heard. But let me tell you the best part."

An office chair on rollers stood a few feet away. Reaching out, Price grabbed it, drew it across the floor and sat down.

"Like I said before, tell me something good."

Kurtzman clapped his hands and rubbed them together.

"Good? Hell, an hour ago I found something great. It's what led me to this bank in Nassau. I had all this data from Blackwell. Tons. The guy has a million of these limited liability companies that he uses to buy up stock in other companies. And he operates these from behind the veil of other LLCs."

"LLCs?"

"Limited liability companies. Haven't you been listening?" He shot her a wink to let her know he was kidding.

"Sorry, but when you talk on a higher plane," Price replied, "it's hard for us little people to keep up."

"Fair enough," he replied, grinning. "Anyway, he has these LLCs that he sets up. He operates them from behind a veil of other shell companies all of which are set up by third parties."

"Sounds pretty standard so far."

"It is. Some of them are shady. But on the surface, at least, none of it screams international intrigue, right? Sneaky and opaque, maybe. Tax dodge possibly. But nothing all that much different from other rich folks who invest overseas, as best I can tell."

He took another swig of coffee.

"But I kept looking for strange things and hit on something. About a year ago, our friend got involved with a venture called Dark Coast LLC."

"Sounds mysterious."

"You don't know the half of it. On paper the whole thing

was based in New York. But that's on paper. It was started by Maximilian Blackwell, the investor. But then we start unwinding the thing and we find out it's a front."

"A front for…?"

Kurtzman shrugged. "I don't know, not exactly. But I'm finding it has a lot of foreign connections. Not such a big deal until you also see that it's been buying up pieces of U.S. and Israeli defense companies."

He pointed to a list on his computer monitor. "Including QF-17."

"The company Briggs and Rabin were involved with?"

"None other."

Price chewed on her lip and pondered what she'd just learned. They already knew several of the players involved in the scheme to take over QF-17. If they'd found the entity— or entities—behind the takeover attempt, that'd give them an edge in undercutting their foes.

"How far into Dark Coast do you think you can dig?"

Kurtzman grinned. "Bank accounts, stock trades. Whatever you need. Just give me a little time."

# CHAPTER TWENTY-SEVEN

*Brazil*

Jose Antunes knew something bad had gone down.

The attorney had just finished a four-mile run when his telephone buzzed, announcing a text message. He'd opened the message and read it. Immediately, his mouth had gone dry and he cursed under his breath. The message itself was nothing if not succinct. It simply read: new concerns.

The number had been blocked, but Antunes already knew the sender's identity, Xu Chin.

He also knew the brief message—new concerns—carried major connotations. It was a preset code indicating Xu needed help of the extra-legal variety.

That was a specialty for Antunes.

The Brazilian had begun his legal practice as a criminal defense lawyer. It hadn't been his first choice, because it paid less than other specialties. However, his firm had needed someone to take the role, and he'd been new, so it fell to him to deal with it. Though he knew for a fact he had nothing in common with his clients, he took to the work quickly and found he talked easily with murderers, rapists and thieves. In fact, when it came to the violent crimes, he found his appetite insatiable for even the smallest details: Did he beg for his life when you showed the gun? How did it feel when you drove the knife into her? How long did it take for him to die? What sounds did he make before he slipped away?

Sometimes the clients would answer; sometimes they'd

silently stare at him, unsure what to say. One or two actually laughed and had the audacity to suggest he try killing for himself. One bastard, a tattooed psychopath who'd moved from raping women to torturing and dismembering them, had assured Antunes he'd love it. The man had leaned forward and flashed the lawyer a gap-toothed smile. "It's a fucking power trip," the guy had growled. "Sick fuck like you'd love it. Get started, you'll never stop."

Antunes stiffly had assured them that, no, it wasn't that. He didn't like hearing about; he just wanted to get all the information he needed to defend them.

But he would ruminate over the details repeatedly, imagine the events as they must have unfolded, always from the killer's perspective. At one point, he'd wondered if the thoughts ever would leave him alone. He'd found peace only when he realized he didn't want them to leave him alone.

*Sick fuck like you'd love it.*

Even now the experiences played through his mind again, an endless loop.

*Get started, you'll never stop.*

It'd been the damn truth. Some smelly, toothless crook, a son of a bitch with barely enough brains to tie his own shoes, had been right.

That was when he'd met Xu Chin.

Xu ran a big part of the skin trade in Rio de Janeiro. Word was, he had some mysterious financier, another Chinese man, who'd helped him build a line of brothels, peep shows and porn theaters throughout the city. Some said the guy was Chinese mafia, others claimed he was a spy.

All Antunes knew was that Xu—and his mysterious benefactor—owned a lot of people in the country, including the young lawyer.

Antunes heard from more than one person that Xu was the go-to guy for just about anything when it came to skin. After a lot of thought, Antunes had asked the guy if he could help him fulfill a fantasy of his own. He wanted to kill someone, maybe do some things to the remains, sick things he didn't want to say out loud. Could Xu make it happen? Pick a victim, clean up the mess?

The guy had been only too glad to oblige. That should have been Antunes's first clue.

Unbeknownst to Antunes, Xu also had taped every minute of it. And the time after that, and the one after that. Xu owned him. If the tapes fell into the hands of the police, he'd be in jail in a heartbeat and his face plastered on the news all over the world. So, yeah, Antunes did as he was told.

Slipping into his office, he closed the door behind him and tossed his gym bag onto a nearby armchair. He considered taking a quick shower before calling Xu, but dismissed the idea. Xu didn't like waiting and it had already been several minutes since he'd received the text.

The hair on the back of his neck prickled. He turned and caught a vague impression of something flying at his face and slamming into his jaw. He stumbled back a couple of steps before he collided with a wall.

He shook his head and instantly was aware of the coppery taste of blood filling his mouth. As his vision came back into focus, he saw something that prompted him to inhale sharply.

A man togged head to toe in black stood a couple of feet from him. The guy's right hand was curled into a fist. In his left, he clutched a big silver pistol. At first, it almost was hard to believe the guy had struck him. He stood still, his face impassive. Eyes like chipped ice were locked on Antunes and his gaze seemed to have a weight all its own. Antunes felt stuck in place, like a dead bug pinned to a piece of cardboard in some kid's science project.

"What do you want?" the lawyer asked.

"Xu Chin," the other man said.

The Brazilian swallowed hard. "Who?"

A humorless smile ghosted the other man's lips. "So that's how it's going to go?"

"Honestly," Antunes said, "I have no idea who you're talking about."

"Let me be more specific."

BOLAN SIZED UP the lawyer. Even if he didn't have files from U.S. intelligence linking the Brazilian with Xu, he could tell the SOB was lying to him. After so many years of chasing savages and psychopaths, the Executioner had developed a sixth sense about such things. The man quivering in front of Bolan practically stank of innocent blood. He wanted to shoot the guy on the spot.

"Let me be more specific," Bolan said. "I came here to find Xu. I don't know where he is. You do. Understand now?"

The other man swallowed hard, nodded and held Bolan's stare.

"You do work for Xu, right?"

"I've never represented him if that's what you mean."

"No, that's not what I meant," Bolan said. "I think we both understand that."

The Executioner raised the Beretta and leveled the muzzle at the other man's chest. The weapon was set for 3-round bursts, and Bolan figured that many 9 mm slugs in the other man's heart at this range probably would do the trick.

"What I'm saying, Jose, is this. You're a hot-shit criminal defense attorney. Supposedly one of the better attorneys in Rio. Of course, part of the reason you get so many people off the hook is because you're not afraid to pay out bribes. Am I getting warmer, Jose? I think I am. But that's the public side. You have a couple other sides, too. One of them is that hanging out with so many criminals has made you, well, connected. If someone needs something, let's say high-quality passports or government IDs, maybe a crate of AK-47s, they don't have to look too hard. They just call you."

Bolan wagged the barrel toward a nearby chair.

"Sit," Bolan said.

The other man complied.

"What do you want?" Antunes demanded. "If you have a gripe with one of my clients, go find him. Or her. Don't drag me into this."

"I wish it were that easy," Bolan said. "Problem is, there's no space between you and your clients. Right? You defend them in court. You provide them with criminal tools and contraband. They provide you with victims. It's a vicious cycle."

The other guy tensed and his eyes went wide.

"Yeah," Bolan continued, "I know about that side of you. The cold, psychotic side."

"How?"

"Apparently, your buddy Xu sent an encrypted video file of you murdering some poor bastard to his bosses in China. Someone, somewhere, nabbed it and shared it with certain people in the United States."

The guy licked his lips.

"What? You didn't think anyone was watching him? Guy's either a criminal or a spy, right? And you think nobody's watching him?" Antunes opened his mouth to speak, but Bolan silenced him with a wave of the Beretta. "So somebody, somewhere, gets the video and identifies you and identifies the sender and here I am, ready to put three holes in your chest."

"You can't prove anything," Antunes said. A sheen of perspiration had formed on his forehead.

Bolan shrugged.

"Let me see the video," Antunes said.

"Where's Xu?"

"I don't know."

"Wrong answer."

"Wait, I really don't know. The guy moves a lot. He told me it was because he'd pissed off the Russian mafia a few years ago. He never sleeps in the same place twice. He has a couple of body doubles, like that guy from Iraq."

"Saddam Hussein."

"Yes, that's it."

"It worked out for Saddam," Bolan said. "Until it didn't."

"Listen, he has a couple of close friends and trusts them implicitly. One is usually with him. Both know his location at all times."

"Give me names and phone numbers."

Antunes nodded. He spit out the information and Bolan memorized it.

"By the way," Bolan said, "on your way up here, you got a text message. Don't look at me like that. Of course we were tracking your phone. Looked pretty mysterious. That was Xu, right?"

"I get lots of texts and phone calls," Antunes said, staring over Bolan's shoulder.

"Is that the best you can do?"

The other man chewed on his lower lip. His right leg jumped up and down nervously and the sweat was now rolling off his forehead and into his eyes, occasionally causing him to squint.

"It was him, wasn't it?"

"Yes," Antunes said.

"What does the text mean?"

"He needs something."

"Like?"

"I don't know," the attorney said. Bolan's eyes narrowed and the other guy held up his hands defensively. "Seriously. I have no idea until he contacts me."

"When will that be?"

Antunes shrugged. "Hard to say."

"Try."

"Tonight. He'll contact me tonight, I would guess. He never contacts me at the office. He usually sends someone to my apartment. They stick me in a car, blindfold me and take me to see him."

"And you hop to."

"Fuck you."

"I thought you only did dead people. Yeah, that was on the tape, too."

Antunes's mouth worked for a second, but no sound came out.

"You're a bastard," he said finally.

"And I'm only getting started." Bolan gestured at the other man's gym bag with a nod. "Grab it and let's go."

## CHAPTER TWENTY-EIGHT

Antunes navigated his car off the street and onto a ramp that ran into the garage beneath his apartment.

Bolan was riding shotgun. The Beretta was clutched in his right hand, and he pushed the handgun's muzzle into the other man's ribs.

"Play it cool, counselor," the soldier warned.

The other man kept his eyes focused straight ahead and nodded.

A voice crackled in Bolan's earpiece. "You okay?" It was Grimaldi.

"Affirmative," Bolan said into his throat mike.

"I couldn't follow you into the garage," Grimaldi said. "The gate closed as soon as you guys pulled through it."

"Understood," Bolan replied. "Park your car and get into the building. And keep an eye out for Xu. You saw him at the apartment so you'd recognize him. Once you get inside, come up to the apartment and watch the front door. Flag me if something looks wrong."

"Will do."

Antunes pulled his car into a spot between a red SUV and a black BMW sports car.

Bolan held out his left palm and after a couple of seconds Antunes dropped the keys in his hand. "Stay here."

The soldier exited the vehicle, slipped the Beretta into the shoulder holster and slammed the door. Walking around the back of the vehicle, he came up on the driver's door and pulled it open. He knew there was a chance the other man would lock himself in the car, though after that his options were limited. Bolan had taken the guy's phone and made sure he wasn't carrying a gun. The best the other man could do is lock himself in the car and honk the horn until someone came to help. Antunes probably didn't want to do that because he was arrogant enough to believe he still could negotiate something with the American. That was probably a more attractive option than having Bolan out him as a murderer.

Sure, the guy had seemed overwhelmed back at his office. But the soldier guessed Antunes would recover enough to try to bargain his way out of his current situation.

The Brazilian climbed out of the car. Bolan grabbed the guy by the triceps, his fingers digging hard into the flesh, and guided him from between the vehicles.

They rode the elevator to Antunes's floor and made their way to his apartment. The lawyer unlocked the door and pushed it open. Bolan shoved him inside and followed on his heels, the Beretta drawn by the time he closed the door behind him. He wagged the pistol's barrel at a couch and ordered the other man to sit. Five minutes later Grimaldi arrived, a gym bag slung over his shoulder. Bolan knew the bag contained submachine guns and other hardware.

"So we have no idea when Xu's people will come for this douche bag?" Grimaldi asked.

Bolan shook his head.

Grimaldi sighed. "Guess I'd better brew a pot of coffee, then."

Bolan looked at Antunes. The attorney was staring after Grimaldi, his mouth opening to say something before he slammed it shut. He snapped his gaze back in Bolan's direction.

"Look…"

"Shut up," Bolan said.

A minute later Grimaldi reappeared, carrying a device about the size of a tablet computer. He was humming and staring at the screen as he moved slowly through the apartment. Antunes opened his mouth to speak, but Bolan warned him off with a sharp look. Antunes pressed his lips together in a tight line, but said nothing.

A few minutes later, Grimaldi returned, his eyes still locked on the screen. The smell of freshly brewed coffee had begun to fill the air. The pilot walked around the luxuriously furnished living room for a couple of minutes, pausing here and there. Finally, he said, "No signals. I think we're good."

"Thanks," Bolan said.

The Stony Man pilot left them alone again.

"When you meet with Xu, he has guards, right?"

The other guy nodded.

"Give me a number."

"Ten, eleven. They mostly ignore me."

"But they're all carrying weapons, right?"

Antunes nodded affirmatively again.

"How many people does he send here?"

"To pick me up?" Antunes shrugged. "Two, maybe three."

"Including the driver?"

"Yes."

Two sets of sliding-glass doors stood on the other side of the room, each opening onto a wide balcony. A pair of skyscrapers stared down on Antunes's high-rise apartment building. Bolan marched across the room and pulled the curtains shut. The room grew dark and the soldier flipped a wall switch to turn on some overhead lights. He also pulled the blinds on the windows.

Grimaldi sauntered back into the room. The tail of his jacket was pulled back and tucked behind the grip of a Browning Hi-Power that was holstered on his hip. The Stony Man warrior leaned his right shoulder against a nearby wall and crossed his arms over his chest

Antunes seemed to ignore him and, instead, was focused on Bolan. "What are you doing?" he asked the warrior.

"I'm guessing his people are smarter than you are," Bolan said. "They probably look in on you, try and see whether you have company. Paranoid group, your friends."

Antunes shrugged. "I have no idea what they do," he said.

A mahogany bar stood along one wall. Bolan moved to it and splashed some whiskey from a crystal decanter into a glass. He carried the drink to Antunes and set it on a table next to the guy. "Drink up," Bolan said. "It's your lucky day."

The other man scowled.

"Hardly," he said.

Bolan found an armchair across from the guy and backed into it.

"All depends on how you look at it," Bolan said. "I'm giving you a chance to clear your conscience and tell me everything you know."

"About the murders?"

Bolan shook his head. "I'm not here about the murders," Bolan said. "That's just another stick to beat you with. No, I'm here about other issues. Like your friend Xu. And his employers. I assume he doesn't work on his own."

"I don't know what you're talking about," Antunes said.

"Of course you don't. Whole world's a big damn mystery to you."

The other man took a drink of whiskey. Bolan thought he detected small tremors in the guy's hand.

When Antunes set the glass on the table, Bolan said, "How did you first get hooked in with Max Blackwell? And if you say, 'who?' I'm going to open a third eye in your forehead."

Antunes cast his gaze to the floor. "I know Blackwell," he said.

"No shit," Bolan said. "Tell me how you know him."

The other man swallowed hard, licked his lips.

"He needed some help, I helped him."

"Like you help Xu?"

"He needed some front companies set up in the Caymans. I set them up."

"What? He found you at random?"

"A friend of a friend of a friend. One of his lawyers in Manhattan started the ball rolling, setting up Dark Coast LLC, and I ended up doing all the work. That way, there were three or four layers between Blackwell and me. That was a couple of years ago. I made it all happen. I was discreet."

The guy had drained his glass. Bolan snatched it from the table and carried it to the bar.

"And the friend was Xu, right?" he asked as he refilled the glass.

Antunes hesitated, but only for a heartbeat. "Yes. But I don't think he was working on this by himself."

"Because?"

"It's not his style. He deals in skin and violence. He sets up front companies, but he uses them to launder money. The companies I established dealt with stocks and market trading. All of it in the defense and technology sectors. That's not something Xu would stick his nose into. He's more likely to set up a shitty restaurant, a trucking company or an auto-parts store to launder his cash."

"He was setting it up for someone else." Bolan held Antunes's glass out to him.

The Brazilian snatched it from his hand and drank deeply, nearly draining it again.

"Most likely," he said, dragging his forearm across his lips, wiping them clean.

"You think he set up Dark Coast LLC for someone else."

"Sure," Antunes said, shrugging.

"Jiang?"

"He'll kill me."

Bolan said nothing. Instead, he let an uncomfortable silence build between them.

Antunes muttered an oath. "Oh, what the hell? I'm in trouble, anyway, right?" He paused and looked at Bolan who stayed silent. "Yes, he had it set up for Jiang."

"What's Jiang doing with the stock? Or Blackwell, for that matter?"

"Hell if I know. I just set these things up. I don't get involved in their day-to-day operations. I have too much to worry about as it is."

"Like killing people for thrills?"

"Look, I only did it once. Okay, a couple of times. I told you what you want to know. Why don't you just let me go? Walk out of here and I'll never tell anyone we talked. You want to stay here until Xu's men come for me? Fine. Take them out."

"That's the plan."

The other man looked relieved.

"So you're really not here about the murders. The people I killed?"

"Right."

"You're not going to arrest me, then?"

"Right."

"And you're not going to kill me?"

"Wrong."

Antunes whipped the heavy whiskey glass at Bolan's head. It missed, and the Beretta coughed once. A single hole opened in the lawyer's forehead before bursting through the rear of the man's skull. A spray of blood, brain matter and bone fragments exploded from the guy's head and splattered over the couch.

Grimaldi looked at the corpse, then glanced down into his coffee cup.

"If I find a bone fragment in this cup," he said, "I will not be happy."

# CHAPTER TWENTY-NINE

Four hours later, the intercom in Antunes's apartment buzzed. Bolan answered tersely and the front-desk security told him two men were in the lobby waiting for him. He asked if he could send them up. Bolan said yes.

The soldier left the front door open a crack. He flattened himself along the wall the door was on and positioned himself so it would block their view of him when they came through the door. They'd moved Antunes's body, dumping it in one of the bedrooms, and had covered the blood-splattered couch with a blanket.

A brick fireplace rose up through the center of the living room. Grimaldi stood behind it. The fireplace provided cover for the pilot, who had the muzzle of his Browning pistol trained on the door.

The door swung inward slowly and a male voice called out Antunes's name. The first man swaggered into view. The Executioner crept toward the door and sized up his opponent. The guy was just a couple of inches shy of six feet tall. He was togged in blue jeans and a black windbreaker. His hands were empty, his brow wrinkled as he swept his gaze over Antunes's apartment. A second man, in faded jeans and a tweed sport coat, moved more cautiously, his hand already fishing beneath his jacket, probably for a gun.

The Beretta sighed once and the Parabellum slug drilled into Professor Tweed's head. His body swayed for a stretched second, his arms falling limp, like a marionette with its strings cut. Blood splattered on the other thug's right cheek.

In a single motion, he wiped at his cheek and shot his partner a questioning glance. When he saw the other man crumpling to the ground, he ripped his blood-covered hand from his cheek and shoved it under the windbreaker, clawing for hardware.

By then Bolan was on him. The grim avenger brought his right arm down in an arc and struck at the guy's head with the Beretta's grip. The guy jerked his head out of the gun's path, but collapsed to the ground nonetheless. An instant later, his right leg swept around and struck Bolan in the ankles and knocked his feet out from under him.

Bolan landed on his back on the ceramic tile. Bolts of pain shot through his back and shoulders, which bore the brunt of the fall. Air hissed through his clenched teeth. His fingers uncurled and the Beretta fell from his grip, clattering a few feet out of reach.

The other man raised himself into a crouch. Leg muscles coiling and releasing, he lunged and landed on top of Bolan. His fist came down and struck the soldier in the jaw. The blow snapped his jaw to the right. The soldier was faintly aware of the coppery taste of blood filling his mouth. His opponent drew back his fist, telegraphing another strike.

Bolan's hand, fingers extended and stiff, darted out and bit into his attacker's solar plexus. The guy's mouth popped open, emitting a croaking noise, and his eyes bulged. As the other man faltered, Bolan grabbed a handful of his shirt, jerked him forward and greeted his approach with a right jab to the chin.

Grimaldi's lanky form came into view just behind the hardman. Bolan saw the Stony Man pilot bring his hand down in a vicious arc and heard a thud as steel struck bone. Eyes rolling back into his head, the man's body went limp and he pitched forward onto the Executioner, who threw up a forearm to stop him. He shoved the hardman aside and drew himself into a sitting position.

Grimaldi had used the Beretta to crack the thug's skull. He handed it back to the soldier.

"Lose something?" the pilot asked, grinning.

"Took you long enough."

"I wanted to see if you've still got it."

"And?"

"You have a bright future in daycare security."

Grimaldi moved to the unconscious thug. Kneeling next to him, the Stony Man warrior rolled the guy on his back and checked his pulse.

"Breathing," he said. "But he may be out for a while."

To Bolan's left, a telephone buzzed. He cast a glance at the hardman whose head had stopped a bullet. Moving toward the guy, he gingerly peeled aside the man's blood-soaked jacket and found a phone clipped to his belt. Grabbing the phone, Bolan studied the screen. The word "restricted" flashed in time with the rings.

"The driver?" Grimaldi asked.

"Could be getting restless," Bolan said. "Let's bum a ride."

BOLAN STEPPED FROM the elevator. He scanned the apartment building's sparsely populated lobby, looking for a doorman or another employee. He spotted a well-groomed man dressed in a black suit. A plastic name badge was clipped to his right lapel and a card laminated in plastic hung from a lanyard looped around the man's neck. A clipboard was tucked under his left biceps.

Nudging Grimaldi with an elbow, Bolan turned and walked to the man, who greeted him with a wide smile. The luxury high-rise apartment housed a number of American and British executives. Bolan hoped it meant the high-ranking staff spoke English.

Bolan kept his own expression grim. He pulled a leather wallet from his pants pocket. It contained the Justice Department credentials for Matt Cooper. He flipped the wallet open, long enough for the man to get a vague impression of what it contained, then closed it again. The man's smile faded slightly and uncertainty crept into his eyes.

"Two men came to see Jose Antunes, yes?" Bolan said.

The man nodded.

"We're private security, hired by his law firm," Bolan said. "Those men work for one of Antunes's clients, one who's unhappy with his legal representation. They were harassing Mr. Antunes."

"Should I call the police?"

Bolan shook his head. "We took care of them," he said. "Gave them a little scare. Chased them out through the garage." He shot the guy a wink. "They won't bother anyone anymore."

The man heaved a relieved sigh that struck Bolan as more theatrical than sincere. "That's good."

"I can assure you Mr. Antunes appreciates your concern. He's heading to the airport right now," Bolan added. "We're sending him out of town for a couple of days. Just until we can get things settled."

"Of course."

"Those two men," Bolan said. "Did they come with a driver?"

"Yes. They came in the sedan parked in the street. See it?" Bolan peered through the window and saw a four-door BMW sedan parked next to the curb. He could see the outline of one man sitting in the driver's seat. The air above the car's hood and around its exhaust pipes undulated as the forest green luxury sedan was idling.

Bolan drew a wad of bills from his pocket, peeled a few off and handed them to the man.

"Thanks," Bolan said. "Let's keep this talk to ourselves, all right?"

"Of course," the man said as he stuffed the cash into the breast pocket of his jacket. "We pride ourselves on discretion."

"Of course," the soldier said.

Bolan stepped outside. The evening was still hot and muggy. He moved to the sedan, walked around to the driver's side and rapped on the window. The driver shot him a questioning look, and Bolan gestured for him to roll down the window. The guy shook his head. Bolan brought out the Beretta and used it to smash the window. He jammed the muzzle into the guy's neck.

"Have I got your attention now?" he growled.

The man nodded. Bolan reached down and pulled open the door. He gestured for the man to slide into the passenger's seat, which the man did, while Grimaldi climbed into the backseat.

"Where's Xu?" Bolan barked.

The driver, his hands raised, muttered an address. Bolan wheeled the car into traffic and headed off to find the killer.

# CHAPTER THIRTY

Xu rolled off the woman and lay next to her, panting and staring at the ceiling.

Air cooled the sweat on his chest and belly. He grabbed a sheet and used it to wipe away the gathered moisture. The woman next to him propped herself up on one elbow, raked her hair from her face and smiled down at him. With an index finger she traced random, swirling patterns on his stomach.

Her name escaped him. He only recalled that he'd helped smuggle her from Fujian province a year or so ago, promising to send her to the United States where she could join distant relatives in New York.

Instead, he'd brought her to Rio, told her she owed him $20,000 and forced her to work it off as a whore. She was nineteen. While he guessed she could repay her debt in another seven years, after a life of prostitution and drugs had left her aged beyond her years and undesirable, he also guessed he'd shoot her and dump her in a landfill somewhere. His hookers all carried expiration dates. By the time they'd reached it, they'd usually seen and heard too much. They knew his clients. They caught snatches of talk about murders, drug shipments and other crimes.

That made them liabilities, ones he couldn't tolerate. For Xu, it came easily. He'd killed more people than he could count.

"That was good," the latest liability said. "Want to go again?"

"Where the fuck are my cigarettes?" Xu snapped. He didn't

bother looking at her, but instead concentrated on a jagged-edged water stain on the ceiling.

She drew back her hand. "Sure," she said. Rolling over, she swung her legs off the side of the bed, sat on the edge for a second, before rising. As she padded across the floor, Xu stared after her. He admired the swing in her hips and the curve of her calves before they tapered into slim ankles. If he didn't have pressing business to attend to, he would indulge himself in another round with the woman.

But he was getting pressure from his bosses and he wanted to make the pressure go away.

Athens continued to haunt him. He'd killed the woman, but he'd lost his team and failed to slay the two men in the apartment. Xu's handlers had told him ahead of time to expect a fight. He'd rolled his eyes. A team of his killers against two or three Americans? He'd expected—no, anticipated—a slaughter.

It hadn't gone that way. Now his connections in the triad, Jiang and even elements in the Chinese government were looking down on him. He'd hoped working out some stress on one of his hookers might ease his anxiety. It hadn't. As much as he hated Jiang, he needed to find a way to redeem himself with the bastard or he'd spend the rest of his life looking over his shoulder. Jiang was powerful. He had the ear of many powerful people in China and he could make Xu's life such a living hell he'd wish for death.

Xu's khakis were folded and draped over the back of a wooden chair. The hooker lifted them from the chair and carefully ran her hands through the pockets until she found his cigarettes and lighter. She returned to the bed, and, keeping her eyes cast at the ground, laid the pants on the mattress and handed him the smokes. Sitting up, he plucked one from the pack and put it in his mouth. As she lit the cigarette, a knock came at the door.

Muttering a curse, he snatched the cigarette from his lips, handed it to the woman and grabbed his pants. "In!" he yelled.

As he turned toward the door, it swung inward and a thickset man entered the room. One look at the expression on the face of Soong Ying, his security chief and logistics man, telegraphed more problems for Xu. The burly man always wore a dour expression, but his scowl looked even more severe than usual.

"What?" Xu asked. He caught a trace of apprehension in his own voice. The realization angered him and the need to lash out surged up inside. "Spit it out!"

"Jiang called."

Shit.

"Okay," Xu replied.

"Kassem's dead."

Xu paused in the middle of buckling his belt. "What happened?"

"He got taken out in Algeria. Him and his whole crew."

Xu looked at the woman and pointed at the door. "Get the hell out."

The two men waited in silence, Xu slipping on a shirt, while the woman pulled on a robe and exited. Soong shut the door behind her.

"Who did Kassem?" Xu asked.

"No one is sure," Soong said, shrugging. "With all the damage they did, the high body count, that took a whole team. Maybe the U.S. Navy SEALs or Israeli commandos. Whoever it was burned the place to the ground. The Algerians swooped in and locked the place down. They even found a dead Chechen there, so maybe the Russians did it. There's no way to know for sure what happened."

Nausea passed through Xu's gut. By now he'd finished dressing and was shrugging on a shoulder rig loaded with a Beretta 92.

"It had to be the Americans or the Israelis," he said. "They want blood for what happened in Athens. Not the job we did. They wanted to even the score for the Israeli and the American woman Kassem killed."

"It doesn't matter," the other man said. "It's the least of your worries at this point."

"What the hell does that mean?"

"The Americans from Athens are here in Rio."

"They're after me."

"There is no other explanation."

"How do we know this?"

"Jiang."

"Shit, Jiang's sources are impeccable."

"They used the same jet to fly from Athens to Algeria to here. Spotters logged the tail numbers onto one of those websites. It registered with someone in Beijing."

"Sloppy."

"Good for us, though."

Xu nodded. "When did they get here?"

"Six, maybe seven hours ago. Jiang has people on the ground trying to retrace their steps since then. See if they rented a car, paid for a hotel room, whatever."

Xu found his cigarettes and lit another.

"What about Antunes?" Xu asked.

Soong checked his watch. "I sent a team for him about forty-five minutes ago. They should be here any minute."

"You heard anything from them since they left?"

"No."

"That doesn't worry you?"

Soong shifted nervously on his feet.

"Not really."

"Are you an idiot? The Americans are here, in Rio. Our guys don't check in for forty-five minutes. That doesn't strike you as odd?"

Soong cursed and pulled out his cell phone. He punched in some numbers, switched the phone to speaker mode and pointed the speaker in Xu's direction. With each ring, his stomach clenched tighter and his breathing became more rapid.

"I'll let the others know," Soong said.

"Go!"

The bulky security man pivoted and left the room. He hadn't bothered to close the door, and from outside the room Xu heard him shouting the names of Xu's other gunners.

Xu stepped into the hallway and found the thickset security chief clustered with four members of his team.

"Lock this place down tight," Soong was saying. "If these people have grabbed our people, they could be on their way now. We need to prepare for that."

The gunners peeled away and began beating on doors. One threw open a door and marched through it, prompting shouts from inside the room. A few seconds later, a heavyset man, a sheet clutched in his hand and held over his crotch to cover it, stumbled into view. His cheeks were scarlet, either from exertion or rage. Similar scenes unfolded before Xu as he moved through the building. It didn't bother him that most of his customers were getting sent away decidedly unsatisfied. In all his years in the skin trade, he'd never suffered from a lack of business.

The same went for his work as a hit man. Someone always wanted someone else dead. They rarely wanted to pull the trigger, tighten the garrote or twist the knife themselves, though. Some—crime bosses or public officials—considered it beneath them, like scrubbing a toilet or cutting the grass. Others felt having a buffer between them and the deed somehow absolved them of responsibility. That was where Xu was different; he knew he had blood on his hands. He just didn't care.

And if things unfolded in the next few hours the way he expected, he'd have even more blood on his hands. That realization gave him the first smile he'd experienced all day.

THE WHOREHOUSE WASN'T a house at all. Xu's skin palace was a three-story building with an unassuming redbrick facade, the glass-block windows rendered opaque by black paint and mortar.

Bolan stood across the street and sized the place up. His brief recon had turned up three ground-level doors. One door had been boarded over, probably to keep johns from bolting before they settled their tab or to prevent the women from running away. Doors in front and back were steel security doors, though Bolan guessed they only rarely locked them.

A trio of guards stood outside the front door. One puffed on a cigarette while the others surveyed the street or turned away the occasional customer. None of the hardmen displayed weapons, though Bolan's trained eye could tell all three were carrying.

The soldier had surveyed the back door minutes earlier and had found a similar scene—a trio of guards milling around in front of the entrance. Hidden from general view, though, one of the thugs had a shotgun, while another carried a JS 9 SMG.

Going through the back door made the most sense, Bolan had decided. It was nothing for a brothel to have a bouncer or two on the premises to show a john-turned-jackass the door. Six men, three showing weapons, told a different story. They were expecting him to show. He took it as a good sign that they were turning people away at the door. He hoped it signaled that they'd evacuated customers from inside the building as well as the women. Until he knew that for sure, though, he'd have to proceed as though the place was filled with civilians.

According to the available intelligence, Xu's group was insular. If he approached the guards and tried to bluster his way in, tried conning them into thinking he was a Black Ace, he'd probably end up dead. They weren't going to defer to a foul-mouthed bastard who rolled up and started throwing his weight around. More likely they'd put two in his head and call it a day.

At the same time, there was no way into the building except through the doors. The ground-floor windows were filled with glass blocks and mortar. If he tried to use the fire escape ladders, he guessed the noise would draw attention.

So, yeah, he was going to take the direct route.

He keyed the throat mike.

"Striker to Ace," he said.

"Go, Striker."

"Rear entry is our best bet."

"The jokes all but write themselves."

Bolan allowed himself a grin.

"You watch the three in front. If they suddenly break away and come after me, drop a tone."

"Roger."

After taking the driver's keys, security card, wallet and other gear, Bolan and Grimaldi had locked him in the trunk of the BMW. They'd ditched the sedan in a parking garage several blocks from the brothel and hoofed it the rest of the way, their weapons hidden in gym bags. Bolan guessed the driver would be uncomfortable, but in no danger of suffocating or suffering heat stroke. The evening temperatures had fallen into the 60s and the vehicle wasn't sitting in sunlight. The soldier figured they could drop an anonymous call to the police once all of this was over, and they could pull the guy from the trunk. Bolan had no qualms killing Xu's people; he had no interest in leaving someone to die slowly, though.

Bolan had come looking for Xu. The man had killed one person in cold blood and left one of Bolan's friends in the hospital. But he still considered the guy a symptom of a larger problem. Xu's boss, Jiang, had pulled a lot of strings and left a lot of people dead. Kassem had killed Briggs and Rabin, that much Bolan knew. He'd brought them justice by hunting down and killing Kassem. Killing Xu would close another hole.

But Bolan knew these acts weren't random. From what he and his fellow Stony Man warriors had pieced together, Jiang had much bigger plans than waxing a few people. He wanted to grab a piece of the Valkyrie missile and the U.S. defense establishment for the benefit of his country. Briggs and Rabin had gotten in the way. It had cost them their lives. Bolan knew others were sure to die, too, before it was all over, unless he took out Jiang. So, yeah, if he got the chance, he'd burn the SOB down.

First he had to deal with Xu. There was no guarantee Bolan would survive. No doubt, the bastard had surrounded himself with a small army. No doubt, Bolan and Grimaldi would have to fight their way through waves of trained and determined hardmen before they could reach their target. Bolan stepped into each battle knowing it could be his last. Maybe this was the day when all went black for him.

Maybe.

Only one way to find out. The soldier headed for the brothel.

BOLAN CIRCLED THE brothel, putting an abandoned building between himself and the target site to cover his approach. It was possible Xu, if he was expecting trouble, had put spotters on the street. At the same time, the soldier recalled Antunes telling him Xu usually kept ten or so guards on site. If that included the three Bolan and Grimaldi already had neutralized, the warriors already had cut Xu's security force by a third. If not, the pair still were going to go up against ten armed thugs. Not great odds, but Bolan had faced much worse and done so alone.

He slipped into an alley and glided along the edge of the nearest building. A huge garbage bin stood in the alley. Beyond it, Bolan could see the top two floors of the brothel rising above the steel trash container. It provided at least some cover for him as he made his way toward the brothel.

When he reached the bin, he knelt behind it, unzipped the gym bag and pulled out an MP-5 and a sound suppressor, acquired through a CIA contact. He threaded the suppressor into the MP-5's barrel and fed another magazine into the weapon. The bag contained two more magazines for the SMG, along with a couple of flash-bang grenades. Bolan looped it over his shoulder and, rising into a crouch, came around the bin. He paused just at the container's edge and sized up the men gathered around the door.

It was the same group he'd seen a few minutes earlier during his recon, their weapons still in plain sight. Two of the gunners were facing his way, though not staring directly at him. He estimated about thirty yards separated him from the gunners.

Once he came into view, the numbers would fall fast. He'd have no time for indecision.

He activated the throat mike.

"I'm about to move," he said.

"Roger that," Grimaldi replied.

Bolan surged out from behind the bin, the MP-5 coughing out a stream of 9 mm Parabellum rounds at the guards.

The first volley fell short, ripping out a ragged line in the pavement a few yards ahead of the guards and kicking up geysers of chewed asphalt.

The hardman with the JS 9 caught sight of Bolan first. He stood fast but laid down a sustained burst from the Chinese SMG and swung the weapon in a horizontal arc. Before the fusillade could reach Bolan, he whipped the MP-5 in the guard's direction and cut him down with a withering burst from the H&K. By now the other two guards were in motion. The man with the shotgun had peeled off and was darting to Bolan's left. The other was fumbling under his jacket for a weapon of some sort, his face a mask of panic.

Bolan took him down with a fast blast from the MP-5. The

storm of bullets ripped into the man's midsection and spun him a quarter turn before he folded to the ground.

Mr. Shotgun was now sprinting at Bolan. Peals of thunder echoed in the alley as the guy fired off a couple of panic rounds. The big American was already darting to the right and firing the MP-5. The volley of steel-jacketed slugs went wide, flying past the shotgun-wielding thug and ricocheting against the brothel's brick exterior.

Dropping into a crouch, Bolan triggered the MP-5 again, maneuvering the SMG in a figure eight pattern. A ragged line of crimson dots appeared across the man's torso. He jerked under the onslaught for a stretched second as the bullets drilled through skin and vital organs. The shotgun slid from his grasp, striking the ground and letting loose a final skyward blast before its former owner collapsed on top of it.

Cursing under his breath, the soldier waded through the kill zone. No doubt the shotgun blasts had alerted Xu and his people that they were under attack. Bolan guessed the front-door guards already were moving in his direction looking to deal retribution to the guy who'd killed their comrades, or at least hoping to keep their boss alive.

Bolan ran up on Mr. Shotgun and dropped to one knee next to the corpse. A lanyard around the corpse's neck carried a security card with a magnetic strip. He yanked it off and wiped the splattered blood on the guy's jeans. He ejected the H&K's nearly spent magazine and reached into the gym bag for another.

Grimaldi's voice buzzed in his ear.

"You're about to have company," the pilot said.

Bolan wheeled around and spotted two of the front-door guards creeping up on him, one in front of the other, hugging the wall of the brothel.

The soldier slammed the fresh magazine into the MP-5 just as one of the hardmen raised a pistol and drew a bead on him.

WHEN GRIMALDI HEARD the first shotgun blast, he knew things were heading south, fast.

The three guards stationed at the front door froze for a microsecond as the blast split the air. An instant later, one of the men began talking rapidly and gestured toward the back of the building. Another of the security team pulled a small SMG from beneath his jacket, while thug number three brought a pistol into view. Both started for the rear of the building. Another shotgun blast rent the air.

The man who'd stayed behind pulled a phone from his jacket pocket and began tapping in a number. His back was turned to Grimaldi.

The pilot moved up to the edge of the building and closed in on the guard. He'd threaded the customized sound suppressor into the barrel of the Browning and stuck the pistol back into the gym bag. He kept his hand inside the bag, his fingers wrapped around the pistol's grip.

By the time he got within twenty feet of the guard, he heard the guy begin speaking into the phone. He drew the Browning from the bag. In the same instant, the sole of his boot scraped against the concrete. The noise registered with the guard, prompting him to turn. His free hand was already drifting underneath his jacket by the time he was facing Grimaldi.

The Browning coughed once, and a hole opened in the guy's forehead, a half inch or so above the left eye. The slug burned a path through the guy's brain before it ripped out the back of his skull. The resulting spray slicked the wall behind with blood and brain matter.

Grimaldi radioed Bolan, alerting him to the two killers coming his way.

He moved around the corner of Xu's building and started down the alley, falling in behind the two shooters.

The nearer man had to have sensed the Stony Man Farm pilot's approach and wheeled around to meet the threat. The hardman's sound-suppressed pistol chugged bullets. The slugs sliced past Grimaldi's head, missing his right ear and his temple by inches.

The Browning coughed twice in Grimaldi's hand. Bullets pierced the other man's torso. He grunted under the onslaught, stumbled sideways, the SMG's barrel canting skyward. His trigger finger tightened again, causing his weapon to churn out another fast burst even as his body withered to the ground.

Even as the guy did a headlong dive into hell, Grimaldi was looking for another target. The third guard already had grabbed some distance. The chatter of his comrade's SMG apparently wasn't enough to stop him in his tracks.

Grimaldi saw the man drawing down on Bolan who was crouched on the ground. Swinging the Browning in the guy's direction, he lined up the shot. His finger tightened on the trigger. He needed to help Striker. One shot should do it.

Before he could squeeze off a round, something in his peripheral vision registered with him, making Grimaldi hesitate for just an instant. Something—a human form—surged at him, seemingly from nowhere. The body slammed into his midsection just as he depressed the Browning's trigger. He lost his footing and the barrel of the pistol arced up as it spit a single round skyward.

BOLAN HEAVED HIMSELF sideways to avoid the thug's first shot. The bullet slapped into the asphalt and would have drilled into the big American had he hesitated a microsecond.

He squeezed off a fast burst at the pistol-wielding thug. The bullets flew just wide enough to miss his attacker's head by inches before they slammed into the brothel's exterior wall.

The Executioner's opponent stood his ground and swung the muzzle of his pistol at the American even as Bolan was adjusting his own aim. The H&K snapped out a punishing burst that savaged the other man's midsection. The man collapsed to the ground in a dead heap.

Bolan heard scuffling to his right. He jerked his head toward the noise and saw a man armed with a knife rushing at Grimaldi.

THE WEIGHT OF his attacker, combined with the angle the guy struck him from, made Grimaldi easy to put down. His body slammed against the cracked asphalt and he grunted in pain.

The man on top of him was big. If he'd had the presence of mind, Grimaldi likely would have put the bastard's weight at 250 pounds, maybe more. And despite his soft appearance the guy was anything but.

Grimaldi brought around the Browning, figuring he could solve the problem with an up-close bullet to the head. The bigger man's hand lashed out and fingers encircled Grimaldi's wrist in a steely grip, squeezing hard enough that the pilot swore his bones were being crushed to dust.

The bigger man drew back his fist, ready to hammer Grimaldi's face.

The fist shot forward, connecting with the pilot's chin. The Stony Man warrior rolled with the punch, but it still felt as though he'd taken a swing from a Louisville Slugger baseball bat.

The fist pulled back again so the guard could deal more punishment to Grimaldi.

The pilot turned his wrist, angling it so the Browning's muzzle was moving in the direction of the other man's head. The pistol coughed once. The guy's body jerked and his head snapped back. He let go of Grimaldi's wrist and brought both hands to his face, slapping them protectively over his forehead.

Grimaldi pushed the guy off, rolled a couple of feet away and stood.

He stared down at the other man, who was writhing on the ground, bloodied hands covering his face. The pilot assumed the slug had creased his opponent's forehead. The

Browning spit a mercy round into the man's chest and his body went still.

He sensed someone approaching, looked up and saw Bolan.

The soldier jerked his head toward a pair of luxury sedans parked next to the building.

"This way."

BOLAN AND GRIMALDI moved through the rear door of the brothel.

The door led into a maintenance room filled with brooms, a couple of electric vacuum cleaners, a sink and a washer and dryer. The johns apparently appreciated clean sheets. While Bolan had used the seized key card to open the door, he saw the door was wired with alarms, and he couldn't be sure his entry hadn't triggered warnings of some kind with the security team.

The soldier noticed that bars covered all the windows, and he wondered if they were to keep intruders out or the hookers in.

The Stony Man warriors crossed the room, their eyes sweeping it for cameras or sensors, and headed for a door on the other side. When they reached the door, Bolan tried the knob. It wouldn't turn. He stepped back, aimed the MP-5 at it and fired a short burst into the space between the knob and the doorjamb. The bullets chewed through the wood, ripped apart the latch and the door swung open.

Seconds later, they were in a long corridor. Bolan heard the slap of shoe soles, lots of them, striking the floor. From inside his pocket, he withdrew a small black box. He thumbed a sequence of numbers on a small keypad on the detonator, bringing it live, and flipped one switch, then a second.

A pair of explosions erupted outside. The force shook dust loose from the ceiling and caused the floor to vibrate. Bolan guessed the blasts had also shattered the windows in the maintenance room, though the guttural roar of the explosions drowned out the sound.

He caught the screeching sound of twisted metal striking the earth and guessed it was the flaming wreckage of the sedans he'd just blown up.

"Xu should call a cab," Grimaldi muttered.

THE WHUMP OF explosions caused Xu to freeze. His entourage of several guards also stopped, forming a protective ring around him. One of his guards stared at the screen of his smartphone for a second.

He turned the device toward Xu. On the screen was a video feed from a security camera. Xu saw a pair of cars, or at least, their remains. Smoke-tinged flames lashed out from the interiors of the ravaged vehicles.

"They took out the cars," the man said.

"I can see that, idiot," Xu snapped.

"What should we do?"

Xu gestured toward the back of the building.

"They probably came through the rear door," he said. He spit out the names of several guards.

"Go find them!" he ordered.

# CHAPTER THIRTY-ONE

Driven by fear and a primitive desire to live, Xu raced through the halls of the brothel until he reached the elevator. Gunfire crackled behind him, occasionally accompanied by the strangled cries of one of his men catching a bullet. He punched the elevator button and, while he waited, pivoted, his AKM held at hip level as he searched for targets.

He knew the American was coming for him, like an unstoppable, almost supernatural force. The man was tearing through Xu's small army of gunners. Once he'd seen his escape vehicle burning in the back alley, Xu knew he was going to need to make a stand. He'd strategically left behind a second small group of his security entourage to further slow the American's progress. But Xu knew the truth: he was just buying time. His adversary wasn't going to stop until they faced each other.

So, fine, Xu would face him. But he'd do so on his terms.

The elevator door opened behind him and he backed into it. Just as the doors closed, he spotted the American come around a corner. Xu heard a bullet strike the elevator door just as it shut, felt his heart skip a beat. The car jerked into motion, and he began his ascent to the fourth floor.

When it shuddered to a halt and the doors parted, Xu jabbed the maintenance stop button on the control panel so the elevator would stay put. He exited the elevator car and prepared for the American's arrival.

ONE OF XU'S shooters darted into Bolan's path from an adjoining corridor. The guy's AKM was spitting a blistering of hot lead at the Stony Man warriors. The bullets drilled through the air next to Bolan, just missing him and Grimaldi. The soldier reciprocated with a punishing barrage of his own from the MP-5 that took the guy down.

Two more gunners entered the corridor, their assault rifles spewing fire and destruction. Grimaldi had traded in the Browning for an Uzi that had been stowed in his duffel bag. The sound-suppressed weapon churned out a wave of fire that scythed down one of the men, while Bolan took down the second with the MP-5.

They burned through another trio of gunners before finally reaching the first-floor elevator. Bolan watched the numbers on the elevator's indicator panel tick up to four and stop.

He guessed Xu would switch off the elevator to limit access to the top floor, forcing the soldier to hike up four flights of stairs to reach him. Even if Bolan moved at a dead run, Xu still had bought himself at least a minute.

"You stay here," Bolan said to Grimaldi. "He may try to double back and escape."

Grimaldi scowled, but nodded in agreement. Bolan moved up the steps as fast as he could without pounding his feet and creating a lot of noise.

By the time he'd reached the third floor, it occurred to him that he was doing exactly what Xu expected. He moved onto the third floor and headed down a long corridor in the direction of the fire escape.

Twenty yards or so ahead, the corridor veered into an L-shaped turn. The soldier rounded it slowly, his SMG held at shoulder level and leading the way.

Another, shorter corridor lay before him, with doors on either side of it. Moving to the nearer door on the right, he opened it and entered the room, and found what he'd been looking for—a window that opened onto the fire escape.

Bolan raised the window and pushed himself through it onto the platform. Moving in a crouch, he made his way to the angled ladder leading to the next floor and climbed onto the next platform. He crouched next to the windows, which were covered in black paint, and listened for any signs of Xu.

He heard nothing.

Bolan studied the window, but saw no wires indicating an alarm. He pulled up on it, but it held fast. Bringing around the MP-5, he drove the butt of the weapon into the glass. He tried to temper the strike, hit the pane just hard enough to crack it. But he misjudged the hit and the brittleness of the glass. The window exploded inward in a shower of sparkling shards of glass.

The Executioner muttered an oath. Using the MP-5 again, he knocked away any remnants of the glass jutting from the frame and climbed through the window.

Enough light filtered in through the opening to provide some limited visibility. Bolan could make out a double bed in one corner, a cushioned armchair and a rectangular coffee table topped by an ashtray and a wine bottle lying on its side. The room stank of perspiration and stale cigarettes.

A short, horizontal slit of light at the bottom edge of the opposite wall told Bolan the location of the door. He crossed the room, pressed an ear against one of its panels and listened, but heard no sounds on the other side. Gripping the doorknob, he turned it slowly and pulled it open.

The door swung inward and Bolan moved into the hallway. He swept the MP-5 from left to right, but saw no threats. After a few yards, another hallway opened to his right and he turned into it. Doors lined both sides of the corridor. Again, he smelled traces of perfume, incense, cigarettes and other things, but it all seemed faint, as though no one had been up here for days at least.

He continued toward the elevator and stairs, guessing Xu was waiting for him there.

The hallway eventually opened into a large room outfitted with a bar, couches and several high-backed leather chairs. The elevator was on the other side of the room, the doors locked open and emitting a soft beep. The stairwell door, located a few yards from the elevator, was closed.

He swept his gaze over the room, but didn't see Xu anywhere.

The soldier crept inside, his movements nearly silent. His brow was creased with confusion. Where the hell was Xu? Had he taken the stairs back to the main floor and escaped?

Bolan was about twenty paces into the room when he heard the click of gun's hammer behind him.

He whirled and spotted the Chinese assassin lining up a shot at him. The gun in Xu's hand cracked and a bullet whizzed just past Bolan's cheek. The soldier replied with a fast burst from the MP-5. The bullets found their target, pounding into Xu's midsection and pushing him into a wall. The gun fell from his fingers and he dropped behind the bar.

Bolan marched across the room, ready to confirm the kill. Before he reached the bar something struck him as wrong. He'd hit the other man in the torso. Where the hell was the blood? He came around the end of the bar and found Xu on all fours and scrambling for his pistol.

The Executioner drove his foot into the other man's face, the toe of his boot striking the other man in the chin. The blow split the skin of Xu's chin and he grunted with pain. He made another grab for the pistol, but Bolan dropped his foot on the other man's hand. This prompted a scream from Xu who spit out a string of expletives in Chinese.

Bolan closed in on his adversary and scooped up the pistol from the floor. Ejecting the magazine, he tossed it aside, then disconnected the slide and threw it in another direction. He dropped what was left of the gun on the floor. Reaching down, he grabbed a handful of Xu's jacket, yanked him to his feet and shoved him against a wall. Xu's jacket parted and Bolan could see that the guy wore a black Kevlar vest.

Bolan spun the other man around and shoved out from behind the bar. Xu, still shaky after having his midsection pounded by 9 mm rounds, stumbled and fell to his knees. Switching the H&K to single-shot mode, Bolan circled the other man and pointed the SMG at him.

"Nice vest," the soldier said. "Too bad it won't help your head. Now, where's Jiang?"

Xu tried to haul himself up from the floor. The movement caused him to grimace in pain. He went still again, other than labored breathing.

"You followed me here? From Athens?"

"Yeah."

"Because I killed the hooker."

"Only the tip of the iceberg," Bolan said. "We both know that. With all the crap you and Jiang are into, her death's just a sideshow. Now, where's Jiang?"

"Fuck off."

The H&K coughed once. A bullet ripped through Xu's pants leg and into his calf, just missing the shinbone. He screamed and tried to cover the wound with his hands.

"Please," Bolan said. "Play tough. I've got a full magazine and nowhere to go. And you've got all kinds of unprotected spots."

"He's here in Rio," Xu said. "He came back two days ago."

"Because?"

"Because…" Xu hesitated. Bolan stepped forward and kicked the guy's injured leg, drawing another scream from Xu. Bolan frowned on torture, but considered this play to be a necessary evil.

"Crazy bastard…"

"You have no idea," Bolan said. "Now, why the hell is he here?"

"He has a meeting. Board members from QF-17 are going to meet with him."

"I find that hard to believe. Why would the executives for

a major defense contractor travel here to meet with a Chinese national?"

"Not to meet with him. To meet with Max Blackwell. They've asked Blackwell to join the board and he agreed. They think they're meeting him to discuss the company. They don't know the rest of it."

"What is the rest of it?"

"I'm bleeding," Xu snapped. He'd clamped his hand over his leg wound. Blood leaked through his fingers and was dripping onto the floor. "Aren't you going to help me?"

"Answer my questions," Bolan said.

"Then you'll help?"

"Answer my questions."

"Bastard. Blackwell and his company, Dark Coast, they're just cutouts." Bolan stayed quiet, wanting the assassin to tell the full story. "That way Jiang can put an American face on all of this."

"But he wants it all?"

The other man shook his head. "Not for himself, he doesn't. Jiang isn't grabbing these companies so he can make money. He wants the technology. He wants China to have the Valkyrie missile and all the technology that comes with it."

"And he thinks QF-17's management will just hand it over. No questions asked."

"Not exactly. This wasn't something he threw together overnight. He's been working on it for a year, gathering information, working up dossiers on them. He's got leverage on the executives, enough to make them follow his orders."

"Like blackmail?"

The other man shook his head. "That might work with a couple of them, but not all. He's going for the jugular. Most of them have families. He'll lay out the plans, give them their marching orders."

"And if they don't comply?"

"He hurts somebody. Maybe a spouse, maybe a child or a

grandchild. It doesn't matter. They've already lost three board members. He makes a threat, they will listen."

Bolan nodded in agreement. "I assume that's where you and your gang come in? Chinese intelligence can order a hit and not implicate its own people in the process."

"Yes."

"Where's the meeting?"

Xu recited an address. The guy had finally pulled himself into a standing position and was propping himself up with his left arm. Bolan was deciding what to do with the guy when Xu's hand drifted out of sight for an instant. When it came back into view, he was holding a pistol. Before he could level the weapon, Bolan's MP-5 spit out a single round and drilled a hole through Xu's forehead, killing him.

# CHAPTER THIRTY-TWO

*New York*

Blackwell exited his limousine and ran across the tarmac to his Cessna CJ4 jet.

As he crossed the pavement, his consternation grew. The pilot and copilot usually stood next to the stairs to welcome him aboard the craft. Instead, he saw two men dressed in blue coveralls standing next to the starboard wing.

Neither seemed to pay much attention to him as he neared the plane, which made him angrier.

He paused at the stairs, put his hands on his hips and peered inside the plane. Where the hell were the pilot and copilot?

Blackwell turned to the ground crew. One was bulky. Not fat, but strong-looking. The other looked well-muscled and fit. One had gray hair and the other blond.

"You there," he said. "Where's the pilot?"

The gray-haired man cupped a hand behind his ear, the palm pointing at Blackwell. *"Que?"*

"The pilot!" Blackwell said. "Where the hell is the pilot?"

The gray-haired man shook his head in confusion. He smiled and began walking in Blackwell's direction. The millionaire noticed that the blond man stood still and gave him a withering stare. He probably doesn't understand English, either, Blackwell thought. He clenched and unclenched his jaw in irritation. He was already behind schedule and he knew Jiang was getting restless.

Blackwell was slated to meet with the board in a matter of hours. Without him, there was no meeting and Jiang would have to walk away from everything he'd accomplished. Certainly a part of Blackwell would have enjoyed seeing his blackmailer fail. But as a practical matter, he had a feeling that, if Jiang failed, he'd make sure no one lived to tell about it.

So, while Blackwell wanted the payday Jiang had promised, he wanted even more to live through all this. For that reason, he planned to tread carefully over the next seventy-two hours and follow Jiang's orders to the letter.

The gray-haired man almost had reached him now.

The guy's easy smile suddenly melted away. He reached out, and before Blackwell could react, grabbed hold of his upper arm, spinning him and shoving him toward the plane's fuselage.

"Hey!" Blackwell snapped. "What the hell is going on?"

"Shut up," the man said. Blackwell felt the guy loop something around his right wrist. He yanked hard to get his arm free. Something hard smacked into his kidney, caused an explosion of pain. His knees buckled and struck the pavement.

White spots danced across his vision and the contents of his stomach began to push their way back up. By the time someone pulled him back to his feet, his hands had been secured behind his back. The men in coveralls stood on either side of Blackwell and led him to the stairs. With faltering steps, he climbed onto the plane.

BLANCANALES GUIDED BLACKWELL to the plane's side door and pushed him through it, following a step behind.

Escorting Blackwell to one of the jet's high-backed seats, he shoved the guy into one, took a step back and stared down at him.

"Who are you?" Blackwell demanded. "Are you kidnapping me? Is that what this is? Are you insane? You know who I am, right?"

"Not a kidnapping. Sorry. We're here to speak with you. Let you get some things off your sunken, hairless little chest."

Blackwell, his jaw hanging down, stared at Blancanales for a second before the light clicked on.

"You're cops? I'll have your fucking badges for this."

Blancanales greeted that with a smile. "Good luck with that one, tough guy."

"What does that mean? You are the police, aren't you?"

Blancanales shook his head. He pointed at one of the cabin windows on the starboard side. Two men in suits were dragging Blackwell's chauffeur from the limousine.

"Those are cops," Blancanales said. "My friend and I are something else entirely."

"What the hell? Where are my pilots? I have an attendant. Where is she? What have you done with them?"

"Relax, Max. Your crew is fine. The federal government suggested they keep a low profile for the next couple of days, and they will do just that. No one's going to hurt them. Quite the contrary, Uncle Sam sprang for nice rooms at the Waldorf. No one's going to hurt them."

"Hurt them? Fuck them! What about me?"

"It's all about you, Max. I mean, right? Sucks, too, because your future's become a complicated issue."

BLANCANALES LOWERED HIMSELF into a seat across from Blackwell. By now, the plane's interior had become a hive of activity. The CIA had supplied two pilots, both willing to fly anywhere without asking uncomfortable questions. The unmistakable hum of jet engines warming up filled the craft.

Blackwell glared at Blancanales when he sat down. The Stony Man warrior had left the man to stew for a while, figuring it'd heighten his anxiety and make him more pliable. A few seconds later, Lyons bulled his way down the aisle, brushed past Blancanales and dropped into the next seat with a grunt. The former L.A. detective looked like he was ready to blow a gasket, his face flushed red, his eyes narrowed into slits.

Blackwell's gaze flicked from Blancanales to Lyons and back again.

"I want to speak with a lawyer," he said.

The corner of Lyons's lip turned up in a snarl and he leaned forward. "You little…"

Blanacanales held up a hand to silence him.

"You have a lawyer?" Blancanales asked.

"Of course I have a lawyer. I have several on retainer, in fact."

"You can take your lawyer and shove him," Lyons interjected. "In case my friend didn't educate you, let me. We don't arrest people. That means we don't read people their rights, which means you don't get a fucking lawyer. What you will get is my foot shoved so far up your ass it pops out your mouth. If that sounds like a square deal to you, stand up, turn around and prepare for liftoff."

Blackwell stared at Lyons for several seconds, but said nothing.

"What my friend is trying to say…" Blancanales said.

"What I am trying to say is you screwed yourself. You sold out your country, which puts you several layers below whale shit. There are no lawyers who can help you. You can't call a senator and have them pull strings. You are screwed like a ten-dollar whore."

Blancanales nodded at Lyons. "What he said."

"What do you want from me?"

"Why are you going to Brazil? What's the draw there?"

"I have a meeting."

"With?" Blancanales asked. "We know about Jiang. Is that why you're going there?"

Blackwell nodded.

"And you're going to discuss what?"

"I can't go into that."

Lyons was a blur coming out of his chair. His fist arced around in a roundhouse punch and connected with Blackwell's jaw. It took the man a couple of moments to recover from the hit. When he turned back to the Able Team warriors, a red spot had formed along his jawline and his eyes looked unfocused. He coughed a few times before spitting blood on the floor.

"You son of a bitch," he said, his voice low. "I'll make sure you die for that."

"You're lucky I pulled the punch," Lyons said. "Otherwise, they'd be wiring your jaw up even as we speak. Now, my friend asked you a question. Why don't you answer him? We know Jiang has set up a meeting in Brazil. What the hell can you tell us about that?"

Blackwell shrugged.

"If I tell you everything," he said, "what's in it for me?"

Had the situation not been so dire, Blancanales would have laughed at that one. It was obvious Blackwell had no idea who he was dealing with.

Lyons leaned forward, his elbows resting on his thighs, his lips peeled back in an ugly smile.

"In it for you? Hell, that's easy. Not a damn thing. You think this is a negotiation? It isn't. You have nothing to bargain with. You get nothing. No, wait, I take that back. You get a choice. Either you can tell me what I want to know, or you can get the shit kicked out of you, and then you tell me what I want to know. Sweet choice, right?"

A sheen of perspiration had formed on the financier's forehead. He licked his lips. "You can't tell me what to do. I'm Max Blackwell."

"Lord of the jungle? Master of the universe? How about dead douche walking, because that's what you are."

Blackwell swallowed hard.

"Jiang wants to take over QF-17."

"For the Valkyries," Lyons said. "Right, we know that."

"Oh, you knew that? Okay. Well, they're supposed to have a secondary offering. You know what that is, right?"

"Humor me."

"Yes, I doubt you own a checking account, let alone stock."

"I'm sure you're a fucking laugh riot at the yacht club," Lyons shot back. "But here, on this plane, I am in charge. Understood? Now explain a secondary offering to me."

"When a company first sells stock it's called an initial public offering."

"An IPO," Blancanales said.

"Right. A subsequent sale of new stock is called a secondary offering. QF-17 plans to hold one of those. They want the money to help pay for a new plant in South Carolina to build the missile."

"Okay," Lyons said.

"Our entity, the one I control with him, already owns some shares of QF-17, not quite a controlling interest, but a decent amount of stock."

"But you're going to buy like hell in the next couple of days."

"Right."

"Which is probably why they tapped you for the board," Lyons said.

"Exactly. They knew I was getting a decent stake in the company. I'd made some noises before about stirring up trouble, introducing an alternative slate of directors, demanding they fire management, that sort of thing."

"So they asked you on their board to appease you."

"It wouldn't have appeased me," Blackwell said. "You don't appease me. Not for long."

"Stop it, pencil neck," Lyons growled. "You're scaring me."

"You'd better be enjoying this," Blackwell countered. "I'll have you dealt with. A couple of phone calls from me and—"

Lyons's hand flashed out and he struck the other man with an open-palmed slap to the cheek. Blackwell pulled out his monogrammed handkerchief and spit blood into it.

"The point," Blancanales warned. "Get to the point. Or this guy's going to tear you apart."

"The whole point of the meeting is to bring together some of the QF-17 executives—not many, just a couple—and lay things out for them."

"Wait, you mean come clean about things?" Blancanales asked incredulously.

"Not exactly. They still weren't going to know about Jiang directly. They were going to meet with me at Jiang's place in Brazil. Jiang would be there. But I'd introduce him as one of my executives and an American citizen. He'd stay in the background, keep quiet and watch."

"Okay."

"I'd lay out for them just exactly what I expected as a board member."

"And it would include unlimited access to the Valkyrie project," Blancanales said.

"Essentially, yes."

"Which, of course, they'd say no to, right?"

"Maybe."

"And you guys would just dry up and blow away."

"Hardly. That's where Jiang and his friends would come in. He's been building dossiers on these executives for a year or more. He knows their families, their friends, their strengths and their weaknesses. All of it. If one of their children goes to a private school, Jiang knows exactly what time they leave, the route they take, everything. One of them, the chairman, has a daughter who attends college in New York. Jiang could use his connections to have her disappear one day and end up dead of a heroin overdose, maybe twist the knife a little and leak her death photos to a gossip websites in the U.S. or Israel."

"And you're okay with this?" Blancanales asked.

Blackwell looked surprised by the question. "It's all a means to an end. We have a goal and we need to meet it."

"And you were going to lay all this out for them in Brazil?"

The financier shrugged. "More or less. Hey, we're offering them a deal. If they don't want to take it, well—" he spread his hands in a helpless gesture "—they have to face the consequences of their decisions."

"Consequences?" Blancanales echoed, his voice incredulous. "You call murdering someone's kid a consequence?"

Blackwell hesitated, as though he needed to think hard for the right answer.

"Like I said, we have a goal," Blackwell said.

"And in your case, the goal is to betray the United States," Blancanales said.

"Not the goal," Blackwell countered, shaking his head. "It's just a way to reach the goal. You really aren't getting it, are you?"

"Oh, we get it," Blancanales said. He glanced over at Lyons and saw the guy's neck and cheeks had turned cherry-red. His fists were clenched. "See, we're all about consequences, especially when it comes to guys like you, the ones willing to betray your country. The ones willing to hurt innocent people for your own gain."

"Consequences? What? Like jail? I'm not going to jail, you idiot."

"You're right. You're going somewhere else. But first we need you to make a phone call."

LYONS DIDN'T CONSIDER himself a hyper-emotional guy. But, when it came to righteous rage, he knew he carried a bottomless well of the stuff, and he didn't bother to hide it. When he'd been an L.A. cop, he'd never bothered to hide it when a suspect disgusted him. When it came to interrogation, some guys had used finesse and even manipulation to get a confession or a critical piece of information. That approach had never worked for Lyons, especially when it came to dealing with a dead-eyed psychopath whose only regret was getting caught.

Even a man with no soul was afraid of dying, and once you took things to that level, the cooperation flowed like a proverbial mountain stream.

Lyons was staring at Blackwell, who seemed oblivious to him. Call it blissfully unaware, because Lyons knew he was about to rock the little bastard's privileged world.

Blackwell was saying to Blancanales, "You want me to make a phone call? And who might I be calling?"

"Jiang."

"And I would do that because?"

"Because…" Blancanales began.

Lyons cut his friend off with a wave of the hand and surged from his chair.

"What do you think, you little shit? You think this is a negotiation? Is that it?" When he'd closed the gap between them he bent down, his face inches from Blackwell's. "You think you have some advantage here?"

"You need me to make a call," Blackwell said. "So you need me."

Lyons's mouth twisted into a cold smile.

"We need a contact made from your phone," Lyons said. "We don't need your voice. Ever heard of texting, douche bag?"

Blackwell licked his lips and Lyons saw uncertainty flicker in the guy's stare. The ex-cop stood up to his full height, reached into his pocket and drew out a Gerber folding knife. He flicked it open and the financier flinched at the metallic sound of the blade clicking into place. Lyons grabbed a handful of the other man's hair, brittle with gel, and shoved Blackwell's face downward until he could see the man's bound hands. The man grunted.

Lyons looked over a shoulder, caught Blancanales's stare and nodded toward the door.

"You and the crew, vamoose," Lyons growled. "Max and I need some quality time."

Blancanales nodded, rose from his chair. He gathered the crew and led them from the airplane.

"What in the hell are you doing?" Blackwell sputtered. "Do you know who I am? You hurt me and there will be hell to pay!"

Lyons brought the knife down. The motion caused Blackwell to jerk in anticipation of the knife plunging into his back. Instead, Lyons slipped the blade's tip under the plastic handcuffs and cut them open. Releasing his hold on the other man's hair, Lyons stepped back as the guy's torso sprang up. The Able Team commander took a step back and let a couple of seconds pass, figuring if Blackwell was going to attack he'd do it then.

The guy stayed planted in his seat, rubbed his wrists and stared at Lyons.

The Stony Man warrior gave the guy a second to collect himself, then gestured at the phone with the tip of the Gerber's blade.

"The phone call," Lyons said. "Now."

"And what do I say?"

Lyons told him. The other man picked up the phone, punched in a number with his index finger and waited several seconds before a connection was made. Lyons heard a woman's voice answer and he saw Blackwell scowl.

"Where is he?"

The woman said something that Lyons couldn't quite understand, though he thought he heard the woman say "shooting range" and a couple of other words that struck the warrior as unimportant.

Blackwell cut her off. "We're getting ready to leave," he said. "Yes, I know we're late. It couldn't be helped. We had mechanical problems."

He and the woman spoke for another minute or so. The entire time, Lyons held his gaze, and when the conversation started to drag on too long, the warrior signaled for the guy to cut it short by making a slashing motion across his throat with the index finger of his left hand.

As Blackwell wrapped up the phone conversation, Lyons casually set the Gerber knife on the armrest of the passenger's seat nearest him, turned and took a couple of steps away, grabbing some distance from the small group of seats. Though not as cramped as a typical commercial airline, one lined on either side by seats, the cabin still left little room for maneuvering.

Lyons heard the creak of a leather shoe, followed by the sound of a sole scuffing the carpet and a grunt of exertion.

He stepped to one side and whipped around. The blade, gleaming under the cabin lights, surged past him, missing his chest by several inches. The force of the thrust had left Blackwell off balance, his right knee bent, his right arm hyperextended, his ribs exposed.

Lyons could have tipped the guy over with just a gentle push.

Instead, he balled the fingers of his right hand into a fist and drove it hard into Blackwell's ribs, which snapped under the pressure of the blow. Blackwell staggered, belched out the contents of his lungs and crashed to his knees.

Lyons reached down, clamped one of his big hands over the other guy's face and the other on the back of his head, and twisted violently.

The financier's body went slack. Lyons released his hold on the guy and let his limp form collapse to the ground.

He sensed someone looking at him. Jerking his head to

the left, he saw Blancanales standing on the other end of the cabin, his expression neutral.

"Awkward," Blancanales said. "You need me to come back later?"

# CHAPTER THIRTY-THREE

Just a few more hours, Jiang told himself, and it all would come together.

He stood on a patch of bare earth on the grounds of what once had been a cattle ranch. He brought his hand to his forehead to shield his eyes from the midday sun's glare, and scanned the sky for approaching aircraft but saw none.

A group of QF-17 executives were supposed to arrive in four hours or so. Blackwell, on the other hand, was supposed to have arrived an hour ago from New York. The American's tardiness made Jiang nervous. Blackwell had sent him a text blaming a minor maintenance problem for the delay. The explanation seemed plausible enough, but Jiang still found himself wondering. He was so close. He couldn't allow anything to divert him from his goal.

His cigarette had burned down nearly to the filter. He plucked it from his mouth and tossed it onto the ground. Turning to his right, he exhaled a column of smoke through his mouth. The white-gray smoke rose up and slowly swirled around his eyes, stinging them. Through the haze, he stared at the collection of weapons arrayed on the table.

Selecting an old favorite, an Uzi, he chambered a round and took a couple of steps closer toward the targets that lined the other end of the range. The five silhouette targets stood about forty feet from him. Bringing the Uzi to hip level, he squeezed the trigger. The Israeli-made submachine gun ground through a third of its magazine. Bullets from the concentrated burst pierced the center circle of the nearest target. Jiang snapped to his right and fired off another burst into another target, this time stitching a diagonal line from the target's left hip to its right shoulder. By the time he'd emptied the weapon, it had torn through the third silhouette's center mass and the head of the fourth circle.

Turning, he walked over the spent shell casings littering the ground as he returned to the table and set down the Uzi among the other weapons. A Beretta 92 was holstered on his right hip. He wanted to blow through a few more magazines of ammo before going inside and changing for his upcoming meetings.

A young Chinese man stood near the table. Jiang snapped his fingers and gestured at the line of targets. The young man grabbed several new sheets and moved quickly to change out the targets.

He hadn't peeled off his ear protection yet. But he could sense someone approaching his back. He whirled around and found Wong Mei-Xing walking across the hard-packed earth, her face a mask of worry.

Pulling off his headphones, he set them aside.

"What's wrong?"

"It's Xu," she said.

"What about him?"

She stopped just a couple of feet from him. "He's dead."

Jiang took a step back, shocked by the news.

"Dead? What happened to him?"

She cast her eyes downward and shook her head, as though trying to piece together the story while also disbelieving it.

"He was shot. It happened at his place in Rio, the one near the docks. Everyone was shot."

"Everyone?"

"Not everyone," she said. "The women and the customers appear to have gotten out fine. Most of them have dispersed and we have no idea where they went."

"Find them," Jiang said. "Last thing I need is a bunch

of mouthy hookers running around telling everything they know."

"Of course."

"But you said 'everyone.'"

"His entire security team is gone. Our information says the place was littered with bodies. Whoever it was took no money, no weapons. There was five kilos of cocaine hidden in there, weapons, hundreds of thousands of dollars in cash. The police recovered all of it." She swallowed and glanced up at him. "All the laptops are missing, though. From what little I know, they found no cell phones in the place. Tablet computers, hard drives, all of it is gone."

Jiang muttered a curse.

"All our information," he said. "It's been compromised."

She nodded in agreement.

"It had to be the American," he said.

"Or maybe the CIA."

"No, this is the American, the one from Athens. The one who killed Kassem in Algeria."

"Matt Cooper."

"Yes."

Wong closed her eyes. "He probably knows how to find you," she said.

"I can deal with him."

"Perhaps..." She paused.

"Perhaps what? Say it!"

"Perhaps we should go underground. You have the place in Sudan."

He brought his hand around in a wide arc and delivered a stinging slap to her cheek. The force of the blow whipped her head to one side, causing her to stumble. She yelped in pain and surprise. When she looked back at him, he could see the slap had left an angry scarlet mark on her cheek. Her eyes burned white-hot with anger. Her breath came in hard pulls through clenched teeth, and her fingers curled into fists.

He set his palm on the Beretta's grip and pinned her under his gaze.

"I will not leave," he said, his voice even. "I will not hide. I will not run. QF-17 is going to have its initial public offering in three days. There will never be another chance like this. This will move forward. Just the suggestion of running shames me."

He expected her to apologize. Instead, she silently glared at him for several seconds. Her quiet defiance surprised and angered him. He considered fisting the Beretta and taking her out with a shot to the head, but checked himself. There'd be time for that later, he assured himself.

"Summon more security," he commanded. "If the American comes here, I want to make sure he dies."

JIANG FIRED TWO more magazines through the Uzi before calling it a day at the range. Setting down the weapon, he unloaded the gun, set the empty magazines on the table. Gesturing for one of his attendants, he ordered the man to clean and store all the weapons.

Jiang headed for the house and pondered the meeting set for later in the day. It wasn't his style to sit back and let someone else take control, particularly someone like Blackwell. In this situation, though, he felt he had little choice but to keep a low profile rather than derail their efforts. Besides, if the QF-17 executives took a hard line, he would have the chance to speak up, to describe for them in great detail the hell that awaited their loved ones if they refused to play along. He almost hoped one of them would try to make a stand so he could step off the sidelines and destroy them.

Jiang had sweated while standing on the range, shooting. Best to take a shower and change clothes before the others began arriving, he told himself.

Just as he stepped onto the brick patio that surrounded his Olympic-size pool, his phone vibrated. He pulled it from his belt, stared at the screen and frowned. It was Xu's number. But the man was dead. Had the police recovered his phone? Were they combing through the numbers stored in the memory, looking for leads to the killings? An instant later, Jiang remembered what Wong had said. All the phones, the laptops and other hardware had been taken from the brothel.

He clicked on the phone. "What?"

"Hello, Jiang," a male voice answered.

"Who is this?" Jiang demanded.

"I think you know who it is," the caller said.

"Is this Cooper?"

"Are you ready for me?"

"I've been ready for you, Cooper. But you seem to go after everyone but me. Perhaps you're scared?"

"Petrified," the American replied.

There was something in the American's voice, cold, confident and deadly. Jiang shuddered. Instinctively, he looked around to determine if anyone had seen it. A second later, an idea formed in his head and he walked briskly toward the house. He just needed to keep the guy talking.

"You killed Xu," he said.

"Yeah."

"And took his phone."

"Among other things."

"I don't get it, Cooper," Jiang said. "I never took you for a thief. My sources say that you work for the Justice Department. Why take those things?"

"I take all kinds of things, Jiang."

There was something in Cooper's tone that further unsettled Jiang, sent alarm bells clanging. "What does that mean?"

"There's more than one way to cripple a man, friend. You just need to know where to hit him."

"You're talking in riddles," Jiang said, his irritation rising. "You're making no sense."

"Yeah? You'll understand soon enough. But you won't like what you learn. Your buddy Xu sure didn't."

The line went dead. Jiang, now moving through the kitchen, halted and stared at the phone for a stretched second. What had Cooper meant by all of that? Jiang passed through a dining room and into a large living room. He found three of his men sitting on the couch in front of a big-screen television, watching a soccer game.

He walked to the nearest one, a man named Bo Chen. Bo was a beefy guy with his hair trimmed into a flattop. Drawing his arm back, Jiang tossed the phone at the guy's head. His target batted the phone away, sending it skittering across the floor. If the assault pissed him off, the guy's facial expression remained calm.

"I got a call from Xu's phone." The guy opened his mouth to speak and Jiang waved him off. "Yeah, I know he's dead. Shut up and listen. It wasn't him who called. It was the man who killed him. Got it?"

Bo nodded his understanding. The other men, both of whom had been lounging when Jiang first entered the room, now were sitting upright, staring at their leader.

"Get a track on Xu's phone number. You can do that, right? Get a track on his number and track it down."

The guy nodded again.

"Good. And let me know when you find it."

Without waiting for the man's reaction, Jiang wheeled around and marched from the room. A plan was forming in his head. The American thought he was smart, using Xu's phone to torment Jiang? Thought he'd gotten one over on him? Cooper had underestimated him. It would prove to be a fatal mistake for the American.

AFTER HE'D SHOWERED and changed, Jiang adjourned to his office and settled in behind his big desk. Unlocking it, he pulled open the top right-hand drawer. He took from it a

Smith & Wesson Bodyguard BG380 pistol. The weapon carried six .380 cartridges in the clip and another in the chamber. It was outfitted with an Insight laser for targeting. He clipped the holstered weapon onto the waist of his pants, in the small of his back.

A knock sounded at the door. He stood and said, "Come in."

Bo entered the room. He walked up to Jiang's desk and stopped a foot or so away from it. Jiang stared into the other man's face and found it, as always, devoid of any emotion.

"We found the phone."

Jiang nodded.

"It's in a warehouse."

"In Rio?"

The guy shook his head.

"Belem."

"What?"

"Forty-five minutes from here."

"Okay," Jiang said. "Get a team together. Eight, maybe ten men. Hit the place. Take him out."

"Understood," the other man replied.

A PAIR OF black crew wagons crept up on the warehouse. Almost in unison, the doors of the cars flew open, and the killers scurried from inside the vehicle and moved toward the building. One man worked on jimmying the lock while the others circled around him, waiting for him to complete his work. Thirty seconds later, he succeeded and the door came free. He stepped aside and motioned for the others to enter the structure.

The last gunner slipped into the building and closed the door.

Ten seconds later, a rumble sounded from within the building. The structure shook for an instant before orange-and-yellow columns of flames shot through the windows.

Grim-faced, Bolan stepped out of the shadows, the detonator in his hand. He watched as fire began to consume the building, choking the sky with a thick, oily black smoke.

He'd left Xu's phone inside the building, figuring Jiang would track the device. He'd counted nine thugs moving into the building. That meant he'd just taken a big chunk out of Jiang's forces.

Now it was time to go for the big man.

"THE WHOLE TEAM is dead?" Jiang asked in a voice tinged with disbelief.

Wong nodded. "Every last one of them is gone," she said. "It was a trap from the beginning."

"And I walked into it. Is that what you're saying?"

She shook her head. "I'm not saying that."

"Where the hell is Blackwell? Has anyone heard from him?"

"No."

Jiang ground his teeth together as his thoughts began to race through his head. The whole thing was falling apart. Despite all his careful planning and work, the whole damn thing was disintegrating right before his eyes. Maybe he should follow Wong's advice and leave. They could hop on his private jet and head for Macau Island. He had a casino there. They could keep their heads down, wait for the storm to pass.

No, he told himself. If he failed at this, there likely would be no second chances. The Chinese government had trusted him with an operation of massive importance and it was failing.

His telephone beeped once, announcing that he'd received an email. Frowning, he grabbed the phone, tapped on the screen a couple of times until he'd opened it. His heart skipped a beat. It was from Xu's account, which probably meant it was from Cooper.

"Check your accounts," the email read. "Dark Coast is broke."

Jiang suddenly felt light-headed and he stumbled back a step, bumping into the edge of his bar. He slammed the phone onto the top of the bar. He caught the look of concern in Wong's expression, the unspoken question it conveyed.

"Check our accounts," he said.

"Which ones?"

"All of them," Jiang shouted.

FIFTEEN MINUTES LATER, Wong looked up from her tablet computer. Her eyes were wide with fear and shock. She opened her mouth to speak, her lips working for a second or two before she could form words.

"It's all gone," she said. "The money, the stock we'd acquired. It's all gone."

Jiang started to say something, but froze. He heard the rattle of autofire outside. He looked at Wong, who had jumped up from her seat and was moving to the nearest window for a look.

"They've come for us," she said.

# CHAPTER THIRTY-FOUR

Bolan had learned many lessons as he'd fought his endless war. One of them was the value of breaking an enemy long before you engaged him face-to-face.

It sometimes was a risky proposition. A man with nothing left to lose could be a formidable and tenacious foe, especially if he had time to ponder his losses, realize he had nothing left to lose. But a man still in the process of losing everything labored under the illusion he could stem the tide, stop the bleeding, rebound and even thrive. He was still in shock, trying to assimilate all the things happening to him, wondering how to respond. Even a man as strong as Jiang would lose his mental footing under the barrage of setbacks he was facing.

Bolan was counting on it.

The soldier tossed the grappling hook onto the wall and heard it strike something. He gave it a tug, found it was firmly in place and scaled up the side of the wall. When he reached the top, he paused and swept his eyes over the grounds while Grimaldi climbed up behind him.

Swinging his legs over the side of the wall, Bolan lowered himself until he was hanging by his fingertips before letting go and falling to the ground. Grimaldi, who'd covered him as he'd lowered himself, followed while Bolan watched for Jiang's men.

The pair distanced themselves from each other and headed for the house. Bolan had come here wanting to hunt down Jiang. They'd been able to divert the plane filled with QF-17 executives, and Blancanales and Lyons had intercepted Blackwell before he could cause more havoc. Bolan knew the Valkyries wouldn't fall into the wrong hands, but he wouldn't rest until the man who'd set these events in motion was dead.

The warriors had covered a dozen or so yards when the mansion's front door swung open and a trio of gunners came into view. The thugs immediately began unloading their weapons when they saw the intruders. However, their spray-and-pray method of combat didn't produce results. The bullets bit into the ground in front of Bolan and Grimaldi, destroying the landscaping and accomplishing little else. Two of them were moving through Bolan's field of fire. He cut loose with the MP-5 and hosed the gunners down with a punishing burst from the SMG.

At his left, Grimaldi had dropped into a crouch and was firing off a burst from his M-16. The bullets lanced through the air and pierced the third shooter, who danced crazily under the vicious swarm of 5.56 mm rounds. The thug's own assault rifle fired into the air, chewing into the mansion's wooden facade.

Bolan sprinted up the front steps and moved in on the front door. When he was just a few feet from the entrance, another gunner came into view, the guy maneuvering his AK-47 to acquire Bolan as a target. The Executioner knocked the guy down with another burst from the MP-5. The soldier went through the door, stepping over the hardman's corpse, and rolled into the foyer. Grimaldi followed behind him, covering Bolan's six.

Two more shooters sprinted into view. One of them let out a loud war cry and ran directly for Bolan, his submachine gun spitting autofire. The bullets sizzled just past Bolan's cheek, and the gunner's poor marksmanship gave the soldier a chance to unload a burst into the thug's midsection, the spray of bullets eviscerating him. The second man squeezed off a frantic volley of slugs at Bolan and Grimaldi. The Ex-

ecutioner dropped into a crouch, darted right and took the
guy down with a sustained burst from the MP-5.

Gunshots at his six prompted Bolan to wheel around in
time to see Grimaldi hosing down three more shooters with
his M-16. Gun smoke hung in the air and spent shell casings
were arrayed all over the floor.

One of the men Grimaldi had shot was writhing on the
floor. Bolan moved past Grimaldi, knelt next to the guy and
waved the MP-5's barrel at him.

"Where's Jiang?" the soldier barked.

The guy smiled up at him, blood trailing down from the
corner of his mouth. "You're too late."

The thrumming of an engine reached Bolan's ears and he
shot Grimaldi a look.

"Helicopter," Grimaldi said unnecessarily.

Bolan uncoiled from the floor and surged out the front
door. He reloaded the MP-5 as he exited the building. The
whirling rotor blades were just rising up into view of the
rooftop, the rotor wash whipping around the tree branches.
The side door of the craft was open and Jiang stood in it, his
body secured by a harness. Jiang squeezed off a long burst
from his assault rifle and swept the weapon in a long arc. The
murderous onslaught rained down on Bolan and Grimaldi,
forcing them to run in separate directions, each moving in
a zig-zag pattern.

When Jiang's magazine ran dry, the fiery rain ended.
Bolan raised the MP-5 and cut loose with a fast, final burst.
A couple of slugs struck the helicopter's body, sparked and
whined before they spun away. The chopper continued its rise.

Bolan saw the door slam closed and knew he'd lost Jiang.
For now.

# CHAPTER THIRTY-FIVE

*Macau Island*

The courier arrived just as Jiang downed his second whiskey on the rocks.

The man's slim body was clad in a dark blue suit. A tie with diagonal red-and-blue stripes was set against a gleaming white shirt. He greeted Jiang with a nod and muttered a name that matched the one Jiang had been told to expect.

Jiang offered the man from Beijing a seat.

The guy shook his head.

He offered a whiskey and was similarly rebuffed.

The man plucked his glasses from his face, folded them and stuffed them into his breast pocket. Several of Jiang's personal security detail were seated around the room. The man ran his gaze over each of them, his lip curling slightly as though he were looking at something unclean.

Jiang felt his hands curl into fists.

"If you won't drink my alcohol and you won't sit on my furniture," Jiang said, "tell me why you are here. Or get out."

Jiang heard someone in the room snicker. The man fixed him with a hard stare and a scowl, apparently meant to intimidate. Jiang kept his own face a stony mask.

The other man pursed his lips, and the lines on his forehead deepened for a moment. Apparently speaking didn't come easily to this low-level bureaucrat.

"The American who caused so much havoc in Greece, Algeria and Brazil is coming here."

Jiang felt himself stiffen. A cold sensation raced down his spine, and he felt the hair prickle on the back of his neck. He cast his eyes down at his drink and stared at the white rectangle undulating on the whiskey's surface, a reflection of the fluorescent light overhead.

He could feel his guards' eyes on him. He guessed they were looking for his reaction, trying to gauge if he was scared. If he panicked, it was only a matter of time before others did, too. Before they realized he wasn't really in control. Once that happened, he could expect one of two outcomes. They'd either abandon him and look for an employer with some balls. Or one of them would sense an opening and take it. They'd put a knife in his back or a bullet in his head, maybe even take over his operation. None of them had the brains to run the operation, he assured himself. That didn't insulate him against a mutiny, though. He'd met plenty of people whose ambition dwarfed their intellect but still fueled their decisions.

Regardless, the end result was the same. Him dead. He'd lose everything he'd worked for. Unacceptable.

He cleared his throat and hoped his voice came out sure and strong.

"When is he coming?"

"Soon."

"Be more specific."

"No."

"Because?"

"Because we don't know."

"How do you know this much?"

"Sources."

"I need to know more."

The other man shook his head. "Beijing says otherwise. I've told you what your country wants you to know."

Jiang felt his cheeks and neck burn hot with humiliation. He glanced at a couple of his men and noticed a couple of them avert their eyes. He could feel he was losing control of the situation, and he needed to do something.

"If Beijing doesn't know…"

"Of course we know. We have sources."

Jiang nodded. He looked at a couple of his men then back at the Ministry of State Security courier. "So Beijing knows when the American is coming here. The MSS knows how and where he is arriving, this man who has killed several of its countrymen. But it just doesn't want to tell us."

"That's not how it is."

"Yes, I believe it is. I believe that the MSS, for reasons that escape me, wants to leave these men, faithful servants of China, to face off against a murderer. And the MSS doesn't have the decency to at least give them enough information to prepare. Or maybe the MSS is just so incompetent that it really doesn't know."

Gripping the arms of his chair, he pushed himself erect and took a step toward the other man.

The courier swallowed hard but held his ground. Jiang's gaze drifted past the courier's shoulder until he caught the eye of one of his hardmen. He gave the guy a slight nod and two of his men converged on the messenger, each grabbing an arm.

The man shot Jiang a questioning look.

"It's really a shame," Jiang said. "You shouldn't have pulled a gun on me."

The courier struggled against the men holding him.

"What are talking about? I did no such thing!"

"That's not what Beijing will hear."

Jiang drew the Beretta, pointed the muzzle at the other man's chest and pulled the trigger. The bullet tore through the man's torso and drilled into one of the overstuffed couches. A crimson spray exploded from the man's back, splattering blood on the furniture and the floor. Jiang noticed some dark flecks of blood on the tips of his shoes. He gestured for a towel.

"Dispose of the body," he barked. "Then get back here. We have to prepare for the American."

# CHAPTER THIRTY-SIX

The double glass doors slid open and Bolan moved into the casino, about five minutes behind the Chinese courier.

NSA had initially caught wind of the courier's mission about twenty-four hours ago. Fort Meade had sent the translated dispatches from Beijing to the U.S. President. The Man, in turn, had shipped the information to Brognola and Stony Man Farm.

The soldier wore a black linen suit with a black T-shirt. Underneath the jacket he carried the Beretta in its shoulder sling. There were extra magazines in his jacket pockets.

A Gerber folding knife was stowed in his front left pants pocket. He hoped the casino's security system didn't include metal detectors, and none were evident.

Sunglasses with black, rectangular frames covered his ice-blue eyes, and the soldier had streaked his hair with gray. He had also adopted the halting gait of someone plagued by a chronic injury. Padding in his jacket made his shoulders look rounded and weak. His jacket carried the faint smell of stale beer and cologne.

Bolan knew the disguise alone wasn't enough. But years ago he had mastered role camouflage, the ability to blend into and function in strange and hostile environments, even when surrounded by people who wanted to kill him. It was as much about attitude, the way he carried himself as anything else.

The soldier scanned the casino and found a whirlwind of activity. Bells rang on slot machines. Lights flashed red, green and yellow on screens. People milled around between blackjack and roulette tables or sat on high stools next to them. A haze of cigarette smoke hung in the air.

As he wound his way through the casino, he looked beyond its most obvious features and began to tally up the stuff that mattered. He counted six uniformed guards, all armed with pistols. Half of them were clustered around the cashier's station.

Four bulky guys in suits, their faces grim masks, screamed "hired muscle." They maneuvered between the patrons like sharks winding among swimmers, just below the water's surface, ready to strike. They occasionally bumped into a patron or knocked a cocktail waitress off course. None seemed particularly interested in Bolan, leading him to believe he hadn't set off the metal detectors.

The warrior shambled up to a slot machine. With a grunt, he dropped onto a stool, shoved in the plastic card he'd loaded and spent several minutes letting his money disappear as he lost to the machine and watched the guards. If they were concerned about him, they were doing their best to hide it. More likely, though, the security team was looking for someone able to unleash mayhem on multiple continents. At the moment, Bolan didn't appear to fit that bill.

The soldier had come here with a single purpose. He wanted to kill Jiang, make sure the guy received justice for the deaths he'd caused. But more important, he needed to short circuit any repeat performances the man might decide to undertake in the future.

Bolan wove his way through the crowd. As best he knew, Jiang had no photographs of him, so Bolan guessed he didn't need to worry about facial-recognition technology betraying his approach.

He stopped along the way, taking a couple of minutes to watch a guy on a winning streak at the blackjack table. Again, the guards didn't seem to have noticed him.

Bolan reached the rear of the casino. A set of stairs led to the private area where Jiang kept his offices. A silver chain stretched across the steps. A plastic sign that hung from the chain read Employees Only in English and also Chinese. He cast a look around but saw no one close by paying attention to him.

Unhooking the small chain, he moved onto the first step and put the chain back into place. At this point he guessed he had just a few moments before someone tried to intercept him. Dozens of smoke-colored half globes that covered surveillance cameras stared down from the ceiling. Maybe his walking up to the steps wouldn't draw attention, but moving onto the stairs would spur even the most complacent guard to come down hard on Bolan.

As he climbed the stairs, the warrior reached inside his jacket, wrapped his fingers around the Beretta's grip and freed the gun from its holster. He kept the gun tucked up against his leg as he climbed the stairs, maintaining his limp as he moved.

It was only a matter of time before someone confronted him. But whether they saw him as a confused visitor, one struggling to navigate the big casino, or an able-bodied man remained to be seen. He hoped keeping the gun hidden from sight against the black fabric of his suit while moving on the dimly lit stairs would buy him a couple of seconds and hide his true motives.

Once the gun came into play, the numbers would fall fast and hard. Any edge Bolan had would evaporate.

A man in a charcoal-colored suit appeared at the top of the stairs. He held out an open hand, palm facing Bolan, and gestured for the Executioner to halt. He'd tucked the tail of his jacket behind the butt of a pistol holstered on his hip. His palm rested on the pistol's grip. He said something to Bolan in what the soldier guessed was a Chinese dialect.

Bolan made eye contact. He furrowed his brow and shook his head in feigned confusion. The move allowed him to climb another step and close the distance between him and the other man.

The man repeated what he'd just said, only in a louder voice.

The big American shook his head again.

At the same time, he surged up the stairs. His opponent, apparently surprised by the aggressive reaction, took a step back and began to draw his pistol. Before he could clear leather, though, the soldier had closed the gap. He brought the Beretta around in a sideways arc and struck the guy in the temple with pistol's grip. Grunting, the man's eyes rolled back in his head and his body sagged under its own weight. Bolan shoved him aside before he could fall and stepped onto the mezzanine. A dozen or so unused slot machines were stacked along the wall along with a dozen or so cardboard boxes, the tops flipped open.

He'd only taken a couple of steps when three more gunners came into view.

The two hardmen closest to Bolan seemed surprised by the violence unfolding before them. Both had their guns in view, but not directly pointing at the Executioner. They were walking close together, making it easier for Bolan to take them both out. The third man lagged behind the other two and was clawing underneath his jacket for a holstered gun.

The Beretta chugged out a half-dozen rounds and the closest guards fell under the onslaught from the Italian-made pistol.

Bolan adjusted his aim fast. The soldier double-tapped the trigger and cut loose with a pair of 3-round bursts. The third guy jerked and his pistol slipped from his hand and struck the floor.

Another trio of thugs was advancing on Bolan. The two in front were brandishing pistols while a behemoth lumbered behind them. A pump shotgun cradled in the man's arms looked ridiculously small next to his massive frame.

One of the pistol-wielding men dropped to one knee and tried to line up a shot on Bolan. The gun cracked and unleashed two shots in rapid succession. The slugs whistled past Bolan's right ear and buried themselves in a wall at the soldier's six. The Beretta cut loose with a 3-shot reply. The rounds blazed past the shooter, but came close enough to force him to throw himself sideways instead of attempting another shot.

At the same time, the man-mountain swung his shotgun in Bolan's direction. The weapon thundered. Bolan guessed the shots from the small-caliber pistol had been dampened, but not drowned out by the din of the casino: soft-rock ballads of a 1980s vintage, the dinging of slot machines, the aural haze of a couple of hundred people talking all at once.

The thunderous peal of the shotgun changed that.

A corner of Bolan's mind was aware of the din of voices subsiding, like someone turning down the volume on a television. He guessed patrons were trying to wrap their minds around what they'd just heard, especially those unaccustomed to gunfire. One more shotgun blast and Bolan knew all hell would break loose downstairs.

Police would swarm the place. Bolan knew if he stayed long enough he could find himself on the wrong end of a cop's gun. He'd sworn a long time ago that he'd never fire on a cop.

That meant he needed to move.

The Beretta 93-R whispered again and another of Jiang's gunners folded.

The man with the shotgun was twisting in Bolan's direction, lining up another shot.

"HE'S HERE," ONE OF Jiang's men said.

Jiang nodded. He'd already heard the shotgun blasts and the frantic chatter on his security team's two-way radios. He'd figured the American would show eventually, though he hadn't expected it to happen so quickly. A small part of him had hoped the bastard would leave him alone. Take his victory and move on to some other mission. Cooper had already destroyed Jiang's efforts to grab the Valkyries, had caused millions of dollars in investments to evaporate and had killed nearly all of Jiang's network. And, after they'd fled Brazil, Wong Mei-Xing had deserted him, returning to Beijing. Her departure certainly didn't break Jiang's heart; he cared little either way. But it was another humiliation, another reason for the bastards in Beijing to ridicule him.

All that should've been enough for the son of a bitch.

Yet here he was, knocking on Jiang's door, ready to cause more havoc. The American wasn't going to stop until one of them was dead. So, fine, Jiang would accommodate him. This ended now, this day.

Jiang, his Beretta holstered in the small of his back, uncoiled from his chair. He felt the eyes of his security team on him as he crossed the room to the security monitors.

"Uniforms are moving patrons out the exits," he said. "We should have a full evacuation in minutes."

Jiang greeted the news with a shrug. At this point, he cared little about his patrons, his security team or anyone else who got between him and Cooper. All he cared about was the American who had tracked him all over the world, had humiliated him in front of his own people and his country. The way Jiang saw it, if he had to sacrifice a few gamblers in order to make Cooper pay, then Jiang would do it.

Jiang shot a glance to his right. Two of his security guards were seated at a small, circular table, one smoking, the other reading a newspaper. Their weapons lay on the table. A third one, a massive guy from the Xinjiang province who shot steroids like a diabetic taking insulin, stood at a small drink cart. He had been pouring himself a whiskey and soda, but had paused and was looking at Jiang.

"Go," Jiang said. He jerked his head at the door. "Take care of this."

The big man nodded. He looked at the pair at the table and gestured at the door with one of his thick arms. The men grabbed their weapons, rose in unison and started for the door. The big gunner fell in behind them and hit the nearest guard in the back with an open palm, shoving the guy forward.

When the door closed, Jiang wondered for an instant how they might fare. He dismissed the question with a shrug. Hired muscle, even trained killers like the team he'd just dispatched, was a commodity, cheap and easily obtained. If they failed to make it back, he had more he could send. Even if they didn't kill the American, they'd wear him down, perhaps injure him, leaving him vulnerable.

Jiang felt excitement surge through his stomach. Within the hour, Cooper would be dead and he'd dance on the bastard's corpse.

BOLAN PRESSED THE release bar with his hip and pushed open the door.

As he eased through the opening, his micro-Uzi held at hip level, he felt his heartbeat kick up a notch. Silhouetted in the doorway as he was, he knew he made an easy target and he half expected a swarm of bullets to come screaming at him. He switched the Uzi to his left hand and with his right closed the door. His eyes scanned the room that lay before him, a large rectangular area. Folding tables, their legs tucked under, leaned in rows against one wall. Bolan also saw more decommissioned slot machines standing stacked against another wall. He also counted three exits and an elevator door.

The soldier rolled across the room toward the elevator. His eyes and ears strained for some warning of an attack. If his intelligence was right, he knew he was closing in on Jiang's operations center and he guessed he'd run into some stiff resistance before all was said and done.

He covered a couple more steps before one of the exit doors slammed open, smacking hard against a wall, the sound as shocking and violent as a gunshot. Three of Jiang's men surged into the room and immediately fanned out.

The soldier dropped into a crouch and squeezed the Uzi's trigger. The small weapon chattered out a line of fire. One of the hardmen was sprinting to the ten o'clock position and was lining up a shot on Bolan.

The Executioner raked the Uzi in a low arc. The bullets ripped into the guy's chest and cut his sprint short.

Another of Jiang's thugs snapped off a couple of shots from a pistol. The bullets whizzed just inches over the soldier's head. Bolan turned the Uzi on that guy and pummeled his gut with a relentless storm of 9 mm shredders.

The biggest of Bolan's three attackers held a JS 9 mm submachine gun snug against his thick torso. The weapon, with its bull-pup design, had a rate of fire of 400 rounds a minute and a muzzle velocity of more than 1,000 feet per second. At the moment, the Chinese hardman was turning that firepower on Bolan. The rounds struck the floor just a few feet in front of Bolan and began cutting a path toward him.

The soldier darted right while his Uzi cycled through the rest of its magazine. The bullets sprayed harmlessly over the head of Bolan's opponent and drilled through the ceiling tiles. Even as the Stony Man warrior's SMG clicked dry, he fisted the Beretta and brought it to bear on the other guy. A tri-burst of subsonic rounds chugged from the Beretta's barrel, and the bullets savaged the hardman's torso. Dark, glossy patches of blood formed on the fabric of the man's shirt over his lower abdomen and on the left hip of his jeans.

He staggered and pitched forward.

Bolan slipped the empty Uzi into the harness beneath his jacket and headed for the fallen thug. Bolan fed a fresh magazine into the Beretta as he moved. By the time he reached the man, he'd rolled onto his back. Bloodied hands clutched at his stomach. The man's eyes were squeezed closed and his jaw clenched with pain. Perspiration gleamed on the man's forehead.

Bolan knelt next to the gunner and pressed the Beretta's muzzle to his forehead.

The thug's eyes snapped open and he glared at Bolan.

"Jiang! Where is he?" Bolan said.

Speaking through gritted teeth, the man said something in rapid-fire Chinese. Bolan couldn't understand the words. But the man's tone, angry and defiant, was unmistakable. Before the soldier could think of another way to pose the question, he heard a door opening behind him. The injured man's eyes drifted to a spot over Bolan's shoulder.

JIANG HAD WATCHED the security monitors as his gunners had closed in on the American. Before the first of his men had fallen, the Chinese spymaster knew his men weren't up to the task.

Muttering a curse, he looked around at his last two guards. Both men were former PLA foot soldiers and both were armed with JS 9 mm submachine guns. They were decent shooters, aggressive and loyal. Stupid, but loyal. They stared back at him, their eyes vacant, as though they had no idea how to act unless someone told them. Well, he was going to do just that.

He nodded toward the door.

"Let's go," he said.

The first man to the door opened it and poked his head through it, looking left and then right before turning back to Jiang.

"It's safe."

Jiang nodded. He pushed past the guy and moved into the hallway, filling his hand with the Beretta before he moved through the door. He headed to the elevators, summoned one and waited. His mind raced through the possibilities. A helicopter was parked on the casino's roof. He considered for a moment sending the last two guards after the American to run interference while he made a break for the chopper.

He could pilot the craft himself. By the time the American had gotten through these last two hardmen, Jiang would be in the air. He could fly the craft to a small executive airport located a mile or so from the casino, where he could charter a plane and seek a new refuge, perhaps Sudan as Wong had once suggested.

He dismissed the idea almost as quickly as it occurred to him. His own government, the people whom he'd devoted his adult life to serving, had turned on him because he'd failed. Wherever he went, the Chinese would come after him and mete out a fatal punishment for his failure. He'd spend the rest of his life on the run from his own country's intelligence service. And it probably wouldn't be a very long existence at that.

Unless…

Delivering Matt Cooper, the man who'd derailed his plans, could change things. It might not erase all the damage. But it would buy a little goodwill with his government handlers and gain him a second chance.

He couldn't bring Cooper in alive. The bastard was too resourceful, too tough, too damn good to keep under wraps for long. Jiang knew his best option was to kill the guy, drag his corpse back to Beijing and hope that appeased his leaders.

And if it didn't work?

He couldn't think about it.

The elevator came to a halt and the door opened. He gestured at the double doors that stood several yards away from them. The chattering of a submachine gun was audible through the doors.

"Go through there," he said. "Shoot anything that moves."

The men stared at him for a second, their eyes telegraphing an unspoken question.

"I said anything. That includes our own. You go in on my signal."

One of the men shrugged. But they both turned and headed for the door.

Jiang stared after them for a couple of heartbeats. Once he was certain they'd follow his orders, he turned and doubled back past the elevator doors. A hallway opened to his left and he turned and followed it. The room the American was fighting in had several entrances, one of them located in this corridor.

He heard the guns fall silent on the other side of the door. An instant later, he heard a man's voice speaking sharply in English.

Jiang keyed a mike he wore at his neck and ordered them to burst into the room.

"Now," he snapped.

A heartbeat later, more gunfire sounded from inside the room. A smile ghosted Jiang's lips as he counted to three and listened to the carnage unfold on the other side of the door.

BOLAN THREW HIMSELF forward. He felt bullets tug and tear at his jacket. A stinging sensation in his calf registered with him. He gritted his teeth and his eyes squeezed shut for an instant. He guessed a bullet had grazed him.

When he struck the floor he rolled onto his side and brought around the Uzi, looking for a target. He found the two gunners still bunched up and coming through the door. Their weapons were chugging indiscriminately, the rounds drilling into their injured comrade's torso, killing him instantly.

Jagged muzzle-flashes erupted from the Uzi as Bolan, firing with one hand, hosed down the two hardmen with a hail of 9 mm rounds. A bullet fired from Bolan's six sizzled just past his ear followed by a second.

The Uzi still firing, Bolan dug under his jacket for the Beretta and rolled toward the gunfire.

He saw Jiang standing on the other side of the room, lining up another shot at him. Rounds from the Uzi lanced through the air and stabbed just past Jiang's head. The guy flinched as he squeezed the trigger. The movement threw off his aim. The bullet burned past Bolan's temple and drilled into the floor behind him.

The Beretta 93-R sighed and loosed a burst. The subsonic rounds hammered into Jiang's torso, causing him to jerk in place. A second burst from the Beretta sent the Chinese spy crashing to the ground, dead. His handgun slipped from his fingers and hit the floor several feet from his body.

Bolan hauled himself to his feet. When he put weight on his injured leg, he winced involuntarily, but ignored the pain. He glanced down at the injury and saw the gash in his pant leg, the area around the injury dark and wet.

He keyed his throat mike and called for Grimaldi to meet him on the casino's rooftop.

## EPILOGUE

At first, he swore the sun would burn out his eyes.

It seemed like forever since Dale Roberts had seen it. As he exited the hospital, he squinted against the afternoon sun's brilliance.

He was unsure how many days he'd spent in the hospital recovering from the injuries he'd suffered at the Pearson estate. Once his condition had stabilized, he'd been put into a secure room inside the hospital, one without windows, television, internet, calendars or any other links to the outside world.

Sure, the Americans had fed him well and he'd healed nicely. Neither of the bullets that had drilled through his torso had hit vital organs. He'd found himself able to move with a minimum of pain. What was left, he drowned with enough painkillers to keep him mobile without slowing his mind.

From what he'd gathered through overheard snatches of conversation among his FBI-agent guards, the British government had gotten wind of his capture somehow and wanted the U.S. to return him to England so he could answer for old espionage charges there.

While the lawyers for the two countries squabbled over the details, Roberts had devoted as much time as possible to mending his injured body, a regime of resting, eating well and following the doctor's orders to the letter.

A couple more weeks, and he guessed he could start real exercise. Word was he was headed for the United States Penitentiary, Administrative Maximum Facility in Florence, Colorado. Years ago, he'd read an article about the place, the so-called "Alcatraz of the Rockies," and knew, at least from his perspective, he was about to plunge into hell. The place housed the worst criminals and terrorists: killers from the Gangster Disciples to the Aryan Brotherhood to al Qaeda.

And now him. He probably should have felt honored.

One of the guards, a grim-faced guy with U.S. Marshall's credentials pinned to his suit coat, tightened his grip on Roberts's upper arm and guided him to the right.

"This way, sir," the man said, nodding at a black panel truck.

Roberts kept his mouth shut and shuffled toward the van. To his surprise, the guards had cuffed his hands behind his back, but hadn't used ankle irons or other restraints on him. He would have considered it an oversight, except that every time they came within a few feet of a nurse, doctor or orderly, the big man squeezed Roberts's arm hard enough to cause him to sharply suck in a lungful of air. The guard then would let his free hand drop to the grip of the pistol strapped around his waist and he'd scowl at Roberts.

Roberts wasn't an expert on non-verbal communication, but he got the message, loud and bloody clear. Do something stupid and take a bullet, on the spot.

Truthfully, he had no intention of trying to escape or take a hostage.

He needed time and he needed a plan.

He guessed the legal wrangling would leave him languishing in prison for months, if not a year or more. That would give him plenty of time to orchestrate something. He had friends—or at least professional contacts, clients, really—who'd willingly supply him with many of things he needed to pull it off. After years in the private espionage business, he knew where a lot of bodies were buried and he'd be only too happy to share that information with the federal government if his various customers refused to provide him the money, clothes, vehicles, tools and other items he'd need to pull off an escape. He just needed to make it known that he was feeling like talking and the offers of help would pour in.

Once he hit the streets, he'd get the hell out of America, find a way to some Third World shit-pile country where he could rebuild. It'd take some time, but he could do it. He knew that about himself. No matter where he was, he was the smartest damn guy in the room, able to do anything once he put his mind to it.

Before he left the country, though, he'd make one last stop.

He'd pay a surprise visit to Sandra Pearson. He'd put the bitch in the ground for shooting him, hell, for humiliating him. With all her snooping, he knew he could find someone, somewhere, who was willing to offer up the money and the gear necessary to take her out. He'd also track down her new-found friends, the Latino and that blond-haired asshole, and put them in the ground, too.

But all that was a little way down the road, he reminded himself.

First, he needed to get to his new luxury suite in Colorado and think things through.

When he came within a couple of feet of the van's rear doors, the big guard said, "Wait."

The guard rapped twice on the door with his knuckles. After a couple of seconds, Roberts heard electronic beeping inside as someone punched in a code of some sort. After another long beep, the lock gave and the doors parted.

Another guard—a small man with a Marshall's badge hanging from a chain around his neck—pushed the doors apart and stepped from the rear of the van onto the pavement. Wordlessly, the guards helped Roberts onto a step. He then moved through the door and into the van's rear compartment, which reminded him of a package-delivery truck with enough headroom to stand.

As his eyes adjusted to the more subdued interior light, he took a couple of steps farther into the van. Something crinkled under his feet. He looked down and saw clear plastic drop cloths had been spread over the floor. A check of the van's interior told him the walls also had been covered with plastic.

What the hell?

He opened his mouth to verbalize the question racing through his mind.

The other man growled, "Stay."

Roberts halted. Keys jingled and a second later, he felt the other man tug on his handcuffs, unlocking them.

Roberts turned and looked at the other man.

The guy was slipping the cuffs into a small pouch on his belt.

Roberts didn't bother to utter his question. He already knew where this was going. He lunged for the other man, hands grasping for the guard's throat.

BOLAN THREW HIS left forearm up in a blocking motion and knocked aside Roberts's hands. He chopped down with his right hand and struck the other guy in the side of the neck with the edge of his hand.

Roberts crumpled to the ground, but his foot lashed out at Bolan's knee. The soldier sidestepped the kick, though he could feel the sole of Roberts's shoe brush against the fabric of his pants.

For a man who'd spent the past few weeks recovering from an injury, Roberts was surprisingly fast. Bolan guessed adrenaline and the reality that he was fighting for his life were fueling the Briton's vicious attack.

Roberts was back on his feet, fists raised. He threw a jab at Bolan. The soldier blocked it easily, but another punch came at him from the opposite side and thudded against his chin. Bolan's head snapped to the side, but he held his ground. Roberts tried to press his advantage.

He rushed Bolan and thrust an open hand toward Bolan's solar plexus. The Executioner stepped aside and pushed the strike away. At the same time, Roberts grabbed for Bolan's holstered pistol.

The soldier dropped a protective hand onto the pistol's grip and at the same time threw an elbow into Roberts's face. The blow flattened the man's nose and Bolan felt the warmth of blood soaking through his shirtsleeve.

Bolan used his superior weight to knock the other guy to the ground. Dropping onto Roberts, he grabbed the guy's head and twisted until he heard the man's neck pop.

Climbing off Roberts, Bolan rolled the man's body in the plastic tarp. Though he hadn't tangled with the guy previously, Bolan had figured that, given the chance, Roberts would pursue a blood vendetta against Pearson. Maybe he'd hire out the killing, even from within the walls of a federal prison. Maybe he'd do it himself. Regardless, Bolan wasn't willing to take the chance. Roberts, like Jiang and the others, had left a trail of blood and betrayal in the pursuit of money and power. For that, he needed to face the ultimate justice.

And the Executioner had given the man a fighting chance. It was more than he deserved.

* * * * *

# The
# Don Pendleton's
# Executioner®
## ROGUE ASSAULT

**A West African drug lord sets his sights on America.**

The traffickers of Africa's first narco-state, Guinea-Bissau, have worked their way into the U.S. Mack Bolan is unable to legally confront the drug kingpin of the country, so his mission is to go in under the radar. But Bolan soon learns that everyone—from the corrupt leaders in the military to the police department—is part of the drug ring. There's only one way justice can be served, and the Executioner is determined to be the last man standing.

**GOLD EAGLE®**

*Available in August wherever books are sold.*

# TAKE 'EM FREE
## 2 action-packed novels
## plus a mystery bonus

## NO RISK
### NO OBLIGATION TO BUY

GE13

# JAMES AXLER

# DEATH LANDS®

## Dark Fathoms

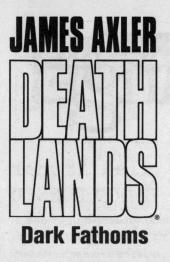

**Between the devil and the deep blue sea…**

Miles beneath the ocean's surface, a decaying redoubt barely protects Ryan and his companions from a watery death. Battling cyborgs programmed by artificial intelligence to kill them, they're desperate to escape. But above the waves a new threat awaits: a massive predark supership banished to the seas of Deathlands. Decades of madness have led to civil war between the citizens of the upper and lower decks. Now pawns in a bloody game, Ryan and the other survivors must destroy the ship or face their certain end at sea.

*Available in September wherever books are sold.*

## AleX Archer
## BLOOD CURSED

### A local superstition or one of history's monsters come to life?

Deep in the Bavarian forest, archaeologists unearth a medieval human skull with a brick stuffed in its mouth. When Annja Creed catches wind of the strange discovery, the TV host and archaeologist rushes to join the dig. But the superstitious locals fear the excavation has angered one of the chewing dead—those who rise from their graves to feast on human flesh and blood. Then a child goes missing. Suddenly ensnared in the Czech Republic's black market underworld, Annja must wield Joan of Arc's sword to protect the innocent....

*Available in September wherever books are sold.*

When a thirst for blood signals certain death....

GRA44